Philip Kerrigan was born in Bristol in 1959, but was brought up in Norfolk, where he still lives with his wife and child.

CW01402453

By the same author

Dead Ground
Survival Game
Blood Libel

PHILIP KERRIGAN

Weatherspy

Grafton Books

A Division of HarperCollinsPublishers

GraftonBooks
A Division of HarperCollins*Publishers*
77-85 Fulham Palace Road,
Hammersmith, London W6 8JB

Published by GraftonBooks 1991
9 8 7 6 5 4 3 2 1

First published in Great Britain by
GraftonBooks 1990

A CIP catalogue record for this book
is available from the British Library

ISBN 0-586-20365-6

Printed in Great Britain by
HarperCollinsManufacturing Glasgow

Set in Trump Medieval

Nothing is illegal if a hundred businessmen decide to do it, and that's true anywhere in the world.

Andrew Young

For A. and M.

PART ONE
Foreshock

1

Five minutes before the disaster, no one had ever heard of Santo Caraz. It was a scrubby little town standing at the conjunction of two river valleys below the Chiarroca mountain in the High Andes of Peru. Its population was something over seven thousand, evenly split between the *blancos* and *mestizos* – descendants of the Spanish invaders – and the *campesinos* – the second-class citizens whose ancestors built the ruins the tourists come to see. It had two main roads running into it. There were five churches, seven bars, a hotel, a couple of foreign-owned factories – one American, one German – a school, a football field, a hospital, and a cemetery on a hill where the statue of an adolescent angel raised her arms and wings to heaven.

Five minutes before the disaster, it was an ordinary Monday morning, a little after dawn on January 27th. The smoke of a thousand fires made a thin mist over the rooftops. Cold was sweeping down from the heights of Chiarroca.

Down in the main square, Juan Chequilla unlocked the doors of the Paraíso bar and began to sweep the floor. His son, Tomás, had cleaned up after closing the previous evening, but he was never comfortable until he had seen to it himself. He was a small, tidy man, with only odd wisps of carefully greased black hair left on the top of his head. He ran the broom across the tiles, driving invisible particles of dirt out of the door and into the square. He gave them a last flick and straightened up to survey the morning.

The square was damp and grey. A jeep was parked

11

in front of police headquarters, a couple of uniformed boys lounged at the door, smoking cigarettes. A black cat hunkered in the dust, watching a bird on the lip of the broken fountain. Juan smiled. The cat had not been around much lately. Perhaps it was something to do with the dogs. For two nights now it seemed every dog in town wanted to join a choir.

He turned back to his premises. The floor was now spotless, the counter polished, the bottles neatly arranged. Even the pictures, copies of old masters cut from magazines, were straight on the walls. In the kitchen at the rear his wife sang along with the radio; a song by the American, Michael Jackson. She could not hold a note, but he liked to hear her. He rubbed his hands: he was ready to face his customers.

The town began to stir. Smells of breakfast cooking wafted from the steeply packed adobe houses. Radios blared. Babies squalled for the morning feed. A garbage truck bumped down the road from the next village and rattled through the narrow streets, waking grumbling men who had indulged too well in bars the night before. In back yards children appeared and threw corn to chickens. Bells began to ring all at once, and black-clad figures left their homes and moved slowly toward the churches.

The mayor, a long, serious, scrawny man of late middle years, yawned in his bed and rolled over to face the open window. He stretched out a hand for his wife, as he did every morning, and was reminded, as every morning, that she had been gone for ten years. He felt the usual residue of sadness. He had only realized in the time since her death how fond of her he had been. He had tried having one of the girls from the house down by the river sleep with him once, but it had not seemed proper. The ghost of his wife still lay in the bed they had shared. When he felt the need of feminine company now, he went to the house.

He blinked myopically at the open window. The scent of snow was in the air. He yawned again, belly rumbling. Today he had to make serious representations to the Governor about pay in the foreign-owned factories. It was not a matter he relished. He was a man of bookish tastes and demeanour. He was mayor chiefly because no one else seemed to desire the post. Given the occasional dangers a holder of such office could be exposed to, that was not surprising. Only a month ago, the mayor of the next village had been dragged off a bus by masked men and shot. Some said it was the *Sendero Luminoso*, others blamed the Rodrigo Franco death squad. It might as easily have been the government's security forces. The mayor knew little, cared less. But on occasion, he had to make representations to regional government on this or that matter, because his people expected it of him.

He rose and pulled down his nightshirt. It had ridden up past his hips during the night. He went to the window and gazed out. From the window of his residence he could see a great deal of the town. The jumbled rooftops, the meltwater river tumbling down from the glacier, the valley rising steeply away to the west, and Chiarroca shining white and pure eight horizontal miles and ten thousand vertical feet distant.

He breathed lungfuls of crisp air. He was sure that his interview with the Governor would proceed in a civilized manner.

The garbage truck whined and clanked its way through the streets. The teacher at the school unlocked the doors and strode through the classrooms, thinking about the girls and boys in his charge. A hooter blew three times at the German-owned factory.

Ana Barbajas, an eight-year-old from the street just

13

below Cemetery Hill, was helping her Grandmother toward the Church of the Saints at the corner of Tarija and Nazca Streets. She did this every morning because Grandmother was blind, and no one else in the house could spare the time. She did not like it. She was frightened of Grandmother, who was old and half-crazy, whose blind eyes stared fixedly at no one when she spoke. But she took the view that the sooner she had done her duty, seen Grandmother to her seat, the sooner she could say her prayers and set herself right with God for the day.

The town was awake but sluggish. A 'paper boy wandered into the square as the soldiers got into their jeep and started the engine in a blue snort of exhaust fumes. The cat in the road ran for cover, and the bird on the fountain fluttered into the trees. An old man, out early for a stroll, watched the bird, and decided to rest a moment on one of the benches round the fountain.

Juan poured the first cup of coffee from the urn at the back of the bar, added a pinch of sugar and drank it down in slow, pleasurable sips. Above, Tomás was being harried out of bed by his mother. Juan heard the thump of his wife's steps on the floor. She always walked on the balls of her feet, therefore she sounded like a small army tramping through the upstairs rooms. That made him smile too. He smoothed the lick of hair on top of his head, keeping it in place.

Through the window, he watched the 'paper boy cross the square. He waved to attract the boy's attention. He liked keeping up with the news: miners' strikes; attacks by the *Senderos*; the continuing story of the economic crisis. But, also he wanted to see if – miracle of all the miracles – he had won the lottery this month. Unlikely, but there were always the sports pages for consolation.

14

Over his head, the sound of his wife's feet on the floorboards grew louder. They seemed to merge into each other, to become a rumble. He saw the old man sit up on the bench beneath the trees, and the boy come to a halt, a copy of the 'paper held out like a flag. Juan glanced round at the bar. The liquor in the bottles on the shelves trembled ever so slightly.

He realized.

He put down his coffee cup, where the dregs began to shudder also, and started to call out to his wife and son.

He was going to fetch them down, hurry them out of the house, make sure they were safe in the open. He moved swiftly toward the rear door.

Too late.

The epicentre of the earthquake that hit Santo Caraz that morning was some ten miles out in the Pacific Ocean, one hundred and fifty miles away from the village. It registered a magnitude of 7.7 on the Richter scale. Magnitude 5 is sufficient to cause damage to buildings. There was no great disturbance of the sea, no *Tsunami*, which most people inaccurately call a tidal wave, because the fault lines along that side of the Pacific tend to slip sideways rather than up and down. There was much damage across the country — houses flattened, hill slopes subsiding, thousands of people killed. But as people said afterwards, it could have been much worse.

Except in Santo Caraz.

In that small, unheard-of town there were special factors. First, it was densely built, most streets no wider than lanes. Second, the majority of the houses were of adobe, which has little internal strength. Only the mayor's residence, the factories, a couple of municipal buildings and the school were built of concrete. Third was the lack of a warning. A major earthquake some-times announces itself well in advance. Faint tremors and shiftings give people time to get out of their homes. But the 'quake of January 27th was heralded only by that slight tremor at 7.15. Perhaps five seconds passed between the shivering of the liquor in the bottles on Juan Chequilla's shelves and the major strike.

It came like a hammer blow. Juan was thrown to the floor by the force of it, his head striking the side of the bar. He lay on the red tiles, feeling them move beneath his hands. He heard his wife screaming, then she was blotted out by the sound of thunder. He tried to get to his feet, but nothing would stay still. Bottles were falling from the shelves, spraying glass and liquor in all directions. He started to crawl toward the door, praying silently. He had experienced one other sizeable earthquake. That was twenty years ago, when he was little more than a boy. It had shaken down some houses, killed a few people, but it had not been bad in the town. This, he already knew, was very bad.

He was almost at the door. Morning light fell on the square, where the old man and the 'paper boy lay flat in the dirt. Water slopped over the sides of the fountain. The deep wrenching of the earth was under him, and his bar was shaking apart. He saw cracks opening around the windows and the door. Roof tiles fell on the sidewalk outside, pieces of plaster began to drop around him. He was almost there.

The bar collapsed. Its walls buckled and appeared to explode into the square. The old man and 'paper boy stared wild-eyed as other buildings followed. The square came down like a pack of cards.

All over town, people were stumbling into the streets, only to be buried as their houses gave way. There were a few open spaces near homes in Santo Caraz – the main square was one, the football field another. But people had no time to reach them. As streets became blocked by debris and bodies, they were trapped, panicking and jostling together as more houses fell.

In the Church of the Saints, Ana's Grandmother was the first to realize what was happening. She was old enough to know all the signs, perhaps her blindness also made her more sensitive to them.

She straightened suddenly, while the rest of the congregation was muttering prayers, and grasped Ana's arm.

'Take us out of here,' she hissed.

Ana was confused, afraid to move while the service was in progress.

'Quick, child, outside.' Grandmother started up by herself. Ana saved her from tripping over and led her along the row of chairs toward the doors. The prayers had petered out now, and the candles on the altar were flickering strangely. Glass and silver began to chink. The priest called for them to be calm. His face was pale. Grandmother pushed roughly onward, repeating: 'Outside. Outside, in the name of God. You want to die in here?' Others were rising, there was a sharp smell on the damp air of the church. Everyone knew, even Ana. Chairs toppled as they struggled toward the doors.

Ana and her Grandmother were outside when the shock wave struck. It threw them to the ground. Ana picked herself out of the dust and saw the church trembling like a sheet of paper in the wind. A window broke and fell in a rain of coloured glass. The bell swung and pealed frantically in its crumbling tower.

Grandmother lay on the ground, the fat wife of Marilla the baker sprawled across her legs. 'Get us away from here,' she shouted above the noise. 'Away from the church.'

Ana pulled her free, dragged her into the middle of

the street. It was impossible to walk now. The ground was moving so violently that it seemed to be swatting her. Those who had escaped from the church huddled together, clutching each other as if they would fall off the world if they let go. They whimpered and cried, the men as well as the women. Ana looked toward her home. The street had disappeared. In its place was a mass of rubble. The garbage truck stood in the middle of it, buried past the wheel arches. A fire had started somewhere in the heart of it and thick black smoke billowed into the calm sky.

On the steep slopes above the town, field walls slumped and pebbles sifted down the ploughed furrows. All along the valley above and below, terrace slopes in alluvium and glaciofluvial gravels failed and slid. Higher up, snow turned into small avalanches. The river foamed and splashed as if it were boiling. The banks gave way in places, and rocks dropped into the torrent.

Most of the soldiers in the barracks on the square were killed when their headquarters collapsed on them. The ceremonial gun, a Howitzer 25-pounder they kept on the parade ground, was shaken from its restraining chocks and danced around like a prancing horse. The town's fire engine, housed in a new concrete building, was unharmed, but its exit was blocked by the fall of houses in the streets outside. Most of its crew were already buried in the remains of their homes.

The 'quake lasted approximately 45 seconds in Santo Caraz, which is no more than the average.

As the final vibrations faded, the mayor crawled out from under his bed. He lay for a moment, listening, letting the floor become still. The great turmoil of the earth was replaced by the pounding of his heart. He opened one eye. The bedroom was a shambles; his books scattered like dead birds, pictures off the walls,

18

the shutters loose and swinging, dipping him in and out of slatted darkness. He did not say a prayer – he had lost his faith long ago – only thanked his good luck and the builders of his residence. It was a mess, but it remained standing.

Wary of possible aftershocks, he got up. He could scarcely breathe, his legs were hardly strong enough to hold him, and he stumbled to the bed. He had to think. What must he do? First, find out how bad it was. Then something else. He raised his head and listened again. Perhaps they were safe, perhaps this was all there would be.

He picked his way cautiously across the floor, testing to make sure of its strength. All his volumes of poetry and literature lay open at his feet. He gripped the shutters and pushed them open.

He was somewhat prepared for the sight. He had seen a good deal of destruction in the last big 'quake, had spent several days helping to clear streets and dig out bodies. But he did not remember having such a clear view last time. Now it lay before him in all its detail: the order of the town dissolved in rubble, the smoke rising as fires started, the bodies.

But it was not the sight. It was what he heard. Now that the earth had ceased grinding, there was an unnatural silence. No traffic moving, no voices shouting or dogs barking, no horns or sirens. Just a breath of wind and the faint crackle of the fires, an occasional sob or scream, which seemed distant and part of another scene.

Transfixed by the world so completely changed, the mayor did finally utter a prayer, for everyone in the town, himself included. And he tore his gaze from the devastation, because there was something else he had to be sure of.

He looked up, past the sides of the valley, into the

distance far above the town where the sun shone bright and clear.

Chiarroca is one of the highest mountains in Peru. Its summit is more than 20,000 feet above sea level. It is always covered by snow. Just below the summit on the western face, there is an almost vertical drop into a basin where a great glacier lies. As the last houses in Santo Caraz slithered belatedly to the ground, the mountain began to move.

The mayor thought he saw it shifting. He knew that he heard it. Others in the town heard it too. Faces that had been pressed into hands or covered with clothing turned toward the head of the valley. The noise was like a faint echo of the 'quake, as if storm clouds were rubbing together.

The snow on the slopes above the western face had been weakened by the tremors. Now a section of it half a mile across and a quarter-mile long began to slip. Moving in one solid piece, it slid over the edge of a three thousand foot drop.

The mayor stood transfixed. Down in the shattered streets, he saw people struggling from the rubble. He leaned over the balcony and shouted to them. They paid him no heed. Their attention was fixed on the mountain, and the gathering thunder that issued from it.

The snow had scoured rock from the mountain. When it hit the glacier, pulverized and partially melted by friction, it threw up thousands of tons of rock, ice and moraine debris. Clouds of snow billowed up in the basin, and the new mixture continued its fall down the glacier toward the narrow mouth of the gorge where the meltwater stream that fed Santo Caraz began. Bursting through, it gathered speed, moving finally in excess of 250 miles an hour. It flowed like liquid mud, crashing down the valley so fast that at times it rode on its own air cushion, skipping over bushes and leaving them untouched.

Ana's Grandmother said: 'Is it the mountain?' Ana whispered: 'Yes.' People were standing up, gazing at the mountain. Their faces had a stupid look, as if they were waiting for an explanation. Others were already running, trying to get around the ruined houses. The fire near the garbage truck forced them back.

'We must go to the hill,' Grandmother said. 'Come, you must find the way.'

'What about Mama and Papa?' Ana asked, helping the old woman to stand.

'They're in God's hands,' Grandmother said. 'We all are. Hurry.' The roar from the mountain was gathering force.

The upper part of the valley was home to a few farmhouses and some fields of sheep and cattle. These were wiped out as the mudflow crashed down. Fragments of the mountain twenty feet across were bowled along like pebbles. The river disappeared, the valley floor was buried for a width of two miles in places where the flow was momentarily dammed. And still the basin fed the surge.

The mayor was out of his residence, yelling at people to move quickly to high ground. He still wore his nightshirt. He carried a copy of a novel by Saavedra, the one thing he had paused to pick up as he hurried from his room. He started running toward Cemetery Hill himself, joining the crowds who were trying to do the same thing. Most of them knew what had happened before. They knew the last great avalanche had been diverted by the ridge above the town, had bypassed it and flowed down the southern valley, almost swallowing the next village. That had been a miracle. He had no great certainty they would be smiled on again.

21

They were screaming. A lot of them were screaming. He tried to see what was happening up ahead.
Taller than most, he saw the front of the crowd
pushing against a blocked street. Doctor Cazar was
clambering onto the remains of a roof, calling for
them to try another route. The people ignored him,
driving children and old people to the ground. The
mayor attempted to help the doctor, calling out and
pointing down another street. But panic had set in,
the crowd was out of control. The mayor raised his
eyes for a moment and saw the angel on Cemetery
Hill. He thought: If only we had her wings. The birds
were better off than all these people now. The smallest
fly was more blessed than anyone in this crowd. He ran
from the mass and headed back toward his residence.
Maybe the flow would not hit the town, maybe it
would be small, maybe his house could withstand the
flood as it had survived the 'quake. He clutched his
book, realizing that he was as frightened as everyone
else. He thought of the angel.

The mudflow took four minutes and thirty-one seconds to plunge the eight miles down the valley to
Santo Caraz. Four minutes was not long enough for
a fit young person to run from the centre of town to
Cemetery Hill, even before the houses had sprawled
into the streets. Not long enough for the injured to pull
themselves from the wreckage. Not long enough for
some to even realize what was going to happen. Some
were still scrabbling at the remains of their homes,
trying to pull relatives out, some wept hysterically at
the places where familiar streets had been. Those who
knew made for any high spot they could find. But there
were few such places in Santo Caraz. Just Cemetery
Hill and another rise where the school stood.

Ana ran, Grandmother wheezing and complaining
of her heart all the way. People were passing them,

dragging children, shouting at the tops of their voices, but the thunder from the valley head grew closer and louder, drowning out the cries. Some people were already on the hill, clustering round the angel, balancing on fallen pieces of other graves. Ana thought: I shan't get there with Grandmother. She doesn't go fast enough.

The mudflow hit the ridge a quarter-mile above the town, stripping the mountain road away like paint.

Thrust forward by the crowd, Ana lost her grip on Grandmother's hand. She screamed, saw the old woman fall and her lips mouth the words: 'Don't stop.' She had no choice in the matter. The crowd drove her on at such speed that her feet sometimes left the ground. Crushed and breathless, she fought them off, trying to keep herself in one piece. They were streaming through a tiny opening in the rubble at the end of Jacita Street, the noise behind was shaking the earth, the entrance to Cemetery Hill was near. She glimpsed the gates and a portion of the wall still standing. Then she was through and the crowd spread out over the broken ground. Released from its grip, she fell on her knees, then clambered up and continued running for the heights. She ran for her life as the roar engulfed the town.

The mudflow divided at the ridge as it had done before. Part of it continued down the valley to the west, straight toward the next village. But there was too much of it this time, and it moved too fast. It climbed the ridge, overtopped it and swept down on the town. The river bridge disappeared, the football field was swallowed, the school and the town square were crushed and swamped. The mayor's residence lasted no more than the blink of an eye. The wave from the heights of the mountain smothered and crushed everything.

Ana reached the top of the hill as the wave broke around it. It was one hundred and thirty feet high by then, the crest curving like an ocean breaker. She saw it crash down on the people who were still making for the hill. She watched the town vanish, saw the cemetery gates blip out of existence. A friend from school screamed just a moment before it took her.

Next moment the hill was no more than an island in the flood, and the sixty-three people who had managed to reach the high slopes beneath the angel put their hands over their heads as stones and small rocks fell on them.

That part of the wave that topped the ridge came to rest half a mile beyond, contained by surrounding hills. Once it ceased moving, the earth and rocks solidified again, packing so hard that it could be walked on not many minutes after it had drowned the town.

The rest did not run itself out until it passed into the next valley. The debris flow engulfed half the next village, narrowly missed the hamlet at the junction of the two rivers, and carried on for ten miles down the Río Verde before halting just outside the large town of Marias. That valley was not densely populated. The damage to property was small; a further 6,000 people lost their lives.

There was one piece of good fortune for the German and American owners of the factories in the town: both had recently been on part-time working while old equipment was removed in preparation for a refit with new plant. But that was the only good news. Cemetery Hill, where all the dead of Santo Caraz lay, became the only living part of it. The old dead were only buried six feet beneath the earth. The 7,000 people who died that morning lay in a common grave eighty feet down.

It was a remote part of the country. But by dawn of the next day half the world's media had flocked to the

24

area to get a slice of the story. It was the usual scramble: the visually interesting part of the disaster was over in five minutes; there was nothing for the cameras to do but film the aftermath. Specially hired 'planes flew over, photographing the path of the mudslide. It was just a mountain and a valley with a smear of dirty soil like melted chocolate running for miles down its centre. Santo Caraz was no longer there to be filmed. Reporters from the States and Europe ran around trying to find someone who had seen the tragedy, who could speak whatever language it was their viewers spoke, and who might give a vivid eyewitness report. It was the next best thing to pictures. Otherwise, they focused on the crowds who came from miles around to lend a hand. They spoke of 'this politically troubled, economically crippled Third World country, where even the rescue forces are underfunded'. They took moody shots of the angel, and sought out weeping relatives. A British crew paused to film Ana as she sat on a rock with a neighbour, slowly realizing that her entire family was gone. The camera sucked on her grief, and the sound man held a boom toward her to catch her sobs. Later she saw a reporter giving his piece to camera, while behind him a work party with picks and shovels toiled to uncover a section of the school. There was some hope that people were alive under a slab of fallen roof. News teams who had realized that there was little to record until the international rescue effort arrived sat around, complaining about the lack of food and drink, wondering where they were going to sleep that night if they had to stay in the area. One long-serving correspondent pointed out that the last time something like this had happened to the valley, the rescue work was given up after a couple of days. 'You can't dig people out of this crap,' he said. 'They just let 'em lay and hold a mass.'

The day after the disaster, every television and radio service, every newspaper with a decent foreign desk was in Santo Caraz – rather, above it, as one journalist remarked – and the people who had survived were growing accustomed to being asked obvious questions by embarrassed translators while a sharp-eyed foreigner and his camera looked intently on. It was just another part of the suffering. They were too numb to be offended.

There was one strange thing – not that anybody noticed in the confusion. One crew had arrived on the scene much earlier than the rest. They drove in early in the afternoon of the first day; four men with lightweight video cameras. They carried no logo of any broadcasting organization, and there was no reporter to address the cameras; just the four men moving unobtrusively around the area, filming at great length, even going so far as to drive and walk far up the valley to take more detailed studies of the original snowslide. They gave trouble to no one, asked few questions, and were gone by nightfall. Most people thought they were some kind of scientific expedition that happened to be close by. But they were really very early compared to the rest. Almost as if they had been waiting for it to happen.

PART TWO
The Butterfly Effect

2

When his father drowned in Aberdeen's Victoria Dock, Paul Quillet was twenty-eight years old. When he decided to keep the old man's ship, a Dutch motor coaster called *Provider*, running, a lot of people told him that small cargo vessels were a dying way of life, and he ought to chuck it. But he ignored them.

He was a quick, well-built man, with a sardonic gleam in his green eyes that offended every jumped-up harbour master and bank manager who thought he deserved more respect. He had been raised to think for himself, and he did that when the matter of his father's ship came up. Yes, the way of life was dying, yes, he should chuck it. But he had spent all his life working the old tub, and the chorus of voices advising him to take the money and run only made him more determined that he was going to keep her going. He would show them, all the snotty money men, the smart ones in good suits, the grasping little blokes hocked up to the eyeballs to keep their own vessels floating. He knew it was the right thing to do. He had always known it was right.

Except on a morning like this.

He stood up, wiping his hands on a filthy rag and blinking at the other two. 'How bad is it?'

Reiny helped Sam to lever himself off the engine housing. All three of them were up to the armpits in grease and oil. Reiny's iron-grey hair was streaked. Sam breathed raggedly. He scratched himself through his overalls. 'Rotten,' he said. ''Bout as rotten as you like.' His Suffolk accent made it sound like a curse. 'Pistons buggered, gearing's up the spout. I dunno.'

'Reiny?'

Reinhardt Forst, the master of the *Europa Belle*, had been working short-sea traders between the Channel ports for forty years. He knew what was possible.

'It is how Sam tells you.' His eyebrows bristled like metal shavings. He was clumsy with English, preferred French. 'You can't do it yourself. It costs you money.'

Paul worked his shoulders to get the stiffness out. 'That's it, then. We're finished.'

Sam picked up a spanner and stared into the guts of the engine. He was a little old man now, tough but wizened, a year off retirement. Next to Reiny, he looked like a monkey. 'Must be somethin' we can do. We can rig somethin' together, get us across to Hamburg and back one more time.'

Paul shook his head. It felt strange admitting it.

'We rigged her and strung her to get back home this time,' he said. 'There's no more.'

'Bugger.' Sam turned and drove his boot into the crate he had been sitting on. Several important parts of the engine were in pieces on the floor. The three of them had been working on it since ten-thirty the previous night. Reiny had come over from his own tub to give them a hand, and stayed to see the worst. The engine room was dank. The lights ached in their cages. There was a heavy stink of fuel. 'We can get the money to fix 'er. What about another loan?'

'Where from?' Paul rubbed his neck, leaving smears of oil. 'We've been through every bank in town. They've all got signs outside specially for us. They say: "No Chance!"'

'Same ones they made for your papa.' Reiny joked, but it went flat.

Sam bent over and coughed into his sleeve.

Paul looked at him. 'You all right?'

''Course I bloody am.'

Over his head, they exchanged worried looks. Paul picked up his shirt. 'Come on, no one could say we've been warming the bell. Let's get out of this pit.'

They climbed the companion ladder to the crew quarters. Sam panted a bit on the last couple of rungs. Paul helped him up.

Ian was flat out on his bunk, mouth hanging open, a Batman comic spread on his chest. He had been making tea until the small hours.

Paul kicked his foot gently and chanted:

> 'At last the day begins
> In the East a-breaking.
> In the hedges and the whins
> Sleeping birds a-waking.'

The boy gawped, half-asleep. 'What? Whassa matter?'

'Put some water on to boil. Your Grandad's up to his neck in grime.'

As the boy stumbled up and got the stove going, Paul bent to one of the portholes and rubbed the mist off. It was seven-thirteen on a bleak Saturday morning on the east coast of England, a thin drizzle falling on Lowestoft's North Quay. Someone on a tanker across the water was dumping slops over the side.

'Paul.'

He turned. Reiny was pulling on his coat.

'I have to get back,' he said. 'We sail in two hours.'

'Okay, Reiny. Thanks for hanging around.'

'What else do I do?' He grasped Paul's shoulder in the usual pincer grip and shook him affectionately. He and Dad had been drinking pals in the old days, the friendship rooted in the discovery that they were both at Dunkirk in 1941: Dad on a merchantman picking up stragglers, Reiny shooting at him. These days, whenever they were in port at the same time, he

31

would turn up, slap Sam hard enough on the back to rattle his false teeth, and insist they all go to the nearest bar to sink a few glasses 'for old Bernard's sake'. Reiny still titled Paul 'My English nephew' in honour of his friendship with the old man.

'Anything I can do,' he said, buttoning his collar tight. 'Anything. You call me, yes?'

'You know it,' Paul said, though he didn't think there would be much point now.

'You'll think of something.' Reiny made an attempt at his usual grin. 'Like father like son, eh?'

He went out, letting the door clang behind him.

Paul shivered and sat down at the galley table, wedging himself in the corner. Some coffee, stone cold, remained in the pot. He poured it into a cup and drank a mouthful. Everything tasted of oil.

Sam warmed himself at the stove, shifting from foot to foot. 'Must be somethin' we can do.'

Ian made fresh coffee and put a cup in front of him. He stirred three sugars and cream into it, his face pinched and thoughtful. Then he reached under the table, brought out a half-empty bottle of Jameson's, and tipped a shot into the cup. He left the bottle on the table.

Ian made an enquiring face at his grandfather. Sam blew out his veined cheeks and shook his head sorrowfully.

The cabin began to warm up and steam from the big pan of water made the air moist. Sam sluiced himself down in the shower first, then Paul took a turn. They changed their clothes. Then the young man and old man and the boy gathered round the table again.

'I just thought,' Sam said at last, 'I could 'ave a word with old Matty. He might let us have the bits we need on account.'

'Matty doesn't run the business any more.' Paul reached for his cigarettes. 'It's that little prat Davey now. He wouldn't give you a dirty look on credit.'

'Only a thought,' Sam said.

'Anyway, we're supposed to be in Hamburg Monday night. We can't get the gear and put that senile bucket of rust together in time.'

'We got to,' Ian said. He was a bit slow. He worked aboard the *Provider* because he was Sam's kin. But his heart was in the right place, and Paul was uncomfortably aware that the boy looked up to him. 'You could get someone to lend us the money.'

Paul's cigarette glowed. 'How many millionaires you acquainted with, kid? There's no one this side of the Channel'd stump up a penny. My old dad pissed in the well for us a long time before you came along.' He drank, staring at the table, and whispered:

'Nor leave
Thy debts dishonoured, nor thy place desert
Without due service rendered.'

Then he said: 'Jesus.'

Sam put a scarred hand on his shoulder. 'Don't let it craze you, boy. We'll think of somethin'.'

Paul sat back, took the cigarette from his lips.

'Look, lads, let's stop whistling up the wind. We're meant to have this lump of ballast in Hamburg Monday night, and we're contracted to take a load of grain in on the tide at Wells the following Thursday. If we don't get it there – which we won't, short of God sending and fitting a new engine for us – then not only don't we get paid, we also have to scrape up the forfeit. Add on that we still haven't paid for the last overhaul to bring her up to regulations, that my overdraft looks like a row of tyres, that the Inland Revenue's on my back for taxes I can't pay, and the customs boys're all over me 'cause they think we might be doing business with the druggers in Amsterdam, and you'll see we're in the deep end.'

'Been a bad year,' Sam said.

'Bad decade.' Paul smiled. It was as if he didn't care any more.

'It's not your fault.'

He said nothing to that.

'You had expenses last year,' Sam insisted. 'My bloody doing, if it's anyone's.'

'Leave it, Sam.'

'You shouldn't never've paid for me to go in that hospital.'

'We didn't know what was wrong with you.'

'Wasn't nothin'.'

'Might've been.'

'Shouldn't've done it. Be all right if it weren't for me.'

'Look, belt up, will you.'

The subject was closed. Sam drank some coffee, muttering to himself.

'How much do we need?' Ian said.

Paul looked at him. 'Why?'

'I was thinking, I could ask Mum. She might lend us some.'

For a second he thought he was going to explode. But then he laughed and scuffed the boy's head.

'Don't bother your mum, all right?' He rested against the wall, eyes closed. He had seen Sam smile faintly, knew he was thinking kindly of him. Sam had a sentimental attitude to the son of his old employer. Once, in his cups, he had told him he was a better man than his dad had ever been. Sam had always been around, like a good uncle.

'So, what's the plan?' he asked, after a time.

34

Paul stubbed his cigarette and shrugged. 'Must be breakfast time. What say we retire to the Weary Well and partake of some fairy bread?'

Sam snorted. It was how Dad had always raised the subject of meals at the café.

They put their coats on and went out on deck. The harbour buildings were quiet. A few gulls bobbed around on muddy waves. Paul led the way down the gangplank. He stopped on the quayside to light another cigarette. Sam gazed out from under his cap at the *Provider*.

She was a hulk of old white paint and rust streaks, insignificant alongside the big freighters and colliers. Keel laid at Rotterdam in 1948, she was designed for operating in estuaries, rivers and canals. Shallow draft, engines and accommodation aft, electric cargo machinery and a hull strong enough to lie well on the ground at low water. One hundred and thirty feet long and 400 tons gross tonnage.

Sam said: 'Poor old gel.'

Paul threw his match away. It flared and died on the ground. He could hear a train rolling into the station beyond Commercial Road. A milk float rattled over the swing bridge. Beyond it, beyond the trawl basin and outer harbour, the sky was the colour of newspaper left in the gutter. A seagull got tired of gliding in the mist and flopped down to perch on the sign outside the gates.

BRITISH ASSOCIATED PORTS
NORTH QUAY EAST

They strolled toward it, Ian trying to recite the familiar words with him:

> 'Come up here, O dusty feet!
> Here is fairy bread to eat.

35

Here in Ma's retiring room
Children you may dine.'

He heard himself sounding like Dad, swooping low and suggestive on the mention of 'fairy bread'. Sam loved it. Paul knew that he sometimes felt it was thirty years ago, and nothing had changed; not the world or the money troubles. It had always been like this, all his life. Dad always got them through, and he was sure in his heart that Paul would manage it too. Only thing was, Paul no longer had the same confidence.

'You're not gonna give up, are you?' Ian said.

'Give up? Not a chance. Since when did the crew of the old *Provider* lie down and die?'

He sounded like Dad, but not much like himself.

He noticed a car, a blue Daimler, on the other side of the road as they passed out of the gates. It was parked by the harbour control office, blocking the entrance to the Trawl Basin, and he was wondering why the police hadn't moved it on when he heard the engine start.

He tensed. The Daimler leapt across the road, swung hard over and slewed to a halt. Two men in casual clothes got out.

'Paul Quillet?' the bald one said.

Sam started to protest. 'What's goin' on? –'

The driver grabbed Paul's arm. Paul shook him off and backed away, giving himself room. Then he saw Ian move as if he were about to tackle the bald one. He stepped between them before the boy could get hurt.

The bald one flashed an identity card.

'Special Branch, Mr Quillet. We'd like you to come with us.'

He said: 'Oh, yeah?' But he knew where he stood now.

'Just get in the car.'

He got in.

'He hasn't done nothin',' Ian cried, close to tears.

Paul rolled the window down.

'I'll sort it out. You two have some breakfast, get some sleep.'

'What's it about?' Sam demanded, rapping furiously on the passenger window. 'What's the game, you buggers?'

The driver gunned the engine.

Paul said: 'Don't worry.' Then the car jumped away, tyres squealing as it swung across the road and sped off over the bridge.

Sam bawled oaths and curses after them, shaking his fist and calling down seven kinds of doom. The car passed the yacht club and disappeared round the Royal Terrace.

'Bastards,' he concluded. He glanced at Ian, who was looking more anxious than angry now. 'What's up with you?'

'Grandad, did you see that bloke's card proper?'

'Sort of. Why?'

'They're going the wrong way for the police station.'

3

Paul was thinking the same thing as the Daimler raced
past the guest houses on Marine Parade. He clenched
his fists in his pockets, left hand around the grey and
white stone he always kept there. But he sat tight. He
had suspected something when they came for him, but
had not wanted Ian and Sam to get hurt. He had no
idea who the men were or what they wanted. Maybe
someone had been telling lies about him. There were
plenty of dodgy characters round the docks. He had
crossed a few in his time.

The bald one gazed out toward the Esplanade
and the dishwater February sky. 'Can't even see
the beach. Complete boghole, this.' He was in his
late thirties, with a Mexican bandit moustache and
crinkled little eyes. Empty polystyrene coffee cups
and chocolate bar wrappers lay all over the dashboard
in front of him.

They got out on London Road South. He looked for
chances to get out of the car if things turned nasty, but
the driver was good. He was younger, thinner and more
serious. His chin stuck out from the rest of his face
like the toe of a winklepicker shoe. He threw the car
about with scant regard for speed restrictions or road
markings. It was still early, so there was little traffic
to get in his way. At the roundabout he turned without
a pause down Arbour Lane. The metalled surface ran
out and became a muddy track. Paul was curious. He
knew of the occasional murders that had been done
in out-of-the-way parts of town. He wondered who he
might have offended.

'Come to sunny Lowestoft,' the bald one said. 'You from round here?'

Paul nodded.

'How'd you stand it?'

'I like scuba diving and the tropical weather.'

'Boghole,' the bald one said.

He studied the bald one. 'I am a kind of farthing dip,' he said slowly. 'Unfriendly to the nose and eyes.'

'What's that?'

'Nothing.'

The lane became potholes and puddles. The car slowed. He could have jumped out then, but he thought he had seen shoulder holsters under their jackets. He waited.

They ran into a trailer park. It was closed for the winter. A few caravans hunkered on drab grass by the wash house. The North Sea moved sluggishly beyond the cliffs. No one seemed to be about. He noticed another car behind the wash house, a Range Rover, spattered up to the doorhandles with mud.

They pulled up. The bald one said:

'End of journey.'

They got out. The driver moved toward Paul again, but there was no one else to worry about this time. He stood ready, hands out of pockets, the stone in his fist. The driver sensed the change. His mouth twitched, but he decided against laying on hands.

The bald one indicated a long luxury trailer sitting by itself.

He thought about making a break for it, but he was interested. And he was tired. Very tired. The sky was close, the sea and everything that had been so important ten minutes ago were far away. At least this was a change.

The bald one knocked at the trailer door. A booming, well-educated voice answered. Paul ducked as he entered.

It was the usual thing. To the left was a lounge, wood-look surfaces and tweedy brown covers on the seats, a portable gas heater hissing orange flame. At the end was a table with a picture window letting in a rectangle of grass, sea and sky.

The man behind the table was big. Bigger than Paul.

'Ah, Mr Quillet,' he said. 'Please, come and sit down.'

The floor creaked under his feet. He sat, squinting into the light, trying to make out the big man's features. He looked like a gentleman farmer. Straw-coloured hair flopped over a high forehead, little square-framed spectacles balanced in the centre of his ruddy face. Barbour jacket, cashmere sweater. There was something familiar about him.

A packet of Dunhills and an expensive gold lighter lay on the table. He pushed them across.

'You smoke?'

Paul took one, lit it and drew the smoke down. The big man watched him. Paul knew what he was thinking. He generally sensed what was on people's minds. The big man was thinking how disreputable he looked; the weathered face with a couple of days' growth of beard, the hair a little shaggy, the old pea jacket. He returned the scrutiny.

The big man tapped a crimson folder that lay under his hand.

'Mr Quillet,' he said. 'I'm sorry to have dragged you away from your breakfast.'

Paul waited.

'I'm, uh, Chief Inspector Provost. I take it my men told you who they were.'

'I almost believed them.'

'Oh, they're genuine, believe me.'

Which is more than you are, Paul thought. He had

40

never heard of a police inspector with such a classy accent.

'I had you brought here because there're some questions I'd like to ask you.'

Paul nodded.

'You have a brother, do you not?'

That surprised him. He said: 'No.' A knee-jerk reaction, covering while he tried to see a connection.

The inspector drummed on the folder. His spectacles glinted.

'You are Paul Quillet, aren't you? Born the 30th of June, 1954? You have black hair, green eyes. Well, I can see you have. You're left-handed, I think.'

Paul waggled the fingers of his left hand.

Provost continued. 'Your father was Bernard John Quillet, a man with a rather gamey reputation where the customs and excise are concerned, your mother was Mary Trendle. She died of leukaemia in 1959. You have a brother called Charles. He's your elder by two years. The pair of you were brought up chiefly by your father, mainly aboard the *Provider*. You followed your father into the family business, but Charles went to college and then university to study computing. He did very well. Your father passed away in 1981. He left the *Provider* to both of you. Charles wasn't interested, so you're now the master of the vessel. You haven't seen Charles since the funeral.' He pulled a questioning face. 'Now, *do you* have a brother after all, or do I have the wrong Paul Quillet?'

'You've got the right one,' Paul said.

'Good, good. You don't get on with him, do you? . . . I mean, when last you saw anything of each other, you didn't get on?'

'I don't remember.'

'I'm sorry. It's none of my business. But it *is* odd: brothers who have no contact for almost ten years.'

41

'I've got it,' Paul said. 'You're working for one of those Surprise-Surprise programmes. Long-lost relatives reunited, whether they like it or not.'

'I suppose Mina has something to do with it.'

Paul thought about grabbing the big man and ramming his head through the window. Instead, he stared at him through the tobacco smoke.

Provost adjusted his spectacles. That flash of familiarity again.

'Have you kept track of Charles at all?'

'No.'

'So you have no idea how well he's done for himself? That's a pity. You should be proud of him.'

He blew a little smoke in Provost's face.

'He's become quite an authority in his line. Spent several years in America, travelled all over the world helping to install computer systems he designed. Several awards. Research post at Cambridge.'

'Good for him.'

'Mr Quillet, do you know where he is?'

'No.'

'Are you quite sure?'

'You know so much about me, you've probably had me watched. I haven't seen him. What d'you want him for?'

Provost took off his spectacles and rubbed his eyes. Paul had seen the gesture before. He knew this man. Where from?

'He's wanted to assist in our enquiries.'

'Charlie?'

'Yes, Charlie.'

'You've got the wrong bloke.'

'I am afraid we haven't.'

'What enquiries?'

Spectacles back on, Provost pursed his lips. 'Your brother was, uh, doing some work for a government

42

department. Special projects. I can't be more specific. The problem is, he's disappeared, and so have some rather important programs. We don't know for sure, but it looks rather as if he took them.'

Paul shook his head. 'This is bullshit. Charlie's too straight to do anything funny.'

'It's not funny. It's government business.'

'Government,' Paul said. 'That's it! . . . You're Chandor.'

The big man paled, unsure what to do. He glanced over his shoulder, searching for the Special Branch men.

Paul enjoyed his discomfort. 'Saw you on the box once. You hold East Norfolk, don't you? Shouldn't go around pretending to be a policeman, not without a false beard.'

The big man smiled. It was a charming, purser's smile, that tried to suggest that, yes, he had been caught out, and of course he was ready to own up, and wasn't it all rather amusing? Paul saw weakness. This was the kind of man who had always been popular; well-liked at his public school, favoured by everyone he met. He would probably do anything to stay that way.

'Well, you've rumbled me. Must say, I didn't imagine I was as well-known as all that. Teach me to underestimate my own fame, anyway.'

'So, what *is* this about?'

'The, uh, attempt at acting, you mean? Well, it's not as sinister as it might appear. A lot more stupid, I'll give you that. It's just that I'm doing my level best to keep this business under wraps at the moment.'

'What business?'

'The things I told you about Charlie are true. He was working on some things for the government, and he

43

has disappeared in what can best be called questionable circumstances. As you so astutely realized, I'm the Honourable Member for East Norfolk. I also have responsibility for the projects Charlie was involved with. They're nothing in the defence line, I can tell you that. If they were – well, things wouldn't be proceeding as they are. It's chiefly to do with agricultural planning, to tell you the truth. Not very glamorous, I'm afraid. Trouble is, that would make no difference to my superiors. If he *has* done a moonlight flit with the programs and research materials, then he's stolen from Her Majesty's Government, and they won't like that at all.'

'He can't have done it. He doesn't have the guts.'

'He'd been under a great deal of strain lately. His funding was being cut. The research wasn't going forward at the rate certain people would have liked. There was some question of the project being taken away from him altogether.'

'So why would he run away?'

'I don't know. Who can guess what goes on in the mind of a genius?'

Paul almost sneered.

'Oh, he's a very bright man, Mr Quillet, believe me. Very bright and very certain of himself. He may think he can interest others in the work. Probably sees the whole thing as his personal property. You must know how autocratic he can be.'

'You know him?'

'Charlie is a friend of mine.' Chandor bit his lip. 'At the moment, I rather wish he weren't. But that's why we're sitting here this morning. This is how things stand: at present, I'm the only person, apart from a couple of his very close colleagues, who knows what's going on. Because of my friendship with him – not to mention a certain interest in keeping my personal

responsibility for this mess out of the general ken –
I'm trying to contain the story and get him and the
programs back before anything comes to light. I won't
pretend it's not to save my face as well, but it is for
Charlie's sake – if this reaches the ears of my superiors,
it'll be the end of his career – and for Mina's.'

Again the mention of her name struck him like a
kick. But he didn't let Chandor have the satisfaction
of seeing it.

'Can't help you,' he said. 'I'm the last one he'd
come to.'

'I'm aware of that. But you see, asking you questions
is only a preliminary. I want you to find him.'

'Do me a favour.'

'You can understand why, I'm sure. It's impossible
for me to use any of the ordinary channels to find him.
Even the gentlemen who brought you here know nothing about the real reasons for this. The moment I ask
for help, the entire matter goes up in smoke. So, I have
to turn to someone who has no official connections,
but who does know the man I'm after.'

'I don't know him.'

'You grew up together. You're his only surviving relative. You have a better chance of understanding how he
thinks. Besides, there's nothing suspicious about one
brother looking for another. You're the obvious – not
to mention the only – choice.'

'Put it another way. I don't want the job.'

'This is your brother we're talking about. And what
about Mina?'

He held the anger down. 'I've got a business to run.
I'm trying to keep my boat on the water.'

Chandor considered for a moment. Another act. He
was all gestures and camouflage. 'Yes, your boat,' he
said. 'You're in some fairly serious trouble with it,
aren't you?'

Paul watched him, kneading the stone.

'I have plenty of information on the subject, Mr Quillet. I know about your father's questionable activities – even if hardly anything was ever proved. I know how he rarely made ends meet, and how you've just about lurched from one crisis to another. You're up to your neck in debt, you have a boat that won't move from its berth, and the harbour police are keeping a close eye on everything you do.'

The Special Branch men were not close. He could wreck the MP's face for him. It would be easy.

'I'm aware that you're in a tight corner,' Chandor said, uneasy behind the gleaming lenses. 'I'm not expecting you to do this for nothing. There will be payment.' He cleared his throat noisily. 'On the other hand, the negative aspect of this is that, uh, if you refuse to assist me, I can bring every government department you've ever heard of down on your head. You think you have problems now. I'll tell you quite honestly; if you don't help me with this, you won't have a boat to keep afloat.'

The positions were finally declared. It had taken time, but it was out in the open now. Chandor was with the big boys, all that weight behind him. Paul was just livestock.

He rolled the stone between the thickened skin of forefinger and thumb. A tanker slid along the horizon. He knew how to deal with people like this. Dad had always said: 'Tangle as much as you want with your own sort, but steer clear of the big buggers.' By this, he meant those who could have power over you – the police, the banks, tax inspectors, the rich and powerful owners of big firms. So what you did – no matter how much you wanted to snap back or lash out – was just sit still and hold your tongue, and say whatever was necessary to get yourself out of whatever fix it was.

46

There was no point in angering a man who could crush you, laying into a bloke who could call down all manner of trouble on your head. Save that for a punch-up in a bar. He didn't care for it, but he had learned it. So he sat and listened to Chandor, and tried not to show the contempt he felt.

Still avoiding his eyes, Chandor opened the folder. 'He was last heard of in Cambridge. The date's here, along with some names and addresses that might be useful. You merely go along and pose as the long-lost brother. I'm sure you can give any number of reasons for wanting to find him. You might want to bury the hatchet after all this time. Or perhaps you're after money.'

'One more crack,' Paul said softly. 'One more, and I'll put you through that window.'

Chandor blinked. He was sweating heavily.

'I'm sorry . . . It's been a stressful time. No offence was intended. I was simply suggesting – '

'You're so helpful.'

'I hope I'm going to be.' He pulled an envelope from his jacket, tossed it across the table. Currency bulged from it; all the colours of the Bank of England. 'Some of that is to assist with your present difficulties,' he said. 'The rest is towards any expenses you incur. If it should happen that you need any more, there's a number here you can 'phone. Don't use it unless you have to.'

The money, at least, looked good.

'I don't want regular reports or any nonsense like that. You should only make contact – with me, personally, no one else – if you need more money, or if you find him. Clear?'

Paul picked up the envelope and took a rough count. The money looked very good.

'And if I don't find him?'

Chandor touched the rim of his spectacles again. 'That won't be your problem. But I hope it doesn't arise.' He tapped on the window. The driver opened the door. 'Take Mr Quillet back to the docks. We're finished here.'

As the driver disappeared, Chandor added: 'You won't, of course, mention any of the things we've discussed to my men? Or anyone else, for that matter.'

Paul regarded him coldly. It would still be a pleasure to lay him out.

Chandor stood up. He had to stoop under the curving ceiling. Paul expected him to offer his hand, but perhaps he realized it was not suitable to the occasion. 'I'm very grateful you've agreed to help,' he said.

'Pleasure,' Paul said.

He stepped out of the trailer. The car waited, engine running. He got in. The Special Branch men looked disgruntled. Maybe they'd been hoping for something livelier.

'North Quay,' Paul said, relaxing back in his seat. He kept his hands in his pockets. One holding the smooth, cold pebble, the other on the envelope full of money.

4

Ten minutes later, driving his Range Rover along the Norwich road, the MP lifted the car 'phone and punched in a New York number. The day was brightening toward the west. A touch of sunshine lightened the shabby fields and woods he passed. The 'phone clicked and fizzed against his ear. He tried to concentrate on the road. Then the ringing stopped.

'Yes?'

'Drazel?'

The voice was southern Californian. 'Who's calling, please?'

He hesitated, reluctant to use his name over the 'phone.

'Chandor. I want to speak with Mr Drazel.'

'Ah, Mr Chandor.' Waves of synthetic warmth beamed down the line. 'I'll put you straight through.'

It wasn't straight through, though. He waited while static crackled louder, wedging the 'phone with his shoulder as he changed down a gear to overtake an invalid car.

'Hello, Anthony.' Drazel's voice was raised, as if he were greeting him from across a room.

'Drazel, I've done it.'

'You know, it's past three A.M. here.'

'You said you wanted to know as soon as possible.'

'Yes, that's very good, Anthony. I take it he accepted the story?'

'I suppose so. He didn't seem very bright.'

'Well, as long as he can find his way around.'

'Look, I can't talk now.'

'Why the hurry?'

'I'm in my car. It's dangerous to drive and talk like this.'

'You sound a little anxious.'

'Of course I am. You don't know who may be listening.'

'Oh, don't concern yourself. You have nothing to fear. Not unless something should go wrong.'

'It'd better not.'

'Well, that's how I feel about it, Anthony.'

'I don't like all this.'

'Pardon me? You keep fading.'

'This hole and corner stuff. It puts me in an invidious position.'

A drawn-out silence. He thought he had been cut off. 'Drazel?'

Drazel said: 'Anthony, maybe you should've considered your position some time ago.'

He was on the bypass near Beccles, speeding too fast above flat green marshes. The river was a sheet of cold iron.

'You shouldn't worry,' Drazel said, urbane once more. 'I'm sure Mr Quillet will come through for us.'

'If this gets out – '

'It won't. You go home now and carry on doing the job you do so well. How's Julia, by the way?'

'Fine. She's . . . fine.'

'Good. I was saying to Barbara just last week, next time we're over we have to spend some time with Anthony and Julia.'

'Yes, you must.'

'By then all this will be history.'

'Yes.'

'I'd better get off the line. Need *some* sleep before I go to Chicago.'

'Right.'

'Anthony, thanks for doing this. You'll see, it'll work out fine.'

'Yes.'

'And Anthony?'

'What?'

'Don't worry.'

He put the 'phone down. A Navwind 24 cruiser was moving upriver, tacking into a faint breeze. It looked clean and free on the empty water. He rubbed his eyes, wishing he were aboard.

5

They dropped him at the gates. Some kids he knew were using the open space for a makeshift skateboard park. They circled him, asking if he had any money to play in the amusement arcades. He warned them off with a growl and went into the port. The *Provider* waited for him.

He had lived and worked on her most of his life. She was the result of a piece of Dad's famous 'luck'. After the war – to be closer to home and his new wife – he had got out of cargo ships and bought a little tug with back pay and some money he was 'lent' (that was what he always said, even if the authorities had their suspicions). One stormy night in the mid-fifties he and Sam came across a tanker floating loose near South Cross Sands. A fire had broken out in the tanks and the crew had abandoned her for fear of an explosion. He got full salvage value by taking her in tow – at risk of being blown to kingdom come. Then he bought the *Provider*, which was in a sorry state at the time. To Paul, she was more of a home than anywhere on land. And this morning he had hated every last rotting rivet in her miserable hull. Hated the port and all the other dead-and-alive places she had taken him to. But this was his life, as he had made it. Until this new thing, like a lifebelt thrown to him, like an escape hatch.

He thought of Sam and Ian, and felt guilty. That rekindled anger against Chandor and all the faceless organizations that could reach into his life and put him in the rattle like this. It was bitter to swallow being told what to do by such people. He didn't believe Chandor. Something stank. But he needed this money.

He spat in the dirty water and went aboard.

Sam and Ian weren't back. He was relieved. He went to his cabin and packed a bag: one canvas holdall to contain a few clothes, spare cigarettes, a battered Walkman, cassettes of Hendrix, the Stones and Warren Zevon. He paused at the shelf of books above the bunk. Old pocket editions, mostly: the Macmillan Kipling, the Chatto & Windus Stevenson. More verse than fiction on both counts. Dark red and gold spines on the Kipling, dark green and gold for Stevenson. All of them ragged with thumbing and mildewed by years aboard the ship. He was not a reading man, but these books were as natural to him as eating and drinking. He had had one of those eccentric educations, hardly ever in school. The old man couldn't fill in his tax returns, but he quoted RLS and 'Kippers' by the yard. Lines, whole poems were rooted in memory by Dad's voice. He ran a finger along the spines, picked out Stevenson's collected poems and stuffed it in the bag.

He heard the clatter of boots on the gangplank, walked into the galley to wait.

Ian came first. His mouth dropped open. Sam wheezed in behind him.

He cut the questions off by handing over a tenner and asking Ian to get a half-bottle of Jameson's. Then he returned to his cabin. Sam followed, saw the bag.

'What's this?' he said, eyes narrowing.

Paul handed him the money.

'Christ,' he said, and sat down on the bunk.

Paul folded a couple of shirts and stuck them in his bag. Sam watched him. He held the cash as if it were something poisonous.

'What is this, Polly?'

'Money. Know you haven't seen any for ages, but you remember what it's for.'

'Don't bloody cheek me. What's the bag for?'

'Going away for a few days.'

'Where?'

Paul picked up his shaving gear, avoiding the old man's gaze.

'What's wrong with you, Polly?'

'Nothing.'

'You march round looking like thunder, and you tell me nothing. I know you, boy. Something's been up for ages.' Paul was surprised. He didn't know it had been so obvious. 'Now this. I don't like it.'

He emptied his pockets of things he would not be needing. Sam suddenly roared:

'Where you bloody goin'?'

'To see Charlie.'

That stopped him cold. Paul sorted through cassettes to give himself something to do. He heard Sam stomp out, closed the door after him. It was hard enough keeping his temper, without having to explain.

After a while he heard Ian come back, then the murmur of lowered voices. Charlie's name was mentioned, and Ian asked who Charlie was. Funny to think the kid had to be reminded. But he wasn't much more than a baby the last time Charlie had been around.

He listened until he'd had enough, then zipped up the bag and went out to the galley. He caught them huddling over the table. They separated guiltily. He poured himself half a cup of coffee and drank it down. The silence was heavy. Sam was listing parts they would need for repairs. He looked at the ill-formed words. Sam had never really learned to read or write.

'Don't go to Davey, remember,' Paul said. 'His stuff's crap.'

'I know that,' Sam grumbled. 'You eaten yet?'

54

'Get something on the way.'

Ian handed him the whiskey. He slipped it in the bag.

'How long you going for?'

'Don't know. You help your Grandad put this tub in working order, all right?'

'You're coming back, ain't you?'

'What d'you think?'

Sam looked doubtful.

He turned toward the door. 'Right, I'm off.'

Sam followed him out, limping a bit. Saturday traffic was roaring over the swing bridge.

'There ain't no trouble, is there?'

'No,' Paul faced him. 'Don't get stewed up, Sam. Get on and fix her.'

Sam coughed. White breath streamed from his mouth in the cold air. 'You're not right, boy.'

'Never was.' He went down the gangway, conscious of the eyes following him. The quayside was busier now. A couple of Germans were hobbling back to their ship after a long night out.

'Don't get lost,' Sam yelled after him.

6

He had no particular name. Sitting at a table under the palms in the bone-white sunshine of the garden, he heard the 'phone ring. He put down the Charleville flintlock pistol he was cleaning and turned toward the villa, peering into the shadows of the lounge.

Tai, the houseboy, came to answer the 'phone. He spoke in the clipped English phrases he had learned specifically for this duty, then placed the receiver on the table and came to the patio door.

'From America,' he said, plucking at the coarse material of his jellabah.

He went into the cool shade. Tai shuffled out, slippers flapping on the tiled floor.

A Californian voice said: 'Is Mr Dern there, please?'

He said: 'I'm afraid he's out.'

'Oh, that's a pity. You see, I have a job for him.'

'Perhaps I might take a message.'

'Well, thank you. Could you tell him that the job is in England. Looking after a man called Quillet.'

'Quillet.'

'That's correct. If Mr Dern could fly in as fast as possible, the details will be waiting for him when he arrives.'

'I'll pass your message on.'

'That's very kind of you.'

'My pleasure.'

He replaced the receiver and called Tai. The boy reappeared, solemn eyes showing bright in the thin Berber face. He asked where Madame was, learned that she was in the town, shopping. He gave instructions to call the airport and arrange the first possible flight to England, then to pack him a case for the trip. The boy listened carefully as he detailed exactly what the case should contain.

He returned to the garden, paused, drinking in the heat and sunlight. Over the rough wall that bordered the garden, he saw the long beach of Agadir gleaming like snow. The Atlantic was a dazzle of deep blue. A few tourists wandered the sands, pestered by boys selling rainbow-striped rugs.

He was a man of a little below the medium height, compact and muscular. He wore a white shirt and shorts. There was no waste flesh on him. His skin was lightly tanned, not bronzed. His head was well-moulded, the brown hair carefully greased back, and his face was almost boyish, making it hard to tell whether he were thirty or fifty. He looked as if he might be Breton French. When he spoke, his accent was odd, like a foreign language broadcast from a Russian radio station. A European might have said he was from the States or Canada, while an American would probably guess he was a Scandinavian who had studied English with an American instructor.

In the Moroccan town where his expensive villa was situated, he was known to be a dealer in antique weaponry. He was married to a French woman, and they kept very much to themselves. The villa stood amid trees and other smaller homes on the beach below the Palais Royal. It was protected by security devices and employed three full-time staff – all Moroccans – who could rarely be drawn to discuss their employer. One houseboy had, in a boastful moment, divulged that the villa contained a large room like a giant safe which was completely given over to a gun collection. The boy was sacked not long after his indiscretion. Aside from that, the Monsieur was occasionally to be seen taking a swim from the beach, or drinking afternoon coffee with his wife outside a café on the hill going up to town. They tended to avoid the town during the high tourist season.

The Monsieur was known to travel abroad often.

He crossed to the pool, stood with hand on hips, the glitter of blue water pricking his eyes. Then he stripped off his shirt and launched himself into the water.

After the swim, he gathered the Charleville, the oil and cleaning equipment onto a tray and went inside. He passed through the lounge, with its luxurious furniture and paintings, through a small but fully equipped gymnasium, and padded along a cool passage to a steel-lined door. He took a bunch of keys from his shorts pocket, fitted three of them into locks at top, centre and bottom of the door, and let himself into the gun room.

It was a large room, as the unfortunate houseboy had claimed, windowless and carpeted in soft brown. All along the walls glass-fronted cabinets of antique oak housed his collection.

It began with one of the earliest forms of handgun: a fourteenth-century construction, three wrought barrels held together by iron bands, all mounted on a pole and touched off like a cannon. It went on to cover all the developments of the form: battleaxe-pistol combinations; Japanese matchlocks; a seventeenth-century Snapchaunce revolver; an Elgin Cutlass, its blade mounted under the barrel. They were subtly lighted to bring out the rich colours of brass and maple, blue steel and walnut. Other cabinets were given over to modern examples, with an emphasis again on the unusual: the Dardick .38 Model 1500, with the rotary ammunition carrier; and the Gyrojet 13mm Mark 1, which was nothing less than a hand-held rocket launcher. All the weapons were originals.

He admired the collection as he put the tray down. He breathed the still air of the room, a subtle tang of gun oil, black powder, and the many volumes of his library. This was the still centre of his world. It was a pity he had to leave so soon after returning from his last job. His wife would be unhappy, of course. She would ask again what was the point of having a pleasant home if he was never there to enjoy it. He felt some agreement with her as he polished the Charleville and replaced it in its retaining clips. On his desk in the centre of the room, correspondence from Griffins in Canada and Ward and Van Valkenburg in Fargo awaited answers. Several interesting pieces had recently come onto the market. He consoled himself with the thought that, after finishing this job, he would be able to afford more of them.

7

The first thing Paul did after leaving the docks was stop at the public 'phones across from the railway station. He dialled the number Chandor had given him for Charlie's home, let it ring a full minute. No one answered.

Crossing the road to the station and boarding the Norwich train, he couldn't help noticing an unfamiliar feeling. He tried not to think about it. But as the little two-carriage train jolted out of the station in the brightening mid-morning, as he looked to the left and saw ships on the North Quay slipping away, he knew what it was. He was off the *Provider*, out of the port, out of the dingy little town.

The feeling was relief.

He dozed till Norwich, then had a forty-five-minute wait for the Cambridge train. He ate Traveller's Fare sandwiches in the bar and scoured the 'papers, but they held nothing about a computer expert disappearing in Cambridge. Only the earthquake in South America, diplomatic troubles with Iran, a new famine getting started in some African state, and a train crash in Bristol.

The Cambridge train departed ten minutes late. He was in the second carriage, alone except for an old woman knitting, and a young mother with a couple of unruly toddlers called Malcolm and Stacey. He regarded the mother with what Sam called his 'practised eye', took in the fact that she was a size 12 but her dress was a 10, that her blonde hair owed something to the bottle, and that she wore no ring. She had the harassed expression he always read in the faces of people who had taken on responsibility too early. She caught him watching her, wasn't offended. But little Malcolm, who obviously favoured his father for red hair and pale, chubby skin, started yelling for his crayons. So that was the end of another beautiful romance.

He settled down to catch a little more sleep as the train rolled out of the city. Red council estates gave way to rolling farmland and bare black trees. He went through the head-dropping, jerk-awake routine that is sleeping on a train, and Charlie was on his mind, so things he held down while awake got behind his eyes.

Thinking of his brother always led back to the start, to Mum dying. He never saw her at the end. She was in hospital by then, where the leukaemia had finally beaten her down. Auntie May considered her too 'worrying' for the boys to see. Maybe she was right.

Mum had been fading for so long that, to him especially, she was just this sick person whose bed was made up in the front room. He used to go and sit with her sometimes. She liked to see him drink tea from her saucer. She would carefully tip a drop from her bone china cup with the marigolds painted on it, add more milk, and tell him to be careful not to spill it. He would sip from the tiny lake as she watched and smiled, and then she would hug him – he thought even then how bony and light she was – ask for a kiss, and let him climb down. Back in the kitchen, Auntie May would say: 'Good lad,' and ask: 'Were you nice to your mum?' He always said yes. He always was.

Charlie didn't get the same treatment. He was older, perhaps he understood what was happening better. At any rate, he got to be nervous and reluctant about going into the front room. He didn't like the dark wallpaper

61

or the old brass bed and its patchwork quilt. He hated the half-closed curtains, the smell. Eventually he got so bad that he would cry if Auntie May asked him to go in.

Dad wasn't around much. He never had been. In the days before Mum got ill, his homecomings were big events. Sometimes he came in the middle of the night – it seemed like it to them – but he turfed them out of bed anyway and played with them, gave them sweets, bawled bits of poetry. He smelt of beer. His returns now were subdued. He would enter quietly, prowl past the front room door as if there were something bad in there. If he found them in the kitchen, he would take Auntie May aside for a murmured conversation. 'How's she doing?' 'Oh, you know . . .' Auntie May's slow, deep voice would go.

On the day Mum died, he happened to be in port. Just after breakfast, a neighbour came running from across the street – they had no 'phone of their own. The boys were shepherded upstairs. They sat in their bedroom, staring at each other in half-comprehending silence. Peeping round the door, they saw Dad go downstairs in his one good suit. He and Auntie May went out, leaving them in the care of the neighbour.

He remembered that they spent most of the day playing street football and looking at comics.

The adults returned well after bed time, but they were still awake, hunkering at the window to see. By the light of the streetlamp on the corner, they watched Dad open the gate and unlock the front door. His face was expressionless, but he was carrying a bottle in a brown paper bag. Auntie May came behind, sobbing quietly into an enormous handkerchief. She came up to see them, and her face was a red puddle. She whispered: 'Your poor old Mum's gone to the Lord at last.' And she gave them each a toffee, tucked them back into bed and went down again.

Late into the evening, they could hear Dad's voice rumbling below. They fell asleep to its rise and fall, like waves, like the sea.

After that they went wild. The idea was that Auntie May stayed on to look after them. She stayed all right, but most of the time they didn't.

Dad's solution was taking them aboard the *Provider*.

''Least I know where you buggers are,' he'd say. And at least they were fed regularly and had something constructive to do there. By the time Paul was eight, he was working hard for his Dad.

Charlie did the same, but as he got older, he was less happy about it.

Disconnected memories.

Lying in his bunk, aged seven or eight, watching from under the blankets as Dad and Sam polished off a bottle of gin between them, their talk growing more and more sloppy and raucous. The mysterious men who were invited aboard in every port they visited, from Aberdeen to Bremerhaven – men with no official status except in police files. Thin-lipped types whose eyes burned under their caps; big, bearded, expansive chaps who laughed and pinched the boys' cheeks if they got the chance.

He came awake again as the train moved out of Borden. A fight was developing between Malcolm and Stacey. He dug the Walkman out and slotted in the Hendrix tape. The guitar came thrashing out from 'sixty-eight and caught him unawares. He remembered the old Pavilion Theatre out on the South Pier. Gone now. Back in the 'fifties and 'sixties it was a major concert venue. Buddy Holly played there. The Animals, the Stones, Chuck Berry pre- the respected legend era,

63

Fleetwood Mac before Peter Green grew his fingernails and gave it all up. And that time when he crammed to the front of the stage and watched Hendrix throttle the neck off his guitar during 'Voodoo Chile'.

Hell of a thing to expose a thirteen-year-old to.

Charlie had been there. Afterwards, in the snooty way he had, he said: 'Lot of row, wasn't it?' Paul jeered back at him for all the cissy flower-power stuff he liked. Charlie said something else, and he replied in kind, and it ended in a fight on the quayside.

He tried to make a picture of Charlie in his mind. It was hard. A complete image didn't come – just odd things: the superior tone of his voice when he was being clever-clever; the glint in his eye when he tried to wind you up; the loose-jointed way he walked, so easy to imitate.

How could Charlie do anything illegal? It didn't sound real.

He heard Dad complaining, for maybe the fifteen hundredth time: 'Why can't you two get on? One of these days you'll bloody well need each other. You're brothers, for God's sake.'

Brothers, maybe. But you wouldn't have known it by looking. They had both grown up taller than average, but that was about all. Paul looked like his father, Charlie was the male version of their mother. Taller, lighter coloured. He had his mother's long face. The only real resemblance was the colour of their eyes.

Their characters were equally at odds. After the council caught up with them, forced Dad to make them live ashore with their aunt and attend school full-time, Charlie took to it well. But Paul still played truant, went with his father whenever he could persuade him.

He was running with his own gang. In most ports, there are these children who live lives outside the experience of their peers. They travel, they tend to be beyond the reach of the rules most kids have to obey. They get a reputation for being 'bad'. In their day, Paul and Charlie were probably the best-known examples of the breed. They had status, which Paul hung onto even after the authorities tried to hobble them. They were pretty rough, always running close to the law. Charlie left that, started passing exams and getting scholarships, becoming one of the sneerers.

Of course they didn't get on. How could they? They had nothing to get on with.

Another tag of memory. Both of them in the wheel-house one lunchtime during one of the truces they occasionally struck until they hit their teens. Dad and Sam were in the Anchor on Commercial Road, getting legless. Charlie wearing Dad's pea coat and cap, hanging on the wheel as he mimicked the old man bawling 'Requiem'. They had seen him doing this plenty of times, usually at night, in rough weather, at least two or three over the eight. Sometimes it was Kipling's 'The Vampire' or 'The Storm Cone', more often Stevenson's 'My Ship and I'. Beginning with that great swooping chant: 'O it's *I* that am the captain of a tidy little ship'. But he usually wound up with 'Requiem'. The *Provider* would be wallowing along in a heavy sea, the windscreen spinning to fling rain off, and he would launch in with: 'Under the wide and starry sky,' playing it like an old ham actor. Often as not they all joined in, even Sam.

So Charlie was doing his impression, and it was a good one. Paul stood behind him, joining in on the last word of each line, rocking in time. Finally, they had to give up because they were laughing too hard. They had been sipping from Dad's 'hidden' bottle of Red Label, so everything was funny. Paul pulled himself up to the window and peered out at the quay. Charlie took off the cap and hung it on the wheel.

"'Course,' he said, 'he's a drunk.'

Paul said: 'Whatcha mean?'

'He's a drunk,' Charlie said. 'A drunkard.' He was eleven then, learning a lot of new words now he was in school properly. He savoured it. 'Drunk-ard.'

'He's not,' Paul said.

'Bloody is.'

'Isn't.'

And they went on, swapping back and forth with increasing irritation, until there was another fight.

Half their childhood seemed to be spent clouting seven bells out of each other. Charlie was bigger, Paul more vicious. They used to come out looking like victims of the beatings they'd see sometimes outside the Anchor, or bars in foreign ports.

And that was before Mina.

Helping Dad take his boots off one night after a series of heavy sessions in some Cherbourg bars. The old man grinding out something he said was by Tennyson – with alterations:

> 'They should've stabbed me where I lay,
>   Bottom upwards!
> How could I rise and come away,
>   Bottom upwards?
> How could I look upon the day?
> They should have stabbed me where I lay,
>   Bottom upwards –'

Bellowing with laughter all the while. Then, as he pulled the blankets over him, a tear in the wrinkled brown corner of his eye.

'Here, son. We do all right, don't we?'

'Yeah.'

A thick, calloused hand gripped his arm. 'Since your Mum passed over, I dunno. You're all right?'

'Yeah.'

66

'And Charlie?'

'He's all right.'

'I dunno,' Dad said. The tear ran loose and zigzagged down the folds and creases of his face. 'I hope she'd approve.'

He supposed that, by modern medical standards, Charlie was right; their father was an alcoholic. But a lot of people were, by modern standards.

He closed his eyes on endless black fields.

Chandor said it was strange; brothers who had no contact, who didn't even know what the other was doing any more. Maybe in Chandor's comfortable patch it was, but not where he came from. The ships were full of men who seemed to have no relatives, no past. Yes, there were good family men among them, but plenty worked the boats so they could get away from that snake pit.

He patted the money in one of his shirt pockets. The money was what he had to concentrate on. He was only doing this to get the cash to put the *Provider* back in working order, plus perhaps enough to sort out some other long-standing problems. All he had to do was pretend to look for Charlie. Once the money was spent, Chandor could go mate with himself on the floor of the Commons if he wished. And so, for that matter, could his dear departed brother. He wouldn't mind seeing some kind of upset in the 'papers with Charlie's name sticking out of it.

Hendrix was pounding his ears with 'Stone Free'. Despite the naps, he felt like one of the rags off the engine-room floor. Also thirsty. He dug around in his bag for the half-bottle, lifted it and took a pull. The old woman frowned over her knitting. He offered her the bottle. She turned away, needles clattering.

Malcolm and Stacey were spreading their argument

to adjacent seats. The mother glanced at him, checking whether he was the sort to get bad-tempered about it.

He lit a cigarette, closed his eyes, and wondered what it was really all about.

8

It was nearly four o'clock when he reached Cambridge. Darkness coming in, the cold starting to clamp down again. He passed through the station building to the taxi-rank. A sour-faced old man was hunched behind the wheel of the first one in the line, studying the pictures in a copy of *Knave*. He gave Paul the once-over as he got in, obviously didn't like the look.

'Where to?' he said, flipping the meter on. An identity card on the dashboard said he was Ronald Borrel. His mugshot seemed to have been taken after a rough night.

Paul gave him the address, and that made Ronald scowl some more.

They pulled out of the car park into a busy road. Paul read the signs all over the cab's interior. 'Thank you for NOT Smoking.' 'Please make sure your shoes are clean.' 'This cab is not a litter bin.' 'If you feel sick, please stop the taxi or open a window.'

He saw little of the Cambridge he expected, none of the stuff made familiar by films and television. No ancient seats of learning in time-worn stone. Ordinary, shabby streets. He asked Ronald where the university was.

'Don't go through none of that,' Ronald said. 'Less you want a detour.'

Charlie's house was in the New Chesterton part of town. A big Victorian place facing a park. High bay windows, the front door in a porch with stained glass portals. A low wall at the front gave on to gravelled parking space.

'This it?' Ronald asked, doubtfully.

'Wait here.'

He approached the house. Chandor was right about Charlie doing well. It was the kind of house Mercedes and BMWs parked outside. Through the windows he saw tall bookshelves. Exotic houseplants hung in baskets in the porch, wilting.

His hands were sweaty, his heart had speeded up. His reflection in the glass needed a shave, not to mention a bath.

He leaned on the bell push.

No one came. Not even a dog barked.

He wondered suddenly if they had kids yet. What would their children look like? Hope to God they got their mother's looks.

He gave the bell a few more stabs, peered through the door. Letters were scattered on the floor beneath the slot inside. He signalled to Ronald that he was going round the back. Ronald hated that. He started rolling his window down to protest, but Paul was already gone. He cut round the left side of the house, going down an alley made by a tall privet hedge. A neat lawn was edged with flower beds and bounded at the end by fruit trees. Charlie's doing? He never lifted his eyes from the keyboard long enough. Mina's? He couldn't see it. More likely they got someone in to fix it for them.

The back door came out through a conservatory. Inside was a scruffy old couch, a threadbare Persian rug and a bamboo coffee table. Just the place for evening drinkies with university friends. He hawked on the patio slabs and looked up for signs of life. No lights, no staring faces.

A car horn blared three times. He hurried back along the alley. Ronald glowered at him.

'What's your problem?'

'Wondered where you was,' Ronald complained. 'Walking off like that.'

'Ronald, you keep your hand off that bloody horn. You're a taxi driver, not a burglar alarm.' He got in. 'Now, take me to a nice, clean, cheap guest house.'

Ronald didn't like his tone. That was clear by the way he crunched the gears pulling away from the kerb. Paul wondered where Mina was. Charlie going on the run, documents and computer discs falling out of his swag bag was one thing, but a fugitive from justice taking the missis along, that was something else. Chandor hadn't mentioned anything about her.

Ronald took him to a guest house off the Newmarket Road, the kind of place he stayed in when ashore; only the language spoken changed. This one was a three-storey terrace in a row of similar, called 'Parkside'. Pink lampshades in the lounge and a dining room in the basement. It looked clean enough.

Inside, a Greek woman about forty-five years old and sixty inches tall let him have a twin-single room at a low price because it was winter. No register to sign, just cash in hand. She took him up to the first floor. It was better than he was accustomed to. Bathroom across from his door on the landing, good beds with duvets rather than blankets, the carpet soft, the curtains actually thick enough to keep out morning light. When he was alone, he opened them and looked out on pointed rooftops and the orange blush of the city night. He was the only guest, apart from an American couple doing Europe on forty dollars a day. Occasionally he heard their voices above.

He switched on the 14-inch colour set in the corner and watched the news while the kettle boiled for coffee. Nothing about missing scientists. Only the earthquake, another American senator resigning due to allegations about his sexual behaviour, and the Prime Minister visiting the train crash victims in hospital.

71

A tail-end item on the local segment showed a Peter-borough school which was going to raise a hundred thousand pounds' worth of clothes, food and medical supplies to aid the 'quake survivors.

He went out, buttoning his jacket up to the neck against the chill air. Traffic was jockeying out of the city along Newmarket Road. He walked toward town, stopping in a newsagent's to buy a town map. A couple of doors down was an Indian restaurant. He was given a table in the powdery darkness at the back, hidden from the couples who were dining before going on somewhere. Over dinner and a couple more whiskies, he studied Chandor's list and the map. He found one address that was an easy walk away, just off Gonville Place. Dr Brian Coppel.

Dr Coppel's house was like Charlie's. Same bay windows, same pleasant, tree-lined street. The difference was that the garden looked less well-tended, a black Volvo stood out front, and the lights were on. He trod his cigarette into the pavement, climbed three steps to the front door, and rang the bell. It gave him everything Charlie's place had not: a dog yelped and came tumbling down the hall; a child yelled, 'Door! Door!'; a female voice shouted, 'Brian?'; and music that was thumping from the lounge to his right faded quickly. Through frosted glass panels he saw the hall light come on and the shape of a man approach.

'Bit early, aren't you – Ah . . . sorry, thought you were the babysitter.' Coppel was a very tall man, six feet five, at least. Fair-haired, thinning on top, with a reddish beard, long nose, and blue-green eyes that peered in a surprised way. He wore a cardigan, brown cords and training shoes, carried an old leather-bound volume. An Irish setter bitch leapt and yapped round his legs. 'Quiet, Amber.'

'Dr Coppel, I'm Paul Quillet. I'm looking for my brother.'

'Brother?' Coppel's mind was still on his book. The setter didn't help his concentration. He flapped a hand at her. 'Amber!'

'Charlie Quillet,' Paul said. 'Charles. You're a friend of his aren't you?'

'Charlie? Yes, yes, of course.'

Coppel's wife came down the stairs behind him. An attractive redhead in a Laura Ashley dress. She was putting in her earrings. She gave the situation a glance and disappeared down the hall with the setter.

'I came to see him,' Paul said. 'Turned up at his place this afternoon. No one's there.'

'Ah.' Coppel shifted uneasily, as if decisions were not his strong point. 'Look, why don't you come in for a moment?'

He led the way into a high, comfortable room done up as a study. A leather-topped desk stood in the bay, a home computer in one corner. Books grew like weeds in every space, and a Marantz hi-fi surrounded by compact discs was pushing out a fast, folky tune. A child's drawing of a house and family with red dog was propped up on the desk. Coppel motioned him to a wing-backed leather armchair, then swayed over to the desk and put his book down.

'Offer you a drink?' he said.

'Thanks. Whisky, if you've got it.'

Coppel poured a generous measure, then noticed there was no soda. 'Ah, hang on a sec.' He went out. Paul heard the child calling down the stairs: 'Who is it?' Then Coppel and his wife conversing in hisses down the hall. The stereo started singing about red and gold being royal colours.

Coppel returned with a bottle of mineral water. 'There we go. Not too weak?'

73

'That's fine, thanks.'

He sat on the edge of his desk, fiddling with his own glass. 'So, you're Charlie's brother? I didn't know he had one, tell you the truth.'

'I'm the black sheep.'

'Really? Lowestoft, isn't it? Where you come from? He told me once his dad worked on the boats.'

'I still do.'

'You don't look much like him.'

'He's the handsome one.'

The wife called from above, asking where the car keys were. Coppel told her they were in the bathroom. The wife said: 'Where else?' and Coppel grinned sheepishly.

'So, you've come up on a family visit, and he's not here?'

'Looks that way.'

'Well, we haven't seen him for – oh, must be a fortnight now.'

'Do you work with him?'

'No. We see each other socially.' He tipped his head to the music's rhythm, long neck stretching like a swan's. 'College functions, that sort of thing. We're not in the same line, you see.'

'You're a doctor.'

'Only of philosophy. The one thing I know about computers is that mine keeps losing my golden prose somewhere in its electronic bowels.'

The stereo was onto a song about a beggar.

'What is that?' Paul said, making an interested face.

'That? Oh, Fairport Convention.'

'Sounds different to what I remember.'

'This is recent stuff.'

'Saw them once, long time ago, back in the sixties.'

'With Charlie? He was the one who put me onto them. I've only seen the modern version, of course.'

74

'Good stuff,' Paul said. He wanted to get on Coppel's good side.

'You think so?' He jerked his head toward the ceiling. 'Wife hates it. Wailing folkies, she calls it. Thinks we're all ageing hippies. Suppose we are. I've got nearly everything they've put out.' He crossed to the stereo, touching a line of discs and cassettes. 'Everything but "Gottle of Geer". Difficult to find that one.' He gazed dreamily at them.

'However, this isn't helping you with Charlie.' He turned. 'He hasn't been around for a week or so. Took an impromptu holiday.'

Paul sipped the whisky. 'The house looked empty. Did Mina go with him?'

Coppel's tongue pushed against his left cheek. 'Ah, you don't know, then?'

'We don't write much.'

The wife's voice came again. 'Brian, we've got to be at the Reves' by eight-thirty.'

'Just a minute.' He scratched his beard. 'It's a . . . a bit difficult . . . Um, you see, Mina's left him — sort of.'

Paul felt cold. He didn't know what his expression was saying to the other man. He didn't know how he felt himself.

'Sorry it's me who gets to tell you,' Coppel said. When Paul didn't reply, he went on: 'It's not something that's generally known. I mean, everyone round here knows, you can't keep a damn thing private with the bush telegraph so efficient. It's the one thing academia's still good at. But it's very sketchy, even to us. Mina upped sticks and went off — what? — about six weeks ago, probably more. Just a holiday on her own. She's been working hard lately, the costumes and all.'

'Costumes?'

'She and a friend run this costume rental business. Uniforms and so forth. Lately it's been getting a lot of TV and film work. So it's quite reasonable that she would need a holiday, and Charlie's usually too busy to go away. That was the public face, anyway.'

'But?'

'Well, you know how it is. Mina and Janet – Janet's my wife – they're quite close. They talk a lot. So we know that there's more to it than needing a break. When Charlie did a bunk as well, I assumed he'd gone after her. Bloody ought to.'

A voice on the stereo started singing: 'Deep and dark are my true love's eyes.'

The wife came in, asking whether Emily's elephant, without which she refused to go to sleep, was some-where in the room. Also to complain about the non-appearance of the babysitter. Also to get a better look at the visitor. She had a fine figure, good legs too. She nodded good evening and went rooting under the desk for the lost toy.

'I was just telling Mr Quillet –' Coppel said.

'You've had a bit of a wasted journey,' she sympa-thized, dragging the elephant into the open. She held it to her stomach as she looked at Paul.

'Do you know where Mina went?' he asked. 'I mean, if Charlie's with her now?'

Something in her eyes suggested knowledge – not of Mina's whereabouts: something judgemental, as if she were weighing him up against what she'd heard.

'She was just going to drive around and stay where she stayed,' she said. 'The West Country. That's all I can tell you.'

Paul gazed at her. They understood each other. He didn't like it.

Coppel hadn't noticed anything. He was gathering papers on his desk.

'I'd better let you get on with your evening,' Paul said, standing up.

'Yes,' Coppel said. 'Sorry we couldn't help. Sorry we were the ones to tell you, come to that. I'd offer you another drink, but you can see –'

'You've been very kind.'

'Maybe if you tried some of Charlie's colleagues . . .'

'I've got some addresses, thanks.' He left the glass on the marble mantelpiece. The wife swung the elephant against her stomach. Then the doorbell rang, and she said: 'The babysitter,' and whipped out to answer it.

In the confusion that followed, Coppel took him to the door.

'If you should find him – or them,' he said, 'give them our best, won't you?'

'I will.'

The door closed, shutting in the light, the warmth, the music and the voices.

He walked away, sour and annoyed. He was irritated that Chandor had not told him of Mina's leaving, but there was also Coppel's wife staring at him like a detective who had something on him. He thought about the spacious, comfortable house, the life they led, imagined something similar for Charlie and Mina.

Sam was probably still in the *Provider*'s engine room, directing some engineer in the repairs. Ian would be sprawled on his bunk with another comic. His cabin, with its bunk and single bookshelf, chair and table, would be dark and cold.

He made his way down Lensfield and into the town centre. Now he was in the tourist heart, the college buildings along Trumpington Street and King's Parade. Well-dressed people were going into wine bars and pubs. He seemed to be the only person on his own. He was used to it. Most of the time.

After an hour of wandering, he found a suspect-looking pub in a shabby side street and went in. It was what he expected: smoke and noise; unbeautiful people packed in like herring, getting determinedly smashed. He got talking to a brash, ravaged blonde with large breasts and a taste in clothes that leaned as far from the Laura Ashley of Coppel's wife as it was possible to get. Her heels were so high she was almost his height when she finally stood up to leave with him at closing-time. Her name was Sally. She took him back to her bomb-site of a house not far away, and put on a Lionel Ritchie record while they did what they did. She was even drunker than him. She kept saying: 'You're nice. You're nice.'

At three o'clock in the morning he got up, dressed silently and went back to the guest house. His head was splitting. He took another drink from the half-bottle, and fell back into sleep for eleven hours.

When he woke, it was to someone knocking on his door.

He rolled over, bouncing the whiskey bottle on the carpet.

'Wait a minute.' His mouth tasted like a slop bucket, his eyes were shrunken and gritty. The knocking continued. He clambered up, pulling his trousers on. He had a faint flash of unease – who could it be? – but was too groggy to stop. He fumbled the lock, heard someone outside say: 'Maybe he's ill.' Then he got the door open.

Mina stared at him.

9

It *was* her. He didn't believe it, but it was. The
momentary difficulty of fitting what he saw now
to the memory passed. She was much the same.
The eyes, so black they were purple, had a couple
of thread lines under them; a pair of little creases
bracketed her mouth; the thick black hair was longer,
shoulder length; figure slender as ever. Much the same.
But the clothes were more expensive. Everything more
expensive. A full length black swagger coat, red wool
dress with a wide belt, and black medium-heeled boots.
He stared back at her, already losing the old image
as it melted to fit the new. She was as lovely as he
remembered.

Behind her, arms folded and face set, was the landlady.

'Is this right?' she said, the Greek accent soft.

Mina nodded slowly. 'Yes, this is him.' She sounded
sorry. He caught a whiff of her perfume. Different frag-
rance, but the same spiced underscent, which was her.
He backed into the room, reaching for a shirt.

The landlady glanced at Mina. 'You be all right?'

'Yes . . . Thank you. It'll be all right.'

'No trouble, okay?' She went down the stairs slowly.
American voices whispered above.

She entered, looking uncertainly round the room.

He opened the curtains and went to the sink, turned
the taps on and splashed his face with cold water. His
brain throbbed regularly behind his eyes as he bent
down. He drank four glasses of water one after the
other. She stood near the door, holding a sort of

portable typewriter case in front of her. She watched him with bleak eyes, then moved toward the window, catching her toe on the bottle. Outside, low afternoon sun emptied itself on the rooftops.

He cleared his throat. 'You're a surprise.'

She nodded. 'Janet Coppel told me you'd been to see them. I went through the guest houses in the 'phone book. That woman told me there was a Mr Quillet staying here.'

He filled the sink with hot water, fetched his shaving gear. 'Not the right one, though.'

'I wasn't expecting Charlie.'

'He wouldn't be seen dead, place like this, right?' He lathered up and ran the razor over his face.

'What're you doing here?' she said.

'Looking for you.'

'Me?'

'And hubby, of course.'

'Why?'

'Missed you both.'

'Oh, stop it.'

'I'm not starting.'

Her eyes flashed. 'You bloody are. You –' She caught herself. In the mirror he saw that she was drawn tight. 'Back in the old routine,' she said, the smile bitter. She put the case down.

The razor nicked him. He wanted a drink.

'Why're *you* here?' he said.

'I think I need your help. Charlie needs your help.'

The foam washed away, his face emerged, creased and pallid. 'I'm not very clear just now –'

'I can see that. What were you doing last night, scuba diving in a distillery?'

'Why would you need my help?'

'Do something for me, would you? Go look outside, and tell me if there's a silver-grey car in the road.'

She was serious. Anxiety had always honed her temper to sarcasm. Shrugging, he let himself out of the room and padded along the landing to a window facing the street. A silver-grey Vauxhall Carlton was parked near the end of the road. The windscreen reflected sky, he couldn't make out whether anyone was inside.

Back in the room, she said:

'I knew it!' She rubbed the collar of her coat between finger and thumb. An old gesture when she was nervous. 'Is there a back way out of this place?'

'What?'

'Please. Get us out of here.'

They left the house through the kitchen and the back yard. The landlady didn't care for it, but he paid her another night in advance, which helped her keep her thoughts to herself. The passage behind the houses led onto the road at one end and Midsummer Common at the other. He helped her over a low fence – the touch of her hand made him shiver – and they went off across the Common. It was a fine afternoon, there were plenty of people about. He offered to carry her case, but she hung on to it, hung on to herself. She kept glancing back, but he saw no one.

McDonald's didn't suit her. She belonged in a different atmosphere altogether. She was too sleek, her Indian blood made her exotic as an orchid among the weeds of an English Sunday afternoon. But she wanted to be somewhere public and safe. At a table out of sight of the windows, surrounded by people, he ate a late breakfast and told her his story, up to the interview with Coppel and his wife.

She listened, sipping at a cup of what passes for coffee in such places, not tasting. She was wound tight.

When he finished, she said:

81

'Tony asked you to do this?'

'The MP, yeah.'

'Charlie was right, then.' Forefinger and thumb rubbed at the wool of her collar.

'What about? You're supposed to be in Cornwall.'

'I was. I've spent the last four days running around trying to lose that silver car.'

'Why?'

She reached into her pocket and put a folded sheet of paper on the table. Perforations down both sides.

'It's computer printout,' she said.

'I know. I've seen them before.' He opened it. It read:

15.28 29/1/89
MINA
'TAHEIA, THE PIT OF THE NIGHT CRAWLS WITH TREACH-
EROUS THINGS,
SPIRITS OF ULTIMATE AIR AND THE EVIL SOUL OF
THINGS.'
COME BACK. NEED YOUR HELP, WEATHERSPY. *DON'T
GO TO POLICE. TRUST NO ONE. WATCH FOR FOLLOW-
ERS. WILL COMMUNICATE AGAIN BY THIS METHOD.
PLEASE, THIS IS REAL.
CHARLIE.

He turned the paper over, checking the other side, then looked at her. 'So?'

'Recognize it?'

'The quote? Stevenson.'

'I didn't, at first. He means a lot to you and Charlie because of Bernard, but I had to borrow a copy of the verses to make sure.' She produced a slim volume and opened it to the relevant page. 'That was the hero of the tale telling his girlfriend that she shouldn't come to help him in the night. This is what she replies:

"Rua, behold me, kiss me, look in my eyes and read;
Are these the eyes of a maid that would leave her
    lover in need?"'

'Very pretty,' Paul said. 'I don't get it.'

'This came through on my computer on Wednesday.' She indicated what he had thought was the typewriter case, presently between her feet under the table. 'It's a little portable Epson. Charlie gave it to me. I use it for planning the business, doing accounts, and for the electronic mail.'

His face must have shown a blank.

'It's like a postal service. You have a modem, a connection from your computer to any 'phone line you happen to be near. You have a password that lets you into the computer equivalent of a sorting room. They have a file with your name on it, and anyone who's on the same network can write to you. You key into the system and get out any correspondence you've received.'

'Amazing,' he muttered.

'It saves on postal strikes. When I went away –' she skipped over that awkwardness '– I took the machine so I could keep in touch with business. When I keyed in on Wednesday, that message flashed up as soon as I hit the button. It stayed for a few seconds, printed up all by itself, then erased. It's not supposed to do that. Even if there wasn't the verse, no one else I know can fiddle a computer to do that sort of thing.

'I didn't know what to do. It looked so mad. I thought it might just be some kind of plea for me to come home, but that's not Charlie. He's never pleaded for anything. I rang the house but he wasn't there. Then I tried his office at Robersman.'

He wiped a smear of ketchup off his fingers. 'What's Robersman?'

'The company he works for some of the time. They

have a place in Silicon Park. He did a lot of jobs for them in the early eighties. They part-fund his research work now.'

'The agricultural stuff Chandor talked about?'

'I suppose so. Anyway, I tried the office. That was when I found out he'd been gone since last Friday.'

'Weren't you keeping in touch?'

She looked down, the tip of her tongue pressing against her top lip; another gesture he knew. 'Let's not get into that now, all right?'

'Whatever you like.'

Anger flared again. 'Don't say it like that.'

'I'm not saying it like anything.'

'You're gloating.'

'I couldn't care less.'

'You bet you couldn't. You're only here because someone waved a wad of cash in your face.'

'Lay off.' He glared at her. The other customers listened intently, hamburgers suspended halfway to their mouths.

She subsided, smoothed her hair back, the palm of her hand sliding down her neck. Delicate ears with opals in the lobes.

'I did go away,' she said wearily. 'Before Christmas. Because I wanted some time to think. The complete cliché: wife runs off to remote country hotel to consider her life and crimes. But we hadn't split up. Not officially.'

What did that mean? What did it need, a printed form?

'At the beginning I *did* 'phone – but all I got was the answering machine. My voice. Myself talking to myself. I realized I wouldn't have a lot to say even if he answered. So I stopped. He knew where I was: he didn't call me either.'

Over Christmas, he thought. They didn't even talk to say Season's Greetings?

'The girl at his office told me he was taking a short break, but she didn't know where. When she started asking where *I* was, I got off the line.'

He examined the printout again. 'You believe this?'

'Well . . .'

'Doesn't prove a thing. Sort of backs up what Chandor told me.'

'You think he's lost his marbles?'

'What's "Weatherspy"?'

'One of his projects. He didn't talk about it.'

He shook the printout at her. 'Spirits of ultimate air and the evil soul of things.'

'Just what he needs, his own brother thinking the worst.'

'*I* didn't leave him to stew.'

'Don't lecture me on human relationships. You don't have the right.'

'Chandor said he was under pressure.'

'He's always under pressure. He arranges his life that way. Running research programmes, lecturing, developing new software for Robersman. It's how he operates.'

'Maybe he's not so invincible as he thinks. Maybe it got to him.'

'I know things were brewing. He told me that much. Robersman were messing him about. I began to think he was getting as disillusioned with them as I am.'

'Disillusioned?'

'They're a big company. Some of the things Charlie did for them, well, they weren't particularly honest.'

'Par for the course.'

'On the one hand they talk a lot about the health of the planet and good works, on the other Charlie'd be writing programs to organize chopping down

85

rain forests. He has scientist's tunnel vision: sees his work, not the consequences. He always complained. He couldn't stand other people's failings and mistakes. But lately he was more annoyed about interference.'

'Same old Charles.'

She bit off whatever reply she might have made. 'I don't believe he'd run away just because they were trying to close a project down. And he certainly hasn't curled up and died because I left. And what about that car?'

'I haven't seen anything,' he said, throwing the remains of his quarterpounder back in the foam. 'Only a car parked in the street.'

'They were behind me from the moment I left Cornwall. I've spent four days trying to get rid of them.'

'Could be Chandor's people.'

'He told you no one else was involved.'

'They threaten you?'

'The one time I tried to face them they drove off.'

'Sure it's the same car?'

'I'm not one of your bubble-headed tarts,' she said.

'Calm down.'

Her words spilled out like an adult explaining something to an annoying child:

'I don't know where he is. I came back and he's not here. There hasn't been another message since this one.'

'You seriously think friend Chandor – an MP, for Christ's sake – is involved in something criminal?'

'I don't know. I don't know what "Weatherspy" is either. But this is the first time Charlie ever needed anyone. I have to do what I can.'

'And you expect me to do the same?'

'Oh, no. You've been paid your wages.'

He could have hit her. He had done it before. The old familiar tightening of his stomach, the cold fury washing through him. 'You think I owe him any favours, that's your lookout. He'd probably shoot himself before he took anything from me. I'm here because they threatened to take my boat away, that's the only reason.'

'So what will you do?' There was challenge in her eyes. Something strong he'd never seen before. If he had hit her, she would probably have lashed back.

He was itching for a drink. He stood up. 'Come on.'

When they returned to the guest house, the grey Carlton had gone. It didn't make her any more relaxed. She hung near him, not touching, looking nervously up and down the street.

He packed his gear while the landlady protested that she could not refund his money. He told her that was fine, and went to the bathroom for a minute so he could take a drink from the bottle. He was angry. Mina automatically assumed he was going to fall in with her. If she needed help, why didn't she ask her smart friends?

'So you leave,' the landlady said, as they went past her down the stairs.

'That's right,' he said. 'Urgent family business.'

He heard her derisive 'Hah!', then they were gone, out of the door and into the street where Mina's car, a crimson Volvo 343, waited. She insisted that he keep the computer on his lap as she drove. 'It mustn't be damaged.'

On the way back to the house, he felt her closeness like the warmth of a flame. He kept thinking of how his insides had flipped over when he first saw her. He hadn't expected it, thought he had kicked that fire down.

She said:

'How's Sam?'

'Fine.'

'He must be getting on.'

'Always was.'

'Still doing the same trips?'

'More or less. Not so much coastal work.'

She smiled faintly. 'I used to think the seven seas were just outside the harbour, the way Bernard went on about it.'

'Delusions of grandeur,' he said.

'The poet in his soul.'

He looked at her dress where it stretched over her knees. 'Where were you last night?'

'Banbury. Friends put me up. I didn't want to stay in a hotel. I haven't felt very safe on my own since Wednesday.'

'Been to the house?'

'Looked in this morning. I think someone's gone through it. There's nothing I could show for proof. All of Charlie's work things were gone, but he might have taken them himself. Everything else was neat and tidy, just as I left it. But there was something . . . off centre, you know? When I stood back I could see it: books put on the shelves in the wrong order, clothes not quite straight in drawers. I could feel it, you understand?'

He understood that you could feel and see an awful lot of things when you were already jumpy.

She flicked the indicator and turned into her road. 'Look out for the car.'

They went slowly, and it was like a repeat of the previous evening. The last of sunset was hollowing the sky. The park faded away on the right into mist. No silver-grey Carlton.

She slipped into a space well short of the house. 'They could be inside.'

'All right,' he said. 'Let's go see.'

They got out. He held on to the computer, but he wasn't concerned. He figured anyone who was smart enough to follow her all the way from Cornwall was not going to get caught red-handed knocking over her home. They walked side by side to the gate, across the gravel. She rustled the key from her pocket, opened the front door. He went in first, noticing only that she had watered the plants. No one waited for them. Coming in behind him, she flicked on lights. He saw good furniture and tasteful decoration.

'Home,' she said, in an almost embarrassed way. He followed her into a big sitting room.

'Put the computer on the table, will you?'

He put it down next to a printer and a telephone, stood back while she made some connections and plugged the computer into the mains. When she switched it on, black characters appeared on the white screen in the lid. She sat over it, typing into the keyboard. He watched her work, the tense concentration of her face, the way her fingers dabbed the keys.

'I'm telling him you're here,' she said.

'He'll be pleased about that.'

The machine made small whirring noises, went blank.

'It's ready,' she said.

They waited, but nothing occurred. Her lips pressed together, then she got up.

'I need my briefcase. It's in the car.'

He went with her only to stop her worrying. Everything was cold and still outside. They collected the briefcase and returned to the house, eyes adjusting as they stepped into the shadows of the yard.

It was the dark that made it possible. That and the fact that he had already decided there was nothing to worry about. Someone broke from the alley by the side of the house, plunged toward Mina. She yelled, raised her arms to fend off attack. He dropped the case to go to her, reached them as she struggled loose, overbalanced and fell. He grabbed, fingers digging and holding on the sleeve of a quilted jacket, hauled the attacker round and saw a vicious white face. He drove his forearm hard into it. The attacker went over in a spray of gravel. He followed, avoided the lashing boot that tried to cut him in half, dragged the attacker up by the collar and swiped him across the side of the head. It felt good. He lifted his arm again.

Mina cried out. He heard the skid of shoes behind, realized there were two of them now, the other one peeling off from the alley and going for Mina. She kicked, but this one was big and fast. He caught her up, clamped a hand over her mouth and dragged her toward the road. Paul started after them, sensed the first attacker was up again, tried to swing back.

The blow caught him on the back of the head. Something metal, solid. A glancing impact, otherwise it would have smashed his skull, but it drove him to his knees, made everything come up dead like a vessel running aground.

He forced his head up, gazed stupidly at headlamp beams, heard an engine roar. The Carlton screeched to a halt in the road, engine revving. The two attackers were carrying Mina. She fought like mad, but they got the back door open and jammed her in.

Get up, get up. He staggered to his feet, pushing nausea back down his throat. They moved like water, one running round the car to the other side. Doors opened and closed. He threw himself at the car, collided with it, got a flickering view of Mina's screams blocked by a gloved hand. He pounded the window, then the car shot from under his grasp. He tried to hold it back by main force, whacked furiously at the boot, but it was gone. He spun and fell, choking in a wash of exhaust fumes, lifted his head and saw tail lights disappearing. Screech of tyres taking a corner. Sudden fall of silence. Darkness again. String of street lamps receding. No one came out of the houses. Nothing moved. Nice civilized area.

He rolled over to the gutter and threw up.

10

When the sickness passed, he found it relatively easy
to get up. Vision disturbed, but no worse than the time
he'd fallen in a heavy sea and smacked his head against
the deck machinery.

> 'Pity the bird that has wandered!
> Pity the sailor ashore!
> Hurry him home to the ocean,
> Let him come here no more!'

Weaving a bit, he crossed the gravel and retrieved
the case. The front door hung open. He let himself in.
The hall lights stabbed his eyes. He leaned against a
wall and tried to focus. Saw her saying: 'I could *feel*
it, you understand?' He'd been so condescending. He
lurched into a sitting room, put the case down. He was
conscious of his legs losing power under him, then the
fact that his hand, reaching for support, struck a side
table and scattered a stack of magazines on the carpet.
Then he was down, then he was nothing.

He came round hearing the chirp of a 'phone, levered
himself up in confusion, searching for it. Couldn't be
the one hooked to the computer. It was on the floor by
the couch. He crawled across and fumbled the receiver
off its cradle.

'Quillet?' A man's voice. Low and indistinct.

'Yeah.' He turned over and rested his back against
the couch. He wanted to vomit again.

'How's your head?'

He swallowed hard. 'Never mind.'

'Called the police?' A Yorkshire accent.

'No.'

'We forgot something.'

'Like?' He thought he knew, but played it more stupid than he felt.

'The box.' The voice faded a little, like a radio signal going off beam.

'Box?'

'The box of tricks. The computer.' Was he using a public 'phone? There was background noise like the sigh of wind through long grass or trees. 'Lady tells us if we've got the box we don't need her. So . . .'

'She all right?'

'She's not with me, so you can forget about talking to her. We're going to arrange a swap.'

A burst of sound in the distance. The cry of a bird, the flutter of water as it took flight. A grunt from the voice, a *thunk* as the sound was closed out. He gripped the receiver tight.

'You won't be calling anyone, will you?' the Yorkshire voice said.

'No.'

'You wait.'

'Hang on – ' The connection broke.

He dropped the 'phone back in place, hauled himself up on the couch, sprawled there fighting off waves of dizziness and the longing to sleep.

Think. *Think.* Come on. There were things to be grabbed out of this mess.

He focused on his watch. Three minutes past six. They'd arrived at the house just after 5.15. The scuffle took no more than a minute. Say they were driving out of the city by 5.20. Yorkshire said Mina was not with him, so it could mean they had her stashed away somewhere. Assume they did. Assume also that they'd questioned her in the car on the move. How far could they get, given the maximum time on the road, at an average fifty miles an hour?

> 'Under the wide and starry sky,
> Dig the grave and let me lie . . .'

Come on, use your brain. Come on.

Say between thirty and forty miles. That was maximum.

And he had a fairly good idea where the call had come from. Not a public 'phone; a carphone. That accounted for the signal fading, and the grunt before the background noises stopped. Yorkshire had rolled his window up.

He tried standing again, found he was pretty good at it. At least as proficient as a two-year-old. Touching the back of his head, he felt a beautifully rounded lump, but no blood.

He looked over the bookshelves, but didn't find what he wanted. Shambled out to the kitchen and located a bottle of Paracetamol in one of the cupboards. He took three, then went out to Mina's car. Cautiously this time, now it was too late. He got the map book and returned to the house. No one seemed to be watching the place.

The map scale was four miles to the inch; detailed enough. He figured out a thirty-five mile radius and drew it round the city with a stub of pencil.

The bird whose flight and cries he had overheard was a snipe: the grating splutter of its alarm notes told him that. Years going up and down estuaries, fishing with Sam upriver from Bredon Water, had taught him to tell a moorhen from a coot, a common snipe from a jack. He knew he had heard one being disturbed from its nest. Snipe haunt marshes and moors. There were no moors round here, and the map said there was only one lake. Grafham Water, west of the city about twenty-five miles. A tiny yacht on the lake indicated sailing facilities, and a caravan park on the north side was fed by a minor road. A few black squares ranged along a B road to the south showed the nearest village. Nothing else within a mile and a half.

He didn't get excited. His head was the size of a dinner gong and ringing just as loud. Besides, he was angry with himself. They had taken him like some stupid kid. Ever since Chandor had him picked up he'd been walking around like an idiot, and they'd dealt with him like one. He hadn't taken Mina seriously. Now he had to get her out of this, if some miracle gave him the chance.

The room pulsated, the ringing in his ears made him gag. There was nothing he could do yet. He had to be here when they rang back, and he had to rest, try to get over some of the shock to his system.

> 'In dreams, unhappy, I behold you stand
> As heretofore.'

He had always been practical about trouble. There had been a lot of it to be practical about. The house was locked, no one could walk in and surprise him. He swivelled on the couch, putting his feet up. The 'phone was on the floor, in easy reach. He forced Mina to the back of his mind. He closed his eyes.

Mina Anjana Woulding. He always thought how bad the English surname sounded stuck on the end of her Indian forenames.

She appeared in town during his fifteenth year, summer of 'sixty-nine. A new girl in the gang, thirteen going on fourteen. Even then people looked twice. The golden skin, the eyes already that unsettling purple, like the sky before a big storm. But not only the colour: the expression too, of watching but not wanting to be watched. Although she got through the early taunts about being a 'darky' and a 'Paki' to become an accepted part of the gang, there was something that set her off from the others. Part of it *was* her blood, the announcement it made in her face. African blacks off the boats were a common enough sight in town, but not Asians. She was only half-Indian, but she had a grace to go with her height that none of the others had. She made most of the girls look like carthorses.

You could tell she was around by the way the boys acted – shouting, showing off, all the usual kiddy stuff for impressing the girls. A lot of older boys – ex-gang members who had graduated to the adult section where motorbikes replaced bicycles – started turning up in their old haunts that summer. They were seventeen, eighteen, but that made no odds. Paul knew several thirteen-year-olds who were getting knocked off by married blokes of thirty or more.

Then there was her accent. She was born and raised entirely in Britain, but her voice had a little of the foreign lilt, and a soft hint of Scots, and it leapt like music when she laughed, not like the giggling Suffolk girls with their hard, flat voices.

She didn't laugh much with him, not early on. More often she was silent, watching, looking at him with those eyes. As if she knew things about him she was too clever to mention.

He had a reputation. Having her around was good for that. It was understood that she was to be his, if anyone's. That was how things worked then. But somehow it didn't go the way he planned it. He became aware that people were making fun of him – behind his back, of course – because she was always near him. He made a joke of it. That was also how you treated girls. But even Dad noticed eventually.

'Who's that muffin?' he said one day, when they were in the wheelhouse fitting a new compass. 'Muffin' was his word for a town girl, any town. Chopped down from 'Ragamuffin', but applied only to girls.

Paul didn't lift his head. He was forcing a spanner to turn a rusted nut. 'Some girl,' he said, as neutral as possible. 'She still on deck?'

'Playin' with my wireless.'

The sound of her tuning the portable radio across the medium wave stations was audible in the dense heat of the September afternoon.

'What's she doin', then?' Dad said.

'Hanging about.' He was cool, sure no interest tinged his voice.

Dad squinted out of the window. 'Pretty little bit.'

'Just a kid.'

'She got a touch o' the tarbrush?'

'Mum's Indian. Dad married her when he was in the army over there. He's a Jock. Works at the cannery.'

'Be a nice little thing, few years' time.'

'Hold it steady, Dad.'

The radio lighted suddenly on Radio One. The d.j. was jabbering about 'the number one fab platter from the band that matters', and Zager and Evans started wailing 'In the Year 2525'.

'Bloody row,' Dad said.

She must have agreed. Zager and Evans tuned out, replaced by a German voice.

He reached for a screwdriver. 'Why's she hangin' around by herself, then?'

'Nothing else to do,' Paul said.

Dad's eyes narrowed, going pouchy in the fat, sun-burnt face. ''Ere, don't you go gettin' into nothin'.'

'What?' Incredulity. Good impression.

'You know what I mean. Your Mum'd never forgive me if I let you lads go to the bad.'

He was a moral man, in his way. After Mum died, his visits to the knocking shops of whichever port they

97

happened to be in were just part of the routine. And he always made friends with the girls. Sometimes Paul would have to go and find him for something, would track him to a favourite bar, and he would be sitting there, surrounded by friends, his arm round some tart or other, and they would always be having a good time. Plenty of beer, lots of cigarette smoke. 'Son, say good evenin' to Monique', or Krista or Anya, or whoever she was. Dad favoured girls who were slightly inflated versions of his late wife. Bosomy brunettes with wide, laughing mouths. Somehow, he managed to find one wherever the *Provider* put in.

'I don't do nothin',' Paul lied. He knew damn well shy old Charlie didn't. 'I turn round, there she is. Not my fault, is it?'

The radio whined and whistled. She rocked the dial back and forth, making the Stones and 'Honky Tonk Woman' fade in and out like an echo.

'She could settle for one thing or the other,' Dad said, irritably. His bald pink head gleamed as he bent over to see where the obstruction was. 'Give her another turn with the spanner.' They worked the old compass off its mounting and started fitting the new one. The Stones were replaced by Radio Caroline, playing an album track by the Moody Blues. Charlie music, Paul thought. Anything gentle was Charlie music.

'Don't she get bored?' Dad asked, craning to get another look at her.

Paul snorted. 'She don't have to sit there. I'm not forcing her.'

Later on, the old man would give him a hard time about the way he treated her. That was a long time after, when they were seen as 'a couple' – not that he ever talked of it that way. It was what everyone else said. Mina was his girl. Among the people he spent most of his time with in his late teens – blokes off other boats and the town layabouts – that meant he could do whatever (whoever) he liked, but she was restricted to him.

He never thought anything about it. It was how things were. And Mina didn't appear to mind. At least, she never said anything at the time.

He woke after a couple of uneasy hours. The headache was bad, but he could see straight. He made a cup of coffee, drinking it black because the fridge was empty, then went looking through the house.

It was tasteful and expensive. Lots of old wood, lots of books. Several bedrooms, unlived in. The master bedroom, with a king-sized bed, one side table stacked with science books, the other with art volumes. On the dressing table was a silver-framed picture of Charlie and Mina at some temple in India. Charlie's Lennon glasses made his face look longer. He grinned at Mina. She wore a vivid orange *sari*. She looked as if she belonged there.

In one of the chests of drawers, he found soft silks and lace. He lifted one of the camisoles and pressed it to his face, breathing deep the traces of her scent. His eyes, when he glimpsed them in the mirror on top of the chest, were lost and empty. He shut the drawer and went out.

The room next door was given over to a study with a double-sided desk. A dustless rectangle showed where a computer or typewriter had stood. The wall beside it was solid with books and files, except one gap where everything had been cleaned out. But he found some Ordnance Survey maps there. Charlie did not let him down; he had always been one for having maps of wherever he lived.

Downstairs he got one small surprise. In among the records and discs by the stereo, all the Fairport

Convention, the Beach Boys and the Paul Simon, was Zevon's *Sentimental Hygiene*. Trouble waiting to happen, all right. Was it Charlie's or Mina's? He put it on, and sat down to study the big map.

By the time the call came at 9.15, he was close to despair. The Ordnance Survey showed what the map book had not: that the country around Huntingdon and Grafham Water was laced with waterways; marinas, gravel pits, ornamental lakes. Any one of them could be a home to the snipe. It had been a nice idea, but a very long shot.

When the 'phone rang, he folded the map almost guiltily and snatched it up.

'Quillet?' the Yorkshire accent said.

'Yeah?'

'Get a pen and paper.'

'Got them.'

'This is what you do. There's a village just off the Kettering road, other side of Huntingdon. It's called Easton. Got it?'

He searched the map. 'Yeah.'

'Carry on down the road toward Stonely. You go through woods. Take the first left. It's a loop, used to lead to an old hotel. There's a red bridge over a river.'

Easton was two miles from Grafham Water. The Stonely road, a lonely minor route, crossed one of the rivers that fed it. The loop did the same. He kept any note of excitement out of his voice. 'Got it.'

'Be there, on your own, one o'clock tonight. With the computer.'

'What about –?'

The line went dead. He put the 'phone down. It looked as if he were right, after all. But knowing the area didn't give him the exact location. He was still at their mercy.

As he sat there, Mina's computer gave a beeping alarm. He glanced up – he'd forgotten it was still on – and saw words appearing on the screen. He went over to it.

The words said:

LAKESIDE HOUSE, GRAFHAM WATER.

He stood there, made still by surprise. The words faded suddenly. He reached for the keyboard, but he didn't know how to work it.

LAKESIDE HOUSE. He walked away from the table, not understanding. But now he was grinning slightly. If Yorkshire had been in the room, he might have been frightened at the way it made him look.

By 9.45 he was driving along the old Roman road to Huntingdon through a moonlit night.

A bag on the back seat made clinking sounds, and a scent of petrol was strong in the car. The computer was tucked away under the passenger seat. He needed it to make the swap if all else failed. Not that he believed they would go for anything so friendly. More likely they would try to end it with Mina *and* the computer in the Carlton, and him lying dead in the river.

Easton was easy to find. A few houses ranged along the road. They wouldn't be there. He guessed that Lakeside would be in an isolated position. The Ordnance Survey showed only two near enough to the water for him to have heard the snipe take flight. They were both in the woods on the north-west side of the lake, near the marshy head, both with tracks leading off the Stonely road.

He found the first easily enough. It was signposted 'Addington Lodge – Private Property'. The second

101

opening he almost missed. It was unmarked, concealed on a bend. He drove on, past the sign for the loop, then over a bridge and out of the woods to Stonely. Turned in a pub car park and went back, dousing the headlamps as soon as he was clear of the village. Just short of the woods, he steered into a field and parked behind a haystack out of sight of the road. He got out, peering into the darkness. The moon showed fields and the scratched mass of bare trees at the edge of the wood. He felt for his torch and pocket knife, loaded up with the bottles, locked the car and set off along the road.

Nothing moved. A frost was on the land. No passing car forced him to take cover in the hedges. Walking with cap pulled low on his forehead, he was pretty well invisible. The cold worked on him.

Grafham Water was deep and clear for boating at the eastern end. This side, where the river flowed in, the Ordnance Survey showed marsh stretching almost up to the bridge. Of the two houses, he favoured the second. 'Lakeside' was probably the second house. It was in among the trees. More private.

He thought of what they might be doing to her, and worked his hand around the stone in his pocket. How the hell could Charlie get her into something like this? And where was he, leaving the despised brother to do work that was his? Difficult to see him prowling through the night, though. Not clean old Charlie. It was just like him, expecting her to walk into trouble on his behalf. He had never shown much care for her.

And you did?

Never mind.

Once over the bridge he started moving more cautiously. The woods had closed in, overhanging branches shut out most of the moonlight. He had to assume they were watching for trouble, even if Yorkshire's voice had suggested over-confidence.

A light through the trees, flickering as he approached the entrance to the track. He got off the road, into the woods. Boots cracking dead frozen twigs, he went from one tree trunk to the next, using them for cover, for handholds in case he tripped. Eyes sharpening to pick shadow from fallen branch, lips compressed, breath streaming pale and ghostly from his nostrils.

An owl called high overhead. His reaching hand met a net of chicken wire at waist height. He crossed it, saw the light more distinctly now, the shape of the house. He peeked round the rough trunk of a tree, saw a door with an outside light hanging over it. The rear of the house.

And a silver-grey Vauxhall Carlton parked at the side.

Beyond it lay glistening blackness, reflecting light that came from windows at the front. He made out long reeds patching the water. The trees gave way to an overgrown lawn, blades of grass stiff with frost. Keeping well back, he skirted it, reached the water's edge. The house stood about ten yards from the water. French windows faced a paved square and the lawn leading down to a rough jetty. An upstairs room was also lighted. The curtains in the french windows were half-open. He broke cover and followed the reedy bank until he could see into the room.

A black man was laughing. He was in profile, sitting down. When he stopped laughing he raised a can of beer and drank.

A little further and he could see someone else. A bearded man, dark colouring.

He backed up to the trees again. Even if Mina was in the upstairs room there was no way for him to climb up. And he knew there were at least three men involved in this.

Call the police, reason said. They won't kill her.

103

The police were the enemy, always had been. Harbour variety or land-based, they were the ones to keep clear of. He could do this himself.

The car gleamed like ice in the moonlight. He put it between him and the house and got in close, looked over it carefully. On the driver's window, next to the engraved security number, was a sticker: PROTECTED BY MAGVOX ALARM. That was fine. Magvox were the vibration-sensitive type. He ducked back and found a long, crooked branch from the rank tangle of dead undergrowth. Quick upward glance to make sure that the trees actually overhung the car. It was fine. He squatted down in the dark, started emptying his pockets.

'One more of those,' Rouse said, 'and that's your lot.' He had to raise his voice above the television. His Yorkshire accent got broader when he shouted.

Micher turned from watching a situation comedy about a mobile disco.

'I can have the rest, can't I?' He tapped the remains of the six pack by his armchair, his big black face asking for sympathy.

'One more,' Rouse said, and got up. Micher went back to his programme, laughing whenever the audience laughed. Rouse strutted into the narrow hallway and looked up the stairs. Whinyard was sitting on a tilted dining chair at the top, feet on the banister rail, facing an open bedroom door.

'All right?' Rouse asked.

Whinyard nodded lazily. It annoyed Rouse. Everything about Whinyard annoyed him. He was so thin his associates called him 'Blade'. Rouse thought about going to check on the woman, but she was safe enough. He pulled his sleeve back and checked the time on his Rolex.

'Couple more hours,' he said.

Whinyard looked down at him sleepily. 'Hope you're right about this.' His accent, pure East End of London, made it sound like an insult. Rouse hated the accent. It was distilled arrogance. All Londoners sounded like that to him.

'It'll be fine,' he said, preening before the hall mirror. He smoothed his neat beard, straightened the double-breasted jacket of his suit.

'Ain't what we were told to do, though, is it?'

'This, Blade, is what you call taking the initiative.'

'They got someone comin' over special for this.'

'And when he arrives, we'll have got the wife, the computer, and the whole thing wrapped up.'

Whinyard nodded.

'Prove we don't need any bloody foreigners to sort things out for us,' Rouse added, tapping the side of his nose.

'It ain't what they said.'

'I don't give a monkey's what they bloody said. It's all here, ready for us to take the chance and gain the prize. You think how pleased they'll be when we solve their problems for 'em. You want to stay in this line of work all your life? It's all about promotion and prospects, Blade.'

'You sound like a fucking accountant.'

'Business is business. Any business.'

Whinyard looked unconvinced. He yawned and pushed his chair further back on two legs.

Rouse left him to it. Blade and Micher were errand boys, both of them Bow Bells cannon fodder. He, however, was on the way up.

Back in the sitting room, Micher was already on his last beer. He glanced up brightly. 'All right?'

'All quiet on the Easton front,' Rouse said, but Micher didn't get the joke.

'Blade still griping?'

Rouse sat down. 'He's all right. Has no vision, that's all.'

'He don't like it you won't let him play with her.'

'She's had enough bad experiences for one night. I want her in decent shape to show the brother-in-law.'

'You're not going to do the swap, are you?'

'What d'you bloody think? You just drive the car. I'll do the thinking.'

Micher's attention wandered back to the television.

Suddenly, a horn started blaring in the night.

Rouse sat bolt upright, reaching under his jacket. 'What the fuck's that?'

Micher looked at the window, brow furrowed. 'Ah, shit, it's the car alarm. Fuckin' 'undredth time it's done it this week.' He got up, hooking the keys out of his jeans pocket. 'Too sensitive, see. Only have to look at it, it starts screaming.'

'Go and shut it off.'

'All right, keep your hat on.'

Rouse shook his head wearily. This was how it was: brain dead field men and dodgy vehicles. That would all change when he was in charge.

Blade poked his head over the banisters.

'What's going on?'

Micher grinned. 'Nothin', man. Don't shit yourself.'

He zipped up his jacket and pulled his woolly hat over his ears, unlocked the door and stepped outside. The dead, frozen air and the darkness made him shiver. He had a quick look round, then crossed the lawn. The car alarm was loud in the stillness, echoing off into the trees. Micher rubbed himself to keep warm. He hated the countryside.

When he got close, he saw what had happened. A branch had broken off one of the trees hanging over the car. It had fallen on the windscreen, almost breaking through in one place. That had set off the alarm. He sighed. Have to get the thing fixed when they got back to town. It was a pain. He went round to the driver's side, fingering through his keys.

Paul hit him as he bent down to unlock the door.

The black guy grunted and fell against the car. He tried to touch the back of his neck where he had been struck, mumbled thickly: 'Hey, what –'

Paul hit him again. This time he shut up and toppled over.

The alarm still braying, Paul turned him on his back. White slits showed in the dark face. Out for any number of counts. He unzipped the jacket, feeling for a gun. It was there, a small automatic, all neat and clean in a shoulder holster. He snatched it out. It was warm from being next to the man's body. There was a box of shells in one of the pockets. Definitely the right house.

The alarm was still going.

'Micher, for fuck's sake!' The yell came from the house. He froze for a second. 'What're you doing?'

He snatched the hat off the black man's head and jammed it on, bobbed up from behind the car, hoping the light from the house wasn't bright enough to show he was the wrong colour. In the doorway under the exterior lamp, the beard was shading his eyes to see, a petulant look on his face.

'Turn it off.'

He waved loosely, ducking down again. Where were the keys? Micher had been about to use them. Must have dropped in the grass. He felt for them. Couldn't see a bloody thing. And any minute now the beard would decide to come and see what was going on for himself. The alarm mocked him with its deafening row. His fingers padded the earth. Come on, come on . . .

He touched metal, grasped a leather key ring, bobbed up and started trying them. Wrong one, wrong one, another jammed in the lock. He glanced at the house. The beard threw up his arms in annoyance, turned to speak with someone inside.

Finally, the right key. He yanked the door open and scrabbled under the seat for the control unit. He had the key ready. He pushed it home, twisted, and the noise finally died. It echoed away through the woods.

Breathing hard already. Adrenalin wouldn't do as it was told. He pushed himself up on the front seats and had a look at the house. The doorway was empty, a sliver of light showed it was still open. The beard had gone inside.

Now what? Fine to lay one of them out, but how does a man who makes his living sailing cargo from one port to another deal with professional hard men? The question made him pause for the first time. He had done his share of fighting, more than his share, perhaps, but the gun in his pocket proved this was serious. He wondered if he knew how to use it. He'd seen plenty of guns in his time, but never fired one. How did automatics work?

He realized he was scared. Couldn't remember the last time he had cared one way or the other what happened to him. Not since that bad October night in the Channel when a couple of boats went down, and the *Provider* was almost one of them. He smelled the expensive leather of the car's upholstery. Something on the back seat caught his eye. He reached it, held smooth glass, pressed the button on top. Mina's perfume misted in the air. It must have fallen from her coat pocket when they were bringing her here. Bet she struggled.

He studied the house again. She was in there. He had to get her out. Simple.

Simple?

'What's he doing out there?' Rouse muttered, adjusting his tie.

'Very proud of that car,' Blade said. 'He goes out to fetch something, and before you know it, he's stripping her down and giving her an oil change.'

Rouse flicked stray hairs off his shoulders. 'He's a clod.'

'He drives well.'

Satisfied with his appearance, Rouse went into the sitting room and channel-hopped the television, hoping for the news. Sunday nights were 1930s detective nights, he noticed, or opera, or nature programmes. He left it on some beautifully photographed scenes of an African river valley under threat from developers and sauntered over to the french windows. Through them he could see moonlight lazing on the water.

He heard the front door open and close, and Micher's footsteps in the hall. He shouted: 'About bloody time.' What was that out on the water? Looked like a bird. He squinted harder through the glass. Micher came into the room. He started to turn and face him.

The general impression was fine. Same jacket, same hat. But the skin was the wrong colour.

He muttered: 'Shit!'

The brother-in-law pointed an automatic at him. He didn't appear too happy with it, but he was squeezing on the trigger. Squeezed harder. Nothing happened.

'Safety catch,' Rouse hissed, and went for his gun.

Paul charged headlong. The beard was side-on to him and badly off-balance, otherwise he would probably have made it. As it was, he had his pistol just out of the holster when Paul hit him. He clamped the beard's arm up against his chest. There was no way to stop. They went through the french windows in a shattering of glass and wood. The beard howled, his gun flew loose from his hand. Shards and splinters were all around them, catching the light as they fell. Paul was protected from most of it by the beard's body.

They hit the ground. He was still on top. His weight drove all the breath from the other's lungs. But the beard was game. His head and face were covered in blood, his suit was ripped, but he got his hand up and went for the eyes. Paul grabbed his head and slammed it back on the slabs. Once, and the beard's thumbs were seeking out his eye sockets. Twice, and the hands fluttered. Third time, they fell.

He leapt aside, showering bits of glass, rolled on the lawn to face the remains of the windows. He fumbled with the gun until he flicked the safety catch off, cursing himself.

Up on his feet, back into the house. He switched the TV off, listened. Not a sound. Where was the third man? Where was Mina? Stomach churning, he moved over to the wall and kicked the door open, going into the hall with the gun ready this time.

He had expected it to be fast; either he would get them or they would get him, all over in a few seconds, before he had time to think. This was not in the plan.

What if the other bastard was upstairs, quietly levelling a gun on Mina's head?

He saw the stairs. Anyone on the landing above had a wonderful view of the hallway. As he walked underneath, he would be a perfect target. He edged forward, head tilted back, waiting for a gun barrel to stick through the banisters, for a face to appear over the rail. None of that happened. He turned slowly, silently as he brought more of the stairs and the landing into his sight, swivelling right round until he was facing the way he had come, the front door behind him.

That door was closed, he knew that. But there were two others off the hall. One leading to a kitchen, the other to a dining room. Both were unlit: both, as far as he knew, were empty. As far as he knew.

He started toward the stairs, his mind on what waited above. When he heard the scuff of feet on the carpet, he was too slow.

There was a loud exhalation, almost a 'Hah!'. He caught the flash of yellow teeth, and a knife travelling up, aiming to end somewhere under his ribs. He swung back to block it, and the blade went into his arm. Hot wire through the nerves. He cried out, dropped the gun, but pain made him react. The smiler was struggling to pull the knife free from the awkward mass of jacket it had tangled in. Still yelling, Paul reared and struck him a stunning blow.

Knife came out, smiler fell, still clutching it. Paul staggered back against the stairs, gritting his teeth and clasping his arm. This was pain. No one had ever got a knife into him before. He hadn't known it could hurt so much.

Blade had seen Micher go past below, seen the jacket and the woolly hat. His own alarm bells should have gone off when Micher didn't look up and grin his big, stupid grin. But it had been a long day, and he was more interested in watching the woman.

When the crash came, he knew they had been rumbled. He didn't know who by, but he wasn't taking any chances. Staying with the woman, doing the old 'one step nearer and I'll slit her throat' routine might not cut any ice with whoever was doing the major rearrangements downstairs. So he got down into the dining room and waited in the dark to see what happened. The brother-in-law happened, and he had just missed his first chance to end the inconvenience. But as he clambered up from the floor, his knife was still in his hand, and he saw plenty more coming his way.

Paul felt his own blood on his fingers. The sleeve of his jacket was getting heavy with it. The gun was on the bottom step. As he went for it, smiler went for him. Again the underarm, streetfighting grip on the blade. He kicked out, and the blade slashed at his leg. He scrabbled backwards up the stairs, trying to get some distance between himself and the sliver of steel.

'Punch-ups is all right,' Dad used to say, when they witnessed a fight in a bar. 'But blades is very nasty.'

Too fucking true. He had to hold his ground. If he got too far from the bottom, smiler would be able to pick up the gun. He lashed again, and smiler backed off.

'Gonna kill ya,' smiler said, 'Gonna do ya.' He lunged, slicing through the ankle leather of Paul's boot. Knife through butter. Paul took the moment to use the other boot. He slammed smiler's shoulder a good one. It felled him again, folded him nicely into the corner by the front door.

He pulled one of the beer bottles out of his pocket. It was undamaged, but some of the petrol had soaked out round the rag stuffed in the neck. Newquay Steam Beer, the label said. One hundred per cent natural ingredients. Even Charlie's vices were good for him. He ripped the rag out of the neck, transferred it to the right hand and threw it with all the force his position allowed.

It hit the wall two inches short of the corner. He had feared it wouldn't break, but it broke. Brown glass and petrol showered down. With no time to get out from under, smiler threw his hands over his head. Paul whipped the cigarette lighter from his pocket.

Smiler was on his feet, shaking his head to get fragments of the bottle out of his hair, spitting petrol off his lips. He was breathing hard, looking evil. He started toward the stairs.

Paul turned the wheel on his lighter. Flame leapt up.

Smiler hesitated.

Paul drew his hands closer together. Little yellow flame, petrol-soaked rag. He gazed at smiler over them, got to his feet.

'You don't want me to,' he said quietly.

Smiler's eyes watched the flame closely. The stink of petrol filled the hall.

He knew smiler was trying to judge two things. First, how much petrol did he really have on him; and second, was his opponent the kind to set light to a man? Was he vicious enough to do it?

Head aching again. Left forearm throbbed to the rhythm of his racing heart.

'Unleaded, is it?' smiler said, weighing the knife. The petrol dripped down his face, staining his shirt collar. 'I prefer unleaded. Better for the ozone layer.'

'Don't do it,' Paul said.

He could see thought cutting through smiler's mind. He knew the type. He'd seen them by the dozens. Smiler was thinking maybe there wasn't that much petrol on him, that he could get a good one in and drop his opponent before the flame touched him. Might even be able to blow the lighter out. He was crabbing sideways to get within easy reach.

Paul extended the lighter toward him.

Yellow teeth. Get the knife in under his arms while he's holding the lighter and the rag. The eyes said he didn't believe Paul had the nerve.

113

He dived.

And flamed.

As he drove forward with the blade, Paul tried to fend him off, but his hands were full. Lighter touched rag. There was the *whoof* of reeking air igniting, and smiler turned into a candle. The knife dropped, but impetus carried him onto Paul, screaming louder and louder as his hair frazzled.

Paul shoved him off. Smiler collided with the front door, batting at himself frantically. The flames caught where petrol had stained the walls, and in a moment they were licking toward the ceiling. Smiler rolled on the floor, trying to put himself out. His screaming started to give way to the sound of fire eating the door curtain.

Paul took the stairs three at a time, black smoke billowing after him. He tripped and fell on the landing, twisted to get up, and saw Mina lying on a bed in the lighted room. She was fully dressed, even to the swagger coat, but bound and gagged, her eyes wild.

The smoke was rising and gathering at ceiling level, smiler was still making shrill, stuck-pig noises. He flicked out his pocket knife and cut the packing tape from her wrists and ankles, pulled the strip off her mouth as gently as he could. She struggled up, gulping for breath. He wasted no time talking. They got out on the landing, tumbled down the stairs. The heat from below was getting fierce, and he gathered her to him as they reached the bottom, protecting her from it. Heard her gasp and pulled her head against his chest, tried not to look at the smiler, lying still now at the foot of the blazing front door. They ran down the hall, through the sitting room and out the broken french windows.

The beard was stirring. Groaning, he stretched out a hand to grab his gun. Paul thrust Mina away and kicked him soundly in the guts. Took her arm again

114

and dragged her across the lawn, into the trees along the drive. Smoke wafted on the night air. He had it all over him, the greasy stink of it in his nostrils. He retched, but kept running, half-carrying her when she stumbled.

As they neared the road, there was an explosion of light off to the right, the roar of a car's engine as it came round the corner. They had no time to get into cover. The car screeched to a halt.

Paul grabbed for the gun. He couldn't see who was in the BMW. The headlamps dazzled him.

Mina panted heavily at his shoulder. Any second now another bunch of heavies were going to jump out and smash his brains in, take her for good. He gripped the gun very tight.

But no doors opened. The engine ticked over softly, the lights went on boring into his skull. He squinted into the glare, made out the shape of the driver's head, the dark gleam of eyes regarding him. His finger twitched on the trigger of the pistol, but something told him he would be dead before he ever fired a shot.

'Polly,' Mina said.

Then the engine revved again and the car rolled past them.

He remained where he was for what seemed a long time. He didn't believe it. Tail lights dodged through the trees toward the house. The silhouette and the eyes that he felt rather than saw were printed over everything.

'Paul, come on.' Mina was pulling at him. He pocketed the gun and put an arm round her. One of her heels had snapped off. He took her along the road because it was easier than stumbling through the woods, and they reached the car without further hindrance.

'What's wrong with your arm?' she said.

'Nothing.' Pain was travelling up and down from fingertips to shoulder like current in a cable.

She touched his sleeve. 'You're bleeding.'

'Get in the fucking car.'

She did it. She was too shaky to argue. He got in the driver's seat, started the engine.

'One thing,' he said.

'What?'

'Put her in gear for me, will you?'

The BMW pulled over at the end of the drive. A dark man stepped out, stood looking at the house. The ground floor was well alight now. Windows had blown out and bright flames were gushing from them. The woods were lit in shuddering orange for a hundred yards around. Wildlife of all sorts was setting up a panic in the reeds around the water's edge. And the smoke rose straight into the night sky, blotting out the moon.

He saw movement over by the car. Eyes narrowing, he went toward it.

When he was still fifty yards away, Rouse stumbled up from his knees. At first his hand flickered toward his gun, but then he stopped, called out:

'You Haggard?'

He nodded. That was his name this time.

Rouse clutched the back of his head miserably. 'Brother-in-law found us. Took her away. Blade's still in there.' Behind him, Micher was propped against the side of the car, moaning. The car was low on the ground. The tyres had been slashed.

All this he took in as he was approaching. The disabled car, the two wounded men, the house becoming cinders. Quillet and the wife had done this?

'I suppose we'll have some explaining to do,' Rouse said.

116

Haggard drew an SIG P210 automatic from his jacket and fired point blank into Rouse's chest. Rouse jerked back six feet and skidded spreadeagled on the grass. Haggard never slowed or changed course. Micher had time to cry: 'Oh, shit, man!' Then Haggard's second shot pinned him to the earth.

The heat from the burning house was intense. It scorched the side of his face. Putting his handgun away, he checked both bodies, took away their weapons and proofs of identity. Moving quickly, he dragged them into the trees well beyond the lawn. He returned to his own car, turned it round and drove off. All the way down the drive, he could hear the flames making cracks like gunfire. He tapped a number in on his 'phone, waited, manoeuvred out onto the road toward Stonely. The call was answered.

'Bodies,' he said, thinking of the wife and the brother-in-law as he had seen them in the headlamp beams. 'Two. In the woods near the car. Third one's already dealt with. You'd better hurry, or the fire service may get there before you.'

11

The hotel room was large and modern. A long window looked down on a row of spiky masts and a big, rectangular marina. Beyond that was the river, and the lights of a canning factory on the opposite bank.

They didn't say anything when they came in. Mina dropped her suitcase and flopped down on one of the beds. He eased the holdall off his shoulder and laid the computer gently down, stood looking at the window, so tired he couldn't be bothered to move.

'Paul, sit down.'

His head rang so loud he was surprised she couldn't hear it.

'Look at your arm.'

He wriggled the stiffening fingers. 'Scratch, babe.' Sounded half-drunk.

She came and pushed him toward the other bed. Pulled his jacket off him, made him lie on it. She peeled back the sleeve of his sweater, swallowed hard.

'We should get you to a doctor.'

He sniggered. 'Yeah. "Hello, Doc, I've just been in this knife fight. Give us a couple of tetanus jabs and don't mention it to anyone, will you?"' He lifted his arm, had to twist it to see where the knife had gone in. It was such a little wound. 'See, told you it was a scratch.'

She left him for a time. He drifted.

She had shown plenty of spirit tonight. For the first ten minutes in the car, as he drove like hell to get away from the area, she was silent. Then he snatched a look at her in the glare of oncoming headlamps and saw

118

tears streaming down her face. But that stopped, and she quietened down. When they reached Huntingdon and he didn't know where to go, she said:

'Take the Bishop's Lynn road.'

'That's forty miles.'

'I know somewhere safe.'

After half an hour, he was beginning to be a little shaky himself. She made him pull over, took off her broken boots and slipped into some old shoes she kept in a box behind the driver's seat. She gave him sheets of kitchen paper from a roll in the same place. He did his best to mop the blood off his hand while she piloted the car through the flat calm sea of moonstruck fen country.

Bishop's Lynn at one A.M. He knew the town because of the docks, was usually there about once a month, but he had only read in the local 'paper about the part she took him to. Like a lot of places in East Anglia, the town was becoming a distant satellite of London. Its position on the river at the entrance to the Wash made it perfect for the businessman with a boat. The derelict warehouses fronting the river and the foul little cobbled alleys between the old Custom House and Mill Street were no longer relics of a waterborne past. The old premises of Victorian grain merchants were now luxury apartment complexes, and the South Quay gave berths to yachts and cruisers instead of barges and barques.

He wasn't too clear by the time she drove down one of the alleys and swung into a yard overlooking the river. She said: 'I'll do this. I don't want them to see you too close.'

'Why not?'

'Because you look a mess.'

It was a hotel. When he got out and gazed up at the side of the building, he could see that the frontage had been restored to something like its original appearance. The windows were single sheets of glass, but at the top of the original sign had been re-painted on the brickwork:

'Thomas P. Levitt and Sons – Grain Merchants, Feed Suppliers.'

The interior had been gutted and redesigned. The lobby was glass and polished wood, plants everywhere. Mina was standing at the desk. The night porter gave him a curious look. He stayed by the door until she came back with the keys to a twin-single room. The porter had questions falling out of his eyes.

They took the lift to the third floor in silence. There was no discussion about sharing the room. He knew she didn't want to be on her own.

She reappeared from the bathroom, carrying a bowl of water that steamed with the smell of antiseptic. She sat next to him and started cleaning the wound, bit her lip as he flinched.

'This isn't enough.'

'Do for now,' he said. 'I'll see a doctor if it drops off.'

She worked around the place where his flesh was sticking out of the skin. 'How did you find me?'

'"A birdie with a brownish bill hopped upon the window sill . . ." Telephone line, in this case.'

She didn't know whether he was delirious or not, so she left it. He grunted again.

'Sorry.'

'All right.' He was remembering how she used to do this when he hurt himself on the boat. He used to make fun of her. Any scratch or knock, and she'd be there with the iodine and the plasters. He watched her bent head, the crown of her hair. Felt bad, all of a sudden, in a way that had nothing to do with the battering he'd taken this evening. 'Get the bottle from my bag, will you?'

She frowned, but did it, gave him a glass from the cabinet by the drinks fridge, poured him a large measure. He turned the wall radio on, and she didn't care for that either, but he had his reasons. He found the local station and left it playing inoffensive music at low volume.

'How'd you book us in?' he said.

'Mr and Mrs Quillet.'

He grinned. 'Sort of accurate.'

'I couldn't make up a name. They know me here. We have a boat on Mill Quay.'

'Charlie's got a boat?' He was surprised.

'Just a little cruiser, a Nomad 22-footer. We've bought one of the new flats in the brewery conversion along the way. It isn't ready yet, so we usually stay here.'

'Won't they think –'

'Doesn't matter.' She bandaged the arm, moved to the other bed, gingerly pulled up her dress to dab at the grazes on her knees.

He drank the whisky, watching her as she leaned forward. The table lamp glowed through the rich black net of her hair.

'Still think I'm paranoid?' she said.

'I believe every word. But what's it all about?'

'I don't know ... My God, what's he got himself into?'

'What's he got you into, more like.'

He found his cigarettes and lit one.

'You still doing that?' she said.

'Yup.'

'Government health warnings don't reach as far as Lowestoft, then?'

'Course not. We think passive smoking's something you do to kippers.'

'Very funny.'

121

He flicked the lighter on, smothered the flame. Flicked it on, killed it.

'So, what're you going to do now? You ready to go to the police yet?'

'No!'

'I just knew you were going to say that.'

'Charlie's message said not to call them.'

'What the hell does Charlie know? He's safe and warm somewhere, sending out his fucking messages.' On and off – Click! Hypnotized by the bud of flame. 'This is dangerous.' Click. 'I think I killed someone tonight because of this.' Click.

'Stop that.'

He dropped the lighter on the bed. Everything was at one remove.

'Did you have to do that?' Her voice was raw. 'Set light to him like that?'

'Accident.'

'You poured petrol on his head.'

'Was a threat that went wrong. A threat. Bugger was too stupid to take it, that's all.'

'It was horrible.'

'What did you want?' he said quietly. 'You prefer if I'd left you there so they could take off that packing tape and strap you to the bed with it? You prefer if I'd waited till they'd done what they liked to you? Is that what you wanted? . . . I got you out. I don't know why, but I got you out. Take you back, if you want.'

She covered her eyes. 'I'm sorry . . .' The trembles were back.

He tried to get up, found it was difficult to do. He thought he was moving toward her, but all that happened was he fell over the side of the bed and crashed to the floor.

She grabbed him, helped him up.

'Lie still, will you.' That was good. She was angry

122

again. That made her blot the rest of it out. She settled him back on the bed.

'Did this before,' he mumbled, before he could stop himself. 'Nurse Woulding.'

She stared. Maybe she remembered the time he got pneumonia and she nursed him through it. But it was almost twenty years ago. She probably had no idea what he was talking about. Wasn't sure he did either. He shut up, focused on the window, on the yacht masts and the reflected lights on the river.

Where was she now? He heard her scuffling around on the other side of the room. He lifted up and saw her clearing a vase of flowers and some leaflets off the table. She put the computer down and opened it, took the 'phone off the hook.

He went out of it for a while. He saw her aged seventeen, doing her college homework at the galley table aboard the *Provider*. Noise and bustle all around her — he and Sam were in the middle of updating the charts, Dad was doing the accounts on some scrap paper, The Sweet were screaming 'Blockbuster' on the radio but she worked as if she were in a library.

He kept ribbing her, kept saying things to Sam about the wonders of a good education.

'Look what it's doing for Charlie,' he grinned. 'He's a university man. Everyone should go to yooneeverseetee. That right, Minny?'

'Leave the gel alone,' Sam said. 'She's not hurtin'.'

'We'll need special permission to talk to her soon.'

'This is important,' she muttered, without looking up.

'What? *Howards End*?'

'You haven't read it.'

'Too busy earning a living so you can sponge off the government.'

Sam stared at the Admiralty Notices to Mariners,

scratching his head. 'Wish I'd had an education,' he said. 'You put him down to where he comes from, love.'

'She always does that,' Paul said. 'Gets it from her college friends.'

'Will you belt up,' Dad barked, chewing his pencil.

'Where's this light beacon go?' Sam asked.

'Reading books like that,' Paul went on, 'what good's it doing you?'

She threw her pen down, and he saw he had finally got to her. He thought that was funny. Always gave him a kick to break down her shyness like that.

'What makes you so brilliant?' she snapped.

'Least I do something practical.'

'Is that what you call it?' She picked up the paperback book and held it tight. 'You think everything's so stupid, don't you? Anything anyone else wants to do, you make fun of it. Well, I'm not spending the rest of my life working in Woolworths.'

Dad and Sam shifted uncomfortably in their chairs. The colour in her cheeks changed from anger to embarrassment. She turned back to her essay.

'Makes 'em bolshy,' he said, to no one in particular. 'That's what you get, educating a woman.'

He came back to the hotel room, squirming inside. He was eighteen then. What a prick.

She had the computer linked to the 'phone. He edged upright and moved slowly across to the table. She was intent on the white screen with the black print running across it. He felt obscurely as if he should apologize, but that would be pretty stupid, since she didn't know what he had been remembering.

She hardly looked at him. 'It's strange . . . When they got me to that house, they had a computer there. They seemed to know what had been going on, and they

124

wanted me to use it, to see if there were any more messages from Charlie.'

He sat down carefully.

'But it didn't work,' she said. 'Nothing came. That's why they wanted this one.'

He was lost. The computer was a neat little machine, but it was so much Greek to him.

'When Charlie gave it to me, he said he'd done a few things to it. Once told me it was a *very* personal computer. You know, he loves taking them apart to see how they work. He fiddles around with them; improves them, he says. He was always working out ways to cut through systems.'

'Cheating.'

'He has a reputation for it,' she muttered, pressing keys on the telephone. 'I think he must have put something into it, some kind of automatic call sign.'

'Why?'

'I don't know. Maybe so we could communicate with each other without paying the bills. He likes to do things like that sometimes.'

'Charlie?'

'Yes, Charlie. You think he's so strait-laced, don't you?'

Never mind what he thought about Charlie.

'Part of his reputation is based on the fact that he can do things with computers no one else can do. He's like . . . like an accountant you hire to cook the books.' She didn't sound proud.

He explored the back of his head. The lump was no more than football-sized. 'What's it doing?' he asked, pointing to the screen.

'I haven't tried it yet.'

'Well, hit the button. I want to be around for another of those dippy messages.'

'All right.' She typed in a word he didn't catch, left

125

one forefinger poised over the keyboard, picked up a
pen. 'I don't have the printer, so your memory'd better
be good.' She pressed.

The screen didn't flicker. It made the bleeping noise,
then a single word appeared:

-TAHEIA-

Mina whispered: 'It's him.' She leaned closer. Paul
felt her tension. Somewhere out there, Charlie was
talking to them.

TAHEIA disappeared.

'Now what?' he said.

'Wait.'

There was a ghostly wash of letters and figures. Then
words.

'Yes!' Mina said.

'Here it comes again.' The young man jumped at
the work station as the screen of the computer lit
the code:

-RECEIVING-

Drazel lifted his bulk out of an armchair and hurried
across. 'Can you get it?'

The young man's fingers danced on the keyboard. His
tongue protruded between thin lips as he concentrated.
'Trying.'

'Can you do it?'

The screen flickered.

-NO ACCESS-

He cursed and tried again. 'Damn it. He's got all the
blocks in.'

Drazel leaned over his shoulder, breathing raggedly. 'Come on, baby,' the young man murmured. 'Come on.'

The NO ACCESS notice began to flash. His fingers blurred as he tried to keep it on. Suddenly the screen filled with gibberish. Random lines of letters and figures. The computer bleeped 'error' five times, then even the gibberish blipped out.

'Fuck!' He slammed his fist on the desk. 'Damn, he's good.'

Drazel threw a bunch of papers down and wandered over to the floor-to-ceiling windows of the office suite, mouth working. New York winter roared against the glass outside. Snowflakes carried by the gale ripped upward like paint streaks against the black sky thirty storeys above Manhattan. The office was huge, dimly lit, quiet as a library. The other man, picked out in a cone of light from a reading lamp, sat back from the computer, his spectacles glinting.

Drazel said: 'Martin, I think I want you to give this problem your personal attention.'

Martin Sheal touched a button on the keyboard and played back what had just occurred. He was lithe, smoothly turned-out, not yet thirty. He wore John Phillips suits, shoes by Gucci. No braces. He never took up anything made fashionable by the movies or TV. He was too superior to the herd for that. He froze the screenful of nonsense, searching for a pattern.

'You mean the computing side?'

'Yes.' Drazel regarded the city of lights shining through the snow. Medium height, burly, hair steel-grey, skin deeply browned and lined, he looked like an exquisitely dressed and manicured construction worker. 'This is the third time he's messaged this way. Always too fast for us to pick it up. We don't know what he's saying, and we can't see where he

127

is. I want you to apply yourself full time to break-ing in.'

'He's an expert – maybe *the* expert – at short-cutting. He knows we're looking for him, and he knows the Sneaker program we're using –'

'He designed it,' Drazel growled.

'I can't even tell you how he gets those messages to her. The last one seems to have gone through maybe fifty-five separate systems in different parts of the world. Then, just to make it really hard, the smart son of a bitch fixes a delayed erase on it. Even if we got it, it could take weeks to work the code.'

Drazel turned the heavy gold ring on his left index finger, something he often did when he was thinking. 'Our man's with them now. He's dealt with the prob-lem in the field.'

Sheal smiled to himself. It was a nice way of putting it. 'Haggard? What exactly's he done to them?'

'Taken them out of the game.'

Sheal thought he heard a hint of real anger in his employer's voice. That would be unusual. It might imply he was worried. He always showed his German blood in his thickset appearance, but put the right moustache on him just now, he'd look like Bismarck. Bismarck in a real snotty mood.

'Those dumb fucks went against their orders. They couldn't even do the small thing we asked of them.'

'It's one of the British diseases,' Sheal said.

'We can't have that kind of insubordination. Look at the mess they made. This is supposed to be a quiet operation. Jesus God! If the wife had been hurt, where would that leave us in trying to find him?' The ring spun on his finger like a top. 'No, Haggard's on it now, so we have someone we can trust in the field. We have whole banks of machines and people working on this, but I want extra insurance. I want you to go up against

128

him one-to-one. Try to break his locks and diversions, try to trace him back through the systems he's working and find out where he is.'

'You have any uppers I can take? It'll be a twenty-four hours a day job.'

'Just get started. If you get the messages, even if you don't understand them, pass them on to Haggard. He might be able to use the information.'

Sheal took off his glasses and knuckled both eyes till the sparks came. 'I'd better send down for some *sushi*. It's going to be a long night.'

The message was gone, the screen empty. Mina stared blankly at the words she had scribbled down.

Paul shook his head. He almost wanted to laugh.

COLLECT ROSIE FROM THE WEARY WELL.

That was what it said. That was *all* it said.

She drew a smiley face next to the words, then stabbed it with the tip of the pen.

'What the hell does this mean?'

He held his arm close to his body. The pain was distracting. 'Know anyone called Rosie?'

'No.' She had expected more than this, he could tell. The excitement of a moment before had deserted her. She slumped. 'Collect Rosie from the Weary Well,' she muttered. 'Shit.'

'Now, now.'

She glared at him, typed some more, but the computer had said all it was going to. She sat back, pushing the hair away from her face. 'I'm hungry.'

Flicking absently through the book of Stevenson's verse, she rang down to see if the night staff could rustle up some sandwiches. He lay down again, wondering how much the room and its river view were costing. He was very tired, and it was getting on for two o'clock.

Food arrived. He took a sandwich, watched her devour the rest.

'It's not in the book,' she said. 'I mean, the Weary Well is in, but not Rosie.' She read it to him, though he knew it well:

> '"She rested by the broken brook
> She drank of Weary Well,
> She moved beyond my lingering look,
> Ah, whither none can tell!"'

'Maybe she was called Rosie,' he said.

'Be serious, will you?'

He fumbled for his glass. 'You're not thinking,' he said, feeling vaguely pleased at knowing something she didn't.

'What?'

'Does old Charles, when he's not sending stupid messages by computer, have a favourite pub?'

She was a little slow for once. 'Pub?'

'Drinking den, ale-house, slop-shop. Pub.'

He saw the light dawn. 'Oh, of course,' she said, tutting irritably. 'You know, your father's got a lot to answer for. Why can't you two just call a pub a pub?'

'More fun his way.'

'The Porterhouse,' she said. 'It's in a little alley between Sidney Street and King's Parade.'

'Any particular reason you go there?'

She shook her head. 'Charlie says the real ale's good. If we go to a pub, it's usually that one. The landlord shares Charlie's tastes in music. That helps.'

'They friends?'

'I wouldn't put it that strong. You know Charlie. He doesn't exactly have friends.'

'Maybe he gave this bloke something to look after.'

'Called Rosie?' She grimaced. 'What could he possibly have left there that he'd need now?'

He stretched back and turned the radio up. The news

had just started. The reader went through the national stories, then moved on to local matters. The fire was up first.

'One man has died in a house fire at Grafham Water near Huntingdon tonight. The house, a lakeside cottage on the popular boating centre, was completely gutted by the blaze. Two fire teams were called to the area, but were too late to save the property. The man who died hasn't yet been identified, and police say there may be suspicious circumstances. A car parked near the house had had its tyres slashed.

'Other news: Cambridge postmen have called for –'
Paul turned the radio off.

'They can't connect it with us,' Mina said. 'I mean, the others won't go to the police, will they?'

He was wondering whether he had left any fingerprints in the car. He was wondering which way revenge might come; from the law or from friends of the three stooges. The reality of what he'd been involved in tonight finally hit him.

The empty glass fell from his fingers. She caught it as it rolled off the bed.

'You've got to rest.' She looked in his eyes for what seemed the first time when she wasn't angry. She shrugged. 'Thanks for getting me out.'

'Was either that or call the cops. And I don't get Chandor's bonus if they find him.'

'You think he's going to show his face again?'

'Only kidding. Whatever this is, he's up to his ears in it. Trouble is –' he closed his eyes ' – so are we.'

12

She was already up and dressed when he woke in the morning. He turned over toward the light edging round the curtains, not knowing for a moment where he was. He had been dreaming bad dreams of the frozen moment when the car hauled up next to them in the woods by Grafham Water. In the dreams it kept happening and, each time, the moments of standing there, wondering what was going to happen next, drew out longer and longer. Each time, he leaned closer and closer to the car, trying to see into the dark, feeling the staring eyes like a cold grip on his heart. He knew the face: not someone, but some thing evil. He sensed the death in it. He knew it was going to kill him. Just as he thought he was about to see the face clearly, it would stop, and then run again, except that the last part got slower and more vivid. Waking at last was a relief, except for the disorientation. Then he heard Mina's voice talking into the 'phone:

'I see. Well, thank you, anyway . . . Yes, thanks a lot.'

He sat up, cursing silently when an echo of the knife going in stabbed through his arm.

The computer was switched off and closed. Mina was dressed in jeans and a sweater, her hair tied back. In front of her was the list Chandor had given him and a *Cosmopolitan* pocket diary. She was starting another call.

Still in his clothes, he took a blue hotel robe off the back of the door and limped into the bathroom, feeling as if someone had slipped sand between his flesh and

132

his bones during the night. He stripped off and eyed himself in the mirror. He had a couple of bruises he hadn't been aware of, and a little spot of dried blood showed through the bandage.

He showered with the water as hot as he could get it, shaved and kept staring at his face. There was nothing of Charlie in him. He once embarked on a long campaign to convince Charlie they were sired by different fathers. Didn't work, though. Charlie always knew exactly who he was. He let you shout, while he remained quiet and watchful, then he snuck in behind your back and took the prize.

'Oh, and where has he moved to?' Mina was saying.

She was so confident now. She dealt with things. He supposed that anyone married to Charlie would have to be pretty good at handling the practical side of life, because he wouldn't. And the way she had been talking since they met; obviously she was nervous to begin with, but mostly she was talking back to him like –

Like an equal.

He finished shaving, went back to the bedroom. Breakfast had arrived, a stack of newspapers were spread on the table. Mina put down the 'phone. She had opened the curtains to show the river and the yachts on the quay glazed with bright frost. The sky was pure blue, and the river moved slowly upstream with the turning tide.

More awkwardness as they started eating. Questions about how each was feeling petered out in silence. He kept trying to think what it reminded him of, then realized: they were acting like strangers after a one-night stand. The same unease, the same question in the air: what are we doing here? They broke it by going through the 'papers, looking for anything that might relate to Charlie or the fire.

'Who were you 'phoning?' he asked, when they were down to the toast and coffee.

She touched the list.

'Trying an experiment; before we go back to Cambridge and risk running into any more musclemen.'

'Been through my pockets.'

'I didn't sleep much last night. Had to have something to think about.'

'So.' He folded the *Times* and scoured the home news pages. 'Tell me.'

'All of the people on this list that Tony gave you,' she said. 'They're people who know him, yes. Colleagues from the university, a few people from companies he had contacts with.' She buttered a slice of toast and ladled marmalade onto it. 'But there's not one person here who works with him for Robersman.'

'I thought some of them –'

'Not one. There's a small team of them, four most of the time, five when Steven Minnock came in.'

'We're talking about the "Weatherspy" thing?'

'It isn't just "Weatherspy". There are various projects, and this little group, who aren't company employees – more freelances, like Charlie – they work together in different combinations on different projects to see whether they can get results. They don't even have to be in the same place, since most of what they do is with computers. I don't think they've all been in the same room at the same time since the team was founded.'

'Anyone famous?'

'Only in their own line.'

'But "Weatherspy's" owned by Robersman?'

She bit into the toast. 'I think there's government funding as well, because it's supposed to do with the EEC, but they were actually working for the company.'

'Were?'

'Here's the point. We see a couple of the team socially.

134

I've got their numbers.' She tapped the diary. 'I just tried to contact them.'

'They disappeared too?'

She sipped some coffee. 'Steven Minnock's "left the country to take up a fellowship at Northwestern University", and Anna Hilding went to Japan to work for the Nakasami Electronics Corporation.'

'When?'

'Since Christmas.'

He stopped eating. 'What about the others?'

'I haven't got numbers for them.'

'Where could you get them?'

'I could call Robersman. But I don't think I want to do that.' She twisted her cup in its saucer, and he suddenly saw that she was very frightened. It made him feel better, because the fat worm of fear was slithering in his guts too.

'No,' he said. 'Second thoughts, neither do I.'

They left the hotel at 10.30. She expected him to head for the Cambridge Road, but he went with the Monday morning traffic into the docks area.

'What're you doing?'

'Trust me.' He pulled into a car showroom opposite a sex shop and a launderette.

Kevin Poller was surprised to see him. He was even more surprised when Paul asked how much part-exchange he would give them on Mina's Volvo. 'Whatcha wanna sell it for?' he asked, his pale red hair flopping over his eyes. His suit was a little bit crumpled, his eyes were a little bit shifty, but he was a friend.

In half an hour they had made a deal on a green Ford Sierra, and Mina handed over her keys in a state of some shock.

'I don't know why I let you do that,' she said, as they drove away.

He was getting used to the steering and the clutch. 'If we have to go back to Cambridge we don't want to turn up in the same car, do we? Let's make it a bit hard for them.'

She looked sourly round the car. 'I don't like this make.'

'Get Charlie to buy you a new one when we're done.'

It was a beautiful day. Everything knife-sharp in the February sun, the road easy going. When he glanced at her, she didn't seem scared any more.

He thought: If things had been different, we could be doing this now. Nothing about Charlie or bad guys in big cars. The ring on her finger would be mine. This'd just be a drive out for the day.

Yes. In his wrecked and pitted Granada that someone had borrowed and forgotten to return; not enough money in their pockets; back home in the evening to the pokey little house in Lowestoft.

Not really *her*, not the way she was now. Maybe it never had been. Besides, he'd never bought her a ring, never invited her to try it.

'Why so grim?' she asked. He snapped out of it. 'We've shaken them off.'

They'll find us again when they want us, he thought.

She smacked her forehead suddenly. 'Oh . . .'

'What's wrong?'

'I never showed you the boat.'

'Maybe another time.' I don't want to see your boat, or your luxury apartment.

Then she laughed softly.

'I was just remembering,' she said. 'That time your Dad almost ran the *Provider* aground on Seal Sand.'

He kept his eyes on the road, said nothing.

'You know, the big sand bar at the head of the estuary.'

He knew it. He saw it twice every month, when he sailed in and out of Bishop's Lynn.

'We were waiting for the Pilot to come out, but Bernard thought he could wriggle her in himself.' She laughed again. 'He was so crazed sometimes. It's a wonder they never took his Master's Ticket away . . . Don't you?–' She turned to look at him, and must have read his face well. She stopped. The temperature seemed to drop several degrees.

They made good time through the fens, racing the London train at one point when the line came close to the road.

As they approached Ely, the cathedral shining like an ancient city on the plain, he lit a cigarette. 'Thought any more about "Rosie"?'

'No.' Her reply was sulky. 'You have any bright ideas?'

'Had a girlfriend called Rosie once.'

'You had a lot of girls *once*.'

'Here we go again.'

'What's wrong? Not getting modest in your old age, are you?'

'That's right. Keep myself to myself.'

'That makes a change.'

He tapped the ash off his cigarette and held his peace. After a minute, she said:

'You know, we can't avoid the subject forever. Can't just black it out and say: No talking about that period.'

He gripped the wheel tight, batting the anger down, hearing the sneer in his voice. 'There's nothing to talk about.'

'We've been thrown into this situation –'

'Which ends as soon as I can get out of it.'

'– And we don't know how long it's going to last. We're not going to be able to say very much if we're constantly trying not to offend each other. What're we going to talk about if we put "No Entry" signs all over the last twenty years?'

'Used cars.'

'Oh, grow up.'

He took his eyes off the road to try and stare her out of it, but she was stoked up and running.

'We're not kids any more. If we can't let what happened be and talk sensibly about things, we'll spend all our time silent or shouting at each other.'

'I like peace and quiet.'

'You haven't changed a bit. I thought the chip on your shoulder would've worn down by now.'

'Oh, no, it's a nice big chip.'

'Well, you put it there.'

'I was great until you started.'

'You've been giving me black looks and the cold shoulder ever since we ran into each other.'

'It's all my fault. Everything wrong with you is my fault.'

'I didn't say that.'

'What the fuck are you saying?'

'That we were kids then, but we're adults now. We can at least be civilized.'

The anger broke. 'You go and be civilized,' he said. 'That's what you and Charlie and all your sort are good at. I don't have to be.'

That shut her up. His hands were shaking on the wheel and his headache was back.

She watched the countryside passing for a while. Then she said:

'Funny. I didn't know you were the only one with things to forgive.'

They parked off Bridge Street, not far from the Porterhouse. The cold was biting, but sunshine made the streets vivid. Walking together, they were nervous.

Mina stopped in a shoe shop to buy a new pair of boots. He loitered well back from the shop windows, staggered that she could think about her comfort at a time like this. But, as she said: 'If I'm going to be chased, I'll run a lot faster if my feet are warm.' He kept expecting the silver-grey Carlton to glide past, or the beard's face to pop up at the window.

'So, what's the plan?' she said, as they resumed. 'Just walk straight in?'

'It's full daylight. What can they do?'

'Shoot us, run us over, get the police to arrest us for the murder of that man last night.'

'No one's mentioned our names yet.'

'I don't trust anyone. I can't even go home. What sort of country is this?'

'Same one as before. Just you're the other side of the glass now.'

'Oh, shut up.'

The Porterhouse stood where it had stood for over five hundred years. A narrow, leaning tudor house squeezed between two antique bookshops down a crooked alley. In the chilly shadows, two old men in expensive coats were discussing the price of a Catullus. The whole alley was like stepping back several hundred years.

They glanced up and down to see if they were followed, but there were just the old men arguing about calf or buckram. They ducked through the low doorway and went inside. It was what he expected: either the establishment had not been changed in the last couple of centuries, or someone had restored it to look that way. Now that Britain was a service economy, a theme park, it was difficult to tell whether history was real or recreated. The floor was stone flags, the walls rough plaster, the ceiling beamed, the bar and the tables and chairs old wood. The big fireplace held a modest pile of blazing logs. No fruit machines or video games, no juke box. It was still early, and the only customers were an aged gentleman nursing a pint of stout at the bar, and a younger man over in one corner, reading the *Daily Mail* and sipping a half of lager.

A big, grey-haired man with sideburns, and eyebrows permanently cocked in a way that suggested amusement appeared from the back. He even wore an apron. He was pleased the moment he saw Mina.

'Hello, my dear.' His voice was a low, west country burr.

'Morning, John. How're you?'

'Brighter for you coming in. What'll it be?'

'Half of best, please, and – ' She looked at Paul.

'Pint of Bateman's,' he said.

The landlord got the order, chatting about how glad he was to see her back, had she enjoyed her holiday, what had it been like? It was difficult to tell how much he knew. Mina made polite replies, and it was all very cosy. The landlord kept glancing at him in a way that was less open, until Mina remembered her manners.

'John, this is my brother-in-law, Paul.'

'Pleased to meet you,' John said. 'Must say, you don't bear much resemblance to Charles.'

'He got the good looks,' Paul said, letting the bitter slide down his throat.

'Ah, same with me and my brothers.' The eyebrows twitched up and down. 'I'm the handsome one.'

More customers came in. The place got busy quickly, so busy that no one particularly noticed when the man who had been reading the *Daily Mail* got up and left most of his drink behind him.

They stayed at the bar. Mina drank slowly and relaxed a little.

'It's strange,' she said, after a time. 'We're sitting here, and it feels so safe and familiar. I can't believe what happened last night.'

140

He touched his arm. The sleeve of his jacket was still damp where he had tried to wash the blood out.

He lit a cigarette and took a more careful look around the place. He had no idea what he was looking for: documents, money, passport, a computer disc? Old prints hung on the walls. He found himself reading the titles to see if any of them contained the word 'Rosie'. The clientele seemed to be mostly respectable people in late middle age. Nearly all had received personal greetings from the landlord. Their talk made a polite hum to go with clinking glasses and the snap of the fire. It was the sort of place Charlie would like, right enough. Nothing nasty or tasteless about it.

The landlord had time to talk again. 'Haven't seen Charles for a while.'

'No, he went away,' Mina said.

'Did 'e? Lord, Charles taking a holiday, there's an event. Decided to join you, did he?'

'Oh, no.' She shook her head a little too definitely.

'When was he last in?'

'Ah, wait a second.' He patted his belly as if his memory resided there. 'That'd be – what? – couple o' weeks ago. Can't say for sure. Most days seem alike in this trade, 'cept Sundays.'

'He didn't leave anything here, did he?'

'What, like his umbrella or his briefcase? No. One thing Charles's got is a good memory.'

Two men came in. The only reason Paul noticed was that conversation lulled slightly, as it does when strangers enter a pub full of regulars. He flicked a glance their way. One of them was the man who had been reading the 'paper in the corner. The other was a heavy blond man in jeans and cowboy boots. They went straight to a free table, but Paul thought he caught their momentary stares. He turned back to his drink as the one in cowboy boots came to the bar.

A south London accent asked for a half of lager and a double Johnnie Walker.

Mina noticed his stillness. She made a questioning face at him, but he did nothing to indicate the strangers.

The landlord went out to change a barrel, and Mina leaned close.

'What's wrong?'

'Two blokes,' he said.

She started to look, but he laid a hand on her arm.

'Not certain. Just got a feeling.'

'How could they have found us so soon?'

'Looks like they know plenty about you. Maybe they've posted someone every place either of you might turn up.'

He swivelled on his stool, warming himself at the fire. Out of the corner of his eye, he saw the two men sitting close together over their drinks. They were doing such a good job of not watching him that instinct prickled his skin with increasing certainty.

'No,' the landlord said, wiping his hands on the bar towel as he returned. 'Just had a look round the back. No lost property at all.'

Mina sighed. 'Oh, well . . .'

Someone over by the dartboard called out: 'Here, John, what about some music.' The landlord nodded and bent down behind the bar. Paul saw a bulky old Sanyo cassette deck stashed on a shelf, a row of cassettes next to it. The landlord hemmed and hawed for a minute, then made his decision. Next moment, a folk-based tune started threading quietly from concealed speakers. The group near the dartboard raised their glasses. The two strangers grimaced.

'Maybe this isn't the Weary Well,' Mina said.

Paul was listening to the music. 'What?'

'Maybe Charlie was thinking of another place.'

142

'Got another pub?'

'This is the only one we go to regularly.'

'Maybe Weary Well doesn't mean what I thought it meant.'

'What else would it mean?'

He watched the dancing red lights of the LED on the cassette deck. The tune was familiar.

'What is that?' he asked, as the landlord passed by again.

The eyebrows twitched. 'That?' He went and picked up the case. The title was handwritten. 'Fairport Convention. *Red and Gold*,' he said. '*Gladys Leap* on the other side.'

Mina put down her drink. 'That's Charlie's handwriting.'

'Yes,' the landlord said. 'He did a bit o' recording for us over Christmas. I was saying people were getting a bit fed up of the same old things all the time – matter o' fact, they're probably fed up full stop, but I'll play what I like in my own place. Anyway, he said he had some records I'd probably like. So I got some blank tapes and he took 'em away and did 'em for me.'

Paul risked a look back. The strangers were sitting forward, trying to see what was going on.

'Amazing, you know,' the landlord was saying. 'Ask people if they like this sort of stuff, they'll go: "What? Folk music? Never!" But you'd be surprised how many of 'em get to like it when it sneaks up on 'em like this.' A thought struck him. 'That reminds me.' He sorted through the rest of the cassettes on the shelf. 'There's one here – which is it? – it didn't come out right.' He slid the case off the shelf, handed it over. 'I don't know what it is. Maybe it's his recorder. I tried playing it, all I get is a load o' chirps and warbles.'

Mina had her hand to it first. The case was transparent, and there was no inlay card with details. On one

143

side, the cassette was labelled: 'Fairport Convention – *Unhalfbricking*'. She turned it over. There, in Charlie's handwriting, were the words: 'Fairport Convention – *Rosie*'.

'An album title,' she muttered. 'My God.'

'If he'd made it *Rubber Soul* we might have got to it quicker.'

'So would anyone else.' She smiled at the landlord. 'John, shall I take this home and get Charlie to re-do it for you? He must've pressed the wrong buttons.'

'All right, my dear. Thanks a lot.'

They sat on, the cassette lying on the counter between them. The strangers were looking at the racing pages in their 'paper, marking possible winners.

'There a back way out of here?' Paul asked.

'Through the door to the dining room and the toilets,' she said. 'The old stables.'

He got up, taking the tape with him. He felt the eyes of the strangers on him all the way to the door, made sure they got a look at the tape before he jammed it in his pocket, but he still gave no sign he knew about them.

He passed through the dining room. The old stable forge was now an open fireplace. No doubt they grilled steaks on it. He looked out of the back door onto a narrow yard. At the end of it was a passage leading to Sidney Street. He nipped out and had a look, but there was no evidence of anyone watching the rear. He locked himself in the gents' toilet for a few moments. Back in the bar, he made a meal out of going over to look at one of the prints by the window. The little panes of glass limited the view, but he couldn't see much to worry about out there either. Under the bland gaze of the cowboy and the reader, he resumed his seat.

'Will you do what I tell you?' he said.

Mina frowned. 'Depends what it is.'

'All right. Go to the Ladies, and stay in there for ten minutes. Ten minutes exactly.'

'And then what?'

'Then come out, take a look outside to make sure no one's watching for you, and head back to the car.'

'And you'll be doing what?'

'My best to lose them.'

'I don't like it.'

'I hate it. Get lost.'

She crossed the room, and not only the strangers watched her go with an appreciative eye. It was difficult, telling her to fade into the background. She didn't have the looks for it.

Five minutes passed, and he edged his drink down to the bottom. He noted that the strangers were getting fidgety. Heads close together, they were probably arguing whether one should go out and try to follow Mina. If they decided to check the ladies' toilets first, then he would be in trouble, but he didn't think they would.

As his watch notched the eighth minute he stood up, nodded to the landlord, and walked out the front door. Once he was outside, he dropped any pretence of being relaxed. He hurried down the alley toward St John's Street. At the end, he swung straight into a gents' outfitters that had stopped the century in about 1930. The suits were classic, the shirts all had tails and holes for cufflinks, and hats were on display as if every man in the street still wore one. He ducked behind a row of club ties and watched the street through a gap between a shooting jacket and an Aquascutum raincoat.

The strangers came out of the alley, looking sharply up and down the street. They registered confusion, and he liked that. It made him feel better about the way his arm throbbed and his head still hurt.

The cowboy went sprinting off toward King's Parade,

the reader stayed where he was, hands in pockets, breathing white clouds in the air. Paul moved out of sight. A portly little salesman with a head like a cherry wended his way between the displays of shirts.

'Was there something, sir?' He had taken a quick inventory of Paul's costume and decided he must be in the wrong shop.

'Browsing,' Paul said, lifting a striped silk tie to prove his sincerity.

'Well, if you require any help . . .'

'I'll call, don't worry.'

The cowboy was back. They held a hasty conference on the pavement, and the reader gave the shop a cursory glance, but then the pair of them moved off toward Bridge Street. That was a pity. If they'd gone the other way, he could have headed straight back to the car.

But this was no time to be picky about his luck. He left the selection of ties and the hats, and walked out of the shop under the dubious gaze of the salesman. He stuck his head round the corner, saw them disappearing into the sparse crowds on the pavement, turned down St John's Street looking for the first left turn. He had a fair memory of the earlier walk through the town centre, and if a life on the *Provider* had given him anything it was a sense of direction. He reached the corner of Green Street and looked back. The cowboy was moving toward him, tall in his boots, head bobbing over the rest of the crowd. No sign of the reader. He was probably coming round the other way to close the trap.

Where to now? Just keep walking along the busy street? After all, what were they going to do to him in full public sight? But eventually he had to get back to Mina, and that meant losing them.

He crossed the street between a couple of taxis and ducked down Trinity Lane. This was taking him into the heart of the university buildings. There were few people in the lane. He broke into a trot, looking for places he could hide while the cowboy went past, turned the corner and saw some kind of church, cut right and came out on a big quadrangle fronting the river. A neat path squared off an area of drab green lawn. He stuck to the path because he was certain some official fool would be onto him if he didn't. He loped along by the side of college buildings red and warmly aged by the sunshine. Where he went after the river he didn't know. His arm was beginning to burn, and he was fairly sure he was bleeding again, but there was no time to look. One quick nod over his shoulder showed the cowboy moving along at a steady lick to close on him. And to make things worse, he saw that the reader had finally caught up with them. He was coming down the opposite side of the square, not hurrying, seeing that in the end they were all going to meet for a polite chat.

He reached the river. The bank on the right looked out of bounds, but he was beginning to think that tangling with college security would be a better bet than the goons behind him. He started to run; past a bridge, where some students gave him a surprised look, along the banks beneath a long stretch of beautiful buildings. He thought: Well, I finally get to go to university, and looked back, and saw that they were together, and catching up. He was not much for running at the best of times. He was reasonably tough, good for brute strength, but too much booze and the wrong food didn't give him an awful lot of endurance.

Past another bridge. He thought about going over it, but there was nothing but grass and trees and a busy road a couple of hundred yards away on the other side. So he swerved right and panted toward a gap between buildings. An old door stood open. He ran through it into a tall, echoing stairwell. Marble stairs and stone flags. The marble bust of some long-gone dignitary with a walrus moustache regarded him imperiously from its plinth. Several doors led off the ground floor. All were shut. He heard the footsteps of the strangers rattling toward him, and started up the stairs. Just as he reached the second landing, a little man in some kind of uniform came through one of the doors, saw the cowboy and the reader lunging in from outside. He said: 'Hoi!' But they didn't stop.

Paul nearly collided with a professorial-looking gent on the first floor. The professor stared and clutched an armful of books close to his chest. Paul went past him across smooth, yellowed floor tiles, through a set of double doors into a library.

It was old and brown and full of leather spines and great slab-like books the size of newspapers. More of the marbled dead looked down from their perches, their faces white and impassive. There was a smell of decaying paper and dust. Right at the end, at some long tables, a few students bent over old volumes. No one seemed to notice him come in, all sounds were swallowed by the high-roofed and underlit room. He slowed, trying not to attract attention. The footsteps on the stairs were getting louder. He wouldn't be able to make the door at the far end before they came in. They would see him and know where he had gone.

He noticed some of the walkways between shelves were blocked off by little spring-loaded gates. He whipped one of the gates on the left open and hurried down to the gloomy end, pulled one of the biggest books he could find off the top shelf and held it up in front of his face.

He heard them enter, and slow down the way he had. Funny how the heavy dignity of the place affected even them. But they had something else to worry about. In the distance down the echoing stairwell, a gruff voice was still shouting: 'You can't go up there.' They were pressed for time. He waited, peeping over the top of the book. It was a bound collection of pamphlets from the nineteenth century, something to do with the corn laws. It weighed a ton. He saw the cowboy go past, looking neither right nor left. He stopped his breath from whistling in his throat. The book was dragging his left arm down. The reader went by.

All right. He leaned against the wall, listening for their footsteps carrying on along the length of the room. The air was suffocating. He closed the book, began to move back along the shelves. Voices were talking at the far end of the room. He couldn't tell what they said. He put his left hand on the little gate and pushed it open.

The reader was a skinny little ferret, but he had a good grip. Paul discovered it when his left arm was grabbed and he was wrenched through the gate. The reader happened to grasp him just an inch below where the knife had gone into his arm. He more or less howled when the reader did that. He certainly made a noise that shattered the peace of the library. He saw the reader's triumphant little grin turn to surprise at the strength of his reaction, then he didn't see the reader's face any more because he brought his right arm up, with the big book still in it, and swatted the reader aside with a blow that split the volume in half and probably broke the reader's nose.

As the reader went down, and brittle sheets of old pamphlets flew up in the air, the cowboy came at him. At least he knew about this kind of fighting. No knives, no guns. Just the cowboy bunching a pair of impressive fists and lunging for him. He was at a disadvantage because of his left arm, but he had been in enough situations like this to know that hands were not all you used. The cowboy thought he had him off-guard. He came in without protecting himself. Paul braced his back against the shelves, and flicked his boot up. The cowboy saw it going straight for his crotch, and did an odd little twist of the body to get out of the way. It didn't work. The boot just hit him a little higher, in the belly. He made a noise like a football team being sick in a bucket and collided with the students who were racing up to see what was going on. Holding his arm close to his body, Paul lurched toward the door just as the little uniformed man entered. He pushed him aside without too much trouble and went down the stairs three at a time.

Outside, he ran up the lane toward iron gates. They were shut, but a wicket let into them was open. Another uniformed man stood by them, and he was a good deal bigger and younger than the first. His head ducked toward a walkie-talkie. He blocked the gate.

'All right, what's going on?'

'Been a fight,' Paul said, checking behind to see whether they were coming.

'And what're you?'

'Exhausted. Let me through.'

A big hand stopped him. 'You just wait a minute.'

There was a disturbance in the doorway. A student who probably rowed for the Cambridge team or ate rugby balls for breakfast came staggering out backwards and fell heavily on the cobbles. The security man or whatever he was gaped. Paul heard shouting, then the cowboy and the reader burst from the doorway and came pelting after him.

The security man forgot Paul, started jabbering into the walkie-talkie. Paul slipped by him through the gate, clanging it shut behind him. He was back in Trinity Lane. He headed for the corner and St John's Street, hearing the row as the cowboy and the reader reached the gate and started their own kind of argument with the security man.

He kept running, out of Trinity Lane, across the street in front of a bus. The crowd parted before him as he careered down Green Street. He didn't stop to see whether he had lost them. All he wanted was to get back to the car and drive away.

Left onto Sidney Street, blood warm in the palm of his hand now and the whole arm like fire. He slowed, crossed over and walked briskly toward Bridge Street. A police siren wailed hysterically somewhere behind, nowhere near. He swung into Church Street. The car park was down at the end. A swathe of tarmac dumped down in the middle of old Victorian terraces. He saw the passage Mina had led him through earlier and went down it. Came out at the back of what had once been a saddlery. He crossed the old yard lined with dustbins and trolleys and stood by the new concrete flower bins, looking for the car. There it was, off to the right, and Mina was in the driving seat. She waved. He beckoned stiffly.

Just then, a middle-aged, horsey-looking woman who had passed him going out cried: 'Do you mind!' and the cowboy jostled past her out of the passage, closely followed by the reader. He turned and searched for the car. It was moving around the rows of parked cars, coming toward him the long way round. He pulled himself together and started to run, but they were up with him by then. They grabbed him by the shoulders and dragged him back into the yard. The cowboy pinioned his arms, which caused an awful lot more pain in the knife wound. The reader came round in front of him. His nose was a mess and his eyes were beginning to bruise.

Paul attempted another kick, but the cowboy lifted him by the bad arm, and that stopped him. The reader drew back and hit him square in the stomach.

'That's what it felt like,' the cowboy spat in his ear.
'Do it again.'

The reader did it again. Despite having time to tense
the muscles, Paul thought his guts would spill out on
the reader's shoes. The reader licked his lips as if that
was his intention.

But the cowboy was keeping watch. He said: 'Car
coming.'

The reader had one last go at his stomach, then
jammed in close and went through his pockets.

'Hah!' he said, and took the cassette. He stepped
back.

The distraction made the cowboy loosen his hold.
Paul kicked backwards, connected with shin. The
cowboy roared and let him go. Paul leapt at the
dustbins, snatched up a lid and hurled it saucer-wise.
They scattered as it clanged off the wall.

Mina pulled up ten yards away, shouting at him to
come on. He wanted to go back and finish off one or
other of them, but his belly felt like so much old rope,
he could hardly breathe. He staggered past the flower
bins and barely had the door shut before Mina's foot
went hard down on the accelerator.

'I thought you were going to lose them.'

'I did,' he whispered, trying to get his breath.
'That was a couple of Salvation Army blokes after
a contribution.'

She cut up Thompson's Lane, and they were out on
Magdalene Street again, heading out of town, no one
following. She drove like a maniac all the way out of
town, angry and frightened, taking it out on the traffic.
He was surprised the police didn't stop them, but they
had a clear run out into the country, where she turned
off the Bishop's Lynn road and raced through open
country. She was close to tears.

'They got the tape, didn't they?'

152

He was holding his stomach, trying to keep his breakfast down. 'Don't bother asking if I'm all right, it's okay.'

'They got the damn tape, didn't they?' she insisted. 'You saw them.'

'So that's it. There's nothing more we can do.'

He thought how fine she looked.

'We needed that tape, damn it. Why did you take it?'

He slipped a hand under his sweater, into the breast pocket of his shirt, and took out a cassette. He placed it on her lap.

She almost steered into the verge.

'Rosie,' she said. She picked it up and saw that it was the tape the landlord had given them. She gave him a look with daggers in it, and he couldn't help grinning. It was good to have won something.

'But what've they got?' she asked.

He rubbed the back of his neck. 'Maybe they're Hendrix fans.'

13

Haggard said: 'Something is amiss here.'

He was sitting in his car in the parking area outside Cambridge airport. A 'plane had just landed. The whine of the airscrews rang across the field as it taxied toward the terminal.

On the other end of the line, New York said:

'How so?'

'Your information about the hotel in Bishop's Lynn was correct. Also the change of car.'

'Everyone has computer records these days,' New York said.

'The people you planted here spotted them this morning, and I drove straight here when the call came.'

'What happened?'

Haggard examined the fingers of his left hand. 'I didn't stay to find out. All I know is that the local radio news had something about a disturbance in one of the colleges. Three men. And Mr and Mrs Quillet have dropped out of sight again.'

'They'll turn up. The next time they book into a hotel, whenever they use a card to pay for petrol or a meal. The moment I have something, I'll let you know.'

'Is it possible,' Haggard said, 'that the authorities are involved?'

'No. Why?'

'My instructions are to track them to the brother, cause them no harm until then. But others appear to have something else in mind. For an operation which is supposed to be silent, it's making a great deal of noise.'

'I'll try to find out what's happening on the English end,' New York soothed. 'They should have pulled out by now and left the ground clear for you.'

'That doesn't appear to be the case.'

'No.' New York sighed. 'I have to confess, we thought you'd dealt with all of that last night.'

'So did I,' Haggard said. 'This isn't clean.'

'I'll get back to you.'

'You do that.'

He put the 'phone down and watched passengers disembarking from the 'plane. He did not care for working in Britain. He never felt as if the structure supporting him was quite sound in this grubby, disorganized little island. His car and the equipment he had required – right down to the little Derringer Model 7 he carried as final insurance – had been provided by the London branch of the Factory, and everything was correct. But he would not have been surprised to find that they had given him the wrong guns, or a car that broke down. The bumbling stupidity of the national life appeared to leak even into his line of work.

He had taken several jobs over the years – a troublesome government minister, a drugs baron who had been arrested and was about to spill rather more beans than his old associates could reasonably accept, a research chemist who wished to share too much of his work with the world – but he never felt comfortable, and always hoped that his task could be carried out elsewhere.

Now this farrago: and he smelled worse trouble before it was done. He thought about this man Quillet, who was supposed to be nothing but a stooge, recalled his white, frightened face in the dark last night. This 'stooge' had managed to kill one of the men put onto him, injure two others and burn down a house. Now he had caused more upset in Cambridge. Fascinating. Of course, it could not happen like this anywhere else.

155

Only in England, where – despite the recent dawning of a realistic view of the world – the amateur still held some favoured place. Only in England.

The 'plane was empty now. He shook his head and switched on the car's audio system. Stockhausen drizzled from four speakers.

Yes, there were definitely things he did not care for here.

14

Paul turned from the window and took off his jacket.

'I'm seeing the inside of a lot of hotels,' he said.

Mina placed the computer on the table, the cassette next to it.

'We're both seeing a different side of life,' she said.

She had wanted to go back to Bishop's Lynn, but he figured the more they moved around the better. They had found this place by driving around the country roads beyond Ely. A square red Georgian house by the New Bedford River, the channel that Dutch engineers cut in the sixteen hundreds to drain that section of the fens. The window of the pleasant, old-fashioned room they had taken looked over the high banks to water running above ground level straight and shining to the horizon.

He went to the bathroom and rolled back his sleeve to check the damage. Not so bad. The bandage needed changing, but the wound looked clean. It had stopped bleeding.

Back in the room, she was studying the tape.

'All for this,' she said.

He fetched the Walkman from his bag and slotted the tape in. After a few seconds listening, he turned it over, ran it back and listened again. He passed the headphones to her, but she barely put them over her ears.

'I don't get it,' he said. 'Like the landlord said, beeps and warbles.'

'That's programming,' she said. 'Like on the discs. Like a kid's toy computer at home.'

'So what's on it?'

157

'I don't know. We don't have the bits and pieces to load it.'

'Charlie could tell us. He doesn't mind getting us to risk our necks. All he does is send cute messages.'

'Don't start on Charlie.'

'He's not here. It won't hurt his feelings.'

She pulled herself back from getting involved in another sniping match. 'Look, I think we're safe here for a while. I paid for the room with cash. You need to rest, and I need time to think. Let's just sit still for a while and try to be civil to each other.'

'Civil.' He laughed.

'Oh, all right, then. I won't use any words that you find offensively middle class. How about calling it a truce?'

'Fine by me.'

'You're a sarcastic bastard. Don't you ever give it a rest?'

'Yes. About now.' He took out his cap, pulled it low over his eyes, and started to doze in the armchair.

He didn't sleep long. Too many things were going round in his mind. He put the Zevon tape on the Walkman and played it loud, while the sky changed and the clouds rolled over the far-off horizon of fenland to the west. He watched her working, and sometimes she reminded him of her young self, sometimes she was like another woman entirely. He found himself wondering whether she was still the same when she took her clothes off. Time must have done some damage, but he didn't think it would be too noticeable. And then he started thinking about what she used to do with her body, and that made his thoughts go in entirely the wrong direction. Zevon sang about desperadoes under the eaves, and his stomach ached, and for all that, he felt the old heat.

He wondered if she felt anything similar when she

looked at him. There had been occasions over the past twenty-four hours (and that was all it was, he realized) when he thought some spark jumped between them, but it was so scrambled up with everything else that he was probably misreading. Certainly she was now as cool and impersonal as could be.

And he remembered how they had once been, and how long ago, and thought it was strange that they should be here, in this expensive room in the middle of the country, having nothing in common any more except Charlie, who he hated.

She hooked the computer to the 'phone again before dinner. They waited like characters in a biblical film watching for the Word of God. After ten minutes he went down to the bar. It was filling up with locals – mostly the waxed jacket and green wellington boot brigade; young farmers and computer analysts to a man and woman. A few real locals huddled by the door, discussing the weather's effect on the work to be done next day in the fields.

He got into conversation with Mrs Daubry, the owner's wife. She was a fat little thing with an exaggerated refined accent and eyes with the fixed sparkle of sequins. She was clearly curious about what Paul and Mina were doing together, being so obviously ill-matched. He decided that he was a 'rough diamond' who had got lucky and married a classy girl of foreign blood. He was in the shipping business – which was true in its way – doing well for himself, but never forgetting 'where he came from'. He made himself jovial and a little bit crude, and she swallowed the whole thing. He and the wife, he said, had only planned a long weekend's break, and now here they were carrying on round the country for the fun of it. In fact, he'd appreciate it if Mrs Daubry would do them a favour:

if his office called, would she be kind enough to tell a little white lie and say there was no one by the name of Quillet staying?

Batting her long eyelashes at him, she said of course she would.

Mina came down, and he introduced them formally. He called Mina 'darling', and enjoyed the way she scowled at him when Mrs Daubry turned her back to fill a glass from the optic.

He told Mrs Daubry more about their travels. How they had gone boating, and stayed in Bishop's Lynn to look over their yacht. Mrs Daubry became more impressed, and Mina grew more tense, until he smiled in what he hoped was a fetching way and covered her hand with his. 'Tell you the truth,' he said, 'it's a bit like a second honeymoon for us.'

Mrs Daubry smiled and sighed, and went off to serve someone else.

Mina withdrew her hand.

'Very amusing.'

'Just making our story convincing.'

'I see you still have a way with the ladies. She's all but lying on her back with her legs in the air.'

'Now, now. Remember what a happy couple we are.'

'Oh, ecstatic,' she said, and downed her glass of wine in two gulps.

'I'm trying to get something out of her.'

'Aren't you always?'

He eyed his drink, ordered another.

'I was just saying to the wife,' he smiled, as Mrs Daubry gravitated back in their direction. 'Be nice if we could send tapes to everyone.'

'Tapes?' Mrs Daubry said.

'You know. Along with a postcard of old Ely Cathedral and all that sort of thing, we like to send little tapes.'

'Oh, yes,' the little woman said. 'We have a nephew in Australia – he works for the government there. He does that. Much easier than writing a letter, isn't it?'

'That's what I say. The wife's good for the letter-writing, but I like carrying a little recorder round with me. Instead of saying: "We went to so-and-so place", you can record the sounds on location.'

'What a nice idea.'

'It's more interesting for the kids.'

Mina stiffened, but Mrs Daubry positively cooed.

'Oh, you have children?'

He nodded. 'Two monsters. Little Rosie – she's six, and Charlie – Charlotte, I should say; she's only – what is she, love?'

Mina muttered: 'Four and a half.'

'I love them at that age,' Mrs Daubry said.

'We're fond of 'em ourselves,' he agreed. 'We left 'em with their Grandma this weekend so we could have a proper break, but I think we've been missing 'em since Friday. Anyway, we've been doing this little tape for them, on the spot, as it were, and it's got us talking about where we're going, what we're seeing, and lots of noises in the background. Footsteps in the cathedral, ducks on the river, that sort of thing.'

'How lovely.' She sighed again, and Mina concentrated hard on her glass.

'Trouble is, you know what kids are. Give one of 'em something, the other wants it. Give 'em one thing to share and they fight. 'Course, we could do two different tapes, but I noticed you've got one of those portable stereos behind the bar with a double cassette . . .'

After a little fiddling around to make sure the machine would do what it was asked, they slotted the tapes in. Charlie's tape with the labels removed, and the Stones compilation someone had put together for him. After putting his ear close to one of the speakers to make sure it was running, he slid the volume control to nought and resumed his seat. Mrs Daubry was happy, he and Mina were happy — at least they pretended to be.

They moved over to a table near the fire to eat. Mina asked for a bottle of good red wine.

They ate without saying much at first. They had to keep in mind that they were on their second honeymoon, but their whispered talk only made Mrs Daubry think more kindly of them.

'Try some,' she said, as she lifted her glass and the wine caught deep crimson tails of the fire in its heart.

'I've drunk wine before,' he said.

'I wasn't saying you only swill meths. I was inviting you to try a drop.'

He did so, and it was good. They relaxed a little more, because it didn't seem as if anything bad could happen in a place like this. He got up once during the meal to turn the tapes over, and was surprised how woozy he felt. When he got back to the table he realized that she was also feeling the effects. Once or twice she mentioned something that had happened earlier, and he had to quiet her.

'Sorry,' she said. 'It's the wine. "Beware gazing on the grape when it is red."'

He knew she was quoting Dad. He smiled at the memory before he could stop himself, and she saw that she had got past his defences.

'I remember once he said that the only really dangerous drink in the world was red wine. It had more effect than you thought it would, and left you feeling worse in the morning than any other booze. That was why he always stuck to spirits. That was his excuse, anyway.'

He remembered a party one time when they'd taken her across to Le Havre with them. A big gathering of

162

all sorts of wild types in a bar off the Rue Courbet. It went on until three in the morning, at which point they retired to the ship, dragging several Frenchmen that Dad swore he knew along with them. The Frogs brought wine. Mina drank a bellyful too much, but while she was still capable of holding a conversation, Dad gave her that great impromptu lecture on the debits and credits of various liquors. He still remembered her leaning against him, her bare brown shoulder warm against his chest, as Dad raised his little shot glass and recited a variation on the Envoy to *Underwoods*:

> 'Go, little drink, and wish to all
> Flowers in the garden, meat in the hall,
> A bin of wine (except the red,
> 'Cause it makes me feel like I was dead).'

'I was thinking,' she said. 'If he was still here, he'd only be sixty-five.'

He nodded, and felt the old, familiar hollowness.

'I used to think he was so ancient,' she went on. 'But he wasn't more than forty-six when I first met him.'

'Kids think everyone over twenty's next for the graveyard.'

'They don't give you any training for it.'

'What?'

'Getting older. You whistle along thinking: "Here I am, still sixteen inside." But the mirror's telling you something different.'

It couldn't be telling her anything too painful, but he didn't say that. 'Don't look in it.'

'Have to. It's difficult getting your make-up straight otherwise.'

He lifted his glass. She blinked at him.

'You know, you drink too much. I've been watching. You drink whisky like water.'

'After the last two days, I wouldn't mind swimming in it.'

'What with that and the cigarettes –'

'Yeah, well, it's my liver and lungs.'

She made a long face. 'Beg your pardon.' She was making fun of him. She'd never done that in the old days.

A girl came to clear their dishes. The wine bottle was almost empty. Mina poured the dregs in her glass and studied them carefully.

'You know, that was a bitchy thing to do.'

'Which?'

'All that stuff about Charlie and Rosie.'

'Just trying to get the tape duplicated.'

'You don't have to try and wind me up at the same time.'

'Gets rid of the tension.'

'Adds to mine.'

'Pardon me.'

'Now you're getting scratchy again.'

'All right, let's not get scratchy.'

She raised her glass to him. 'So, this is all we have to do to stay friendly. Drink a couple of bottles a day.'

'Recipe for happiness.'

'And cirrhosis of the liver.'

'To cirrhosis of the liver.'

'Cheers.'

They collected the tapes from the machine, and made their way upstairs under Mrs Daubry's romantic gaze.

'She'll be listening for the bedsprings tonight,' he said as they climbed the stairs.

'We can take turns jumping up and down on our beds.' She began to laugh, and kept laughing all the way to their room. He had to take her arm to stop her weaving all over the corridor. As he got the key in the door, she broke into hiccupping tears. He guided her inside and laid her down on her bed. He didn't turn the lights on.

The room was close and warm, the radiator under the window roared like a high wind in the distance. He opened the sash an inch or two at the top and felt the night breeze chill his face.

Her voice came from the gloom, muffled by the pillow. 'Too much to drink.'

'It's all right.'

'No, it isn't. I'm the one who insisted on going on with this. Got no right to dissolve.'

'You've been through a lot.'

'Haven't I? I go away with nothing more serious on my mind than a cracked marriage, and come back to this. I don't know what's going on. Only that someone thinks it's worth kidnapping me and sticking knives in you. It's difficult to adjust.'

'You'll get used to it. Just like the television.'

'It's not. This is real. If you get beaten up, you have the bruises to show. I keep asking myself what he could have done that makes it so important to find him. I mean, this is Charlie we're talking about, the man behind the keyboard. When I went away he was just the same old obsessive, with his computers and his discs and his printouts. Now I discover he's some kind of public enemy. It doesn't make any sense.'

He took the armchair again. From there he could see her. His thoughts turned slowly, like cigarette smoke in a still room.

'Charlie and Rosie,' she muttered. Laughter bubbled from her throat again. 'You bastard.'

'I thought you'd have a gross of them by now.'

'What, kids? Haven't got round to it.'

'Leaving it a bit, aren't you? I thought –'

'That I'm getting a bit past it, bit long in the tooth? My mother used to say that. She *wanted* grandchildren, hoped they'd hark back to her side of the family. Lots of little Indian-looking children running round to remind

165

her of home.' She sighed noisily. 'An elderly primip. That's what they call a woman having her first baby when she's over thirty. In fact they say it if you're more than twenty-five. But lots of people wait these days.'

'Not anyone I know.'

'That's because you know the wrong kind of people, sweety. I remember how it was – probably still is. Anyone who isn't pregnant at sixteen and a mother of six squalling brats by the time she's twenty-five must have something wrong with her. I know, nearly all the girls I used to hang around with were pushing prams before they were out of their teens. Mother's sister back in Delhi had her first child when she was fourteen. That's what life's like where we come from. But not here . . . Wherever we are.'

Silence. He thought of the girls who were her friends in the old days. He still saw some of them. They tended to look ten years older than they were, lived in council houses, their children getting to the age when they could start the whole cycle again.

'Actually,' she said, 'I was pregnant once. Must've been, oh, ten years ago now, not long after we got married. That was when Charlie was always jetting off to strange countries to install equipment for people. I went with him, for the adventure, the broadening experience of travel. It was an accident, didn't intend starting a family then. Anyway, I miscarried at five months in a grubby little hospital in Chile. Think it was Chile.'

He looked away so she wouldn't see his face. He knew she was telling him things she would regret in the morning. He was determined not to run onto the same rock himself. Had too much to drink? Batten down the hatches and keep the bulkhead doors firmly closed.

'That sort of spoiled the wonders of impending motherhood for me,' she said. 'Don't know why we didn't try again, though. Suppose it must be me. You know what Bernard always said: "If a woman wants something, you might as well let her have it. She'll get it, anyway."'

'You quote him like a book.'

'You forget how impressive he could be – especially to a kid of thirteen. I used to think he was some sort of Lord.'

'On the ship, he was.'

'Uncle Bernard . . . He never let me call him that. It was "Bernard", right from the start. Anyway, he was more like a second dad. The sort of father you'd choose for yourself when you were shy and adolescent and feeling out of place with everyone around you. 'Course, he was a rogue. Found that out as I got older. But for all that . . .'

'He was all right,' Paul said.

'*He* drank too much, too.'

No reply to that. He let her waffle. She was getting sleepier. She'd drop off soon.

'I wasn't coming back, you know.'

'What?'

'Who goes away and leaves her husband for two months over Christmas if she really means to come back?'

He felt the cold stirring out of the night outside the window. Nothing in sight but a few straggling lights along the rim of the fens. Like being on a calm sea.

'I mean . . . I hadn't decided anything. I was just letting one day run into another, then another, and another. Great way to waste time. You can go for months like that. But I realized after I got his message. I wasn't really meaning to ever go back.' The central heating made ticking, rushing noises. 'God, that's loud.' she said. 'I got tired holding the whole lie together. Does that sound callous?'

'I –'

'You being the expert in callousness – Callousnosity. What is it?'

'Never mind.'

'Wasn't a lie, really. That's wrong. After all, we've always been honest with each other. No illusions. That's terribly useful in a relationship, you know. Not having illusions. You live your life on them when you're younger, but you see through everything later on. Then again, even when you're telling each other it's all up front and clear, it's not really . . . I don't think I'm making any sense.' She plucked at the bedclothes. 'I was so frightened last night. I pride myself on knowing exactly where I stand these days, on being strong and carrying a certain amount of clout. Having a nice, civilized house to lock the world out with, having money and being in charge of a business make you feel secure against the bad things. Generally, you just forget the bad things happen a lot of the time. You see it in the 'papers, but that's not the same. It's a disturbing thing, being made to realize how vulnerable you are. Like when I was a girl, thinking I was just like everyone else in my school, and someone would call me "Paki".'

'Yes.'

'When it comes down to it, having no illusions turns out to be just another kind of illusion.'

'So why did you come back?'

'Why? If he'd called you and begged for help, wouldn't you have come?'

He wiped his mouth as if it were wet.

She breathed more deeply. 'Don't suppose you would. You really hate him, don't you? Hate us, I mean.'

Silence was best. Silence is always best.

She rubbed her cheek against the pillow. It made a soft, rubbing sound. 'It wasn't about our personal problems, you see. It was him asking for help. Just because you don't want to . . .' She swallowed. 'Doesn't mean you refuse to help when someone's in trouble. That changes things.'

He sat gazing into the darkness of the room, and she began to breathe regularly, and he thought she was asleep. He probably dozed a little himself. It seemed colder when she rolled on her back and said:

'You're the same, you know.'

He didn't move.

'Different sides of the same coin. Double-headed type.' Pause. The old house creaked. 'Neither head says anything.'

15

Sheal slept if he got the chance.

He had asked for a bed to be brought in so that he need not leave the office. All the necessary equipment was here. Sitting at the keyboard, he was at the heart of a web of information that stretched around the entire globe. It gave him a curious, powerful feeling to think of himself as a spider – some great silver, science fiction creation – electronically covering the planet. A twitch on the web could not escape him, he could reach into the hearts of corporations and governments, plucking information at will.

Of course, being here meant that whenever Drazel was around he could look in and bother him, but it also meant he was on the case twenty-four hours a day.

Which was the way he wanted it.

He had rigged an alarm into the machine. It was set to sound at the commencement of any unusual activity. If Quillet's wife switched on her computer and tapped into the network, if any messages went to her, he would be alerted. It didn't mean he would be able to capture the message, or decode it even if he did; but it did allow him to lay off occasionally to eat, use the bathroom, get some sleep. He got the feeling that Drazel didn't care for his taking any time away from the screen, but even trusted and loyal employees require a few zees now and then.

The matter of Drazel being on his back stirred him in a way that was close to amusement. Drazel was generally a pleasant employer; 'a real gentleman', some of the office girls said. No one would ever have guessed from his smoothed-out manners and ponderous, respectable air that he had started as a coke dealer in Ipiales, down in Colombia. He had come a long way since then: some people dead, some name changes. But his identity now was as secure as the company could make it. He had been trained and groomed, he mixed with senators and corporate heads. None of them knew anything but the official version. Sheal knew because he had accessed certain classified files. Drazel was like Robersman itself: the threads running back to the drugs and prostitution, blackmail and extortion, were increasingly difficult to discern; everything was laundered so many times. And one day, even Drazel would be gone, replaced by a man who had never touched a gun, never handled dirty money. One day there would be no difference between Robersman and any other large corporation.

It was Drazel who had employed him, fresh from Cal Tech, as a favour to Sheal's father. Drazel liked to say: 'I'd have taken the boy on anyway, he's good at his job.' He demanded 120 per cent efficiency, and his temper could be real bad news; apart from that he was okay. But this little can of worms had him worried. Sheal could tell by the way he was taking a personal interest. Generally, he left things like this to his employees, keeping a safe distance between himself and the illegal, just checking progress now and then to ensure that all was well. On this one, he was there all the time. He had cancelled appointments this afternoon to talk with associates in England. His heavy, Germanic face with its slab-like impassivity had taken on an animation which was a bad sign. His voice showed traces of his Ohio origins.

Sheal rubbed his eyes and looked at his watch. It was coming on for midnight. The two Quillets (he thought of the wife and brother that way – like a circus act)

171

had crawled into the woodwork after their escapade in Cambridge. They weren't turning up on anywhere he could uncover. It was night wherever they were. He could snatch a couple of hours maybe.

He sauntered to the makeshift bed, sipped a little juice, loosened his tie, and fell on the pillows.

He was seldom troubled by the human misery his company's actions caused. He never pondered the murder of South American tribes for their land, or the deaths of Indian peasants in villages next to unsafe chemical works. Nor did he think about the slum kids overdosing in the dank streets a few miles away. He had been raised to regard the masses as distant background only, no more than pixels on a screen. If he thought of them at all, it was only to consider that they were not worth considering. What were a handful of savages with bones in their lower lips, a bunch of peasants with toxins in their blood, or the scum of the ghettoes? No ones, nothings, cannon fodder. Here to work and die.

The computer, its screen carefully scrolling through a hotel chain's records of the day's business, toiled on.

16

Paul woke early. It was still dark. Mina lay in a tangle of bedclothes, hair messed, lips slightly parted. He could have reached out and touched her. She was still in her clothes. He had thought of helping her to take them off when she fell asleep, but had known better. In the end he had dozed off listening to Zevon on the Walkman. The man did sad songs occasionally. They were sadder than anyone else's. One was called 'Reconsider Me'.

He dressed in the bathroom, crept downstairs. Mr Daubry was already up, reading a paper in the lounge. He nodded good morning with the same knowing smile the wife had given them. The Daubrys thought they were having a great time.

He let himself out the front door and walked round the house, turning up his collar against the cold, went through some old plane trees and climbed the embankment to the river. It was barely dawn, and the sun was making fire without heat to the east. Nothing moved except the slow-dragging water.

He stood by the river bank, staring into the flat distance, then back at the house. He could see their window, curtains closed, but a light on behind them now. She was up. He suspected she had been awake when he left. Today was probably going to be tricky, and he'd needed this time on his own. He was not used to being with anyone so much. It being her only made things worse.

Last night he had listened to her breathing, watched the dim shape of her moving under the covers. He had been haunted by her younger self, dogged through the dark hours by thoughts of tigereye and gold.

Saturday afternoon, a mild October day. The autumn had been a slow fade, warm and languorous.

He had done it before, the first couple of occasions with a working girl in Rotterdam. Then with two or three girls from town, moonlighting from their boyfriends. The local 'bicycle', of course: a nice girl called Mandy, who was on everyone's list once, and who now had four kids and looked fifty-five instead of thirty-five. They were the usual up-against-a-wall, under-the-pier, or round-the-back-of-the-theatre jobs. Hurried, panting affairs. Doing it so the girls could say they'd done it rather than anything else. When they did enjoy it, they always looked surprised. Nothing beyond the physical relief of it. 'Fuck 'em and forget 'em,' as the blokes he mixed with used to say. Most of them still did.

That afternoon, he wasn't expecting anything. The morning had been spent knocking around the town with her and some other people. The usual things – looking at records, playing the slot machines in the arcades, shoplifting in Woolworth's. They ended up moving toward the Parade, but when they reached the North Quay, the two of them left the group. He heard the jeers and wolf-whistles as they went through the gates, but he didn't care one way or the other. There was something about the way she'd said, 'Let's see if anyone's on the boat,' her face still, eyes placid: suddenly, standing there with all those people, he had experienced a wash of desire like a seventh wave. She wore a cotton dress with a full skirt, an old raincoat, flat white shoes, her legs bare. She didn't say another word until they were on board, in the crew accommodation. Then she said: 'Anyone here?' And he said: 'No.' And then they were all over each other.

He remembered every last touch and kiss, the way

174

some people say they recall their first time. She wasn't aloof any longer. She wasn't shy. She seemed to know already what she wanted, and at first he wondered if she wasn't more experienced than she seemed. But she didn't know – the scared look in her eyes showed that – she was just ready to give herself up to whatever it was he knew. If he hadn't been so excited, he would have been confused. He had never touched her before, now he could hardly breathe. She pressed her mouth against his, sucking on his tongue, pushing against his hands, holding him.

First orgasm: up against his bunk, dress bunched round her waist, his hand in her white cotton knickers. She bore down on his fingers, belly contracting, smooth-haired opening slick and hot, legs trembling, arms hanging loosely round his neck. He pulled his face away from her, watched as her head went back. Eyes closed, a flush spreading from her neck into her cheeks and forehead, lips wide-parted, little sounds coming from her throat. She thrust against his hand, gasping in time with the movements.

They moved into Dad's cabin. She stopped, lifted her dress over her head, dipped to remove the knickers, unclipped her bra. She came into his arms. Tigereye and gold in the dim-lit cabin. She was fourteen, slender and smooth, the first girl he had ever seen completely naked except for the Dutch girl.

He guessed now that she had done it for all sorts of reasons that had nothing to do with wanting him. She was young; she probably thought it was a way of getting him to herself, marking territory. But it didn't change how it felt.

Afterwards, especially after the marriage, he would tell himself that they had not been that good together; nothing was that good. But it was. No one had ever come close to matching her. No matter what else happened to

175

them, the sex was almost always wonderful. He once thought: she enjoys it like a man does. But that wasn't right. She just enjoyed it like herself.

Long after, when she was gone, he would realize that the old cliché had some truth: she had spoiled him for other women. The ones he tried in the years they were together, the ones who followed, they all seemed uneasy, or well-meaning, or just too damned selfish.

One more memory out of that day: Mina lying under him as he finally relaxed, whispering: 'I love you.' And the words almost repeating themselves from his mouth. But something stopped him. Training stopped him. The life he had led since he was five years old stopped him. He never did say it to her, and she never said it again after that afternoon.

He thought about selfishness, and knew he could have invented the word.

She answered his knock at the door in her dressing gown, wet hair bundled in a towel. She looked tired, reluctant. She said nothing, avoided meeting his eye.

The computer was open and plugged in but she had not connected it to the 'phone yet. She stood over it, chewing her thumb.

He opened a drawer in the table. She moved too quickly away from him. He ignored her and took out the writing paper stored there. She disappeared into the bathroom to dry her hair.

They skirted around each other for half an hour. He wrote a letter, she got dressed in the bathroom. When she came out it was nearly breakfast time. She moved round him to attach the computer to the 'phone.

'Hold on,' he said. She backed off, and he dialled a Lowestoft number.

The receiver was picked up with a clatter.

'Yuh?'

'Ma, that you?'

'Hang on, I'll 'ave a look . . .' She grunted as if lifting part of her swollen anatomy. 'Yuh,' she shouted. He held the 'phone away from his ear. 'Me all right, worse luck. Who's this.'

'Paul Quillet.'

'Polly? What you doing calling this time in the morning? Where are you?'

'Round and about, Ma, here and there.' Knew you'd be open. Is Reiny about?'

'He sailed yesterday, love. Dunno where.'

He'd only asked on the offchance. Pity, though. He would have preferred to deal with Reiny. Reiny was a sight smarter than anyone else. 'What about Sam, then?'

'Nah. He came for his breakfast an hour ago. I hear they're doing your boat up.'

''S right.'

'You come into money, then?'

'Something like that.'

'Lucky you. Save us a bit so's I can retire.'

'We'll sail away to a desert island.'

'With eight gramophone records, I suppose? Get away!'

'Ma, listen. When Sam comes in again, could you tell him I'm sending something through the post to his daughter.'

'What, young Brenda?'

'That's it. Don't tell anyone else, will you? It's something for Ian's birthday, and I don't want him to find out.'

'Is it his birthday, then?'

'Soon. You won't forget, will you?'

'Try not to.'

'Okay, thanks a lot. I've got to go.'

'So've I. Who d'you think does the cooking here, anyway?'

'You can do me a big breakfast when I get back.'

'All right, Polly. Look after yourself, love.'

He replaced the 'phone. Mina got up.

'Ma's still alive,' she said.

'Yeah. Joe passed on couple of years back. Someone said she ought to sell up and retire, but she won't ever do it.'

'You're going to send the copy of the tape to Sam?'

'That's the idea.'

'What for?'

'If we don't get it to Charles, maybe he can. Might do us some good too. Sort of a shot in the locker if things get bad.'

'I hope you've made that letter nice and simple. You know he doesn't read very well.'

'Ian can do the hard words for him.'

She was still trying to pretend the room was bigger than it was. That way she could keep distance between them. She set the computer up.

'What will you do if there's no message?' he said.

'Keep trying.'

'They're looking for him too.'

'I know that,' she snapped. 'Why do you keep stating the obvious?'

'Got an obvious mind.'

She bowed her head in a weary sort of way, began to type. He watched over her shoulder, trying to see what she did. The screen changed. A picture like a chessboard came up. She hit another key and it vanished. Blank screen. She said 'Mmm,' then tapped again, and he saw a word appear letter by letter:

- RUA -

A quick jab at the key marked 'Enter', and the screen crowded with gibberish.

'Ah,' she said, and he knew it was happening again.

A second passed before the mass of figures, letters and symbols vanished. Mina had a pen and paper ready. He leaned on the table, but she was too intent to mind now.

A couple of short bleeps, then it came.

-TAHEIA
URGENT - TAKE ROSIE TO PENNY AT STARCRASH -
DON'T USE PHONE - STAY OFF COMPUTER EXCEPT TO
CONTACT ME - AVOID USING PLASTIC -
BE CAREFUL -

The screen crowded again. It swallowed the message, and he saw the letters of the original lines lifting and dropping from their places until nothing was left. Then that was gone too.

'More bloody riddles,' he said.

Mina had the whole thing written down. She stared at it. He couldn't see her face at all. She was poised stiffly over the paper.

'Let's have breakfast and get out of here,' she said.

'What about this?'

'I know what it means.'

If Sheal had been a more excitable character, he might have danced round the office, or at least whooped a little. As this was not his way — a child psychologist once described him as introverted to a dangerous degree — he merely stood up from the keyboard, tore the sheet from the printer, and smiled to himself.

It was the middle of night, and there was no one around to tell, but he had finally managed to save a part of one of Quillet's messages. Yawning, he walked barefoot around the office, studying what he had.

→≃η√<<∀ε↓ {@OSIE≡ɸ@♀{ PENNΣ○♂*⁎⁎←א
<STARCRASH..@ψ

It was scrambled all to hell, of course. Quillet had been playing the game as before, changing all the rules and methods so that this message had come in a different form and via different routes from the last. But the alarm had woken him, and a delay in the transmission had allowed him to get on the signal before the message started. The machine had protested, all kinds of blocks were thrown up, and after he finally broke in for just that nanosecond, the whole thing had gone into automatic dump and left him staring at a graphic of a tank with its cannon pointing straight out of the screen. It made a puff of smoke, and when it cleared, there was the little tank driver grinning its cartoon smile and giving him the finger.

He had smiled at that too. Quillet was playing serious, but he was still *playing*. It was, in some part, still a game for him. He was so good at this that he couldn't resist messing around. Sheal had read his file, and the thing that came through all of the professional qualifications and the amazing developments he had made, was that weird sense of humour. He had once devised a missile program for the Pentagon that, during its trials, suddenly switched from serious business to a game called 'Ronnie and the Evil Empire'. It did not endear him to several colleagues and a couple of Generals. But that was his idea of fun: another example of the way the British had no sense of perspective. Whenever you read of some British kid breaking into a weapons program or a top-secret espionage file, you could bet the little bozo was only doing it for 'fun'. In America, the same kid would have been milking funds out of a multinational or something sensible.

Sheal did not mind. He had this scrambled fragment,

180

even if it made no particular sense. 'OSIE-PENN-STARCRASH'. He would feed it in and see if anything came up.

He thought about 'phoning Drazel, but decided against. Plenty of time for the old man to hear about this.

He resumed his seat, crunching on a handful of multivitamins, and started typing.

They posted the tape from a village upriver, then went snaking down tree-bordered lanes between black fields, heading north.

He took the scrap of paper containing the message off the dashboard. 'Going to let me in on it?'

They bounded over a level crossing. The fen stretched before them, still clothed here and there with frost. She took a deep breath.

'Okay. "Rosie" you already know about. "Penny" I think must be Penelope Leman, one of the team who worked with Charlie. I met her once at a party. Didn't like her much, and I'm sure she didn't care for me. She's one of those American Wasp types who decided to actually do something instead of living off her parents and marrying a good bank account. She was at Yale, *the* bright brain of her year. She's almost as good as Charlie – at least, that's what he said, and he doesn't give praise easily. She made a packet as a freelance, writing software for games, then got into the amusements side. Has her home base over here. Bit of a blue stocking. She's tall and very blonde. She has "good bones".'

He grinned at the way she made it sound like an insult.

'Anyway, she was part of Charlie's team, and she's one of the people who's supposed to be abroad. On holiday, the person I spoke to said.'

'But she isn't?'

'Not if the last part of the message is right.'

'Starcrash?'

'Ever heard of Hallford Castle?'

It did ring some sort of bell. 'Amusement park, isn't it?'

'*The* amusement park,' she said, turning onto a road that ran alongside the river. 'All the American rides. Scare yourself witless for ten pounds a day.'

'What's the connection?'

'Penelope Leman is a close friend of Jeremy Palter, who owns Hallford Castle. You must've seen him. He made his first fortune in the record business. Wonderful eye for a publicity stunt. He bought it five years ago. The house was a burned-out shell, and one of the biggest landscaped gardens in Europe was just a jungle. He got it cheap from the estate of an American called Goldman, who'd been planning to turn it into a theme park, and decided to carry on and finish the job. Poured money in, restored the outside of the house and the gardens to their former glory, then put up big dippers and roundabouts and all those things. And to devise the computerized systems that hold it all together, he brought in the old family friend, Penny Leman.'

'Starcrash?' Paul begged.

'When it opened two years ago, Charlie got an invite to the ceremony. Because of the professional association. He wouldn't have bothered, but I persuaded him. You know how I love fairs.'

He remembered. She would scream and rave on the waltzers and chairoplanes. It was the only time in those days – apart from in bed – that she came out of her watchful shyness.

'It was a grand opening. Television cameras and celebrities everywhere, trying all the rides. One of them was a big, round building without windows. It didn't say what

182

it was. But you queued up, and you giggled about the mystery, and worried what was going to happen. After all, most of the rides there set your teeth on edge, and this was supposed to be the best – or worst, depending how you feel about them.

'We got in, took our seats in some carriages, and then we were off. And what it did was, it winched you round and round, up and up, all in semi-darkness, with spaceships flying past and planets spinning around you, until you stopped dead at the top. Then, after they'd made you wait just a little longer than necessary, all the lights went out, and the whole thing just dropped out from under you, and you were plunging down in the pitch black, being thrown from side to side, not knowing what you might hit.

'Absolutely terrifying.' She overtook a lorry loaded with sugar beet. 'Charlie had to more or less carry me from that one, and I proceeded to be horribly sick on the grass outside.' She pulled in to avoid an oncoming Land Rover. 'And the name of the ride was "Starcrash".'

'Where is it?'

'Oxfordshire, a few miles from Banbury. You don't need to look it up. I know where we're going.'

'And we'll find this woman hiding there?'

'The staff live in the old estate cottages in the grounds. If Penelope Leman wanted to lay low for a while, she could do it there rather nicely.'

He flicked the map book. 'So it's not just Charlie. It isn't him running off with company funds or something.'

'I never thought it was. Everyone involved with that project for Robersman has either been "posted abroad", or disappeared. It's what they were working on. The tape has something they need.'

'If it's a company thing, why couldn't they go to the police?'

'Robersman is big. Multinational, offices all over the world. You know what big companies are like. They're a law to themselves as long as they can keep it out of the public eye.'

'Kidnapping? Knives and guns?'

'Tell me about the big shipping companies.'

He nodded slowly.

'You're the one who always used to tell me that everyone was bent.' she said. 'Any time I let a little thing like idealism creep into my thoughts, you were there to tell me that everyone was corrupt, and the bigger the organization, the more corrupt it was.'

'Okay. Go on.'

'Charlie and the team developed something for Robersman, and the company doesn't want anyone to know about it. Either that, or they just wanted to take it away from the team, and the others said all right, but Charlie and this Leman woman didn't. So Robersman have hired a bunch of heavies to find them and get whatever it is back.'

'Seems about right. We'd know even more if you'd talked with old Charles about his work.'

'Old Charles never talked about details. That's why they make things secret, so no one talks about them.'

'We could go to the 'papers.'

'What with? A wild story about disappearances and kidnappings. We've got no evidence except this tape, and if I know Charlie it's been coded somehow, so even if we played it, it wouldn't tell us anything. The first thing a reporter would say was "Why didn't you call the police after the kidnapping?" You'd end up in jail for murder, and if we mentioned Robersman, some highly paid solicitor would slap injunctions all over us.'

'You've got a wonderful grasp of the essentials.'

'So, we'll go to Hallford Castle, we'll find Penelope Leman, and maybe that'll sort things out.'

'Sounds reasonable. If anything does.'

'You can get out now, if you want.'

'I'll hang around. Hate to get slaughtered in some back alley for no good reason.'

'You're such a comfort.'

Drazel came in. Sheal beckoned.

'What is it?' Drazel said. He looked as though he could use some good news.

Sheal said nothing. He pointed to the screen.

Drazel bent closer, putting on his half-moon reading glasses.

LEMAN, PENELOPE: the file began. He turned to Sheal. 'You found her?'

'With a little help from friend Quillet.'

'That's good.'

'Not brilliant yet, but I'm getting closer.'

'I take it Haggard's with them?'

'A little behind, but catching up. I gave him the information.'

'No more trouble?'

'Not since Cambridge.'

Drazel dropped his briefcase on a chair and pulled down his waistcoat to take the wrinkles out. 'I get the feeling something's going on. Those guys in Cambridge were supposed to do nothing but watch.'

'Maybe the orders were slow getting down to the lower ranks.'

'Inefficiency, God damn it!' He pressed his palms to his eyes. 'Or something worse. You checked the police files?'

'Police, MI5, MI6, Interpol. No one official's on it.'

'How about unofficial?'

'That takes a little longer. And you detailed me to Quillet and Haggard.'

'Yes, you're right. I'll get someone else on it.'

Sheal tried an encouraging smile. 'Don't worry. If Leman's where Quillet says she is, this could all be dealt with by tonight.'

'I wish.' Drazel shook his head slowly. 'That Quillet, he was underestimated.'

Sheal thought: *You* underestimated him. It's your balls in the sling, and you know it. He said: 'You ever meet him?'

'Once. When the project was set up. He seemed like any other genius: on the ball with his own subject but nowhere in the real world.'

Turned out smarter than you thought, Sheal said to himself, studying the weariness in Drazel's eyes.

A secretary came in just behind her own knock on the door.

'Get the fuck out!' Drazel roared, sending her pale and scurrying from the room.

Sheal watched with interest. For a moment, all the gloss had fallen away, and the little dealer from Colombia was there. Then Drazel seemed to shake himself from the inside, and the constructed man reasserted himself. He glanced at the screen again.

'You keep at the bastard,' he said.

'I'm not going anywhere,' Sheal nodded, and went back to it.

They made slow time from Wisbech to Peterborough, and from there on to Northampton. The roads belonged to the nineteen-sixties, the traffic to the 'nineties. There seemed to be roadworks every five miles or so, and eventually, on a long slope going down into a place called Great Billing, a whole line of cars and lorries came to a dead halt. A high-sided container lorry blocked the view in front of them. Paul got out and walked up the line to see what was wrong. An estate car had tangled with a fully loaded brewery lorry. The lorry lay on its side across the road, scratched aluminium barrels scattered all over the verges. A couple had burst, and a smell of beer hung in the air. An ambulance crew was removing an old man from the wreckage of the estate.

Back in the car, Mina said: 'Well?'

'Hour or two,' he said. 'One for the lifting gear to get here, one to shift the mess. But if you fancy a pint while you're waiting . . .'

She grabbed the map book from under her seat.

'It's times like this I wish I'd taken those flying lessons Charlie offered me.'

Despite the cold he rolled down the window and lit a cigarette. At least the view was good. A car came sliding up behind them and stopped just short of their tail. Clever bastard, he thought, regarding it in the wing mirror. Let's all box ourselves in.

Sucking on a boiled sweet, she traced roads across the network of the book's pages. He smoked and thought about Sam getting the tape, hiding it under the floorboards in his cabin, in the place Dad used to use for his little dabbles in smuggling.

Mina said: 'About last night . . .'

'We both had too much to drink.'

'Yes, and I opened my mouth and blabbed a good deal.'

'Wasn't listening.'

'I was. But I'm not ashamed. What I said was true. Booze-enhanced, but true.'

'Even about double-headed coins?'

'Yes. You think you're so different from him, don't you? He's the same. He likes to pretend he has no roots, that he sprang out of the earth full-formed. But you're brothers all right.'

He watched a bird rising from a ploughed field.

She said: 'If only either of you had ever learned to talk about what you felt.'

He saw the passenger in the car behind getting out, coming up to see what the problem was.

'Still,' she said, 'there is one thing different about you now.'

'What's that?' he asked, tapping his ash out of the window.

'You sometimes listen.'

'Thank you for your approval,' he said. He was about to say more, but the gun sticking in his face made him forget what it was.

The cowboy leaned down at the window. 'Hello again,' he said.

17

Paul's cigarette drooped in his mouth. A quick look out of Mina's side showed the reader waiting close by, hands in pockets.

They had done it perfectly. The lorry in front stopped the police or anyone else from getting a close look: the car behind, with another man at the wheel, had them neatly trapped. The cowboy rested casually against the car, the hand with the gun in it just inside the window. Anyone seeing him from a couple of cars back, or strolling past, would think they were chatting.

The cowboy grinned at him, then at Mina. 'Roll your window down, love.'

Mina stared at the gun. It was a little automatic pistol, shiny and new, very small in the cowboy's hairy hand. She did as she was told, and the reader ducked his face near to her window.

'So,' he said, little eyes twinkling.

Paul sucked long and deep on his cigarette. His gun was in the glove compartment. 'Like the music?'

'Hate that heavy metal stuff,' the cowboy said. 'Didn't like it at all.'

'We can't give it back,' the reader said, nodding to his companion. 'He threw it out the window.'

''S a waste,' Paul said. 'After you took all that trouble getting it.' The cowboy's hand was cocked at an awkward angle to keep the gun on him. Even so, it was off target. The muzzle pointed somewhere between the front seats.

'We'd really appreciate you lending us the other one,' the reader said.

'I like Enya,' the cowboy said, 'Vangelis, Jean Michel Jarre.'

'Computer music,' the reader smiled at Mina. His fingers explored her shoulder. 'We both like that. So, how about lending us the tape.'

She swallowed hard. Her eyes were wide. 'It's in the back,' she said suddenly.

Paul stared at the cowboy, at the gun. She knew the tape wasn't in the back. It was in his pocket. Which meant she was going to try something. He would have liked to tell her that this was fine for her, because the gun wasn't sticking up her nose, but that might have alerted the cowboy.

'Would you mind getting it for us?' the reader said, politely.

She twisted round, reaching to undo her seat belt. He watched her hand go toward the belt, but as she moved and the sleeve of her jacket obscured the cowboy's view, she jabbed the handbrake down. The car moved gently forward down the slope. The cowboy said: 'What –', the reader swore and nearly tripped. The car collided solidly with the tail end of the lorry.

He sat back quickly. The cowboy had pushed the gun into his cheek. Mina was crying out: 'I'm sorry, I'm sorry. It was an accident,' and the reader had a hand round her throat, cursing her.

But it had the desired effect. The reader let go of her and straightened up all of a sudden. They heard the crunch of boots on the road, and a Liverpudlian accent yelling: 'What the fookin' 'ell? . . .'

The cowboy stuck his face into the car, close to Paul's. The gun muzzle drilled at his cheek. 'She thinks she's clever. I don't care. I'll take your fuckin' 'ead off.'

The lorry driver appeared. A grey-haired, beer-bellied man with a fixed expression of disbelief. 'Aw, what's this?' he said to the reader. 'Can't you lot keep a bloody handbrake on?' He thought the cowboy and the reader were passengers in the car. He caught sight of Mina at the steering wheel. 'Look, love, why don't you let one of the men drive. Save your bumpers.'

'I'll back up,' she said, twisting the key in the ignition.

'Do that, will you?'

The reader looked as if he wanted to stop her, but couldn't think of a way.

She was nervous, flustered. She revved the engine much too high, and the lorry driver winced. The cowboy, trying to keep his pistol covered from sight, breathed hotly on Paul's face. 'I'll kill you,' he said.

'For fook's sake,' the lorry driver shouted above the engine's screaming.

'Sorry,' Mina said. And jammed the car into reverse.

They shot back so fast and hard that the cowboy lost his footing. He got caught in the window, the gun slithering up Paul's face and pointing at the roof as it went off. They rammed the car behind, shifting it back a foot or so. The impact clicked his teeth together, and his ears rang with the blast of the pistol, but he got his left arm round the cowboy's neck and held him. Mina changed to first, screwed the wheel to the right and hit the accelerator. The lorry driver's jaw dropped and he threw himself back to get out of her way. The cowboy struggled to turn his gun. Despite the pain from the knife wound, Paul yanked him down, crushing his throat against the door, then drove his fist hard up into the face. Bone breaking, blood spraying. He did it three times, and the cowboy dropped. Mina was pulling away from the scene now, speeding up. He punched once more then let go. The cowboy slithered out, rolled loosely on the verge.

'Brilliant.' He pounded his clenched fist on the dashboard. Blood came off on the black plastic, his left arm

191

hurt like sin. 'Brilliant.' He laid the hand on her knee and squeezed it tight. She was laughing. They were both laughing.

They were going back the way they had come, into a village called Ecton. She took the first right and roared through the village, out into rolling country.

'You were great,' he said, still trembling. 'I could've got my head blown off, but you were great.'

Her hair whipped about her face. She looked happy. His hand was still on her knee. He removed it.

They stopped in a village outside Northampton to buy the ingredients for a late lunch, then drove south along minor roads, looking for a safe place to stop. Came to a forest and pulled into a clearing hidden from the road. Ate the makeshift picnic while the afternoon sun slanted low through bare trees. A bottle of mineral water, a brown loaf, some cheese. They took turns swigging from the bottle. Some distance off to the west traffic poured along the M1, but they were safe for the moment.

For a while they continued breaking into laughter. He knew it was partly hysteria, but it felt good anyway. They kept winning the small running battles, and it seemed strange to him, because most of his time in the last few years had been spent losing them. One little thing after another; none important in themselves, just a whole weight of missed chances and bad breaks that gradually mounted on his back and weighed him down. Knowing that he was responsible for many of them didn't change the payload. He was like a cargo vessel crammed with freight that no one wanted. He'd been dragging around the Channel and coastal ports like the Flying Dutchman.

And now here he was again with Mina again, watching her laugh, listening to her. Psychos with guns threatened them, yet they kept getting away. He suddenly saw that, in a childish way, he would like this to go on and on. It was enough; to be moving, to be doing something that shifted adrenalin in his system, to be looking at her beautiful face again and knowing that they only had each other to rely on.

Maybe reflection made him quiet. He found the laughter had finished, that she was sitting half-out of the car, feet on the wet grass.

'Everything's so bright,' she said.

He looked at the damp forest floor, the sunlight flittering on dead leaves. The birds were loud and echoing above them, the air smelled sweetly of earth and rain.

'Sharper edges,' he said.

She nodded. 'I can taste it. It must be true about being scared. It makes you remember how good it feels to be alive.'

'Easy answer,' he said. 'Get some maniac to stick a gun in your face every time you're bored.'

She got out, he followed. They walked away from the car, toward where the sun blinked through branches. 'When you feel like this, you say to yourself: "I won't forget." But you always do. It's no exchange.'

'What for?'

'For how you feel when you're young.' She bent and picked up a twig. A squirrel ran up the trunk of an ash tree, hugging the wood, putting it between itself and them. 'I mean, how I feel now is how I used to feel all the time.'

'What? Scared out of your mind.'

'Partly that. But excited about everything, because it was new. Or because it was hormones. I don't know.'

He was silent, not knowing what to reply.

'That's the trouble with adolescence,' she said. 'It's hell, and all the adults around you say, "In a few years, you'll settle down, and you'll wonder what all the fuss was about." And they're right. But they don't tell you that what you get in exchange for all the highs and lows is just ... flat.'

'Is that how you see it?'

'No ... Not all the time, it's just that, this happening, it's as if it's a chance to climb one of the old hills, and you look back and see how level the rest looks.'

'You're losing me.'

'I don't think I'm keeping track myself. I should shut up.'

They sauntered round the clearing, silent again, until he said:

'What did go wrong? With you and Charlie?'

'I don't like your gloating face. It's too much like before.'

'I don't want to gloat,' he said. 'I don't understand. I saw your house, everything you've got. It's a good life.'

'It is. It was.'

'So why?'

Her hands were deep in the pockets of her coat. It swirled round her like a cloak as she lifted them. 'How do I know? We've had friends who came to grief. They could talk the clock round about the reasons. But what it all comes down to is, you just feel different.'

He didn't know where he got the nerve to ask the next question. It came out by itself. 'How did you feel at the start?'

She was looking away from him. She kept doing it. 'That's a question.'

He knew it was all she was going to say. He tried another tack: 'What's he like now?'

'Don't tell me you're developing a curiosity after all this time?'

Anger bubbled. 'Forget it.'

194

'I'm sorry,' she said. 'Every time we get to Charlie one of us gets prickly about it.'

'He still the same?'

'I thought he was. Still living in a world of his own, spending most of this time at his desk, tinkering with some machine or other. It's what he does. He still comes across to people who meet him for the first time as a bit snooty, a bit superior . . . I know, you think that's true. But you always forget, he's very shy.'

'Balls,' he said.

'Thank you for your kind comments. He's shy, always has been. He doesn't feel comfortable with people until he gets to know them well, so he puts up that front, and he thinks he's being relaxed and at ease, while everyone else wonders why he looks so pleased with himself.'

'He was always a sensitive flower.'

She laughed again, this time at him. 'Is it any wonder? He grew up with you and your dad and Sam, and all those hairy he-men on the boats. It was all right for you; you went the same way. But he did the difficult thing. He tried to be something else. People who start like that often come across as insular. They *are* insular. They have to be to get through it.'

He sensed she was talking about herself too. He wanted to needle her. It was a dark impulse, but he couldn't stop it. 'He used to treat the old man like some sort of peasant.'

'That's not true.'

'How many times did you come to see him the year before he died?'

'*We* didn't make that very easy, did we?'

'We're nothing to do with it.'

'Oh, of course not. Don't be so dense.'

'Whatever argument we had, Dad wasn't in it.'

'But you were there. All the time, you were still there. How could we come visiting as if it were just family?'

'Don't come much more family than that.'

'That's below the belt.'

'The old man thought a lot of you.'

'I felt the same. But you know how it was then. How you made it.'

'It was up to me, was it?'

'We all made choices then.'

'Some choices I didn't know about.'

'Oh, stop. We're coming round to it again –' They started talking over each other as the temperature rose.

'You wanted to be adult and discuss things –' he said.

'– Every time, it comes back like an old song –'

'Pretty adult, isn't it?'

'It's what I said before; if no one talks about anything, you can't complain when things happen.'

'You still make out it's my fault.'

'You did what you did.'

'I didn't know.'

'You didn't care.'

'Making a choice, it helps to know the whole story.'

'What story's that? All the stories you told me?'

'I never –'

'You never, you never. That's right. You never.'

'You knew what it was –'

'And so did you.' She turned on him, fists clenched as if she were going to lay into him. 'Don't keep making out you were the wounded victim. You made all the rules then, you had everything your way for years. All that happened was I finally got tired of it.'

She struck away from him. He stood there, head down as if waiting for something to come at him. He had needled her all right. Just like the old days. His younger self would have been proud. He glowered

at the ground. The day had been so bright, now the
sun was in. He watched her stalk back to the car. He
wanted to hit out at someone. Mainly himself.

> 'Once only by the garden gate
> Our lips we joined and parted.
> I must fulfil an empty fate
> And travel the uncharted.'

Dad used to declaim it when drink made him maudlin.
It hardly fitted the situation now, though. He remembered: in the wheelhouse, both busy with getting the
Provider into Liverpool. Mina and Charlie had been
married the week before. No one on the ship had
talked about it, not since the weekend they came
back from Le Havre and her note was waiting. Sam
tried, and got cursed for his trouble. 'Nothing to talk
about,' the younger Paul had said, dismissively. 'Stupid
bitch went off with Charlie, good luck to her.' Dad said
nothing until they were alone this night. And then it
was nothing much. A song on the radio: Sinatra singing
'The One I Love Belongs To Somebody Else'. The song
finished, and Dad muttered:

'You lost somethin' there, boy.'

Paul ignored him.

'You shoulda treated her better.'

> 'I must fulfil an empty fate
> And travel the uncharted.'

He thought: We never used to argue all the time.

Answer came straight back: You never let her.

He thought: But there were good times. It wasn't all
bad. I can't have been a shit all the time. We had good
things going for us. Why would she have hung around
so long if we didn't?

People hang on to anything if they think there's
nothing better. Some people spend their whole lives
hanging on, because they never know. But she was
clever, bright and pretty, and she made herself brighter,
and there were plenty of people around to tell her. She

197

realized in the end. Realized that she didn't have to be at the mercy of his ignorance, his moods; that there was a lot more to the world than a crummy, rusting old boat run by an eccentric drunk and his stupid, vicious son; that not all men were intent on keeping her 'in her place'.

There were good times, all right. They had fun – they laughed and made very good love. But he never talked to her. *At* her, certainly, but he lived among men who saw women as another species. Men who looked at a woman and said: 'You going out with it, then?' 'Yeah.' 'Got a good pair on it.' 'Wants to get married.' 'Kidding?' 'Straight up.' 'You want to get out of that.' 'Nah, it's a good shag.' Not much chance of a one-to-one relationship there. His notion of the world, bounded by the ports and the people he worked with was the one she had to live in.

He had consoled himself with the thought that she had gone to Charlie because he was 'a better prospect' according to the ideas of the world he hated. Charlie, with his first-class degree and his well-paid jobs, and his nice middle-class aspirations. Any sensible girl, he used to sneer, would go for the bloke with the nice flat, the expensive car and the glittering prospects. He could hate her easily, thinking she had defected from the 'real world' to the snobs and go-getters.

But he knew now that wasn't it. Not all of it. She had just got tired of living in his meagre cage. She tired of his constant denigration – his sniping and sneering. Years of being reminded how unimportant anything she thought or did was. Years of being made to feel small.

He had starved her of any sense that she mattered to him. Not maliciously; just because that was the way people behaved. You didn't get soppy with women or anyone, you didn't let them think they mattered. It placed you in a bad position. At least Charlie said nice things to her. From the beginning, Paul greeted any change of hairstyle or clothing, any attempt to experiment with herself, with mockery; Charlie told her she was beautiful. Paul laughed at her efforts to make her life better; Charlie understood perfectly. Paul treated the idea of love – even her love for him – as a bad joke; Charlie told her she was the best thing that ever happened to him.

So, naturally she went to him. He was the wider world made flesh. He had the nerve to treat her like a human being.

And it was only over the last few years that his mind, undernourished for too long, started going in circles. Only lately that he had thought back on all the missed schooling with something like regret for chances lost. It had taken him until he was past thirty to start questioning why, if all his ideas about life were right, he was so unhappy. And by then she was already gone.

He had never told her he loved her. Ever.

He saw that she was waiting for him to climb back in the car so that they could get on. He thought of his brother, and wasn't sure who he hated more; Charlie or himself.

They passed a sign in the late afternoon pointing to Hallford Castle. It was mounted on a pair of old lodge gates. Beyond them a gravelled road stretched into woodland.

'One of the old entrances,' she said. 'From the stately home days.'

They followed the wall that bounded the old estate.

'We just going to drive up to the main entrance?'

'I can't think of any other way,' she said. 'The place is riddled with security systems. There's only a skeleton staff to look after things until the spring, but we'd set off all kinds of alarms if we tried climbing in over the wall.'

'How d'you know this part of the country?'

'Friends. We met them when we started coming to the festival.'

'Which one?'

'Cropredy. The Fairport Reunion, as it used to be known. Every year in a couple of fields outside Banbury.'

'Fields?'

'Yes. Take your own tent, drink real ale and sit on damp grass for two days.'

'Charlie does that?'

'He has surprises, even for you.'

'Don't see him in with a crowd of hippies, that's all.'

'Where've you been lately? It's all kinds of people. We started going about five years ago. I wasn't very enthusiastic at first, but it grew on me. The atmosphere's nice there. Charlie relaxes. He calls it paying respects at the grave of the good old days.'

'Which were they?' he said, adjusting his view of Charlie a little more.

'When we were young enough to think things were going to change. Cropredy's like remembering that. Never any trouble. People sit around in the sun, listen to the music, smoke a few joints. No one gets hurt. Some of the police ask to be posted there every year because it's fun.'

'Dreamy.'

'I wouldn't expect you to understand.'

The road branched right. They were in deep-rolling country now, layers of field and wood fading into the misty distances of the lowering sun. Another sign announced 'Hallford Castle – 1½ miles' in big, cartoon lettering. 'The Experience Of A Lifetime – All In One Day!' the sign said.

There had been rain. The road was slick with it. They rounded a corner and passed through an open gate. A notice said 'Hallford Castle is CLOSED. Re-opening April 2nd.' The road led into a huge expanse of parking. A few lamps glimmered against the dying blush of the sky. The castle was far off to the south on a hill wooded with firs and pines. Dark stone, a Victorian idea of King Arthur's palace. Next to it, partly hidden by the trees, some kind of big dipper lurked like the twenty-first century.

What would the lord and master of the place in its heyday have thought of this?

Directly ahead was the entrance. A long, low building with turnstiles in the middle. No lights.

'Where's the security?' Paul said.

'Maybe I'm wrong. Perhaps it's just one old night watchman with a brazier and a couple of bottles of beer.'

They parked out front. The cameras mounted above the entrance didn't move to watch them. Nothing moved except a few lonely birds skating high above.

He checked through his pockets, lifting out the gun to ensure that the clip was full. She saw what he was doing, and her eyes got small. He took the stone out too, and she said:

'You still carry that?'

'Some people have a rabbit's foot.'

They got out of the car and walked toward the entrance. He didn't like the stillness.

'Maybe they're having their tea.' He peered through the ticket office window. Calendars and stacks of paper hats. No one about. The other booths were the same. Through the arcade were closed shops, steps beyond going down to the main concourse.

He swung up and over a turnstile. She did the same. They went through the darkened arcade. Tee-shirted teddy bears smiled on them, cheap cameras waited for the coming season's forgetful visitors, a café advertised drinks and ice creams. It was all glittering and clean, and quite dead without customers to make the lights go on and the music play.

They went out of the building, down steps like something from a Fred Astaire film. There was a great oval lake, drained of water, around it ornamental gardens and more shops. Restaurants to cater for all tastes, booths for the happy punters to 'phone their relatives while being photographed with people in animal costumes. Over the rooftops of Swiss chalets and miniature castles and futuristic domes, there were helter-skelter towers and the stilled arms of chairoplanes and rocket rides. Everything was primary coloured, drab in the winter evening.

He kept expecting a voice to yell from a doorway, for some uniformed muscleman to come striding along the walkways, asking what they thought they were playing at. But it was silent. They circled the empty lake. A few wet leaves were piled against a fountain bowl.

'Where would she be?' he asked.

'Not in the Starcrash thing. Either in the control centre, or one of the cottages.'

He saw a map by one of the signposts bristling with directions. The rides were spread all over the estate. It would take hours to walk round it.

While Mina stood by the signpost, trying to remember which way to go, he wandered off behind the 'Texas Grill'. An electric buggy with a canvas top was parked near the doors, keys in the starter. He knocked, but no one appeared.

He didn't see the tail of a uniform jacket hanging from under the lid of one of the big aluminium waste

202

bins nearby. He didn't hear the faint scraping and the moan from inside.

He got into the buggy and turned the key, reversed out to where Mina waited.

They ascended the hill where the castle stood. It flickered in and out of sight among the tall firs, looming like a horror film set. In summer this was a child's dream of what life should be. The stalls made to resemble fairy tale and science fiction buildings, the craning machines that spun and flew, the lights and the ups and downs. Now, though, it was a factory closed down, an entire country switched off at the main.

'Churches of the present day,' Mina murmured.

'What?'

'Something Charlie said.'

The slope flattened gradually as they droned up a long bend. Under the castle walls ahead were fairground rides for smaller children. Roundabouts and dodgem cars, a helter-skelter and a miniature train. At the top of the rise the big dipper, like an enormous geometric exercise, rose slowly into sight, bright yellow, twisting and plunging. 'The Stunt Flyer', the sort of ride that warned you to stay off if you had a weak heart.

'What's that?' Mina said.

He looked where she was pointing. Ahead of them, still a long way off, figures moved at a gateway in the trees.

'That's the way to the control centre,' Mina said.

The light was bad. It was difficult to make out. He thought there were two figures, then three. One of them was struggling. The other two held it tight, moving swiftly toward the Flyer.

'It's her,' Mina said.

He put his foot down, but the car was designed to do no more than twenty. It purred along at the same unhurried pace, and he watched as the struggling figure was pushed and hustled across the tarmac to the gates of the Flyer. They were so far off that no sound carried.

Mina said: 'What're they doing?'

They merged into a single shape again, mounting the steps to the track. One of the men jumped up on the access walkway. He gestured with one hand, probably with a gun. Something else in the other hand. The woman was thrown forward. He saw her sag, then get yanked up. The three moved together. They didn't hear the buggy approaching yet.

'Stop this thing,' Mina said. 'Stop it. We could run faster than this.'

'No, we couldn't. Stay where you are.'

'Paul . . .'

The woman's skirt blew in the wind. They were climbing up the track, the woman shoved onward by the one behind. They became silhouettes as they moved past a gap in the trees.

Mina's fingers dug into the padded dashboard. He heard the shallow breath coming from her mouth. She seemed to know what was going to happen. His stomach was liquid, burning in his body. He reached for the gun.

The figures were twenty feet off the ground, perhaps a little more. They stopped, and the woman threw herself against the safety rail. Her head went back. Maybe she was screaming. It was a silent film, a dream seen from way off. One of the men knelt to do something at her feet.

He had the gun in his hand now, its milled handgrips were cool. He let the buggy roll to a halt and jumped out. Mina was already running, yelling at the distant figures. He wished she would shut up, stay still. He needed to be steady to try anything, and nothing felt steady except what was happening on the Flyer. He leaned against the buggy, trying to aim. The safety

204

catch was off. He squinted over the barrel. The men had shut the woman up somehow. One of them had her by the shoulders. The other was lifting something to her head. He brought the gun to bear, holding it so tight that the metal cut him.

One of the men turned. He had heard Mina. She was still running straight at them, crying out something he couldn't catch. He saw the man's arm rise and straighten. In a rush of panic, he squeezed the trigger. The gun leapt in his hand, slamming back down his arm like a kick. It never stood a chance of hitting anything, but it did what he wanted. The man ducked. The sound of his shot came echoing down the slope, and Mina skidded and veered sideways, making for the cover of a hot-dog stand among the children's amusements. Both men were looking now, knowing they were not alone. The woman slumped between them.

He started walking slowly, as if he had time. The man who had fired at Mina shifted toward him, the other was lifting the woman into his arms. Something trailed. The one with the gun fired again. He kept walking. Mina was off to his right. He heard her shouting each time the sound of gunfire died.

It was possible to recognize them now by the clothes they wore. The reader had the gun, the cowboy was the one holding the woman in his arms. He staggered a little, swung so the woman was hanging over the rail. Paul pulled the trigger again, but the reader replied, and this time he heard a solid little *plunk* as the bullet went into the tarmac. He started firing randomly, trying to stop it happening. The cowboy leaned forward, as if the strain were telling on him. His arms dropped.

Mina screamed.

He saw the woman fall. Sideways at first, then snapping back, stopping dead in the air. Then swinging.

The hammer of the pistol was falling. He had emptied

the clip, but his finger still flexed on the trigger. The reader knelt to steady his hand on the rail.

Mina called: 'Polly, get out of the way.'

He dodged as the shot rang out, streaking silvery on the ground at his feet. Even as he ran to her, he could see the woman's body slowly turning, skirt fluttering as the wind caught it.

He collided with the wall of the hot-dog stand, got the box of cartridges out of his pocket. He was clumsy reloading, fingers stiff, hands shaking. He sneaked a look round the stand. Both men were coming down the track, the reader leaping and disappearing into the crisscross of struts and girders. The cowboy, also carrying a gun now, skittered toward the covered carriages.

Holding the gun in both hands, he squeezed off a shot.

The cowboy clapped a hand to his right shoulder, stumbled and collided with one of the carriages.

Keeping down the surprise at hitting something, he steadied himself to fire again. The cowboy lifted his right arm, but seemed to have trouble. His shot went off before the gun was pointing anywhere near the right place. Paul fired, and this time the cowboy jerked back in shallow imitation of the woman and fell heavily against the rail. He reached out for balance, clutched nothing, and went over.

The reader bobbed up among the girders, his gun flashed. They were close enough for the shots to mean something now, and the reader would be better than him. He hauled Mina to her feet.

'You run,' he said, catching his breath. 'Keep this thing between you and him, get back to the buggy, and run.'

She nodded. It was hard to tell whether she really heard.

He ran low and fast toward the roundabout five yards

to the right, dived in among the child-sized trains and ships as a bullet shattered a pony's head. He crawled round the back of the machinery, lunged across the gap to the helter-skelter. The reader was above him, but caught in the structure of the Flyer.

Another shot splintered the wall of the helter-skelter as he jumped the entrance gate. He mounted into the spiralling dark, reached the first window, saw Mina crouching by the hot-dog stand, going nowhere. Up another circuit to the next window. This was more like it. The deck where the carriages started was in plain sight, he could see the reader squatting amid the struts under the track. He rested the barrel on the window ledge, breathing deep to steady his hand.

The reader saw him, swung and fired, and the window frame jarred to the impact. He took his time, levelled again, pulled. The reader slithered out of sight.

He changed his position, getting more comfortable. He saw a gleam of paintwork and made out the lines of a car parked some yards from the Flyer. The reader appeared for an instant, crawling along the deck. He was trying to get back. Paul aimed between the girders, slightly ahead of him. When he fired this time, the reader gained his feet long enough to slip over the side of the deck into the double-backing path where customers waited their turn for the ride.

Paul took the steps three at a time, curving up to the roof. The reader must have been expecting it. A shot punched the wall outside as he reached the top window. But the reader was in sight again, kneeling, waiting by one of the fences.

Paul swung into the window, beading down on the walkway. The reader was up, jumping the fences like a rabbit. He fired twice, trying to lead him, failing to allow for the speed. The reader made it over the last fence, threw himself at the car, and kangarooed away, steering drunkenly toward a fence until he got control and sped off round the corner.

He clattered down the stairs. Mina had her back to the stand. Her eyes were shut and she was gulping on tears or a scream. He dragged her up to face him.

'Why didn't you go?' he shouted at her. He was furious. 'He could've come for you. Why don't you do what I say?'

She stared up at him as if he was as dangerous as the rest. He couldn't bear the thought that she might have been hurt. He pulled her against him and held her.

The car was gone. There was peace again. All the dead rides frozen in winter darkness. The edge of day was dulling as they approached the Flyer. He wanted to be gone, but the woman swayed faintly in the wind, the rope creaked. Mina tracked along behind him, feet scuffing the ground. They went through the entrance, and walked up and down the zigzag queuing area like machines following a set path. He stopped her and hitched himself over a gate saying 'STAFF ONLY'. A last wash of daylight touched the sky as he stood underneath the body. It turned gently, its feet level with his chest.

She had been tall. Skirt was ankle length, shoes like a man's. Long woollen jacket, pockets bagged and misshapen. Blouse of white cotton with vivid embroidery on the breast. Hair a short blonde bob. The face, in life, must have been long but handsome.

'It's her,' Mina said, close behind him. He jumped a little. He hadn't heard her approaching.

Suddenly he couldn't stand it. He gave her his pocket knife. 'Can you climb up and cut the rope?' His voice as unsteady as hers.

She climbed the steps to the deck and started up the track. He saw her above, at the top of the rope, leaning

208

over the rail. She reached down, sawing at the rope. He waited, arms outstretched.

He almost dropped her. She came so quickly, was so heavy, that he only just managed to grab her by the waist and stop her collapsing like a puppet at his feet. The rope fell loose, swatting his cheek, and her poor head rested on his shoulder. He swallowed his vomit and gently let her down.

Dad's body had been wet. Soaked through, freezing. He had only been in the water twelve hours, so it wasn't as bad as it could have been – the suicides they sometimes dredged from the sea and rivers were usually unrecognizable – but the old man had gone down to the bottom of the harbour, and a diver off the Greenpeace survey ship found him and brought him to the surface. One of the search parties got hold of him with a hook. The hook bit into the collar of his pea coat, into the back of his neck. When they knew they had something, someone shouted for Paul, who had been searching another part of the dock. He and Sam rowed over, and Paul saw the bald head and the jacket, and knew it was his father. Sam began to cry, and he had never heard Sam do that before. The other men held the body in the water until he got there. He leaned over the stern of the old boat, while others weighted the bow. Sam wept. He pulled his father from the cold water. It was January the seventh. There was snow on the harbour buildings, snow on the decks of the ships. Dad's body felt like a sack of waterlogged grain. Someone said: 'Let us help you, son.' But he did it himself, until the body was in the boat, dirty water brimming gently from its slack mouth, yellow eyes filmed.

Mina's hand touched his shoulder. She said: 'We can't help her.'

He straightened the head, trying to conceal the dislocation of the neck. The face was bad. He dug in

209

the pockets of her cardigan and found a handkerchief, covered her face with it. The pockets spilled their other contents: a grubby old calculator, pens and pencils, a packet of cough sweets, a notebook with a few jottings.

Taking Mina's hand, he picked his way through the girders to the place where the cowboy had fallen. That body lay splayed on the ground, a pool of blood under it. The gun was by its side. He refrained from putting his boot into the cowboy; he was dead anyway. He took the gun and some spare clips, and searched the other pockets.

A bunch of keys rattled in his fingers. They were attached to a Hallford Castle key ring: a jolly knight with big walrus moustache and golden armour. Across it was a strip of stencilled tape printed with the words 'Guest Cottage No. 4'.

He stood up, two guns in his pockets now. Mina looked at the keys.

The buggy descended through wooded hills, leaving the machines behind. They came out at the head of a long, deep valley. It faded away in gathering dark and distance. The towers supporting a cable car pricked the sky far above.

They went down, Mina driving. No lights, no signs of life. There was no way of knowing whether the reader was hiding somewhere, waiting to pick them off. Hardly seemed to matter. They were silent.

The cottage peeped at them from smothering trees halfway up the valley's western slope; an ugly little mock-Tudor redbrick, with architectural pretensions about the chimneys and gables. A lane hairpinned several times to reach a garden on the right.

As Mina guided the buggy round one of the bends directly below the cottage, they were hidden for a moment. He touched her arm and sprang out, ducking into the bushes. She kept going at the same pace. Anyone in the house would only be able to see the buggy's canvas top.

Using tree roots and low branches for holds, he made the distance to the edge of the garden before Mina had even reached the next bend. He moved through the damp tangle of undergrowth, pushed twigs aside and looked at the house. He was at a narrow angle, but the place seemed empty.

The buggy turned onto the last stretch. As she topped the crest and reached the parking area beyond the garden, it would be obvious to anyone watching that she was alone. He stared at the cottage again, making sure.

And noticed something.

In the upstairs window on the right, one diamond-leaded pane was missing.

In the gloom it was hard to make out. But as the buggy came over the rise, he saw a glimmer of movement there, the barrel of a pistol resting on the vee of lead.

He fired twice. Another diamond shattered and the barrel was snatched from sight. He yelled at Mina to get down. The buggy stopped halfway into the parking space. He crossed the garden fast, swung round the blind side of the house. The kitchen window had been smashed open. He clambered in.

The reader was upstairs. He had fallen where he was shot, sprawling over a double bed. One of Paul's bullets had taken away part of his head. A smell of offal hung in the room.

He went to the window and shouted to Mina that it was all right, went back downstairs and opened the front door for her. When she reached him, she didn't say anything, just looked, and he nodded, and she knew there had been more death.

211

'Good,' she said, thinking of the woman.

They went into a small sitting room. He turned on the lights.

A laptop computer the same make as Mina's lay open and plugged in on a writing table by the window. Next to it were a printer, a couple of floppy discs in their cases, and a scratchpad covered in figures and diagrams. A stack of fat books were loosely arranged around the scratchpad: atlases, encyclopedias, a number of ringbound duplicated texts. One of them was open. He leaned over it, reading the typed words of the title: 'Newton and the Chaos Theory'.

Mina sat down and switched the computer on. The little electric sound of its motor running whined in his ears as he picked up copies of the *New Scientist* from the floor. An empty mug stood on the hearth, a ring of dried coffee in the bottom.

He climbed the stairs again, found the other bedroom, the one where Penelope Leman had slept. The bed was unmade, a blue dressing gown was flung over a chair. The bedside table held a few bottles and jars. A row of books spilled along the windowsill: *A Philosophical Essay on Probabilities*, one was called, *Principles of Physical Geology* was another.

He sat on the edge of the bed and looked at the blonde hairs on the pillow. The woman was dead. He had seen her in the moment of dying. It seemed strange that she would never come back to this room.

On the bedside table was a photograph in a silver frame. Just a little picture of two people. One was Leman. She had been handsome in life, all right, and in this picture she was laughing, which made the serious lines change into something much more attractive. She was falling all over the man who was with her, her face turned toward his, an arm round his neck.

The man was Charlie.

He opened a drawer under the table. Inside was a bag of toiletries, a pocket diary, and a few letters – all addressed in Charlie's precise hand. One letter had no envelope. He unfolded it the wrong way round, saw the last page first. He read the words, and they only meant one thing.

He pushed the drawer shut, reached to hide the picture.

Standing in the doorway, Mina said: 'Don't.'

18

On Wednesday morning Sam tramped up to Crown Score. It was bitter cold but bright, the alley slithered down the hill in a jumble of old slums and shop premises, and the factories on the beach industrial area belched white smoke into the shining blue.

He knocked hard. It was half-past nine, but Brenda never got up early if she could help it. The paint on the front door was peeling. There was no man in the house to deal with these things, and Brenda didn't care enough to do them herself. It pained him to think how she'd let herself go since her worthless bugger of a husband ran off.

On the third time of hammering, she finally stuck her head out of a bedroom window.

'What's going on?' she yelled, pale brown hair blowing across her pudgy face. ''Ello, Dad. What you want?'

'You got a parcel for me?'

'Parcel?'

He unwrapped a mint humbug while he waited for her to get decent and come down to let him in. At breakfast, Ma had given him a garbled message about Polly sending something important through the post. He left Ian with the engineer back at the *Provider* and went along to see if there were any truth in it.

Brenda opened the door, awash in furry slippers and a purple dressing gown. 'This must be it,' she said, and thrust a padded envelope into his hands.

He stayed for a cup of tea, because he hadn't seen her for a week or two. She was curious to know what was in the envelope, but he kept it in his pocket, talked about where Paul might have got to, and left her with nothing but the rough pat on the head that had always passed for affection from him.

'You see Ian comes home for his tea tonight,' she said as he left. 'He's never home these days.'

'Do that,' he nodded, and trudged back up the alley to the High Street.

Sitting on a bench outside the town hall, a young man in a leather jacket watched over his 'paper as Sam came out of Crown Score. The edge of the envelope was clearly visible, sticking out of Sam's pocket.

The young man bent his head, spoke into a walkie-talkie in his palm. He folded his 'paper, stuffed it in a waste bin, and started off down the High Street, glancing idly in shop windows.

19

'She's sleeping?' Reiny said.

Paul stepped into his cabin. 'Yeah, she's okay now.'

'She is *erschöpft*, exhausted.'

'We were on the road all night. Besides, you know how it is . . .'

'Oh, yes, I know.' Reiny waved him into a chair. 'Come, sit. Take a drink.'

He unlocked a cupboard on the wall of his neat little cabin and took down a decanter of cognac and two glasses.

'Here now,' he said, his blue eyes bright with enthusiasm. 'You try, tell me what you think.' He handed Paul a brimming glass, pushing a pack of cigarettes toward him at the same time.

They sat at the table, and drank each other's health, and Paul felt the brandy go down like a blessing.

'Good,' he said. 'Good.'

'I get it from Jacques Vertus. He has a brother down in Carcassonne who gets it for friends.'

'It's fine,' Paul said, afraid to light a cigarette until the fumes had died down.

Outside the curtained porthole, dock machinery went up and down the harbour. Cranes and container lifts jumbled together in the late afternoon light. The white cliffs hung like dirty sheets in the distance. Reiny had a load of timber on deck that was going to Rotterdam on the evening tide.

'Thanks for doing this, Reiny.'

'It's okay. You say Sam will meet you in Amsterdam?'

He reached for the matches, uncomfortable about

the lies he had told. 'Yeah, we had the repairs to finish, then some stuff to pick up in Grimsby, and we couldn't stop that just for me and Mina. He's getting some help to take her across. Should be there tomorrow. So . . .'

'So you will be able to take your lady aboard in good style after this —' he searched for the phrase, shrugging at his surroundings '— this old bucket.'

'It's a great bucket,' Paul said.

They drank a toast to Dad. Reiny coughed a little on his brandy.

'A fine man,' he said, wiping the tears from his eyes. 'A *Schuft*, but a fine man. How long is he dead now?'

'Seven years last January the seventh.'

'So long. Ach! The good ones go, the bastards stay, it's true . . . I wonder what he would say about this.'

'Wouldn't like it much.'

'No. I think you're right. He used to say to me: "Those boys, they don't get on. *Why* don't they get on? Even about a girl they fight."'

Paul tapped his cigarette on the ashtray. 'We never fought.'

'You were always hitting each other.'

'We didn't fight about Mina.'

'Maybe you should, eh? Save all this now.'

They drank in companionable silence. Men were shouting topside, boots clanking on the deck.

'She is not changed,' Reiny said, smiling to himself. 'Still such a pretty thing. Only now she is a woman.'

He nodded, looking out of the porthole again to avoid Reiny's clever eyes.

'What's that on the cliff?'

'Eh?'

'Looks like there's a guy hanging halfway down.'

'Ah, he's the . . . filler man.' Reiny struggled with a translation. 'The repair man. Er, the cliffs are *krümelig*.

217

They fall on houses underneath. This man is injecting into them to make them safe.'

'Long job.'

'The coast is falling down. I think it is the tunnel.'

'We'll all be out of a job when that gets finished,' Paul said, thinking of work for the first time in days.

'It won't come,' Reiny said. 'It doesn't get finished, or it floods. It's a bad thing, anyway. If I am British, I don't want this tunnel joining me to Europe. One day, everywhere is joined to everywhere else, then how do we know who is who?'

'It's already done.' Paul examined the cognac, the warm heart of it. 'Only it's not tunnels or bridges. It's wiring.'

'Eh?'

He yawned suddenly. Reiny sighed.

'You exhaust yourself with this. Is it so bad?'

'Oh, you know. You remember Charlie?'

'Not so well. He wasn't around like you.'

'He's got crazy over the years.' It was hard to make up stories about someone he did not know, but he had placed himself in this position. 'He's rich, thinks the world belongs to him. I didn't believe Mina when she said he'd hire people to deal with me, but then we ran into them and I nearly got my ass kicked in.'

'He has connections?'

'Like the *Provider*'s got rats. If we tried to fly out or take a ferry, he'd have people waiting.'

'Maybe this is something you don't want to hear, but why not go to the police?'

Paul hoped he looked embarrassed in the right way. 'Look, Reiny, I won't lie to you. She hasn't just left him. She came away with a few souvenirs.'

'Like?'

'Like several thousand quid that isn't strictly hers.' Reiny laughed. Paul knew he had been thinking there must be more to it. 'This is how you can afford the repairs?'

He nodded. 'You got me . . . But it's nothing illegal. The law's not involved. I wouldn't do anything that could drop you in the shit. It's just it happened so fast. We needed a friend.'

'So you think of me.'

The ghost of a rueful smile to give it sincerity. 'Who else?'

The old man turned his glass slowly between finger and thumb. 'You could tell me this at the start, you know that? It doesn't matter.'

'I was hoping you'd see it that way.'

Reiny poured him another glass. 'Ah, once I got myself beaten for a woman with a rich husband. These men see their wives like *Besitzes*.'

'That's how it is,' he said, and Mina's face when she saw the photograph on the bedside table came to mind. Charlie deserved whatever was coming. 'I had to take her away from him.'

Reiny nodded. 'If you did this at the start, things would be different. I remember Bernard said to me one time: "If only the boy wasn't so stupid, he would've kept her from the start."'

There was no answer to that which didn't work deep into his mind and sweat there. 'Yeah, well,' he said. 'We all make mistakes when we're young.'

'Don't look so serious, nephew.' Reiny clapped him on the shoulder. 'Tonight we sail, tomorrow you're in the Netherlands with your lady, and your problems are over.'

He drank down the last mouthful of brandy, thinking: Oh, yeah. All our troubles are over.

She was stretched on the lower bunk in the cabin Reiny had given them. ('No double beds on this ship,'

219

he'd laughed.) She lay on her back, blankets pulled under her chin. Exhaustion showed in the depth of her breathing, in the way she never stirred when he came in.

He pulled a chair up close to the bunk and sat near to her, hands between his knees. He took the printout from his pocket and looked over it again.

Charlie's message said:

```
-TAHEIA
GO TO SCHIPHOL - ASK AT KLM DESK.
BOOK ANY SEATS OR ROOMS NECESSARY. I WILL
PROTECT.
DESTROY PENNY'S NOTES AND DISCS.
RUA-
```

While he had been upstairs, finding the picture and the letters, Mina had used Penelope Leman's machine to communicate. She told Charlie everything that had occurred. The reply took some time to come. She was holding the torn-off sheet when she found him in the bedroom. She handed it to him as she went to pick up the photograph.

It was hard to make her move quickly after that. Her lethargy seemed to increase as she studied the picture, fingered the envelopes. He had to work around her, collecting Leman's discs and notebooks. Coming back up the stairs, he sat next to her and said:

'We should take those too. If the police see them . . .'

'Yes,' she said, distractedly. She made a small, empty laughing sound through her nose. 'No wonder he took so long answering.'

He got her back to the buggy, back to their car. He expected sirens and blue flashing lights any minute, but nothing came. Their car was in the park, untouched. He drove away, trying to keep the pace

220

unhurried. It was full dark by then, they passed no one till they were well away from the grounds.

She sat in the back, staring out of the windows. He drove south, the only aim being to get as far from the scene as possible. He did not think they were followed. After a while she dozed. He stuck to minor roads, referring to the map book, glad to be doing anything to stop his mind from running faster and faster. It was in the back of his thoughts to go to Southampton, where he had friends, then he thought about Portsmouth, and his mind's eye worked all the way round the coast, trying to work out the next move. Sometime around midnight he stopped in a lonely wood, getting the car well out of sight. But there was no sleep, just the Leman woman turning and turning in the air. He thought about her, and about Charlie, and Mina mumbled in her troubled dreams. After an hour or two he gave up and got back on the road.

They heard the first bulletin about Hallford Castle as they breakfasted in a greasy spoon café outside Chichester. A television tuned to 'Good Morning, Britain' showed the bright-eyes in the studio with their 'tragedy' expressions on. Cameras had been sent, but were being stopped at the gates. A bleary reporter spoke to camera as police cars and ambulances zoomed back and forth, and stock footage showed the park in its summer finery. The story was still fresh, the details garbled. At first the police had been talking only about a security guard being attacked and beaten up. Half an hour later there were two bodies, a man's and a woman's. It would take them a while longer to discover the one in the guest cottage.

Mina picked at her breakfast with little appetite, glancing at him with frightened eyes every time the story was repeated. He tried to calm her. They were a hundred miles away from the scene. No one, so far as he knew, had spotted them coming or going.

The news moved on to pictures of English firemen flying to Peru. They were going to assist in looking for survivors still trapped in the rubble of the recent earthquake. A reporter in a factory somewhere up north stood in front of a workbench and said that the disaster had been good for this firm, who made heat-sensing equipment. Orders had been coming in ever since the 'quake.

When they were back in the car, she said they ought to head for an airport, get a plane to Amsterdam as soon as possible. They argued for a while, but her heart wasn't in it. She said it was perfectly possible for Charlie to write a program that would monitor airline booking computers and hotel registers and wipe their names as soon as they appeared. He said that somehow the bad boys had found out about Hallford Castle and Penelope Leman. Maybe they had intercepted Charlie's message to them. He thought they should try to stay low, not go walking into anything just because Charlie said so.

She gave in. They made their way along the coast, first to Newhaven and Folkestone, where he had no luck – the only people he knew well were not going to Holland – finally to Dover. There, as soon as the pubs opened, he found Reiny, and told him the story of cruel Charlie, and how Mina was running away from him to come live a life of adventure and true love on the *Provider*.

Reiny had regarded them with his penetrating stare for a long time: Paul unshaven and scruffy, Mina so broken up. But finally he laughed as if he knew the story was moonshine, said it was a fine way to behave, and agreed to help. Paul hid the car in a long-stay park, then Reiny got them and their luggage into the port, installed them in a cabin, and assured them that Charlie would not get them here.

The cabin was growing dark. He was tired, and the brandy swirled in his head. He had told lies to Reiny to get them a passage to Rotterdam, and he didn't know how long their story, such as it was, would hold up. By mid-afternoon, the radio news was running the Hallford Castle killings as first story. It was mentioned early on that the 'armed raiders' had somehow interfered with the computer-controlled video security system, switching all the cameras off and wiping the tapes of any evidence (he could see Penelope Leman being forced at gunpoint to scramble the system's brains before they led her out). They couldn't work out what it had all been about; a woman hanged then cut down, two men shot. He had wondered about the hanging himself. Presumably, the cowboy and the reader wanted it to look like suicide. But the news people didn't know that. Still no mention of names, but someone had reported seeing a green car leaving the area early the previous evening. He had dumped the guns in the harbour before they entered the docks: they couldn't risk getting caught by the customs boys with a couple of pistols. He imagined the police stringing together all the incidents of the past few days — the fire by the lake, the disruption of a Cambridge college, maybe the business with the guns on the road near Northampton. They had computers too. Maybe some clever bastard at CID was pressing buttons and coming up with connections even now.

It was too much. He had to rest. He gazed down at Mina.

She was beautiful. He wanted to pick her up and hold her and not let anything hurt her any more.

223

He'd never felt like that before, or never accepted it. But it was a big hypocrisy and he knew it. He'd seen her pain as they drove away from Hallford Castle, and it was familiar to him. In the old days, what he mostly did was cause her pain. Reiny had said he might not have lost her if he'd been cleverer. But he didn't lose her at all; he drove her off. One too many nights with other girls, one too many times when he left her sitting alone in a pub to mess around with 'mates', one too many reminders that she was just another girl; a skirt, a tart, a possession he could take or leave. He even used to laugh when she started spending time with Charlie. He thought it was funny. He used to jeer at her and say: 'Getting to like him better than me, are you?' Her silence he mistook for the old submissiveness. Treating her like dirt was part of being a 'real man'. Didn't want anyone in the pub saying he was soft. He behaved as everyone behaved. And for years he could strike the smile of happiness from her face with one cruel word. He was brilliant at it.

Hardly his place to get angry if others were hurting her now. But he still wanted to beat Charlie to the ground.

She groaned and turned on her side. The covers slid down. He pulled them up as gently as he could, and heard Reiny leave his cabin, shouting to someone that it was getting time to be off.

He left her and went up on deck, trying to keep out of the way. The crew were busy, they didn't need him hanging around like a spare anchor.

He stayed up in the after deckhouse as the ship moved away from its mooring. The cliffs were a ghost smudge reflecting the lights of the town. The sea was calm. Drawn tight against the night chill, he watched the clock tower slide away, the ferry piers and Dover Castle sitting high above on the edge of the sky. Deep under his feet the engines throbbed and the ship heaved slowly out to sea, the red light on the southern breakwater changing to white as they passed the Admiralty pier.

20

Haggard drove from Dover to Gatwick and booked himself onto the Amsterdam 'plane. He settled down in the departure lounge to await his call. Sipping at a glass of fresh orange juice, he considered his position.

Tracking them to Dover had not been hard. New York had given him the information about the amusement park shortly after he visited the hotel where they stayed on Monday night. He never intended staying on their tail the whole time, had been content to catch them up when they reached their destination.

But something more had gone wrong. A great deal was going wrong with this job. None of it his doing.

He had arrived at the park late in the afternoon, seen their car near the entrance. He concealed his own vehicle in the coach area, and was about to investigate when he heard the distant sound of shooting.

He retired to his car and waited to see the outcome. There was no point needlessly involving himself. But he 'phoned New York and said: 'Something is happening again.'

'I know,' New York said, his tone a little irritable. 'Another message just went through. I didn't get it.'

'Something serious,' Haggard explained, patiently.

'How so?'

'They're in the park, but someone else is with them.'

'That's not good.'

'Who would these people be?'

'That's a question,' New York said. There was a far-away clatter of typing. 'I don't get it. I can guarantee there's no official action on this.'

'I think guns in the English countryside are hardly official,' Haggard muttered.

'Guns? That *is* bad. You seen these guys?'

'I'm standing back until there's some resolution.'

'Good. I think that's best.'

'You must find out how these people, whoever they are, get their information.'

'Well, yes, that's priority one.'

'But I think if our couple survive whatever is happening, I go underground after this, use my own people.'

'Hey, wait, Mr – Mr Haggard. I don't know that we can authorize that.'

'Someone is finding out things which are supposed to be unknown. I'm tired of being beaten to the line.'

'But this is not just a closedown,' New York said, speaking a little faster as agitation touched him. Haggard almost smiled at the thought of sweat breaking out under the man's arms.

'Either I am in charge of this, or I cease operations now. It's too dangerous this way.'

'Well, hold on. If I could talk to my superior . . .'

There was movement by the entrance. Haggard raised his head. 'I must go now.' He put the 'phone down as Quillet and the wife appeared, walking fast toward their car. He thought: They must be learning. They're ordinary people, yet they keep escaping.

It occurred to him then to wonder if they were not so ordinary. He had been given files, first on Quillet, then on the wife when she appeared, and there was nothing to suggest training.

But, of course, the files had been provided by his employers. And he was beginning to distrust the voice on the telephone. So many things had gone awry in so short a time, he had less and less faith in the organization that was supposed to be making this easier for him. He had his own contacts in Britain, people he had used before when it was impossible to work completely alone. As he followed Quillet's car from the park at a very safe distance, he called some of them.

They knew him, and they knew when he said he wanted their assistance that anything else was to be put on the back burner. He said that he was in pursuit of a certain car, did not want to risk being spotted. He needed two other followers to take over at intervals. His associate said he would call when he had the people. When Quillet stopped in the woods, he took the opportunity to put his helpers on the job.

And so the tail was accomplished. It was an old trick that he was happy with. The two assistants did the job alone while he rested for an hour, then he rejoined them, and all three made it safe as they progressed south down the country. Two bracketing at long distance, one staying close to be sure that an unexpected turn did not result in loss.

He was close to them when they reached Dover. He watched from across the street as they came out of a public house with a ship's master, and discovered with little trouble which vessel they went to, and where the vessel was bound. He even saw Quillet drop the pistols in the sea. He was the only person who did.

So he left them. He would be in Amsterdam in a few hours, and waiting at Rotterdam when the *Europa Belle* docked.

The departure lounge was a warm haven in the glittering night. He watched a tall, well-kept woman stride over to the bar and order a drink. He carried only an overnight case. No weapons. They were all concealed in his car, and the car should already have been picked up from the airport park. When he reached Amsterdam another vehicle would be waiting, complete with the equipment he had itemized in his call to the Dutch office. This was the good thing about working for corporate employers: the practical backup was so complete. When he had first started, long ago, it was a freelance business, except for the regulars who did work for the mob. He worked for anyone who hired him; just a 'phone call and an envelope dropped at a mailing address, his own equipment, and a cheap operation. But, as it had come to the rest of civilization, the corporate world came to his profession. When he was offered this arrangement, working solely for one employer, he had seen the advantages. As the trusted and important employee of a large conglomerate, he enjoyed many benefits. Not security of tenure, of course. His position was judged solely on results. Which was why he did not care for the developments in this job. Something had broken down, and if he did not protect his back, these mistakes might threaten his position.

Even his life.

21

She was awake when he returned. She lay on the bunk, staring at the ceiling. She still looked tired.

He splashed his face with water from the wash basin. He smelled of the sea, of diesel and dirt from the harbour. He blinked at himself in the mirror, looked for cigarettes, but the packet was empty.

Mina got up. She started brushing her hair. Static jumped and crackled. He stood by the door, waiting.

He said she'd better eat. She said she wasn't hungry. Neither was he, but they went along to the galley. It was empty. A black and white portable television held in a bracket on the table was tuned to *News at Ten*. The Hallford Castle story had been dealt with: Alastair Burnet was onto news from America. An arms sale scandal threatened to involve the White House. Pictures of the President playing baseball before assembled photographers and applauding flunkies were overlaid with commentary about his lack of a strong reply to the accusations.

There were the makings of a quick meal in the store-room. He heated it up, brewed coffee. Mina watched the news with low concentration. The picture fuzzed in and out as the ship took the swell. Turkish peasants were being persuaded to sell their kidneys so that private patients in English hospitals could get quick transplants; an investment adviser suspected of embezzling a million pounds of pensioners' savings was living the good life in Spain; another famine threatened in West Africa. And back again at the end to the headlines. Pictures of the rides at Hallford Castle against a grey sky, a doomy voice pronouncing clichés about 'death coming to this child's fantasy land'. The Chief Inspector of Police who appeared at a press conference nodded and said he wasn't ruling out the possibility of gangland killings. One of the murdered men had a long criminal record, but there was no explanation for him being at the park, or for the murder of the American heiress.

Mina covered her face. One of the crew barged in, said, 'Pardon me,' in a heavy German accent, and bobbed out again like a puppet on a string. The appearance was so fleeting that Mina started to laugh. She shook her head, picked up her fork again.

The news finished with the usual jokey item. A man in Scotland had arranged a wedding ceremony for his dog and bitch. A full dress affair, with the local kennel club attending. A fake vicar conducted the ceremony, and the owner slid a gold ring onto the bitch's collar. Interviewed, to prove what an idiot he was, he grinned obligingly for the cameras and said the whole thing had cost upwards of five thousand pounds. The happy couple would spend the honeymoon at a hotel in the north that catered to dogs and their owners. Sir Alastair spoke his final quip and the signal fizzled and faded. Paul cursed disgustedly.

The ship was well beyond Dunkerque now, the television tuned to the eastern region ITV station. A symbol flashed up for the local bulletin.

He asked if she wanted more coffee. She shook her head, yawned. He got up to refill his mug, rattling around in the cramped galley. He could hear the newsreader's voice droning on.

Then Mina said: 'Polly, come here.'

It turned him cold. He went back to her, the empty mug in his hand. Her face was grey. She had turned up the volume, and the silver-haired newsreader was saying: ' . . . Police are not ruling out foul play. The ship, a motor coaster registered in Lowestoft, sank in the harbour earlier this evening after an explosion on board. It's known that at least one man died. He's been identified as Mr Sam Cuddy, first mate of the vessel. Police are trying to trace the whereabouts of the owner.'

He stumbled backwards as the *Belle* pitched into a bigger wave, fetched up against the wall and stood there, staring at the screen as the newsreader moved on to a local council matter. He closed his eyes, and the darkness rocked.

She turned the set off. She came toward him.

He said: 'Go back to the cabin. I've got to —' He didn't know what. Only to be moving, to be doing anything, so as not to let it sink in.

He pushed by her and went up to the bridge. A fine spittle of rain smeared the windows, and Reiny was talking quietly with the first mate. The radio was tuned to a German station. They had not heard the news, they hardly noticed him. He backed out onto the deck, turned and clutched the rail, the empty night stabbing his face. Off to port, the lights of twenty or thirty vessels were strung across the sea, stars shaming them.

He had done this a thousand times, seen these sights a thousand times. He thought of the *Provider*, recalled his relief at leaving her behind. Sometimes lately, in some foreign port or other, he had just wanted to walk away from her, never go back. *His* ship, his father's ship, the life he had defended so pugnaciously all these years. He thought of Penelope Leman's body in his arms, and of the men he had killed and of Sam, calling out, 'Don't get lost.' He gazed down at the white flush of the sea churning past the hull. England slid away, everything that made him who he used to be was sliding away.

He went down into the ship again, through the galley, where there was no solitude because a couple of the crew had come in. He nodded in passing, went along the corridor to the cabin, closed the door. Then there was nowhere else to go. There were the bunks, the table and chair, and Mina, leaning close to the porthole, not moving.

He sat in the chair, hands twisting on the smooth wooden arms. He stared at the wall. You can beat anything alone, as long as you bury it deep enough.

Mina turned.

Bury it deep. That's how you deal with anything that hurts, anything that matters.

He was on his feet again. He started toward the door, then he drove his fist hard into it; the left, the arm with the knife wound. It hurt like hell. He did it again. The door smeared blood from his split knuckles. Choking, he spun round, to stop from breaking his own fingers.

She came to him. He pushed himself away from the door to go to her. She put her arms around him, and he drew her tight, trying to pull her into him, trying to draw back what she had given him a long time past.

They clung hard, and at first it was just to not be alone. He stroked her shining hair, smelling her warmth, the old familiar scent. He wanted to take all her hurt away. She looked up, her fingers touched his face. There was something like surprise, then her expression changed. Tender, but vicious too somehow. Everything. She drew his head down on her shoulder, holding him.

And after some amount of time that did not register, the soothing became loving, the hurt became heat, the past became present.

There was just Mina, and surviving.

PART THREE
Chaos

22

The *Europa Belle* sailed up the Nieuwe Maas to Rotterdam in early daylight.

Paul wiped the porthole clear of condensation and looked out at the Euromast towering in the park on the north bank. The Euro-prong, Sam used to call it. Used to. The cold made him shiver. He stood, naked, watching the industrial sprawl glide by. Most of the town had been blown off the map in the war, replaced with 'fifties and 'sixties architecture. He always thought of it as a giant factory.

The note of the engines changed. The trip would soon be done. He rubbed at his arms to get some warmth.

'You'll freeze,' she said.

He looked at her. She was still huddled on one side of the bunk they had shared. She patted the blankets. 'Come back or put some clothes on.'

He went back, slid in next to her. The warm line of her body against him was like a charge. She laid her arm over his chest and pulled closer to keep warm. Her eyes were closed again.

'What's wrong?'

'Wasn't sure . . .' he said.

'How it'd be when we woke up and realized "what we'd done"?' She breathed deep. 'Bound to happen.'

He was surprised how matter-of-fact she was. He'd expected denial, more cold silences.

'Put us together in a confined space for long enough,' she said, 'it was inevitable.'

'You reckon.'

'Just so.' Her fingers smoothed across his chest.

237

Touched his lower lip, his chin. 'You could say we were in a susceptible state of mind. You did it to get revenge on me – or Charlie; I did it because of . . . what I found out yesterday.'

'Sounds reasonable.'

'Maybe.' Her mouth was close to his ear. Her breath tickled his skin. 'Maybe curiosity.'

He wanted to say: No, none of those things. But he had said enough last night. Any hiding he wanted to do now had to be in plain sight.

Her hand slid down to his stomach, rested there. 'Still, it's nice to know one thing.'

'What?'

'Some things don't change.'

He put his arms round her, pulling her to him again. He kissed her as if he might never get the chance again. Maybe he wouldn't.

'When you opened the door in that place in Cambridge,' she said, 'when I saw you again, it was the same old thing. You'd think it would go away after so long.'

'I couldn't believe it was you,' he said, feeling strange talking about it. 'Then I couldn't believe how gorgeous you looked.'

'You were a wreck. But it was still there. One look in your bloodshot eyes . . .' She shrugged.

Someone passed the door, hammering and shouting that it was time to get up.

She said: 'What're we going to do?'

The question carried a weight of dread and anger.

He said: 'I can't go back.'

'No one knows we were at Hallford Castle.'

'I mean the boat. Right this minute, they're looking to prove I sank her for the insurance. Lay your odds they made it look that way. Happened before. Owners sink a ship for the cash, member of the crew accidentally gets

238

killed. To make it perfect, I'm not around. If you were an insurance investigator, what would you think?'

'You didn't do it.'

He thought: I did it, all right. I sent him the tape, and they tried to get it, and something went wrong, so they covered for themselves and dropped me in the shit at the same time.

He said: 'What's my alibi? "No officer, I couldn't've blown up my boat. I was off killing people in another part of the country." If we go and tell them, they'll say: "Where's the evidence?" Your MP friend'll never've heard of me, Charlie'll be a scientist with a nervous breakdown, and you and me, we'll be aiding and abetting him.' He badly wanted a cigarette now. 'Besides, you think we'd stay on our feet long enough to tell it?'

She propped herself on one elbow, brushing the hair back off her face. Her shoulders were smooth, breasts pale coffee. She said:

'You know how to spoil a romantic atmosphere, don't you?'

He pulled her head towards his, pressed his lips against her forehead. The pain inside was exquisite, sharp. 'We've got to follow through. It's the only way we stand a chance of getting out alive.'

'I know.'

'Anyway, there's Sam.' Mentioning the name twisted him like a rope at full stretch.

'I know,' she said. 'I know.'

They were out of the docks by midday, but only after a sweaty half-hour with the customs boys. The two officers on duty checked their passports carefully, and took a long look at their bags and the computer. They knew his face well; that made them friendly, but careful too. The blessing was that news of the *Provider*'s sinking obviously hadn't got through yet. He managed to bluff it out.

Reiny waved them off at the dock gates.

'Be happy, okay?' he said, chucking Mina under the chin as if she were a little girl. Looking round for suspicious faces, Paul thought about Reiny's idea of them; the fugitive lovers. A memory of last night rose like a hot wave. He wanted to touch her all the time, wanted to feel her good curves in his hands and pressing against him. 'Fugitive lovers' had some truth for him now, but he hadn't talked about it. There was no good to it. She was being cool and adult. That was the way they were playing it.

They found a taxi, and the driver spoke wonderful English. He did not mind that they had no guilders.

'You in trouble?' he said, smiling widely in the mirror as he drove off.

'Had to come over at a moment's notice,' Paul said. 'My brother's sick.'

'That's bad. I have a brother.' He honked the horn at a bus moving into his path. 'You have dollars?'

'Only English.'

'American is best. But for the lady, I see what we can do.'

When they arrived at Schiphol Airport, he converted the fare from guilders to pounds, asked them to check the calculation against the exchange rate in his 'paper, and charged them only that. Paul gave him a fat tip for his trouble, and they left him singing along to the radio as he pulled out and headed back toward Rotterdam.

They walked into the airport building, Paul wary, checking every face, waiting for police to jump them.

It looked fine: not busy, no sign of heavy police presence. People sat on big couches, wandered around the shops. The diamond shops were doing good business. As they passed one, Mina touched her right ear in an unconscious gesture. He looked at the expensive diamond studs and guessed they were a gift from Charlie, probably bought here. How many years would he need to work to give her such a present?

They went to the KLM desk and Mina asked whether any tickets were booked for Mr and Mrs Quillet. The girl behind the desk could not find them on the computer at first. She typed quickly, a frown creasing her bronze make-up.

Under cover of the muzak, Paul whispered: 'Something's gone wrong.'

Mina spoke calmly to the girl: 'I'm sure we're there. If you just run through it once more.'

More flickering keys, and the screen flashing blocks of colour. The girl smiled: 'Ah, yes,' she said, in her American-accented English. 'It's here. I didn't see it the first time.' Paul smiled back at her as she printed the tickets out. There was nothing to pay. It had been taken care of.

He kept watch for strangers approaching. The expectation of a hand falling on his shoulder was strong. It felt like only a matter of time before someone recognized them and called the cops.

'Come on.' Mina touched his arm and led him away.

'Where we going?' he asked.

'Lima,' she said. 'Peru.'

He stopped dead in the middle of the hall, staring at her.

She lifted her arms helplessly. 'South America.'

The tickets were first-class returns. She smiled at that and said: 'Always first class when the computer's paying.'

There was a long wait for their flight. They spent the hours in the Van Gogh lounge, took their lunch from

241

a buffet groaning with food. Then they sat in the deep armchairs, hiding behind English newspapers, looking for mention of their names.

He said: 'Why South America?'

'He's done work there. I don't know.'

'Why from here, then?'

'If you fly from London, you have to change in the States. I don't think he wants us to risk that. Robersman's centre of operations is there.'

He tapped the shirt pocket where the cassette was.

'I thought you needed health certificates and stuff like that to get in.'

She folded a copy of the *Telegraph*. 'You do. I've got most of mine from the travelling we did last year. We'll have to see if we can bribe you through.'

'Great,' he said. He got up and went to the bar for another drink. Music played, everything was warm and comfortable. Unpleasantness did not get in here. There was good food and fine booze, the far-off sound of 'planes taxiing to the runways. Just a touch of madness in the reproduction Van Goghs on the walls.

He left the drink on the bar and headed for the washrooms. An old woman stood at the door of the Ladies', chattering in German to a little blonde girl. The girl was no more than four years old. She smiled shyly at him. He smiled back. The door to the Gents' opened, someone coughed. He turned to step aside.

The man coming out brushed past, they were face to face for an instant. He mumbled: 'Excuse me,' eyes flicking up before he passed on. It was that fast, that mundane.

But it left something cold behind. He hesitated, following the man with his eyes, watching him return to the lounge. It was hardly conscious thought. He just felt the dead emptiness in the pit of his stomach that had gripped him that night by Grafham Water, when the car stopped, and the driver stared at them from the dark, then drove on.

He shrugged it off. He hadn't seen the face in the car. It was a shadow passing.

When he got back to Mina, he didn't say anything to her about it. He looked around, and the man was sitting alone across the other side of the lounge, reading. He waited for him to look up, to stare at them in an obvious way, but he didn't do it.

Haggard listened to a Brazilian diamond merchant talking a stream of fast Portuguese to his mistress. He watched the lounge, Quillet and the wife in particular, over a copy of the latest Robert Ludlum novel. He wasn't reading the Ludlum. He generally found espionage novels funny. But it seemed a good choice for a man waiting in an airport.

He listened to what the diamond merchant was saying: 'But you have no idea. Really, no idea . . .' and thought about going back to Peru. It was a long time since he had been in South America. He wondered idly what Quillet and the wife wanted there, but didn't let the question bother him. He had considered telling New York where he was going, but knew the Dutch office would eventually report his passing. They would know what was happening soon enough. For the moment, he was happy to be alone.

The flight was called at last. He unzipped his bag and threw the paperback into it. Quillet stood up, offered a hand to the wife, glanced round suspiciously. Quillet had never seen him, but there had been something about their little meeting outside the washroom, something about the way he was trying not to look. Quillet's instincts were good. They had pulled him through so far. Maybe there was a touch of subliminal knowledge in the back of his brain.

He would have to be careful, not be obvious. After all, they were travelling on the same 'plane, he could hardly lose them there.

The stewardess came round as soon as they were in the air. Paul said yes to a Jameson's and water, and watched over Mina's shoulder as the lights of the Netherlands dipped and disappeared into low cloud.

'On our way,' she said.

'Interesting to know what for.'

'We'll find out when we get there.'

'You hope.'

She eased the seat back and held her face under the air blower, eyes closed, hair fluttering around her ears. They had the row of three seats to themselves, could talk quietly without fear of being overheard. 'What day is it?'

'Thursday night,' he said, after thinking a moment.

'I've been running for a week now. It was Saturday when I found you, wasn't it?'

'Yes.'

'It doesn't seem real. Feels like we've been doing this forever, and we'll never stop. Just keep going, flying from one place to another, driving all night every night. And never finding out what the answer is.' She swallowed. 'Never to rest again, never to have time to think. Sounds sort of nice, in a way. If only it wasn't so damn tiring.'

'You've got fifteen hours to sleep now.'

'I never sleep on 'planes.'

He still had no cigarettes. Digging in his pocket by a reflex, the stone met his fingers. He took it out and rolled it in his palm. It was rough and cool, with a light, sandy band running through the grey-black granite.

Mina put her hand on the stone, made a soft, laughing sound.

244

'When I was a girl, I thought that was the most romantic thing I ever heard of. All that rubbish about kids off the boats not being able to swim, having their pockets full of stones so they'd drown quickly if they fell overboard. I used to think it was true.'

'Some of it was,' he said. 'I never learned till I was ten.'

'I thought you were so cool.' She threw the stone up and caught it. 'I thought your pockets were full of them.'

He thought of Dad in the harbour, dying the moment he hit the water. The pathologist at the coroner's inquest said he hadn't drowned. The water was so cold that it stopped his heart like a clock. No need for stones in the pocket.

'What did you think of me?' she said, and he came back from the memory with a jolt.

'How d'you mean?' he said, though he knew what she meant. He leaned closer to her.

'Back then,' she said. Her eyes were closed again, her voice was so low it was difficult to hear it above the dull roar of the engines. Her warmth and her perfume were in his head. He could see tiny lines at the corner of her eyes. 'What did you think?'

He drank a little whiskey. It tingled on his palate like distilled fire.

'I was . . .' He faded. 'You . . .' Her eyes were open again, though she wasn't looking at him at all. The stone rested in her upturned palm. 'I never knew what I had,' he said at last, and it felt like tearing a piece away from himself. 'I treated you like shit. That was how I was then.'

'All those years,' she said. 'You were everything to me from thirteen to twenty-two.'

'I was a bastard,' he said.

245

'I realized that myself in the end. You probably still are. I don't believe in reformed characters.'

'Ten years,' he said.

'All the formative ones. It's hard to shake off.'

He knew that was true. He wanted to touch her again, to be inside her. She reclined in her seat, looking up at the cabin roof, weighing the stone in her hand.

'I will make you brooches,' she murmured, 'and toys for your delight.'

And he thought: I *did* say something more than insults. He had forgotten, but now it came back. The times in the dark, when he had been willing to please her, when she couldn't see his face. He had usually finished off by making a joke of it, but he remembered the way she held him as she listened, how she would ask him to repeat the lines.

'I will make you brooches and toys for your delight,' he repeated, the words coming back easily, with an added weight now that was regret.

'. . . Of bird-song at morning and star-shine at night.
  I will make a palace fit for you and me
  Of green days in forests and blue days at sea.'

She turned her hand over, placing the stone in his palm again, but her fingers stayed there, touching.

'Maybe we've made our peace,' he said.

'Oh no.' She shook her head, and her eyes were shiny. 'This isn't peace yet. I don't know what it is, but it isn't peace.'

He watched over her when she dozed off, and through the night hours as the 'plane nosed west. He read from his pocket Stevenson, remembering more. Remembering the last time he had seen his brother.

Dad's funeral. Mina was there too. He had not seen them since before the marriage. They had come up the night before and stayed in one of the good hotels on the High Street. He knew this because they had been in touch with Sam, and Sam told him. He didn't want to know. He refused to speak on the 'phone, even when Charlie wanted to talk about funeral arrangements and the cost of everything. He told Sam to tell Charlie that it was all taken care of. It wasn't, in fact. He had to get a loan to pay for the coffin.

They put Dad in the ground in a little plot in the Lowestoft town cemetery on a bitter cold January Monday.

When it was over, family and friends retired to an upstairs room of the Anchor to drink the old man on his way. It was a big crowd, so there was no call for him to spend time with Charlie and Mina. They'd stood together at the graveside, but that was it. He hadn't spoken a word to them the whole day.

The room soon filled with smoke and raucous talk. Half the crews and dockers from the port seemed to be there, swapping stories about things 'old Bernard' had done or said. Sam was getting tremendously drunk with Reiny, and their laughter boomed over the clink of glasses and the smell of beer.

He was stuck with Auntie May, seeing to it that she dried her eyes and kept knocking back the port and lemon. He wanted to get out and go back to the ship. At that point he didn't know what was going to happen to her, or his life on her.

He looked round the room. Mina was talking to an old schoolfriend. She and Charlie stuck out from the crowd here like lead crystal in a box of paper cups. They were that much better dressed, better turned out than anyone else. He saw Mina smile. Her dark suit fitted her curves perfectly, her hair gleamed in a short bob that he had never seen before. She had gained a extra sheen of class. She had always had it, but before it was something learned from outside; now it was part of her. It made him feel sick.

She glanced at him, looked away.

He pushed his way through the crush, nodding, saying a few words whenever someone spoke to him, and went down the stairs toward the street. As he reached the bottom, Charlie called:

'Paul, hang on.'

He thought about going on, but that made him the loser. He stopped and looked up the stairs. Charlie paused at the top, his usual smooth self. The good suit, the nice shoes, the air of money and success.

'I think we have to talk,' he said. 'The old man left the boat to both of us.'

Here it comes, he thought. The real kick. He told himself he could see it in Charlie's eyes behind the lenses of his glasses: the quiet, sneering triumph. 'I got out of this hole, I got your girl, and now I'll take the boat away from you. Now who's the clever bastard?' He reached for his cigarettes, lit one and waited.

'You can keep it,' Charlie said. 'I don't want it. I'll sign my share over to you.'

He was surprised, but he wouldn't let big brother see it. 'Thanks a lot,' he said, already thinking that Charlie was doing it to prove what a prince he was.

The sound of talk from the upstairs room washed and receded like the tide on harbour walls.

Charlie said: 'I'm sorry. About the old man.'

'He did what he did.' He blew a cloud of smoke up the stairs.

'We should talk.' Officious now; in-control Charlie. 'There are things we should discuss.'

'No there aren't,' he said.

'Look, I know how you must feel . . .' Charlie trailed away, as if he knew it was a stupid thing to say. The superior manner came back. 'It doesn't do any good.'

'Good enough,' he said, and walked out into the drizzling street.

He prowled up the dim aisles. The man from the airport was there, head back, breathing steadily, a book open on his lap. The airline tag on the holdall at his feet said his name was Haggard.

There were three stops. He only half-caught the names: Caracas, Curaçao, Panama.

Morning finally drew level with them. They breakfasted over the Caribbean, so Mina told him. He looked out at mountains of white cloud and the sea glittering blue far below. As the morning progressed, they swung over a mountainous coastline, and he could see that it was bright and clear there. February was back in England, where the *Provider* lay in the black waters of the harbour.

Then they were over jungle, and the cabin staff served lunch. The captain came over the public address system and told them that in Lima it was 8.30. He backed his watch up five hours or so, and they lunched at breakfast-time. He had never expected to cross the line in a 'plane.

Over coffee, he said: 'You think we can get in?'

'That's what we'll find out when we arrive,' she said. 'We've got passports, we've got through tickets. It's only the health certificate. If we were coming in over the border, they might not even ask to see it, and we could offer them a large wad of cash if they did.'

'You've done this before.'

'I told you. Charlie's worked out here.'

'What sort of place is it? They all sound alike to me.'

'There's an undercurrent all the time. You know: don't take your eyes off your luggage, don't walk in the streets at night, don't mess with the police at

249

the checkpoints. They have checkpoints here the way America has tollbooths.'

She grew more nervous as the 'plane banked and descended. He saw a flat, arid land, mountains far to the east. The other passengers were hardly taking the trouble to look. They were first class, had probably done this often. They were prepared for the change in climate, wearing light, expensive clothes, while he still carried his pea jacket. They weren't excited. Despite the circumstances, he was, just a little. To be flying, to be arriving in a strange country, a strange continent, was a hell of a change. Then he thought of Sam, and the Leman woman, and he didn't feel excited any more. Only apprehensive, the way Mina did.

'If we just look as if we're in command,' she said. 'We're first class passengers, we've got money. We can brazen this out. But you'll have to do most of the talking.'

'Me?'

'They're very hot on *machismo* here. Men are men, and they prove it by being tough and dangerous. Women are strictly to be courted or clobbered. Should suit you.'

The 'plane hit the runway with a thump. People got ready to disembark. Paul looked over his shoulder and saw Mr Haggard watching the airfield scud by.

As he stepped through the cabin door, the heat and light slammed him in the face. He was expecting it, but it still caught him by surprise. It was nine in the morning, and he could have used a pair of sunglasses. He paused on the top step, blinking across the airfield to the terminal buildings.

'Come on,' Mina said, nudging him forward.

They climbed aboard the bus, and it started for the terminal. Mr Haggard sat a good distance away from them, talking to an old man in a white linen suit. Paul kept watching for one sign that he was interested in them, but it did not come. He wanted to ask Mina if she knew him, but she was edgy enough already. She kept wiping her palms on the knees of her grey cords, saying nothing.

The bus drew to a halt. They got off and were ushered through the doors into a large hall. The shade was a thick blanket. Blaring music of a vaguely Spanish kind drifted from speakers somewhere in another part of the building. The walls were covered with big carved reliefs of Incas or Mayans, or whatever sort of folk art it was they had in this country. Men in uniform hung about at the far end of the hall. Snub little sub-machine guns hung from their shoulders.

They joined the queue. There were two men checking passports, both thin, dark and heavily moustached. Their eyes held the same boredom. They stamped and threw passport and other documents back over the desk. With luck, the owner caught them before they skittered to the floor.

Mina took out her passport and opened it. He saw the photograph. It was five years old. There was still something of the girl in the face that looked out. Five years ago she was happily married to Charlie. He supposed she was happily married then.

'Where's yours?' she hissed. He took it out. His picture looked positively callow.

They were getting close to the desks. Beyond them was a wall of glass, people milling around outside, battered taxis waiting in a rank. Bright sunlight, open air. He sweated in his heavy clothes.

A fat German took his documents and wheezed through. Mina was up next. The clerk showed a glimmer of interest when he noticed her. He managed a smile full of irregular yellow teeth, bowed his head and murmured: *'Señora.'*

251

The other one beckoned Paul. He slapped his passport down, assuming a confident expression; but he didn't feel it. Too conscious of Mina tense beside him. Her clerk leafed through the pages, studying the stamps, glanced at her ticket.

Then he raised his index finger. Just that, nothing more. At first Paul didn't register it. He glanced at Mina, saw her face drain of colour.

Two soldiers, both armed, appeared from a doorway. The queue melted back like water. One of the soldiers, bald and bull-necked, laid a hand on his arm. The other stood close to Mina, machine gun loose against his right hip.

The passport clerks spoke in low voices, assuring the rest of the passengers that everything was all right.

The bald one pushed him against the desk, then round it, and motioned both of them toward the door. Mina went first, staring back at him with fear in her eyes.

As he was shoved through the door, he saw Mr Haggard in the crowd. He appeared surprised, maybe even angry.

23

The helicopter lifted away from the airport. Paul sat tight, hanging onto a grab-handle. Mina was next to him. One of the men, the sergeant with the bald brown head and bulging eyes, was up front with the pilot. He kept leaning forward, belly straining against the seat belt, joking with the pilot like a child on his first flight.

Nothing had been said since their arrest. They had been searched, then taken to a small, hot room with a single fan whining in the corner and a picture of some Latin film starlet on the wall. They were left there for a quarter of an hour. Voices went back and forth outside the door, none speaking English. He caught odd words, but he knew little Spanish. Most of the Spaniards he met off the ships talked bad English.

The sergeant returned, ordered them up. They were led out across the tarmac. The helicopter was ready to go. Paul muttered:

'Shit, we must really be in trouble.'

The sergeant grunted, touched his lips with a forefinger.

'What is this?' Paul asked. 'Where're you taking us?'

No reply.

They flew low over industrial outskirts, squat factories plastered with slogans. Then the city: a great hexagonal plaza, a statue of a woman with wings. All very grand, but the traffic-clogged streets leading off the plaza were ugly and raw, as if the cash had run out before the plan could be completed.

He said to himself:

> 'I held the trunk with both my hands,
> And looked abroad on foreign lands.'

Mina clutched the computer in her lap like a child with a security blanket. They had not tried to take it away. She looked scared, still defiant, but younger somehow.

The sergeant bawled something to the pilot, began to shake with laughter.

'*Es alta y delgada*,' he said.

Paul thought about dumping the cassette out of the little window on his left, but the sergeant was keeping an eye on them. Besides, it might come in useful later, if they had to bargain.

The helicopter's shadow fluttered past older, pastel-painted houses, then a river, and low brown hills covered with homes made of cardboard boxes, plastic sheet and corrugated aluminium: miles of them. A big neon sign said something about Inka Cola.

'Where're you taking us?' Mina asked.

'*Quieto*,' the sergeant said.

'I love this fucking country,' Paul muttered.

The city fell behind. They were heading south-east. Sometimes the trees thinned for a moment, and a rooftop would flash by, a yard with chickens and goats scrapping around. There were a couple of metalled roads, then rough trails of dust and rock.

They were in the air for more than an hour. The country got rougher, the forest more dense. The sergeant stopped talking. The smell of his sweat wafted back to them.

They hopped over a rise, dipped into a shallow valley. Mina pointed suddenly. He saw a white house with towers and a red roof. They went over at a few hundred feet, saw the concrete circle of a landing pad behind the house. Two lorries and a jeep were parked out front.

254

A wide, well-kept lawn stretched down to a stream. The pilot set her down. The engine slowed to a tired chop-chopping.

'*Fuera*,' the sergeant said. He had the pistol out of its holster.

They climbed out, the blades still swooping over their heads. A couple more soldiers ran to flank them. They looked about twenty, if that. One tried to grab Mina's arm. Tired of being pushed around, Paul moved before thinking. He swung and pushed him off. The guard's eyes narrowed and the gun snapped up. The sergeant barked an order, the gun lowered again. The sergeant studied Paul for a moment, then turned to Mina and gave a courteous bow of the head.

'*Perdón, Señora. Señor.*' He holstered the pistol and walked away. The guards waved them toward the house.

The house was old. Inside it was dark and cool. Fans creaked overhead, and the marble floor radiated cold. Heavy wooden furniture rested against the walls of a corridor that went the width of the building.

'Lowestoft police never had offices like this,' he said. Mina tried to smile.

They were shown into what looked like a waiting room. It was shuttered, pale light spilling through the slats. A few uncomfortable chairs were ranged round the walls, a big old desk held nothing but a telephone. Behind it was a set of double doors and a map of South America, split horizontally, the pieces mounted side by side. A brass spittoon stood by the desk. The guards gestured them to chairs and took up position outside. The doors closed. They were alone.

Mina put the computer on the floor, folded her arms across her stomach and sat forward until her head was hanging over her knees. Her hair hung down, hiding her face. There was a smear of dust on the back of her neck. He swallowed hard, his throat sore. He wanted to sleep.

'What was he talking about?' he said. 'On the way here?'

She pushed her hair back behind her ear.

'My Spanish isn't that good. Some woman he was with last night. Nothing to do with us.'

He got up and went to the desk, tried the drawers, but they were locked. He went round it to peer at the map.

'What're you doing?' she said.

'Want to see where we are. Got no idea.'

He traced across the continent, found Peru, found Lima. They had travelled mostly south-east in the helicopter. He tried a guess at where they had ended up. The map wasn't that detailed. It just showed green, with a thread of road meandering across it.

She raised her face and looked at him. Weariness made her eyes darker.

'I'm sorry,' she said.

He bobbed down on his haunches before her, took one of her hands.

'Getting you into this,' she said. 'I must've been mad. Should've gone to the police or something before it was too late.'

'They came to us.' He smiled, although he didn't feel like smiling. 'If these boys are the police.'

'Oh, they're what passes for it out here.'

'Which doesn't explain why they brought us so far out. They could've driven us down to the city headquarters.'

Her hand tightened on his. She was almost sick with fear, too tired and worn down to flare up and get angry.

'People disappear out here,' she said. 'They just never come back.'

He pulled her close, forehead to forehead. Her fingers cupped his face.

He kissed her lips. They were dry.

The door opened. The guards entered, followed by the sergeant. He had changed his shirt. The guards marched across and flanked the double doors. The sergeant beckoned with a flexing of his fingers. 'Up,' he said. 'Up.'

Paul stood. Mina got up slowly. He thought what a sight they must make, compared to the starched and pressed guards and the sergeant in fresh clothes and aftershave. They were dirty, weary, at the end of their rope.

The sergeant beckoned again. Mina made to bring the computer, but he shook his head. She took Paul's hand. He felt good only because of that. Whatever was coming, they were facing it together.

The sergeant led them to the door, gave a nod to the guards. The doors were thrown open. They passed through into a larger office, where the light was stronger.

'Hello, Mina,' Charlie said. He moved his head slightly. 'Hello, Parrot.'

24

He stood behind an ornate desk by the window, the sun behind him. It was like opening the door and finding a cabin in the *Provider* on the other side.

Mina let go of his hand, but Charlie had already noticed. He gazed at her through his Lennon glasses in a disconnected way. There were flecks of grey in his fair hair, lines in the tanned face. He looked scrawny, as if he'd been eating badly, sleeping worse.

The sergeant was still at Paul's shoulder, but the guards were outside.

'It's all right, Picchu,' Charlie said. 'It's them.'

The sergeant nodded, glancing at Paul. 'You said there was no resemblance. I see resemblance.'

Mina was ready to drop. Charlie seemed to remember his manners suddenly. 'Look, come and sit down, both of you. Do you want a drink? Picchu, get them to bring some tea, will you?'

'What the hell is this?' Paul growled. 'Tea, cakes, fucking croquet on the lawn.'

'Please,' Charlie said. 'Sit down. You've had a long journey.'

'You sit down.' He stepped forward, and the sergeant moved with him. 'Who's this comedian, anyway?'

Charlie said: 'Paul, this is Sergeant Manuel Carvalho. Picchu, my brother, Paul.'

He had turned it into a formal moment. It was so ridiculous that Paul found himself shaking the sergeant by the hand, almost returning his slight bow.

'You have some adventures,' the sergeant said.

'Gets wilder all the time.'

'Now it's over.'

Mina looked up. 'Are we safe here?'

The sergeant took Mina's hand and pressed it to his lips. 'As safe as myself, *Señora*.' He seemed to find the notion amusing.

'What is this place?' she said.

Charlie hid behind the distorting glass of his spectacles.

'It belongs to General Pereiro.'

'Pereiro?' she said. 'Not Benjamin?'

He nodded. 'When you met him he was a colonel, but he's a general now. This is his 'country retreat'. A safe place he uses when times're troubled.'

'Times are always troubled,' the sergeant said.

'Who's Pereiro?' Paul asked.

'He's a very powerful man,' Charlie said, with a trace of annoyance at having to explain. 'At the moment, instead of the usual coups and revolutions, this country's having another stab at democratically elected government. It's mainly his doing.'

'The General has great faith in democracy.' The sergeant smiled. 'Despite all the evidence to the contrary.'

'When I managed to get here, I asked him for . . . sanctuary. He's probably the reason I'm still alive.'

'But what's it all about?' Mina said. 'Why did you have to run, what started it in the first place?'

Charlie looked as if he were trying to make order from chaos in his mind. 'Long story.'

A boy brought tea. The sergeant did the honours. The four of them sat in armchairs round a low table; Paul and Mina on one side, Charlie and the sergeant on the other.

'Perhaps something stronger, *Señor*?' he asked, as he handed Paul a cup.

'Tea's fine,' he said, and felt how stupid it was, how

259

civilized. All the way to South America so they could sit and drink tea like a bunch of chimps. At one point, Charlie said: 'Have any trouble getting the 'plane?' As if they were tourists on a joyride.

Paul shook his head.

'That's good.'

'Yeah. Great.'

Charlie would not look him in the eye. He took off his glasses and studied the lenses carefully.

'I have to apologize, first, for the way you were treated when you arrived. It was the only way we could be safe.'

'You knew we were coming,' Mina said, almost petulantly.

'We knew *someone* was coming,' the sergeant said. 'If it was you, then we had to get you out of sight quickly. If it was someone else pretending to be you, we needed Señor Quillet to see you and be sure. The best way was to have you arrested immediately on touchdown and brought here. I hope we were not too . . . barbaric.'

'Only scared the shit out of us,' Paul said.

'I was watching from the house when you landed,' Charlie said. 'Then I made sure with the closed circuit camera in the anteroom.'

So you were watching us in there, Paul thought. He stared at Charlie, but his brother was breathing on his glasses, polishing them. He said:

'I'm glad you made it. Both of you.'

'It's a real family reunion.'

'Yes.' It sounded like "No". 'Did you bring the tape?'

'It'll never make *Top of the Pops.*'

'May I have it, please?'

'What if I say no until we get an explanation?'

Charlie's jaw worked. He was trying to keep control. 'Don't be stupid, Paul.'

He got angry. Just like the old days. 'Don't "stupid" me. I should've laid you out when we walked in. You've been sitting here on your arse while your wife got kidnapped, cut, shot at and chased all over the fucking place. Sam's dead because of this.'

'Sam?' He was confused.

'They sank the *Provider*,' Mina said.

Charlie touched his brow. 'I didn't know.'

'Didn't your computer tell you?' Paul said.

It caught him off-guard. Up to now, he'd just looked vaguely embarrassed, like a man who'd walked into the wrong room and wanted to keep his dignity and get out. But this knocked him back.

'How did it happen?'

'I sent him a copy of your precious tape.'

'They didn't get it.' Safe ground again. 'It would've showed up.'

'They killed him. That didn't show up. Neither did Hallford Castle.'

For the first time, Charlie looked straight at him. Pain flickered in his eyes. Once there would have been a bitter satisfaction in causing it.

'Paul, please. The tape is vital.'

He glanced at Mina. She urged him with her eyes to do it. He reached into his shirt pocket and took the tape out, tossed it across. Charlie almost fumbled it, but the way he held it, and made sure it was the one, the way he said: 'Thank you,' showed how serious he was.

'So. Explanations,' Paul said.

'I can't now. We have to fly out of here again before dark. Mina, are all your jabs up to date?'

'Except the yellow fever and cholera.'

'There's a doctor here who'll give you injections and anti-malaria pills. You're supposed to have them in advance, but it'll have to do.'

'Where're we going?'

261

Picchu showed him the watch on his hairy forearm and said something in Spanish. Charlie got up.

'I have to talk to someone. I'll tell you everything on the way. Trust me, all right?'

'Trust you, you bastard?' Paul said.

Charlie turned back, angry and shaking. 'For Christ's sake, will you understand? It's not about me or you. It's not just us. It's millions.'

The bedroom was grand like the rest of the house. All the furniture old and ugly in a heavy, European way. Showing him round, the sergeant said:

'You should sleep a little. You have time.'

'The pleasant land of counterpane.'   ·

'Pardon me?'

'Something my father used to say.'

'Ah.' The sergeant hung about at the door. He smoothed his big belly with his hands, like a man stroking a cat. 'The *Señora* will come soon.'

Paul opened his bag and checked the contents.

'She is a beautiful lady.' The sergeant was watching him. He did not seem like a sergeant in any army. He was too clever, too sly. '*Hermosa*,' he said.

Paul got bored of being studied. 'What do they call you?'

'Picchu,' the sergeant said. 'It's not my name, only what they call me. Officially, I am Manuel Candido Carvalho, Sergeant in the National Guard, seconded to the special unit responsible for the protection of the General.' He paused, smiled with his white teeth. 'But Picchu will do.'

'You're not much like a soldier.'

Picchu's chest expanded with pride. 'I have an education. My father was an American. He paid. I was a schoolteacher. Then I met the General, and begged him to allow me to join his guard. He's the only man in the army who cares about the people.'

'Known my brother long?'

'I was in charge of him when he came to make the computers work. We spent time together then; much gin, much talk. I never met the *Señora* before. She came later, I was always elsewhere.'

'Know what he's doing here?'

'I know nothing of computers. The General says he is to be guarded, that is all I need to know.' He took a cigar from his pocket and rolled it in his hand. 'How are you called?'

'Paul.'

'Your brother, when you met, he said "Parrot".'

'It's a nickname.'

'Ah.'

'My father used to call me Polly. Polly Parrot.'

Picchu narrowed his eyes and said: 'Ah,' again. He clearly thought there was madness here somewhere.

Paul threw his Walkman and the couple of tapes he had left on the bed.

'She will come soon,' Picchu said. 'You should sleep.'

But he did not sleep. Once he was alone, he slid back the shutters and gazed out over the lawn. Jungle lapped up to the edge of the clearing where the house stood. Its shadows were deep and green. A couple of guards peered up at him in a bored way. He tried to think about the fact that he was looking at South America, but it wouldn't focus. The heat pushed against him, but there was one thing on his mind.

When he had left the office, Mina stayed. As the sergeant paused to speak with one of the guards, he could see her through the half-closed door. Charlie was facing her. They weren't saying anything.

He went next door. Her case was on the bed. He

263

waited for the tap of her footsteps in the tiled corridor. It was as if the house had emptied, leaving him alone.

She's with her husband, he told himself. With good old Charles, the king of the computers. They're downstairs now, having their reunion. That's what married people do when they've been separated. They reunite.

He thought of his brother's long, expressionless face. The eyes looking out of the tight skin with their certainty of being right. Charlie who used to watch him as if from a distance. Charlie the thinker.

He thought about Mina in his arms, and that made it worse. What were they saying to each other?

He took a shower, let the water run hot then icy cold. The water drummed out other sound, so he was not waiting for her then, but the memories wouldn't go. He saw the knife man in the house by the lake go down, hair blazing; the cowboy pitching slowly from the big dipper track; the woman suddenly snapping back, turning and swinging. And Sam saying: 'You'll be back, won't you?' And Mina straining against him as he entered her, the way she used to, the way she always had.

As he dried off, there was a knock at the door. Picchu was there with a pile of clothes.

'These will fit you,' he said, dumping them on the bed. 'Uniform issue. You'll look like one of us.'

'That's a good idea?'

Picchu snorted. 'There are no rebels in these parts. The radio says so, so it must be true.'

He took the clothes.

'We get you good boots in a little.'

'How about a gun?'

'To get a gun, you must enlist.'

'I'll think about it.'

'Good. We make you the General's personal bodyguard.'

264

'Dangerous job?'

'No. All the General's bodyguards retire with full disability pension – if they live so long.' Picchu smiled again. 'You come down later. The doctor has to fix you.'

'Okay.'

Alone again, he lay down on the bed and tried not to think. It was like trying not to breathe.

He heard her footsteps at last. They came up the corridor, paused next door. He thought: That's it. All over. Things are back as they should be.

Then she knocked. He said: 'Come in,' but stayed on the bed. She opened the door and looked round the room.

'Nice,' she said.

'We're special guests.'

She sat on the edge of the bed. He blinked at her.

'How is he?'

'You could've asked him yourself.'

'I forgot. Other things on my mind.'

'He's your brother.'

'We haven't had much to say to each other for years. What makes you think we'll start now? Especially now.'

She fingered the buttons of her blouse. 'I'll be so glad to get clean.'

'Better hurry. That Picchu bloke said we haven't got long.'

She was waiting for him to say something. He wondered what she would prefer.

'You've gone back in your shell,' she said. 'You were different, now you're the same again.'

'What've you been talking about?' What he meant was, did he touch you, did he hold you?

'I don't remember. He was uncomfortable, so was I. He's obsessed with what he's doing.'

'Big surprise.'

She twisted one of the buttons. 'He knows.'

'About what?'

'About us. That I found out about Penny Leman.'

'You told him?'

'He just knows.'

And what did you say? he thought. She was close enough to touch, but he didn't touch her.

Looking at the shutters beyond him, she said: 'It's not over yet.'

'Maybe it is. Got the army on our side now. The odds're better.'

Picchu coughed. Mina got up as if they'd been caught in bed, not on it.

'It's time soon for the injections,' he said. His eyes had the amused gleam. 'There is not much time.'

Mina headed for her room. Picchu stood to one side to let her pass. He watched her appreciatively.

'Any chance of that drink?' Paul said.

'It can be arranged, if the doctor says it is all right before your injections.'

'Then what?'

'Then the helicopter again. Only this time I fly you.'

25

The journey was more complicated than Picchu had implied. The four of them filed out to the helicopter and strapped themselves in. Again there was the moment of nausea as the ground fell away. But they were hardly in the air two minutes before the jungle gave way to a clearing and an airstrip. A 'plane waited, guarded by more soldiers, a Lear jet.

'All change here,' Charlie said, as they dropped down. 'We're going over the mountains.'

'Anyway, we go in comfort,' Picchu said.

They were out of the helicopter, the wind from the blades beating at them, and crossing the stony ground before Paul had a chance to take it all in. He saw the guards with their guns watching the hills, felt waves of heat from the jet's engines as it warmed up. Then they were into the 'plane, and the cabin door was closed on them. Air conditioning chilled the skin, and the roar of the engines was cut to a dull hiss.

'Courtesy of the General?' Mina said, rubbing a shoe on the carpeted floor.

'He would not have you travel in a troop transport,' Picchu said, going forward to speak with the pilot.

There was little time for talk. They took their seats immediately, and a moment later the 'plane was moving up the strip.

'We'll be transferring again on the other side,' Charlie said, as the trees blurred and they lifted off.

'You really know how to hide out, don't you?' Paul said.

'No point doing it any other way.'

They climbed steeply for a time. When they levelled off the jungle was model-scale beneath them, folds of green hills, mountains blue in the distance. The 'plane turned east. Picchu came back from the cockpit as they released their seat belts, nodding to Charlie.

The surroundings were luxurious. Picchu saw to it that they each had a drink from the well-stocked refrigerator, then Charlie breathed on his glasses, cleaning them with a handkerchief, and said:

'This is what happened:

'I started doing work for Robersman eight years ago. Mina must've told you that Robersman is big. It makes Time-Warner look modest. It's one of those companies that owns hundreds of others. Go into a supermarket, and you see all kinds of brand names on the shelves, but half of them are actually owned by Robersman. They're involved with everything from satellite television to pharmaceuticals, weapons technology to restaurant chains. At first I was employed to get all these different arms organized, so they could summon up their whole operation on one screen.'

'And to fix any little dirty tricks they wanted,' Mina said.

He paused for a moment, then his voice came again, flat and steady. 'If you don't mind, we can go into the ethics of my career later. If you want to be sniffy, my entire reputation's based on a development that, strictly speaking, is illegal. I invented "Sneaker" programs.

'You see, every business, every university, every airforce base or army camp has a computer now. All the information that used to be kept on paper in filing cabinets is on a disc or a tape or a cartridge somewhere. And a lot of them are hooked into telephone lines or radio networks. Imagine the entire world criss-crossed with wires connecting everyone to everyone else. That's how it is now. "Sneaker" programs alight on any point in the web, break into the files, get the information you want, then exit without ever being noticed. Every year it gets harder, but so far I've kept ahead of the competition.'

'Illegal,' Mina said.

'I agree. But that's how it is. Big business wants to know what the competition's up to, governments want information on their enemies and friends. Not to mention the fact that, to protect yourself against hackers, you need to use the same methods they do. A couple of years ago, I was called in to track down some people who got into the CERN nuclear accelerator computers in Geneva. They'd messed up the software controlling a sub-atomic particle beam. That's no joke. Not long ago a terrorist gang tried to fix it so the control systems at one of Robersman's chemical plants in India went out of whack. If they'd succeeded, the explosion would've made Bhopal look like a slip-up with a couple of test tubes.

'Companies pay millions every year to blackmailers who threaten to activate self-destruct programs in their records. A couple of people in France died because some moron tampered with a hospital's intensive care computer. What I've done most of my career is use the methods of a hacker to stop them. It's no worse than a policeman using illegal methods to get an arrest.'

'And you think that's all right?'

He turned in his seat to look at her. 'I used to. When you spend most of your time in front of a screen, locked in an office far away from the things you're affecting, it's hard to connect. The interesting thing is seeing whether you can make something work.

'If I'd refused to do it, I'd be the only one who did. Computers are a grey area. Hardly anyone thinks fast enough to keep ahead of the developments. What's illegal today is just another trick tomorrow.' He stared hard at her. 'Anyway, it's what paid for our life these past ten years, and I didn't hear you complain so much at the beginning.'

She gazed sullenly at him, but he turned away before she could open her mouth.

'And it also made "Weatherspy" possible,' he said.

'Five years ago, it was suggested that I might like to head a team looking into environmental problems. It began as an attempt to accurately predict long-term changes caused by all the things we're doing to the planet: burning the rain forests, depleting the ozone layer – all the things that've since become fashionable. Robersman's motive was that they needed long-term predictions to make long-term plans. It was a large brief, but they told us they had co-finance from several European governments, and they brought a good team together.'

Paul glanced out of the window as the 'plane hit turbulence. They were over mountains now. They glinted far below, shadowed here and there by clouds. In some of the valleys earlier on, bare fields and little knots of houses had shown some kind of tenacity. Now there was only rock and snow.

'It didn't matter to me that Robersman was involved,' Charlie said. 'All I knew was we had been given the funds and the time to work on an important idea.

'We stuck pretty close to the lines we'd been given for a while, but then something occurred to me. It started the last time we were over here. Remember, Mina, we were in Mexico on the way back to the States when *El Chichón* erupted again? It made me think about disasters; not the slow ones we were researching, but the violent kind. 'Quakes, volcanoes, *Tsunamis*–'

'*Tsunamis*?' Paul asked.

'The Japanese term for what's incorrectly known as a tidal wave.' The old impatience in his voice. 'I'd done some work at university on a friend's geology degree. He specialized in volcanology. I helped him organize some figures, and found out that they can plant all kinds of gear on a volcano to help them spot when it's going to blow. Tiltmeters to give readings on the shape of the earth, gravimeters, that sort of thing. Sometimes there're warnings; in Mexico there wasn't.

'It meshed with some points that Penny had been pushing all along; thinking about the planet as a "patient". She'd been playing with the idea for years. If you put a human being through all the medical tests they can do now, you can spot not only the diseases and problems he *has*, but also things that're *waiting* to happen. Like a man with a heart condition; you take his blood pressure and his cholesterol level, and that gives you a pretty good idea he's in danger.'

Paul heard Picchu snort. Maybe the sergeant was having as much trouble keeping up with this line of thought as he was.

'Obviously, it's a lot more complicated than that,' Charlie said, 'but, basically, it's an acupuncturist's view of the world. Or like the Gaia theories. Everything connected, nothing independent. A symptom in one place can be a sign of trouble in another. I tried to look at the world in the same way. After all, these places may be separated by thousands of miles, but they're all lying on top of the same core, and most of the danger spots, the fault lines and the volcanoes, are connected. The whole Pacific perimeter's one big fracture. Central Asia's the same.

'The first thing was to find out how much environmental data was available. You wouldn't believe it. Millions of bytes of information being churned out every day. Seismological readings, the Pacific Tsunami

Warning System, weather satellites, volcano research, all manner of items that don't usually get collated.

'They've known for a long time that there can be other warning signs when a natural disaster occurs. Things not easily noticeable: atmospheric waves; ionospheric variations in reflected radio signals; changes in magnetic fields; lunar behaviour; sound waves below the level of human hearing. Animals in an earthquake area often behave in odd ways just before the shock. Birds go quiet, dogs start howling for no apparent reason.

'The whole thing boiled down to a simple, but excruciatingly difficult, aim; to gather all of this information together – anything that might possibly relate, from anywhere – and work out what it might mean.'

'That's "Weatherspy"?' Paul said.

Charlie nodded. 'It's a word I found in Johnson's dictionary. It meant a star-gazer, an astrologer. Or someone who foretells the weather. I thought it was suitable.'

'No one can tell the future.'

'Look at your watch. I can tell you, with a fair degree of accuracy, that in ten minutes, the hands will be pointing to a certain position.'

'It's just a watch.'

'And a planet's just a planet. The only difference is, there's a great deal more you need to know.'

'And you made it work?' Mina said.

'We pitched the idea to Robersman in terms they'd understand. They have investments all over the Third World, which is where a lot of these things occur. They could see the advantage, in terms of saving plant and people, of having early warning of a disaster. We also mentioned what such a gift to the world would do for their public relations.

'They seemed to swallow it.'

* * *

The pilot's voice came from a speaker in the ceiling. Picchu cocked his head to listen.

'We arrive soon,' he said.

They finished the drinks and fastened themselves in again. For some minutes, they had been descending the other side of the mountains. Greenery had been starting to show like a threadbare carpet on the bare earth. Now the farms reappeared and roads were to be seen twisting through the bottoms of valleys.

They landed at another airstrip in the middle of a flat, tree-covered valley. The only difference was that this one was attached to a sizeable military camp. Paul saw troop transports and cargo 'planes, lorries and armoured vehicles, the roofs of the barracks, as they swung down to the strip. Then the wheels touched with a thump, and the 'plane shuddered as the engines switched to reverse.

There was some kind of official welcome this time. An officer in a braided cap with decorations on his chest stood beside a staff car and saluted as Picchu went down the steps. A guard of four tired-looking men with the usual machine guns stood to attention. Picchu frowned and stayed close to Charlie as the officer jabbered importantly and escorted them to another helicopter, this one a military machine, dark green, with the mountings for a gun.

'You all right?' Paul asked Mina, as the soldiers followed her with their eyes.

'Getting sick of flying,' she said.

The helicopter was ready to go. Picchu checked it over before he took command. He spoke to the ground engineer, studied the maintenance record, finally signed with a flourish, and waved Charlie and the rest of them aboard. The officer saluted again, receiving a perfunctory reply from Picchu, and bawled to his men to back off.

Picchu took the controls. Paul held his breath. He

still wasn't sure how he felt about this kind of travel. The rotors screamed faster, and the helicopter went weightless again. The officer and his men shrank.

Paul closed his eyes for a moment, until the sensation of falling eased, then looked around. Mina was beside him, Charlie up front with Picchu. They all had radio headsets, which Charlie had asked them to put on. He could hear the others breathing through the static and the row of the blades. They gained height and the country revealed itself in the lowering sun. Behind them, the mountains were already receding into gathering mist, cutting out the sun and standing like frozen grey waves under the fading light. They flew south-east again, and Charlie told them the rest.

'We went ahead.' His voice was oddly close and intimate in the headphones. 'The problems were massive. For a start, a good deal of the information was classified. A lot you can get by switching on any desk computer and dialling the right numbers. But newspapers don't like their files being read and some governments guard even their weather satellite data, because they're doing a lot more than just checking the weather. I had to write a lot of new "Sneaker" programs. Russia was hard, but a lot of their stuff is in free exchange with western scientists. Some of the dictatorships here were easy because the equipment and the money behind it was American or European: some of it I installed myself. Britain's never easy, of course; everything's secret there. But what I couldn't handle, someone else in the team could.' He paused, and Paul thought he heard a break in his voice.

'Late last year, we were getting close. We were too late for the San Francisco 'quake, but we had everything on the Armenian landslide except the location. We knew something was going to happen, but we didn't find out where in time. However, it helped us with the next one, the one that came just after, in Tajikistan.

'We were so close to getting it, Penny thought we should give out what we had so someone else might make the connections and save some lives. But they kept saying we couldn't release half a story. At best it'd lead to panic over nothing, at worst, it'd discredit the "Weatherspy" program before it'd even begun. In China in the mid-'seventies, someone predicted one 'quake accurately, but got the next one wrong. The entire population of Peking sat in the streets for three days until they admitted it wasn't going to happen. An American scientist nearly ruined the Peruvian tourist industry by predicting a major disaster here in 1981.'

Picchu turned his head so they saw the gleam of his teeth. Everything seemed to amuse him.

Charlie continued: '"You say it's only a small tremor," they said, "very little possibility of casualties. Why not see whether you're right first?"

'So we kept it to ourselves. And six thousand people were killed in that Russian province because we got the time and the place right, but the magnitude wrong.'

Even through the headset, Paul could hear the anger in Charlie's voice; anger with himself.

'After that, we were desperate to go public. But the order came down from on high. And suddenly we were of great interest to people we'd never heard of.

'The others got worried or began to act strangely. Minnock, for example, and Anna Hilding. Up to a point, they'd been as enthusiastic as we were about publishing the work. Now they were arguing to keep it under wraps until we'd worked the bugs out. We quickly found ourselves in a minority.

'I was buried up to my neck in the work, but Penny never had much love for Robersman. She recommended making secret copies of everything. I did it on an Amstrad machine that wasn't connected to the 'phone lines, on cassettes too, like the one you brought. Penny said she was being watched. I was naive enough then to think she had an exaggerated sense of our importance.

'Then we predicted Santo Caraz.'

Paul had heard the name. For a moment he couldn't think where. Then it came to him from a dozen news reports and pictures: the town that had been buried under a mudslide back in January.

'The program worked it out before Christmas,' Charlie said. His voice was getting raw. 'Anyone doing normal seismological research couldn't have picked it up. There were no warning tremors. That only happens when a fault line slips gradually. This one was locked, so nothing obvious happened until the big one.

'Everything came together just as we'd designed it to. The thing that clinched it was a new satellite the Russians put up to monitor infra-red last September. Probably the most sensitive measuring device of its kind. It detects ground temperature changes in fractions of degrees, even at the sea bed. That was what we got. A rise in the temperature of the eastern Pacific fault lines off Peru. With all the other information "Weatherspy" had, it concluded that a major disturbance was set for late January. I contacted Robersman and insisted we give the information to the authorities.

'That was when the trap really started to close.'

Picchu laughed shortly again, and Charlie stared malevolently at him. 'Think it's funny, Picchu?'

'It's funny you're surprised.'

Charlie took off his glasses, polished them needlessly. 'It wasn't strong-arm tactics, nothing so obvious. They asked for copies of everything we had. They said that everything should be brought under one roof.

They wanted the entire project shifted to the States. The others had already agreed, they said, it was just up to us to make up our minds. We asked when the news would be made public. They said, let's look at the figures first. There's time.

'Next day, Penny was seen by a couple of men purporting to be from MI6, who informed her that the project was now under a "D" notice. I got the same a day later. The rationale behind it was that we now had an awesomely powerful weapon for good or evil in our hands, and it must be protected.

'The mechanical grind of the work was being done in a government computer centre in Cambridgeshire. I'd put anti-tamper devices in, but all of a sudden there'd been a rash of attempts to hack into the system. The security boys said it was kids wanting to play nuclear war, or terrorists.

'Christmas came and went. We were kicking our heels in a kind of limbo. But I knew that you can't evacuate entire towns in a few days.

'Then they finally agreed to go public, but they were going to do it quietly. They had business and political contacts in South America, they could talk to the right people. The main objective, apart from saving lives, was not to cause panic. That would be worse than doing nothing.'

You innocent clod, Paul thought. It was the one thing his brother might usefully have learned from him: never assume anyone's motives are pure. Everyone's out to fuck everyone else.

'My God, I was so trusting. Even when I knew, *knew* in my guts that it was all a lie, I kept hoping. This was my business. I thought I could deal with these people.

'Penny never believed it, though . . . ' He choked. Mina hesitated a moment, then reached forward and put her hand on his shoulder. He seemed to draw strength from it. Paul glanced away. The sun was on the edge of a distant mountain. It slipped abruptly from sight, and the shadow was cold as they flew on.

'All this while, she'd been putting together a dossier on Robersman. Of course, I'd done some checking myself, but never the sort of depth she went into. Her method was simple. She used "Sneaker" programs.

'Not pretty. Very ugly, in fact. No worse than a lot of major companies, but it was still a shock. I was that bloody stupid, or arrogant. There were dirty relationships with other companies, links with all kinds of unsavoury governments, organized crime. Once it reached a certain point, it was impossible even for our programs to sort out the threads. There's no separating them. There're senators and congressmen in Washington, MPs in the European Parliament, Government ministers in Japan, who do whatever Robersman tells them. It's just like all those conspiracy theories we used to get worked up about at college; the whole thing's a big dirty mess, crooked all the way through.'

A flock of white birds exploded from the tree tops far below. The helicopter wound between high, jungle-covered peaks.

'She found other things; the people they use to remove inconveniences that can't be got rid of legally; company employees with strange job titles; arms sales. They were busy getting lost in the morass, but they told us one thing for certain: a lot of activity was going on around us.

'It's a frightening thing to realize there's a gun pointed at your head.

'They were holding off only because they assumed we were a pair of boffins with no practical grasp of the situation. That was the only thing that gave us

278

a chance. That and the fact that they didn't want a word of "Weatherspy" to get out.

'You see, some clever bastard had realized that "Weatherspy" is a wonderful method of keeping the Third World in its place. A lot of dirty minds in the West know that we're on the decline, that eventually, we'll fall like every empire's fallen, and then it'll be the turn of Africa, or South America, or India. But most of the earthquakes, the volcanoes, the tidal waves, that take place are in what we call the Third World, and they cause more loss of life, more damage there, because there's no money, no organization to palliate the circumstances. California's littered with seismological equipment, Peru isn't. Robersman saw how advantageous it would be for their investments to keep such knowledge to themselves. They could get their plant and people out, knowing that any competition – especially competition from indigenous peoples trying to pull themselves up and take possession of their own country – would be ruined. The government of some country you disapprove of opens a mine in competition with the one you founded? No worry, the mine's going to be destroyed by a 7.7 earthquake in six months' time. You can make your plans accordingly.

'The possibilities are endless, and they'd seen it, while we were busy thinking about the good we were going to do.

'We had to get out. But first we had to erase "Weatherspy". I'd distributed my own copies in odd places, one at a time, so they wouldn't be noticed. A few in my office at the university, some more in the boot of the car, and the "Rosie" tape in the pub. I knew they'd have people trying to break the locks I put on the main program, and once they did it, that was it. They'd made access increasingly difficult. We couldn't get in and physically destroy the place. It had

279

to be done through the keyboard. And that was hard, because I designed the security features. I'd made them so complex and difficult to break that even I had trouble worming my way in. And it all had to be timed to a nicety, because if we dumped the program before we got away, they'd be down on us like a ton of bricks.

'We finally broke in on the Saturday before the earthquake, working together, me in Cambridge, Penny in North Wales. We accessed the original command program and planted "bombs" all over the place. Then we ran for it.

'So you see why I couldn't tell anyone what was happening, just had to go, using the computer to cover my tracks.

'I thought I had everything, but I forgot the "Rosie" tape because they were already on my tail. I had to leave it and hope Penny could fill in the gaps.'

'You were going to meet up?' Mina said.

He didn't look round. 'Yes.'

'So I was called in to help as second choice.'

'Penny was there when I needed someone,' he said. 'You weren't.'

Paul saw her flinch.

'I made it to Amsterdam with no trouble. No one looked twice at my passport, and the airline records were erased by the time I stepped aboard the 'plane. But Penny didn't make it. We were supposed to take the same flight. Looks as if she never got out of England.' He stopped again.

Picchu pointed down. Paul looked over his shoulder. Below them, at the summit of a green mountain was a great white dome. In the darkening evening, in the deep, jungled valleys and thrusts of rock, it was the only building, the only sign of man.

'*El observatorio*,' Picchu yelled.

There was a landing pad on a plateau beside the

dome, a square outbuilding, and a road that dropped steeply away down the mountain and disappeared in the trees. Soldiers appeared, guns tracking the helicopter as it circled. Picchu swooped low over them, waving, and the guns lowered. He took her down, setting her on the pad facing east. Only the summits of the distant skyline caught sunlight now. Picchu switched off the engine. A deep silence smothered the last creaks of the rotors. A few bird cries came up from the jungle.

The soldiers came forward. They all wanted to help Mina, behaved with a gallantry born of being too long away from women. All were thin and deeply tanned, their teeth bad, eyes bright. Someone took Paul's bag. He removed the headset and climbed out, numbed by noise and vibration, shivering as the cold hit him.

'The Mount Arequipa Observatory,' Picchu announced, drolly. 'The pride of Peru's astronomical community.'

Charlie was dusting himself down, standing awkwardly beside Mina. 'Let's go in.'

Paul shouldered his bag. The observatory rose like a giant eggshell against the sky. Stars were pricking out of the blue, brighter than he had ever seen them. It was difficult to catch his breath, he felt a little dizzy.

'The problem with running was that I couldn't just run,' Charlie said. 'I had to end up somewhere I could get access to a mainframe big enough to take "Weatherspy". Benjamin was the only man I knew who'd believe me, and had the power to help.'

They entered the outbuilding, passed down a corridor into living quarters. There was a main area where the soldiers were billeted, then a couple of small rooms with camp beds.

'Mina, you'll be sleeping in the first room. Paul can

281

share with me and Picchu.' He was too offhand for it to sound natural.

Paul glanced at Mina. Her face showed nothing but a fierce concentration on letting nothing show.

They left the bags and the computer. Charlie was already heading down the concrete corridor toward a locked steel door.

'This place was built by a Spanish astronomer called Cabrera in the early years of the century. Pure science, paid for out of the fish meal fortune his family made here in the late eighteen-nineties. Now it's also a listening post, established by the Peruvian government with financial and technological assistance from the US. The Peruvians get to keep an eye on the Bolivians, and the American military has a window on the unsteadier regimes in this part of the continent. That's how I know of it; I installed the spy programs. The General brought me in to do several things the Pentagon wasn't supposed to know about. But the Pentagon also asked me to do several things the Peruvians didn't know about. So it all balanced up. Although there's a computer somewhere in the States that reads everything this system does, I also know how to feed it false data. It's Benjamin's pet project. Over the years, he's been able to get the whole place restored and updated using government money.'

'Thought he was a good guy,' Paul said.

'That's a relative term down here,' Charlie said, digging keys out of his pocket. 'But he's better than most of the butchers who pass for authority in this continent. The American Government doesn't like him because he has rather left-wing ideas for a military man. He leads a very precarious life. But he's hiding me here, so, for the moment, he *is* a good guy.' He slotted a heavy key into a lock. Mechanisms

282

buzzed inside. He hauled it back using all his weight. Paul lent a hand when it scraped on the floor at the last.

They stepped through into the main building. Charlie hit the lights. The dome flared white and beautiful, echoing their footsteps. Somewhere off to the left, machines were running. A great telescope slanted up toward the roof. There was much brass and polished wood.

'It has everything,' Charlie said, patting the telescope as he passed. 'Satellite equipment, landlines, everything "Weatherspy" needs.'

Round the corner beyond a wrought-iron staircase leading up to the roof, the machines making all the noise were revealed. Charlie swept his hand toward them with a half-flourish.

'"Weatherspy".'

Paul was obscurely disappointed. He had expected something from a science fiction film. Lots of flashing lights and spinning tape reels; little white-coated figures bustling from screen to screen, writing on clipboards; reams of paper spilling from chattering printers. There was none of that.

There were three wardrobe-sized metal cabinets fixed to the wall side by side. A single red LED burned in the top right-hand corner of each. Next to them were four work stations, each with a screen, keyboard and printer. One of the screens flickered unsteadily as images flicked by too fast for the eye to make them out. He saw what he thought were maps, pieces of a coastline. Another screen was scrolling through an apparently endless document.

No one was in attendance. The machines worked alone.

Charlie went over to the far work station and hit some keys. The screen flashed red, then green, a symbol

283

came up. Charlie typed, and the screen lit with a mass of data.

'It's a lot harder to do from here. We haven't the easy access to government and military files – not to mention the fact that we have to be a lot more careful. They know I'm up to something, so they're trying to keep her out, and every time she gets in, we run the risk of them tracking us back here. The tape you brought will help to fill the gaps.' He put the cassette into a player by the work station.

'But why do you need to run the program?' Mina said. 'The earthquake in Santo Caraz is over. You can't stop it now.'

'Two reasons,' Charlie said, as the cassette ran and the screen above it showed a number climbing from thirty to forty. 'The first is that the only way we'll get out of this alive is to broadcast something so important, so definite, that Robersman can't cover it up. The second is more urgent. When Penny and I had to pack up and run, the program was getting ready to tell us about another disaster. One that'll be worse than what happened in Santo Caraz. Much worse.'

Picchu came in, knocking as if he were entering a bedroom.

'*Excusa*, I've been talking on the radio with the General.'

Charlie stood up. The number hit forty.

'News,' Picchu said. 'From our embassy in London.'

'Tell me,' Charlie said.

'The news programmes are saying there have been murders. A ship sunk, a woman killed.' He gazed at them without the sardonic gleam Paul was getting used to. 'All of you are wanted by the *policía*.'

26

Haggard sat on the verandah of the Gran Hotel Bolívar, drinking a pisco sour and watching the street below.

The Bolívar is Lima's grandest hotel. Indian flunkies in blue and gold livery had greeted him at the Corinthian-columned entrance when he arrived. He had dined last night amid gilt and plush. It did not trouble him that the waiters, in starched white jackets and satin bow ties, wore shoes that were falling to pieces. He had spent too long in countries like this to be bothered by the gulf between the servants and the served.

The *Miami Herald* lay open before him, but he was not reading it. He watched the Avenida Nicholas de Pierola and waited. It was Sunday, yet the street was by no means busy. A demonstration by the Communist Party was taking place in the city today. A Mercedes water cannon was drawn up to the kerb below, behind it a long green articulated lorry, known to the locals as a *gusano*, a worm. The worm was used to remove what the government regarded as undesirable characters. A few policemen in steel helmets and battle dress stood at the corner of the street, accompanied by policewomen looking incongruous in heavy make-up and long black boots. There were even police guards in the hotel, ready to protect the guests from any demonstrator who became too enthusiastic in his denunciation of the bourgeoisie. Haggard had breakfasted this morning in the company of several machine-gun-toting guards.

The buildings across the street were pitted with bullet holes from the anti-government riots of 1977.

All the balcony windows were of bullet-proof glass. Guests of the hotel were able to dine in comfort, and have riots for a floorshow.

A waiter came toward him from the bar, his shoes flapping open at the toes. He was young, with a bright, ready smile. He seemed conscious only of the neatness of his upper half, not of the ruined shoes. He bowed before Haggard and placed a small card on the table before him. Haggard glanced at the message written there, nodded to the waiter.

He reappeared leading a big man in a gaudy floral shirt and a cream safari-style jacket and trousers. The man swayed in a broad-shouldered way between the tables, glancing sharply around with little eyes the colour of emeralds.

'Gimme one of those,' he growled, in a stagey Texan drawl, pointing at Haggard's pisco sour. He pulled out a chair and sat heavily down.

'Morning,' he said, loosening his collar and mopping the sweat off his pink face.

'Dudgeon.' Haggard closed the 'paper. 'Good trip?'

'Usual lousy bullshit,' Dudgeon said, '*Aero Peru*. *Aero Peor*'s more like it. Air Worst.' He laughed without humour.

Haggard knew the joke. It was common in Peru.

The waiter brought Dudgeon's drink. He scowled over it, complaining about the lousy alcohol in this god-forsaken country, but still drank big mouthfuls.

'When do the others get in?' he asked, wiping his mouth with the back of his hand.

'Today.'

'How many?'

'Three more.'

'Anyone I know?'

'You'll be familiar with some of them.' Their profession, like any other, had its well-known names.

286

The only difference was that the names were seldom real.

Dudgeon was thinking. 'Five of us. What's the job?'

'You'll know when the rest arrive. There's been too much loose talk in this already. I want no more.'

'We going into the jungle?'

He nodded.

Dudgeon groaned. 'God, I hate the fucking jungle. All those bugs and leeches and things any civilized country would've sprayed or burned out years ago.'

'You can go home.'

Dudgeon was offended. He drew his head back in the way that gave anyone with an eye for detail the clue that he had once seen time in the military.

'Now don't go getting touchy on me. That ain't what I said. We seen a lot of shit together.'

That was true, Haggard thought. But it was also going back a long time. He had become used to working alone, relying only on himself. He disliked the fact that he was having to gather a team. He had disliked having to tell New York where he was and what was happening. But after he'd seen Quillet and the wife arrested at the airport, he had no choice. Last night, a 'phone call had told him the likely location of his targets and how to go about getting them. It seemed that the brother who was the cause of all this had some form of unofficial-official protection. He had been ordered to get a team together, because it wasn't just elimination his employers required, but also the retrieval of certain items belonging to them. It was not going to be easy, they said, and he agreed with that. Removing someone was easy enough; doing another job at the same time increased the difficulties a hundredfold. He had become increasingly curious as to what this job was all about – a failing he never usually allowed himself. From the beginning the entire affair had smelled bad somewhere, and he had been forced once more to place himself in the hands of people he no longer trusted. Last night, he had demanded to know more. The bland voice on the telephone told him they would provide more information when he had assembled his people.

At least expense was no object. He could afford to call the best available. For all his swaggering, Dudgeon was one of the best. They had worked together in Africa in the early seventies. Dudgeon was still alive after all this time. This alone made him one of the best.

'Damn foreign drinks don't quench a thirst,' he was saying, clapping his big red hands to bring the waiter running.

'Go easily with the drink,' Haggard said, watching a couple of soldiers climb in the back of the worm.

Dudgeon looked at him, one eye screwed shut. 'Hey, you my grandma?'

'I'm your employer,' Haggard said. 'I expect you to do what you're told.'

Dudgeon scowled even harder. Then he grinned a big, nasty grin. Lots of teeth. 'Well, okay,' he said, and clapped his hands again. 'You're the boss. You *are* the boss.'

27

The first night and half the next day were spent catching up on rest. Paul slept badly, seeing the *Provider* and the man with the cold eyes all the time in his dreams, but he slept. Mina suffered a little from *el soroche*, a mild form of mountain sickness caused by the sudden change in altitude.

Picchu made her coco tea. 'It is not the real sickness,' he said. 'You're not high enough.'

'It's real enough for me,' she said.

Paul looked after her, but it was an uncomfortable situation, knowing Charlie was next door. Not that he was much to be seen. He was shut in the air-conditioned cool of the observatory. He stopped occasionally to eat a little, but sleep was something he largely did without.

On the third day Paul familiarized himself with the situation. There were six soldiers with them on the mountain. At first they seemed a sleepy bunch, slouching around outside, reading comics with their feet on their bunks when off duty. They grinned at Paul, and watched Mina with a veiled look that he didn't like. But Picchu assured him they were good men.

'All good,' he said, on Saturday evening. '*Mestizos*, naturally. I picked them myself.'

He got to know them gradually, by doing his share of the work. They swapped him cigarettes for the remains of his whiskey, and Picchu bawled them out for drinking on duty. Most of the time, they neither drank nor smoked, but chewed coco leaves.

'Good for keeping hunger away,' Picchu explained. 'It's what the poor here have instead of good diet.'

One of the storerooms contained a small arsenal. Picchu showed him round.

'We have machine guns, of course. The latest from the States. This is a grenade launcher. You know these things? These are mines. If someone attempts a siege, we plant them. Also we have *plastique*. The General said to be ready for a *guerra pequeña*, so we are prepared.'

'Think you'll have to use them?' Paul asked. It was hard to imagine anyone tracking them here.

'It is to be hoped,' Picchu grinned, as if he would like a war, even a little one.

Picchu, in fact, was his pilot in strange waters. He told him about the mosquitoes, about the things that would crawl into his boots if he stepped into the undergrowth without preparation. In the evening, he showed him round the mountain, pointing out the trails and tracks that might be used by an approaching enemy; and the eastern cliff, where he would later take his turn as guard. It was not truly a cliff; more a very steep hill, with rocks bursting out of the stony soil, odd trees hanging wherever the most tenacious seeds had found a crevice. The guard had a natural cup of rocks and bushes to protect him against any fire from below. Certainly, no one could hope to attack from the tangle of trees two hundred feet down at the base. But it had to be watched.

'What if they have rocket launchers?' Picchu had said. 'In one way we are safe here, in another we are not safe at all. The radio and the satellite dishes are hidden, but this is an exposed place.'

Paul leaned over the long drop, thinking that if Robersman was so powerful, it should be easy for them to fly in and bomb the whole place to rubble. He knew

290

about heat-seeking missiles, that kind of stuff. If they were into so many important offices and companies, wouldn't it be possible for them to arrange a 'tragic mistake' with an air force jet?

Standing in the chill night, Picchu identified some of the sounds that welled up from the forest. There weren't many. They were higher than anything else they could see. The silence of the vast country stretching away in folds of jungle and thrusts of rocky hilltops was like the end of the world. Two tiny, wavering lights showed in all the darkness.

'That's the village,' Picchu said. 'Fifteen kilometres by road, and nowhere to land a helicopter.'

'Who lives there?'

'*Campesinos*. Indians. It's not a place for tourists. Nothing there. Listen carefully, you can hear the river.'

'What river? I don't see one.'

'Down there,' Picchu lit a cigar and pointed vaguely into the trees. 'You see tomorrow.'

Next morning, carrying water cans, they went down the hill with four of the soldiers. The road twisted end over end going down the steep side of the mountain, levelling only when it reached a bridge wide enough for a lorry to cross. The soldiers spilled off the road and clambered down through the undergrowth. Picchu led him onto the bridge. Paul looked over the rail. A hundred feet below, the soldiers were filling the cans from a surging brown torrent.

'Now you see,' Picchu said. 'It's a safe place. The river embraces us like so –' He made a loop with his hands '– north, west and south. And the east is hard to climb. This is the only way for jeep or truck. Anything starts, we mine it, then we are an island. We guard the bridge, we are okay.'

They descended to the river. It was a thick, muddy

flow, icy cold, smelling of vegetation. They filled the cans.

'Take care,' Picchu said. 'The current is strong.'

The wound in his arm twinged when he took weight with it, but it was healing. Picchu had demanded to see it and redress it when he noticed the old bandage.

'Out here, wounds go bad fast. I have medical training.' He did it expertly, muttering, *'Cuchillo?'* when he saw it. Paul nodded. 'You fight plenty?' Picchu asked.

'Only the last week.'

'Either you have much luck, or some talent.'

'Just luck.'

They trudged back up the hill. Paul watched the soldiers going ahead, talking in low voices. The thin, clear air scraped in his lungs.

Picchu said: 'The *Señora* is better?'

'Seems to be.'

'She's been through much, I think.'

'You think right.'

'But she is strong also.'

He nodded, changing the heavy can from one hand to the other.

'You don't want to talk, that's okay.'

He was conscious of Picchu's bright little eyes on him.

'She and the *Señor*,' Picchu said. 'Things are not good between them.'

'You're a mind reader.'

'And you are not happy.'

'I'm never happy when people are trying to kill me.'

'You should stay a while.' He laughed. 'In this country it's a way of life.'

When they reached the top, Mina was up. She had put on the uniform clothes provided by Picchu. She was washing her hair over a bucket. The soldiers put down their cans and milled about in an obvious way until Picchu scared them off. She lifted a jug and poured. The water caught sunlight falling.

'Feeling better?' Paul asked.

She twisted the water out, flipped upright and gathered the towel round her streaming head. 'Almost human. Been exploring?'

'Yeah. Picchu's a human guidebook.'

'He's taken a shine to you.'

'Likes an audience.' He watched her. 'Seen Charlie?'

'I looked in, but he's working flat out, trying to short-cut to the answer, I think. I don't suppose you've talked to him?'

He shook his head, not bothering to tell her that they had already had a meeting that suggested it was going to be just like old times. It was on the first Saturday afternoon, while she was still sleeping off the sickness. Charlie had called out for someone to bring more printer paper. It was in a store cupboard ten paces from the big steel door, he could have fetched it himself. But since no one else was around, Paul hefted out a couple of boxes and took them to the main building.

Charlie was intent over the screens. One was a computerized contour map dotted with points of light. The legend said it was hot spot activity around *El Chichón*. Charlie barely glanced up as he stood there with the boxes.

'Where d'you want them?'

'On the floor there.' Same old dismissive way.

He placed them on the floor by the work stations. Printers clattered like woodpeckers.

'How's Mina?' Charlie said, his fingers not stopping on the keys.

'She's two doors down. Ask her yourself.' He heard his own edge. It was just there, natural as breathing.

'I thought I'd save the trouble. You seem to know all about her now.'

He should have got out then. But this had been waiting since they met.

'You didn't waste any time, did you?' Charlie scrolled a line of figures up the screen. 'I mean, I hope you don't mind my impertinence, but what's the . . . er,' He thought over the word, ' . . . situation with you two?' He was apparently engrossed in the screen, talking about something that didn't really bother him. 'I'm just curious, you understand. You seem to have reasserted yourself pretty quickly. Resumed your old status, shall we say?'

The room was empty except for them. The telescope reared up to the roof. A couple of the screens burst into life, thousands of images passing every second.

'Have you slept with her?' Charlie said. Eyes on the screen, fingers on the keys. Voice level. 'I think that's the least you can tell me, the way things are in this diseased world. I mean to say, with your history of screwing anything that moves. Has she thought about that, by the way? Your legacy from a thousand one-night stands. It's not like the old days. She put up with it then, for whatever reasons she thought were good, but these days it's a matter of life and death.' His mouth turned up at the corners. 'Lot of things seem to be that way now.' He hit the 'enter' key, and a printer began to whirr. 'So, have you?'

Paul sat on one of the units, a leg swinging.

'You don't want to get holier than thou.'

'I'm still her husband. You're the, er, what shall we call it, the "blast from the past"?'

'She knows. She saw the letters you sent that woman.'

Charlie jerked slightly. His knuckles tightened. 'Leave her out of this.'

'You didn't leave her out of it. You dragged both of them in. Mina watched your girlfriend die.'

'That's enough.' Charlie was on his feet.

Paul shook his head. 'Still can't stand it, can you? Being in the wrong doesn't fit your image.'

'Get out.'

'All right, bro'.'

'Get out!'

And that was their first real conversation. Doomed to repeat their old behaviour, it seemed. But Paul got no pleasure from it. Not even the old, twisted kind.

Mina stood up, dragging a comb through her hair. 'Does it look all right?'

'Looks fine.'

A couple of the soldiers went past, on their way to take up guard duty on the eastern side. He wanted to kiss her, but he didn't.

28

The five men flew into Cuzco from Lima on Monday afternoon. They stayed at the *Hostal Familiar*, a pleasant establishment a little way from the *Plaza de Armas*. They were in their thirties or forties; very fit, very unlike most tourists. The apparent leader of the group told the owner of the *Hostal* that they had come down to do some exploring in the jungle around the Urubamba Valley. Some of them were American, and they all had money to spend, but they did not behave as these parties usually did. They were gentlemen. The desk clerk told a chamber-maid that they were clearly not first-time visitors. He would also be unsurprised, he said, to find that they had friends in high places.

They dined together at the *Trattorio Adriano* that night. Their talk was low and quick. They were clearly all in the same business, whatever that was.

They had little time for the ordinary tourist activities. Cuzco may have been the centre of the Inca culture, but the great mortarless stonework that lines the streets might have been breeze blocks to them; they showed no desire to visit the fortress of Sacsayhuaman above the city, or take the train up to Machu Picchu. They were busy all of Tuesday, renting or buying camping gear at 'Inca Treks' and 'Andean Adventures'. Late Tuesday afternoon, two Shogun four-wheel-drive vehicles were delivered. Definitely friends in high places, the desk clerk said.

They left on Wednesday morning, heading, they said, for Urubamba itself.

On Wednesday afternoon, in a reasonably flat clearing in jungle north of the valley, a helicopter set down. The five men unstrapped a cache of arms, the uniforms which would allow them to pass for rebels, and a high-powered but compact satellite transmitter-receiver. They checked the weapons thoroughly, found all of them good, and the helicopter leapt into the sky again, dwindling into the haze until the chop of its blades was lost in the chatter of the jungle.

The two cars moved quickly away from the area along bone-breaking roads, burrowing deeper into the lonely country where tourists never go.

In the passenger seat of the first car, Haggard considered that events had proceeded well. He had four good men, all with their own particular talents to add to a general proficiency. Dudgeon, the specialist in explosives; Scelerat, the Frenchman who was the best with any kind of knife; the Englishman, Runnion, whose hands were offensive weapons in themselves; and Matar, who was South American, though no one knew from which country he came. He had been responsible for many political deaths in Latin America, but the reason for his being on this job was that he knew the country. It was always good, Haggard thought, to have a guide in a strange land.

When they stopped to make camp that night, he asked Dudgeon to set the radio up. It had been ordered that he keep in regular contact with New York. Somehow, a connection had been arranged, probably with computers. This job was all about computers. He didn't like it, but without New York, he would not have known where to find Quillet. The modern world was a very disconcerting place. Some company man with clean hands was sitting at a desk somewhere in New York, yet he was able to do so much.

Not the dirty work, though. That was for him, and the others. There would always be work for them, until someone should work out how to commit murder by computer.

29

The generator started acting up. The reserve cut in and kept the programs running, but it would not last long with the kind of power Charlie was using. After watching the soldiers file in and out of the generator room for a while, Paul took command. It was a big Wilson machine of a kind he was familiar with. He had one of the soldiers to assist, a boy called Jorge, who knew some English. They stripped the generator down and cleaned out the magnetos. It took most of a day, but when they finally had her reassembled and kicked her into action again, she ran sweet. After that, there was a new respect in the eyes of the soldiers. They knew he was useful for something. He made the generator his responsibility. It was safely tucked away beneath the main building, and the room got fearfully hot when it ran, but it was no worse than being stuck in the *Provider*'s engine room. He went down there more than he needed to. Mina was spending time in the main building now, helping Charlie. He didn't want to know what they said to each other, but he thought about it most of the time. And about the boat and what had happened to Sam, about what would happen to them if they actually came out of this intact. He kept remembering the man at the airport, and he did not believe they were safe yet.

But there was the jungle and the deep gorge where the river plunged, the vast hollow wonder of the early mornings, the silence at night, and the stars close enough to touch. He realized that, in a strange way, he wasn't unhappy. When he was a kid, and Dad used to reel off those poems with exotic settings, he would think about boarding the *Provider* and sailing to them. Kid-dreams that he lost, as he lost everything but a good, useful adult cynicism.

> 'Since long ago, a child at home,
> I read and longed to rise and roam,
> Where'er I went, whate'er I willed . . . '

Mina seemed to sense it. One morning, as they went down to the river, she said:

'You look comfortable here.'

He was comfortable, except where she and Charlie were concerned.

30

Sheal walked into Drazel's office. The blinds were partly closed against a grey, snowy sky, and the TV by the bar showed *As the World Turns*.

'What?' Drazel snapped. He put down his fountain pen and covered the papers he was working on. Sheal laid a printout before him. Drazel turned his head slightly to read it. He had just returned from Chicago. He had been seeing important people, and it was clear that the going had not been easy. His eyes were bloodshot, his face had lost its high colour. His usual vigour had a nervous rasp to it. They had been grilling him in Chicago about the mistakes. There had been a number, and one was too many for a man in Drazel's position. He had been sent back, Sheal guessed, knowing that he had better get the rest of it right, or there would be repercussions.

'They're in the jungle?' he said, as if the words on the printout were not comprehensible to him.

'As you see.'

'When do they figure on reaching the place?'

'Couple of days. It's pretty rough country out there.'

'They could've flown in.' There was an empty whisky tumbler beside the 'phone. It was unlike Drazel to drink in office hours. Sheal noted this with interest. 'Why didn't they parachute in?'

'It would've been too complicated to arrange in a short time. They needed a lot of equipment.'

'God damn it. What do they need? Some guns is all. Go in there, deal with the problem, and get out. I could do it myself.'

301

'I'm sure Haggard knows what he's doing.' Sheal felt almost sorry for him. Drazel was unused to being in a bad position. It must be a sweaty experience for him.

'What about the program?'

'He's still running it.'

'Can we stop him?'

'Well, naturally, we know where he is now. That makes it easier. But he's still being very clever.'

Drazel rose, his barrel of a body moving with a jerky suddenness. 'He's clever,' he said, going over to the window and raising the shades a little.

'He's running a lot of protection. I haven't been able to break in yet. For one thing, he's not using only the computers in the observatory. According to the records, they're not that big. Somehow or other he's . . . contracting the work out to bigger machines.'

'That's impossible.'

'Not for him. I have a feeling he's borrowing time from the Los Alamos supers –'

'Feelings are what we don't have time for, Martin. I want *facts*. I want him stopped before he gets any more conclusions.'

'I'm trying to plan blocks to jam the whole system, but I haven't worked it out yet.'

'Well, work it out,' Drazel said, his lower lip thrusting out like a sulky, suspicious child. 'Damn it, you have nothing else to do. Work it out and stop him.'

Sheal bowed out slowly. 'I'll get back on it,' he said.

31

Picchu came out of the radio room. He was smiling to himself, humming some tune. Paul looked up from the table.

'You want coffee?' Picchu said.

'No, thanks.' He had a Browning 9mm High Power pistol broken down on the table. He was cleaning the parts and sliding them back together again. Picchu poured himself a cup from the pot heating over the gas burner and leaned against one of the bunks, watching.

'You sure you don't know guns?'

'Only from last week.' He used the fine oil and the cotton wadding to poke through the barrel. 'A machine's a machine. You should let me have one.'

'Only if you swear to take orders like a soldier.'

'Fine by me.'

Picchu drank, watching the vapour from his coffee. 'Later we see.'

They heard Charlie's voice rising as he talked over the radio.

'Bad static,' Picchu said.

'What's going on?'

'Ah, it's very good.' Picchu sat down and flipped his shirt pocket open to get a cigar. 'Suddenly the General gets telephone calls. The British Embassy has heard a rumour that certain persons wanted by your government are in Peru. American senators also call. Our government is being asked difficult questions by its friends, the Americans, and they ask the General. He says: is there any proof these people are here? And there is nothing to show. All the airline passenger lists are on computers, and none of them have *Señor* Quillet, or the *Señora*, or you.'

'Think they can force him to hand us over?'

The teeth showed in a big white line. 'Force the General?'

He smiled back, but he thought: They know we're here.

Charlie came in, scratching his ears where the headphones had been. He sat down. Paul kept working, reassembling the pistol carefully. Picchu placed a cup of coffee in front of Charlie and walked away toward the storeroom. Charlie looked as if he'd prefer to go too, but he stayed where he was. He drank a little, and leaned his elbows on the table, yawning.

'They're onto us,' he said.

'How long before your program comes up with the answer?'

'Impossible to say. It's just a mass of data now, general trends and global activity building a logic tree. The particulars always come in the last minute.'

'What happens if you do get it?'

'I have a special program. It'll broadcast the details worldwide, every government and scientific computer it can reach. Enough information to convince any specialist worth a damn that they have to take it seriously.'

'Can they stop it?'

Charlie nodded slowly. 'Possible. But we're still a long way ahead of them. They're going mad in New York, trying to dig us out, but I'm better than any of the smart bastards they have up there. At least, I am at the moment.'

They sat on, both uneasy, neither looking at the other. Then Charlie said:

'We have you to thank, don't we? For the generator?'

He was so surprised that his reply came out sounding more arrogant than he intended. 'They could've fixed it. Just gave me something useful to do.'

More silence. 'I said some stupid things the other day.'

'Both did.' Grudgingly.

'Yes, well . . . You were right about one thing: right-eous indignation doesn't suit me. I was still trying to come to terms with what happened to Penny, you see. I always thought she'd be too clever for them. She was so self-reliant, it never crossed my mind to try and stop her doing what she wanted.' He stared into the coffee cup. 'And, of course, it's not easy being found out at the same time you're trying to grieve.' He coughed, drank. 'I cocked things up rather well.'

The gun was back in one piece. It gleamed with the oil. Paul wiped it off. He thought he was going to leave things there, but found himself saying:

'I acted like the same old prick. Maybe we shouldn't talk. Saves trouble.'

'We're talking now.'

'Give it time.'

'Anyway,' Charlie stood, taking the remains of the coffee with him. 'I just wanted to say thanks. For getting Mina through, as well as the generator.'

'Hell, I didn't have a choice. I thought your mate Chandor was going to make me rich if I found you.'

Charlie didn't know how to take that. He went up the corridor toward the steel door.

Picchu appeared from the storeroom, carrying one of the machine guns.

'Come,' he said. 'Let's see if you can fire one of these.'

He was given the weapon outside, an old Sterling 9mm, allowed to get the feel of it, then told to try and hit a broad tree trunk at the edge of the plateau. He did that easily enough, though the jumping of the gun in his hands surprised him. As Picchu said, a machine gun does not require a marksman on the trigger. Just point in the general direction and let off a burst. It usually cuts the opponent in half.

The agreement was that Paul would take orders from him when the gun was required. 'You will be an honorary member of my platoon,' he said. 'A great honour, to be inducted into this army. A privilege usually reserved for boys of twelve years. But seriously, if it comes to fighting, you do as I say, yes?'

Paul agreed. The fact that Picchu had allowed him a gun at all suggested that he thought things might turn bad.

That was when he started taking his share of guard duty. It was slow work, hanging around by the bridge or watching the cliff, but he didn't mind it. When he was paired with Manaro, an experienced soldier about his own age, they watched in easy silence, smoking, occasionally trying out shreds of each other's language.

That night, Charlie ate with them, and eventually the conversation turned to what the 'Weatherspy' program might do. They were on the grass outside the dome in the gathering dusk, just beginning to feel the high altitude chill.

'If it does prove itself,' Picchu was saying, 'and if you can put it in the hands of the right people, what then?'

Charlie savoured a mouthful of wine. 'I've been thinking about an extension of the basic idea.'

'Going from natural fuck-ups to unnatural ones,' Paul said.

'Very perceptive.' A hint of condescension, but it did not annoy him so much. He realized it was simply that

306

Charlie couldn't believe anyone thought slower than he did. 'That's exactly what I had in mind.'

There was a general stir of incredulity. Picchu tore another piece of bread from the loaf between his knees and said: 'So you say: "This passenger jet will crash at four-thirty on Wednesday the twenty-ninth of May"? This is not possible.'

'Why not?' Charlie examined the evening sky. The forest below was alive with sound. 'If there was a computer record of all the tests they do on those things between flights, and if you also had a medical on the captain that said his reactions were slower than they had been *and* you had a weather report that told you conditions were going to be rough on a certain stretch of the journey, maybe it would come up with the prediction. All you need is enough detailed knowledge.'

Mina shook her head. She was withdrawn and silent.

Charlie said: 'I have to confess, that by "detailed knowledge" we probably mean a complete record of the behaviour of each atom in the universe, which would probably *also* mean the computer would have to be about the same size as the universe, but these are small problems for a super brain.'

Each atom? Paul thought. The wine was strong. His brain skidded on the idea. He was most surprised, though, by the fact that he could see his brother's mind working. Charlie played with theories the way he played cards.

'Maybe that's all creation is, anyway,' Charlie said. 'A big computer, in which we're all just logic gates – or illogic gates, given our behaviour.' He laughed softly, with just enough bitterness to be noticeable.

'Newton says the universe is a giant clock, therefore we can know how things'll turn out if we can get a close enough look at the works. The Chaos theory

307

says the universe is too complex, and it's impossible to know enough to predict anything. But I think if I had the time and the resources, it might be interesting to try something on a limited scale. Companies already use character profiles to predict how a prospective employee might behave in given circumstances. If we took "Weatherspy's" long-term predictions for natural world trends, threw in everything you could find on economics, industry – every piece of knowledge available, in other words – and then added a character file for every single person on the planet, maybe it would work.'

'It's impossible,' Mina said. 'It's too complicated.'

'It's just a notion in the back of my mind. But today's notion is tomorrow's breakthrough.'

'Of course, there is another question,' Picchu ruminated over his bread.

'Which is?'

'If you take this idea to its conclusion, you can present each man on the planet with the complete story of his life and death. You would be able to ask your computers when and how you were going to die. You wish this?'

'You're getting too far ahead. You're talking about particulars.'

Mina stirred again. 'If you could punch in a question for "Weatherspy" now, asking what the outcome of this situation's going to be, would you do it?'

He smiled vaguely. 'Depends whether knowing the future means we can change it.'

'That's what "Weatherspy" does.'

'No. It just tells us something will happen so we can get people away from the place in which it'll occur. What you're asking is complete foreknowledge, which is just hindsight in advance: instead of knowing what *has* gone wrong, you'll know what *will*

308

go wrong. You still can't change anything. Just like our lives.'

'Would you do it?' she insisted.

'Only if I were allowed to re-write the program for a happy ending.'

Picchu laughed. 'You English,' he chortled. 'You will be the death of me. I mean this literally.'

After another conversation with the General, Picchu decided it was time to mine the bridge. Paul went down and watched them do it, a couple of the soldiers dropping over the rails on thin ropes to plant the explosive.

As he spooled out the wire back to the road, Picchu said:

'You know anything of computers?'

'No. Charlie's the computer expert. Anything you want to know about boats, though . . .'

'You think your brother can do this? This prediction?'

'Says he already has.'

Picchu rummaged through a box of timers and detonators. 'It is impossible. Earthquakes, hurricanes, volcanoes, these things are acts of God.'

Paul snorted. 'You believe in God?'

'I am a Catholic. What else would I believe?'

'All the things you've told me about this country, and you still believe in a God.'

'Things are so bad, somebody must take the blame.'

God was in the great sky above, and, like God, 'Weatherspy' worked night and day, never ceasing.

32

Sleep came hard one night. Picchu was snoring off half a bottle of rum. He got up, took the bottle, and wandered into the canteen, shivering at the cold. Three of the soldiers were asleep in their bunks. His next watch was not till five. He went back along the corridor, checking that Mina was safe. He tilted the bottle and drank. The rum was unlike any he had tasted. It slithered down and left a brushfire behind. More like dragon's blood than Nelson's. He heard the buzz of the computers in the dome, pulled the door back and looked in.

Charlie was in the usual place. He seemed to be taking root there. His face was drawn and lit with strange colours by the screens' flow of images. Darkness covered the rest of the room.

Paul watched him for a while, then turned to go. He caught a table leg with his foot.

Charlie looked round sharply.

'Who is it?' His voice was terrified.

'It's me.'

'Polly? Christ! What time is it?'

'Half-past one.' He moved closer so he could be seen.

Charlie sat back, rubbing at the base of his spine. Paul put the bottle on the desk.

'For Christ's sake, don't spill it on anything.'

'Try not to.' Paul drank again. 'Have a shot. It's all right.'

There was a twinge of the old judgemental look in Charlie's eyes. The way he used to watch Dad knocking back the doubles. Paul felt uncomfortable.

310

'So don't have one. Don't want to end up like the old man. One of us is enough.'

It seemed to goad Charlie. He searched around on the floor until he found a couple of tin mugs that had contained coffee. He wiped them out with a scrap of printer paper and set them on the table. He regarded Paul in a challenging way. Paul poured what he estimated as doubles.

They drank. Charlie croaked:

'Hate these local brews. They're all made of rope and tar. Ask Picchu.' He downed the rest and stuck the mug out again. Paul sensed he was doing it to prove something. He poured more. Charlie swilled the liquor round a few times and sipped again. Then he patted the casing of the screen in front of him.

'You know, this machine can run itself perfectly well. Set it a problem, it'll go on till it gets the solution. It's my program, but it doesn't need me.'

'Why watch it?'

'Sometimes I can help it short-cut.'

'You ought to get some sleep.'

He was twitchy with lack of it. 'I can't,' he said, shifting stacks of printout around as if one figure in the whole mass might mean something. 'Every time I close my eyes, I see what happened to that village because we didn't tell anyone. Ten thousand people buried in the mud. Countless others killed and injured on the coast. I could've done something, but I was so innocent.'

'You did pretty well.'

'For a man with his head buried in circuit boards.'

'Didn't say that.'

'It's what you think. You always had a low opinion of intellect.'

'Wouldn't call you innocent.'

'Arrogant, then. That's probably more accurate. I just

311

refused to believe that anyone could take "Weatherspy" away from me.'

'They haven't yet.'

'No.' He drank again, washing the rum around in his mouth. They sat watching the screens. 'Even if they do, we've given them a pretty good run for their money. Two computer scientists,' he blinked when he said it, 'the owner of a theatrical costume business, and a merchant seaman. Pretty good, considering who we're up against.'

'The computers helped.'

'Good Lord, Parrot, that's the first nice thing you've ever said about my business.'

'They gave me the address when Mina was kidnapped. Still don't know how you managed that.'

'Every time they made a move, someone somewhere made a 'phone call, and eventually that information ended up on a computer. And I was monitoring everything they did. When I knew they'd taken her, I used the stuff Penny had dug out. The computer just had to run through its list of company safe houses. Of course, if they'd been keeping her somewhere else . . .'

'Clever.'

'Oh, yes.' Charlie tipped the bottle and watched the rum gurgle into his mug. He raised an eyebrow at Paul, and poured him a shot.

'I don't drink much,' he said. 'The old man may not have set us many good examples, but he set us the right bad ones.'

'He liked a drink.'

'Liked it? He and the bottle were like Romeo and Juliet.'

Paul scowled. 'You going to get onto that again? Next it'll be the night he drowned.'

'He was three times over the limit when he fell in the dock.'

'I'd seen him at the wheel in that state.'

'That doesn't make it right.'

'Didn't say it does.'

Charlie sniffed. The drink was getting to him.

'For a long time, I blamed you.'

Paul kept watching the screen. 'There's a surprise.'

'Took me ages to realize it was his own fault. I stopped blaming you and started on him. He just drank too much.'

'That's the truth.'

'You drink?'

Paul waggled his mug. A drop slopped on the table. 'No.'

'I find myself tempted to it all the time,' Charlie said. 'They say alcoholism may be genetic – or perhaps we just follow the examples we're set. I'm always watching myself when there's booze around, thinking about him.' The nearest screen became a satellite picture of the northern hemisphere. The whole planet moving in stop motion, cloud formations and continents jumping over a dark globe. 'You look older,' he said.

'You too. It's the hard living.'

'You hear what Picchu said when you first arrived? We were both sporting three-day growth. He said: "Yes, you are brothers after all." I told him there was no resemblance.'

'There isn't.'

'He thinks there is. Mina thinks there is.'

The mention of her name caused a prickle of discomfort.

'Last couple of years, she was always saying how alike we were. Usually with irritation in her manner, I hasten to add. Apparently we share the same faults.'

Nothing he could say to that. Charlie went on:

'I suppose she'd know, wouldn't she? Between the

313

two of us, we've given her a complete course in why women really ought to avoid men.'

'Don't start,' he said. He was defensive at the same time as a part of him agreed.

'I'm starting on me,' Charlie said. 'There's one thing you can say about having the threat of death hanging over you: it puts everything into perspective pretty quickly. I've been thinking about it a lot.'

'Come to any conclusions?'

'Yes. That she would've been better off if she'd never laid eyes on either of us.'

'But she did.'

'I know. Isn't that the hell of it?' He chuckled quietly, and a printer started rattling off a sheet of numbers.

'Oh, she loved me, I never said she didn't.' He had his feet on the desk now. His glasses were off, and he was leaning back sleepily. The chair looked ready to topple over. They were both better than half-shot. 'Maybe she still does a little. I know I still feel something for her, despite what I've done. I've sometimes thought it was *because* of her. Perhaps I just couldn't stand not being as important to her as she was to me.'

'She married you, didn't she?'

'Of course she did. I think she was so muddled up by the time you finished with her, she would've married anyone who asked her. I was good for her then. I provided warmth, caring when she needed that most. And I was still naive enough to believe that people can be sensible where their hearts are concerned. I thought she'd realized how bad you were for her, and that was all it needed. But warmth doesn't compare very well with excitement. That's what she had with you, though it pains me to admit it, and I couldn't summon that out of nowhere.'

Paul drank. The cup was cold in his hand. Charlie

314

was doing all the talking. He was letting him unravel, giving little in return. What do you want? he asked himself. For Charlie to give his blessing? To say: 'You go ahead and make love to her. It's all over for us, anyway'?

'I think she loves both of us, in a way,' Charlie said. 'But the way she felt for me was always the same. Friendship love. Perhaps she told herself that was enough back then. People do, you know. They get burnt by passion and settle for something safer, friendship love. Let's face it, she didn't have much luck with the other kind, did she?'

'I don't want to talk about Penny,' he said. 'I really don't, all right?' He gazed at the screens, closing one eye. Then, contradicting himself, continued: 'She's probably the reason we're here. She made me see what was going on. Otherwise I might've let Robersman have their way. I was just as easily scared as anyone else.' He peered at the rum in his cup. 'Oh, God, she was ballsy, you know?'

'I didn't think she . . .' The image of Penny Leman's broken figure burned in Paul's eye for a moment. 'She didn't look your type.'

'What's my type? All I know about her was that she knew what she was doing all the time. She told me more about myself, about Mina too, than I'd learned in my entire life.' He waggled the cup to make Paul refill it, took a long pull at it. 'She once told me I was so enthusiastic about predicting the future because I was obsessed with the past. Mina too. And you, for that matter.'

'She never met me.'

'She would've seen it. Look at the way we went. You tried to hold onto it, and I did my best to get right away. Don't you see, we never had a damn thing to

315

believe in. All we knew was chaos, booze, and running from one debt to another, Dad sweating every month when the bills were due. You stuck to it. Penny told me computers were my way of imposing order. My version of God.' He closed his eyes. 'I miss her.'

'Why did I marry Mina? Because I was in love with her, why else? I haven't done everything in my life just to spite you, no matter what you think.'

The bottle was almost empty. If there had been windows in the dome, Paul thought, dawn light would be showing by now. He nursed his cup, chin on his chest. He was as far gone as Charlie, but he was listening. He had not listened to Charlie since they were very small.

'Ever since I met her, I was mad about her. All the time she was going with you, I thought she was the most wonderful girl I'd ever seen. Not so strange: she was like another world. But I never did anything about it until you started being so unbearable that even she couldn't take it any more. I didn't care that she'd been your girlfriend. I wouldn't have minded if she'd gone out with Adolf Hitler before me. Pride doesn't matter one little bit when you feel that about someone, any more than good sense. I probably knew it couldn't work even then, knew she wouldn't just forget about you. But it didn't matter. It just happened, and I was too confused to think about what it meant.'

'Always exploited your opportunities, haven't you?'

'My God, Polly, we were kids. We were all just kids. You behave as if everything was done out of malice by full-grown adults. I was in love with her, that's my only excuse. What the hell's yours?'

He had no quick answer. And, as if he'd been storing it all up for twenty years and become more sad than angry, Charlie said:

'You were a complete bastard to her.'

Once it would have led to a fight, or at least to him snapping back with a mouthful of insults and curses. This time he sat quietly and said:

'I know.'

Charlie turned back to the keyboard. For a while they sat like that, shoulder to shoulder, and Charlie worked, while the screen in front of him flashed graphs and maps too fast for the eyes to separate them. Then he took off his glasses and rubbed his eyes hard.

'Best thing that could happen to her is if she dumped both of us and got out. We've done her enough damage.'

'But what if one of us wants to make it up to her?'

'Then that one has to say so. To her. Not to anyone else. We've both been too fucking private for our own good, or anyone's. She's probably had enough of trying to guess what the hell we want. It's time someone asked her what she wants.'

'Still a fucking philosopher.'

Charlie grinned. 'No point having a brain 'less you use it.'

'Think we'll get out of this?'

'Ah, there's a question.' He stared into the shadows of the dome.

'"All round the house is jet black night;
It stares through the window pane . . ."'

Paul picked up the quote, and they spoke the last two lines loosely together.

'"It crawls in the corners, hiding from the light,
And it moves with the moving flame."'

'Why not ask the computer?'

Charlie snuffed over the swipes in his mug, chuckling. 'She can't handle that just yet. But I'm working on it.'

'I might not want to know.'

317

'That's the problem with complete knowledge. It takes all the fun out of things.'

Picchu stuck his head round the door.

'Paul, it is your watch.' He stopped, staring at them. 'Never mind. I get someone else.'

33

They were coming through the jungle by old tracks that no car had seen for years. Sometimes they had to stop and hack a path out of the undergrowth. Their progress was slow, and Dudgeon grumbled about it. They were supposed to be doing a job, weren't they? Why hadn't they been dropped in by 'plane? Save all this fritzing around with the mosquitoes.

Every night, just after dusk, Haggard would take the radio off to a secluded place away from the camp, and speak to New York. He listened, took note of anything useful New York had to tell him. Generally, the call was for him to move faster. He told the voice that he was moving as fast as he could. Then it started telling him that they would have to remain in radio contact throughout the attack. He said that was a ridiculous request. The voice said it wasn't a request, but an order. New York had to be kept fully informed throughout.

The days were steaming and dull, the nights cold. The men who had never been in these parts before expressed surprise over the frost that met them every morning when they crawled out of the tents.

Once they passed through a village, and saw the Indian peasants in their squalor. The travellers were a big event to the children of the village. They stopped in a bar where the only drink was a foul local beer or coco tea, and Matar asked a few questions of the owner. The army was nowhere around, and there was little rebel activity at present.

Later, racketing over the potholed track down into a valley, Dudgeon said: 'You can bet there'll be rebel activity if they ever catch sight of these here mobiles. Bet they'd love to have themselves some vehicles like these. We'll be fighting the whole population before we ever see your people.'

Haggard relaxed as best he could, and read through some literature from an antique weaponry shop he had visited in Lima. He wished Dudgeon would shut up.

34

Charlie spent almost an hour on the radio. He wore headphones so no one else should hear what was said, but the tone of his voice gave it away.

'They're putting the pressure on.' Paul sat at the table with Picchu, drinking coffee with canned milk to sweeten the thick brew. 'Right?'

Picchu opened his little marble eyes wide and shrugged. 'No one pressures the General.'

'Why's all the fuss, then?'

'Oh, they try to make him uncomfortable. Things are made difficult for other Generals, so the Generals want to know what he is doing.'

'He's only one man. He'll have to tell them in the end.'

'Not if your brother's computer can tell us what we wish to know. Many powerful men here are like tame dogs for the foreigners. If the General proves they were trying to stop him saving some Latino country from disaster, then he will be vindicated in the eyes of the people. It will be very useful for him.'

'That why he's doing it?'

'He does it to save thousands, maybe millions, of lives,' Picchu said, loyally.

'So, what's he going to do?'

'I ask him to send more soldiers. He will do what he can, but his position is bad now. One mistake and they know where we are.'

'We're causing you a lot of trouble.'

'What else do foreigners ever cause here?'

In the evening, Mina disappeared.

The sun was sliding behind the mountains, leaving pale fire. Paul came off his trick on the cliff. In the canteen Picchu was talking to a couple of the guards, mumbling low, giggling occasionally.

He went to his bed, lay down but couldn't relax. He reached onto the floor for the Walkman and the Zevon tape.

They weren't there.

He looked in Mina's room. She wasn't in. He went along the corridor to the dome, poked his head round the door. Charlie was walking back and forth in front of the work stations, reading a page of notes.

He backtracked to the canteen. Picchu looked up.

'Mina here?' he asked.

Picchu shook his head. One of the soldiers said something. Paul caught it before Picchu translated.

'Outside where? How long for?' They hadn't seen her. He pulled on his jacket, slung the Sterling over his shoulder and headed out. Jorge had not seen her for maybe an hour. She had said she was going for a walk. He did not know where.

He called her name as he crossed the grass. His voice emptied into the vast evening, echoing after long delay. Mosquitoes swarmed up. He went down the road toward the bridge.

'Mina!'

The guards at the bridge shook their head when he came down. No, the *Señora* had not been there.

Cursing, he struck off the road into the trees. The shade was colder still. It was like moving through green soup. He kept calling her name, thinking all the 'what if's' it was possible to think. Picchu had told her – asked her – not to go off by herself.

He worked along a path that circled the hill, saw fat beetles the size of brooches crawling over his boots.

He saw her at last in a clearing not twenty yards away. She was leaning against a tree, the headphones over her ears, watching the western sky where night was blowing out the last of the day.

He pulled the headphones off. She turned quickly, frightened and ready to strike out or run until she saw who it was.

He breathed heavily in the thin air, glowered at her. 'What're you doing?'

'Listening to some music.' She stared at him as if he were mad. 'Is that all right?'

'We didn't know where you were.' *I* didn't know. Why didn't he say it?

'I beg your pardon. I didn't realize I needed your permission.' She was spoiling for a fight. Cool like butane about to ignite.

'You should've told someone.'

'I wanted to be alone for five minutes.'

'Stay in your room, then.' Where you're safe, he wanted to add, but didn't.

Her eyes narrowed. 'Don't order me. Don't you dare. You've done enough of that.'

'It's not safe out here.'

'You think we're safe anywhere? We haven't been safe for a long time.' She got up and started kicking at the spongy earth. 'At least down here I'm away from all . . . ' She waved a hand in the direction of the observatory. '– that.'

'What're you talking about?'

'The boys' club, the adventure playground.'

He tried to take her arm. 'For Christ's sake, Mina –'

She pulled away. 'I don't want to be up there any more, do you understand? The smell of dirty clothes and sweat and booze. And all the toy soldiers.' She turned and studied him. The army clothes he wore, the machine gun swinging at his side. 'Look at you.

323

You're like one of them. You're enjoying it. You and Picchu and the rest of the chaps all having a wonderful time, and Charlie sitting over his bloody computers, mourning his lost love.'

'That's not fair.'

'Oh, lecture me in being fair, please. Times have changed.'

That cut him. She shook her head.

'Have a good time last night?'

Ah, he thought, so that's it. 'We had a few drinks.'

'A few. He was so far out of it he was across the border. I found him this morning, snoring his head off under a table.'

'You said he needed a rest.'

'He never drinks like that. What were you giving him?'

'Bottle said rum. Probably diesel.'

'And you had a great time, didn't you?'

'You said we should talk. We talked.'

'What about?'

He was getting angry, but she stayed calm. It was an act, but it was a good one. He thought, we don't need this now. Living cramped up like this, everything has to be kept down or it gets messy.

'I heard the pair of you,' she said. 'Woke up in the dark and heard you laughing. Ten years without a word, and then you get together like a pair of good old boys and get plastered together. Sorting everything out between you. Deciding who I should go to this time.'

The roar of the river pounding the base of the mountain came up through the trees. To the west were dark shadowed hills and the jungle. 'Let's go back up,' he said.

'You go. I'm tired of it. I just want it to finish so I can get away from both of you.'

'No.' He did grab her now. Too hard. She winced. He let her go. 'I'm sorry.'

She was shivering. She did not have a jacket. She folded her arms round herself.

'You've talked more to each other than me. You know that?'

'Maybe we should all sit down with a bottle,' he said.

'And thrash things out like civilized human beings?' She cradled herself. 'There's not much time for being civilized just now.'

'We're all right here,' he said.

'No, we're not. We're not all right anywhere. Don't you see that? It's not just Robersman. Behind them there's someone else, and behind that someone there's someone else. We can't be safe.' She stared out at the stars. 'I'm frightened. I don't think I'll ever see home again.'

He wanted to hold her, sensed she wanted it too. Still he didn't touch her. He thought: I can't do without this. I need this. I need her.

'Aren't you scared?' she said.

'Been terrified so long, it's hard remembering how I felt before.' But he remembered all right. Before being afraid was also before she came back. It was feeling dead inside, thinking nothing was worth a damn any more.

'We'll come through,' he said. 'Charlie'll get the answer.'

'I'm reassured,' she said. 'Never mind what happens after that.'

Night was cloaking the jungle now. He peered over her head into the emptiness.

'You know something?' she said. 'When you used to tell me how rotten the world was, how everything and everyone was corrupt, I used to think you were wrong.

I thought it was just you, the way you saw things. I got more and more certain that you were infecting me with the same disease. I got away. Charlie was sweet then. Like you with all the bad taken out. I thought I could be a good wife to him just by wanting to. And we got all those things that proved you wrong. Nice surroundings, nice people. Nothing bad ever happens to people like that.'

He felt ashamed.

'But here's the good part,' she said. 'You were right. The whole thing is riddled right through. The good parts were all paid for by Charlie working for Robersman. Robersman with its fingers in all those dirty pies, moving politicians around like chessmen. The good things, they're just walls we put up so we won't see the view; all the backhanders and blackmails, the squalid little deals and killings. You were right. I should have believed you all along. It would've been easier.'

He wanted to say that it wasn't like that. But encouragement to look on the bright side would sound like a lot of carny coming from him now.

'Why weren't you kinder?' she said.

Out of the corner of his eye, he thought he saw a flash of light. He looked again. It was a hillside maybe five miles distant.

Her eyes glimmered. 'What's wrong?'

'Nothing. Can we go back now?'

'That's a request, not an order?'

'Request, based on the fact that you're freezing.'

'Maybe you *have* changed.'

'Maybe I have.'

'Well, that's one good thing to come out of this.'

'Is it good?' The importance of the question strained against the words.

She smiled. 'Better than bad.'

* * *

'What did you see?' Picchu asked. They were alone outside the darkened observatory, the night sky a mass of starlight, the country lost in the dark.

'Headlight, maybe. Can't say for sure.'

Picchu swivelled slowly, a pair of field glasses to his face. 'Nothing.'

'They wouldn't light fires to tell us they're coming, would they?'

His tongue clicked against his teeth. 'It wasn't a *chispar*?'

'What?'

'A spark, you know, in the eye?'

'Don't think so.'

The field glasses covered the western hills.

'Nothing.'

'I don't like it.'

'You are not alone.'

'What do we do?'

'Tonight we double the guards on the bridge. I will use the radio. Tomorrow we take the helicopter and look.'

Charlie came out of the canteen. A burst of some opera from the radio the guards were listening to followed him, a tenor weeping Italian. He picked his way over the unlighted ground.

'Anything wrong?'

'Nothing to concern yourself,' Picchu said.

'Polly?'

'I'm imagining lights.'

Picchu threw his cigar to the grass and stamped it out. 'Maybe we should think of leaving.'

Charlie took his glasses off and polished them on his shirt tail. 'I can't do that. It's getting close now. I'm expecting results any time.'

Picchu frowned. 'Then perhaps the *Senōra* and Paul . . . '

'She won't go,' Paul said. 'Neither will I. Haven't had a chance to use this gun you gave me.'

'I will try to contact the General,' Picchu said. He left them there. The door opened, letting a slice of light spill out over the grass, then closed and left them in the silent night.

'How close is it?' Paul asked.

'Can't tell you. It doesn't work that simply.' Charlie gazed up at the stars. 'My God, this is a pretty world.'

Then he said:

> '"I should like to rise and go
> Where the golden apples grow . . ."'

Paul heard his voice going quietly over the lines, and it came back to him, something he'd barely known before. The night Mum died. It was so complete that he could feel the bedclothes over them as they lay side by side in the big double bed they used to share at the front of the house. Charlie, not much older than him, reciting in a whisper his imperfect version of 'Travel'.

> '"I should like to rise and go
> Where the golden apples grow; –
> Where below another sky
> Parrot islands anchored lie . . ."'

He stopped and said: 'Parrot,' several times, because that was his name for his brother. Paul giggled more and more each time Charlie said it. He thought of Mum being somewhere else, and it was a blank.

> '". . . And, watched by kangaroos and goats,
> Lonely Crusoes building boats; –
> Where in sunshine reaching out
> Eastern cities, miles about,
> Are with moss and minaret
> Among sandy gardens set."'

The words he got wrong because he had not read it, only heard Dad chanting it, were part of it. Whenever he thought of it later, Paul always said the same words wrong.

In return he started on another verse. Charlie joined him word for word:

'"The world is so full of a number of things,
I'm sure we should all be as happy as kings."'

Then Charlie said: 'Let's not forget, the old man usually told us that one when he was in the deepest trouble.'

'He usually got through.'

'I wish he'd hung around a bit longer.'

'Yeah.'

He kept looking for signs of movement in the jungle, but there were no lights.

'I'm not leaving,' Charlie said. 'The program's too close. If they run me out of here, I may not be able to get to another mainframe big enough to take it. And then what happens to the next lot of poor bastards who wake up to feel the ground heaving under them? I let those people in Santo Caraz down. It's not going to happen again.'

'No one's going anywhere,' Paul said.

'Mina ought to. So should you. You did enough just getting here. Neither of you owe anyone a thing.'

'She won't go.'

'With you she might.'

'She doesn't give a shit about either of us any more.'

'I can't really say I blame her. You could make her go, though.'

'And miss the fun?' He searched his pockets for cigarettes that weren't there. 'This is the first holiday I've ever had. Wouldn't want to leave before it's over.'

Charlie's face hovered in the dark, pale and moonlike. 'I'm not feeling very brave.'

'No one is,' he said, although in some deep part of himself, he was itching to kick back.

'I hoped it was a noble ideal making me stay,' Charlie

said. 'But it really isn't. I'm just sick of playing hide and seek with these people. They've tried to take everything away, and they've damn near succeeded. I've had enough.'

'So, get back to your computer and get the answer.'

'Easy for you to say.'

'You have my gun, I'll go and play with the computer.'

'I think it's better this way round.'

35

Before dawn the helicopter was ready to go. As the sun glinted over the edge of the mountains, Picchu took a last mouthful of coffee and ordered Jorge to load up the Thompson gun.

'Let me go,' Paul said, as they went out to the pad.

'You should be here with your family, my friend.'

'But I may know one of these people. The one I saw at the airport. I could recognize him.'

'What makes you think he will be here?'

'Let me do this. Let me do something.'

'You are in my charge.'

'You were told to look after Charlie and Mina, not me.'

'You want to go so badly?'

'I want to see if I was right.'

Picchu stared at him for a thoughtful moment. Then he snapped his fingers. 'Ah, go get killed. Go.'

Paul ran into the sleeping quarters and fetched his gun. When he got outside again, the pilot, a lieutenant called Loreto was already in the helicopter, carrying out the checks with Picchu watching over his shoulder. Jorge came, lugging the big Thompson gun with its heavy belts of ammunition. Mina stood watching.

'You'll be sorry if everything starts while you're gone,' she said. It was a joke, almost.

'We'll be in sight most of the time.' He slung the Sterling over his shoulder. 'Anyway, you've got Picchu and Charlie.'

'You might break down.'

'I'll walk back in time to save you.'

She looked up at him. 'Plain as the glistering planets shine.'

'How's the computer doing?' he asked.

'Charlie's excited, but I can't see why. It hasn't told us anything yet.'

He made as if to touch her face, cup her cheek in the old way. But her eyes stopped him. He said:

'Picchu reckons we'll be about ten minutes.'

'I'll hold him to it.'

Picchu whistled to Paul.

Mina stuck her hands in her pockets, 'Go on. They're waiting.'

Paul clambered in behind the pilot. Jorge grinned at him. Picchu made a small salute.

'So, go find your rebels.'

The motor coughed, whined and caught, the blades shimmered into a circle. After the silence of the night, the noise seemed enough to wake the mountains.

They'll know we're coming Paul thought, grabbing the hand rails as Loreto lifted her off the pad. They slid broadside to the south, skimming the trees on the slopes, then pulled up like a toy on a string and moved off west. The guards left on the plateau watched, getting smaller. Mina waved. He stuck a hand out, but he didn't know if she could see him.

'This takes little time,' Loreto shouted. 'Tell me where you saw.'

The country was mysterious under early morning shadows. Mist lay pooled in the valleys; no smoke, no movement. The jungle was so thick down there that a whole army could be advancing and they would not know it. Paul glanced back and saw the observatory dwindling. The chop of the blades made it hard to think.

332

They were two or three miles off before Paul indicated the slopes where he thought he had seen the light. Loreto swung her over, blotting out the observatory behind a conical hill.

They hopped along a ridge, swooped into a valley where a rough track twisted among the trees. They dropped suddenly, rose again, catching the sun as they came up. Jorge saw Paul's hand clenching on the rail, and smiled at him, making a *loco* sign at the pilot.

He peered down at the jungle, wondering what it was like down there; what animals ran; what other dangerous creatures. He was on edge, waiting for something bad to happen, the machine gun across his knees.

They broke over another hill, a big one sloping easily down into a valley.

'Here?' Loreto bawled.

Paul made a thumbs-up sign, signalled him to drop closer to the slope. They drifted smoothly toward the hill, the sun dragging their dark shape over the treetops.

There was a road: what they called a road here. Through the gaps in the tree cover, he saw where it went. He motioned to Loreto to get lower. They dropped another twenty feet, until the wash of the rotors thrashed the upper branches into a frenzy. He took Picchu's field glasses and held as steady as he could to take a better look.

In the mud of the narrow, overgrown track below, he thought he saw tyre marks. He gave the glasses to the gunner and pointed. Jorge stopped chewing, focused, turned as the helicopter swung. Paul made a questioning face. He nodded.

'*Rastro,*' he shouted, close to the pilot's ear.

Paul studied them again. They looked like heavy duty tyres, going downhill. He unfolded the plastic-coated map Picchu had given them, showed it to

Loreto. The pilot lifted her, the blades chopping sunlight over their heads. They moved slowly north.

The map showed the trail as little more than a cart track. Some of it petered out in sketchy dots. But it led eventually to the road between the observatory and the village.

They stayed low, hugging the hillsides, the blades whipping the mist like cream as they flew into it. The observatory was still out of sight, hidden behind a high, rocky escarpment. He put the map back in his pocket and hung out over the long drop, trying to follow the road through Picchu's glasses. It was like keeping track of a tunnel which only now and then emerged above ground. Jorge rested back, his boots on the lip of the door, the Thompson gun tracking idly across the dark green.

The trail slithered round the flanks of a mountain. It looked as if the people who made this road had done the difficult thing every time. Paul signalled to Loreto to hang left, sweeping out over the hillside, over the road and the tree-covered drop below. He was half out of the helicopter now, could see the road angling round the mountainside, and the drop into a deep, rivered channel. A surge of yellow water showed momentarily, then was gone. The road was smeared with tracks.

Jorge grabbed his arm, pointing wildly out the other side of the machine. He pulled himself back into his seat and the gunner heaved him forward so he could see.

Ahead of them, no more than two hundred yards, some kind of big four-wheel-drive machine was pulled off the trail under a hollow of rock and low-hanging trees. The shadows and foliage made it hard to make out more.

Paul tapped Loreto's shoulder, thumbing the car. Loreto swung further out from the mountainside,

334

brought them in opposite the car, sinking to bring it better into view.

'Rebels use cars like that?' Paul shouted.

Loreto shook his head. Jorge did likewise. He was alert now, hands tight round the Thompson gun.

'We get closer,' the pilot said. He was bringing her down almost level with the road. They could see the make of the vehicle, and the mound of tents and sleeping bags in the back. No signs of life, though. Just the branches crashing back and forth in the draught from the blades, and dust from the road scouring up and obscuring.

'Let's get back,' Paul said. Loreto nodded, pulled the stick back, and the machine lifted like a ship going into heavy swell.

He didn't see it – couldn't have from where he was. He only saw Jorge start to open his mouth, and his hands flex on the Thompson gun. Then the machine was punched back. Loreto's left shoulder exploded through his uniform jacket, spraying Paul and the gunner with blood and flesh. He screamed, and the helicopter lurched. Paul collided with the gunner, struck his head on something jagged. Loreto began to whimper, but grasped at the stick. Jorge, thrown off balance, dug his heels in, trying to stay in the machine and get the Thompson gun levelled on something.

They pitched crazily. Paul hung on, saw the pilot's blood pumping from the big wound, strings of flesh hanging out of the tattered uniform. He grabbed his jacket and tried to wad it into the mess.

More impacts, like a hammer smacking the fabric of the machine. The windscreen starred, and Jorge was swearing in his own tongue, demanding that Loreto keep her still so he could shoot. The pilot groaned, sweat pouring off him, trying to hold her. But smoke was coming out of them somewhere. They began to spin, catching the smoke as they turned. It smelt oily and bad. Loreto grunted, cursing the pain, his right hand white on the stick, but they were going down.

Paul managed to snap his seat belt on, wedging the gun. Loreto's head dropped. He tried to reach over him, bumped the wounded shoulder, set Loreto to screaming again. Smoke was in the cabin, black and choking. Out of the open doors, he saw the mountainside blurring past in wild leaps and plunges.

They hit something; a tree, perhaps. It caught the undercarriage and tipped her over. Jorge lost his grip on the Thompson gun, scrabbled after it before he realized they were still pitching. He howled, and Paul lunged for him, but he was gone.

A tearing crash as the blades slashed into trees. The whole machine jarred and twisted, engine kicking, and they broke loose from whatever had stopped them. They fell.

Paul closed his eyes, trying to hold the pilot.

They struck.

36

The sound of running water. He lifted his head painfully, coughing on smoke.

Water tumbling fast through a narrow channel. He put out a hand, realized dimly that he was the wrong way up.

Coughing got worse. The smoke was thick. When he opened his eyes, motes of sunlight were piercing through it.

He started to understand the danger. He was hanging sideways in his seat, held only by the belt. The helicopter lay tangled in trees, branches poking into the cockpit. He tried to get his head up, saw the pilot hanging down out of the door, held and partly impaled by the branches. He shook him by the shoulder. The pilot's blood leaked slowly, dropping through the smoke toward the water.

The fire was growing. He could feel the heat of it at his back. Panicking, he fumbled at the belt, trying to free himself. The machine gun was still in his lap, held by the strap across his belly. He grabbed and heaved it out of his door, hoping it would strike ground when it fell. Then the buckle snapped open, and he spilled over the gunner's seat, falling toward the river.

Icy water closed over him. In the shock of it, he gulped some down and felt a burst of old fear; stones in the pocket. He fought to the surface, vomiting, but there was nothing to hold. The current was fast and hard, and the water cold as the mountain glaciers it came from. He thrashed against it, seeing the shattered wreck of the helicopter receding through the trees on

337

the bank. Low branches passed by overhead, he got a hand up and grasped one, held it while the water beat at him, trying to drag him loose. He swung in the current, twisting to get the other hand up, feeling the old wound pull. Made it just as he thought he must let go. The branch was smooth under his hands. He began to pull along it, legs streaming out behind as the water tore at him.

He heard the dull *whoof* of an explosion. A ball of bright flame rose from the helicopter. It lit the dim green of the valley for a second, swelling up through the trees, sizzling the leaves. The 'copter shifted in the blast, screwed round awkwardly and made a great hissing splash as it fell into the water.

Freezing, shaking, hand over hand, water taking breath from his lungs as the cold worked inward. Another mouthful jolted him out of succumbing to shock. He saw Mina, then bumped against the overhanging bank, the current whacking him against it twice more. Pain sparked under his ribs. He struck out, trying to find a foothold. The bank crumbled, pebbles showering down. The torrent threshed at him. Then his boot caught something, pushed, and he hauled himself up. The branch bent, but he kept doing it.

Mina.

He was half out of the water, a sharp rock digging into his belly. He dug the other foot well into the river bottom, holding it there against the battering of the current, then he pushed and clawed, threw himself forward onto the bank.

He lay there for a time, thinking nothing, shaking with cold or shock. He was maybe a hundred feet from where they had crashed. The 'copter was still burning, the flames crackling through the fuselage, smoke rising straight and black through the trees. He smelled the burning, and threw up, spilling that morning's coffee on the grass.

He could have lain there for a long time. He seemed unhurt by the crash; a couple of deep cuts on his arms and a feeling that his back had been twisted out of shape, but no broken bones. All the same, he felt emptied and beaten. It was good to lie there, even shivering and aching. But he knew they might come to check results. He had to get out of the way.

He rolled on his side. The mountainside rose sharply, the ground soon lost in undergrowth. The air was full of the helicopter burning and the river's roar. Frightened birds chattered in the trees. He couldn't hear anyone. On his elbows, he pulled himself into the ferns, hid there with flies batting at his face, waiting.

They didn't come. They must have seen the way the 'copter fell, maybe they watched the gunner when he slipped out. They could not have seen the final impact, but they could have heard it, and they would see the smoke. They would probably think that it was a long way to climb down, just to make sure of what was already pretty certain. He prayed that was what they thought as he moved again, working back along the bank toward the wreck.

The machine was blackened and broken like an injured cranefly. The rotor blades had snapped off, the tail was crumpled, the canopy was melting into the fire. He could no longer make out the pilot at all, too much smoke. Slicks of petrol occasionally spread with the current and flared briefly on the water. As he came in close, still looking out for the men who had done this, the heat grew fierce, striking through his wet clothes, prickling his face.

It took a while to find his gun, freezing every time he heard movement on the hill, but he saw it at last. It lay under a bush fifteen feet from the wreck. He picked it up, wincing as muscles in his back pulled, and dodged into the trees again.

When he was clear, he checked the gun. Couldn't risk firing it, but it seemed all right. The action was smooth. He felt his pockets for extra magazines. Two were gone, the remaining one dripped water. He only hoped the bullets would still fire if he needed them.

He blinked blood out of his eye. A cut on his head was oozing, and flies swarmed up to taste. He swatted them away and returned to the water, using his neckerchief to mop the blood and tie up the cuts on his arm. He felt dizzy. He drank a handful of the water, then pushed himself to his feet, coming up to balance uneasily on his haunches. He searched the rest of his pockets, found the map in one of them, opened it out and spread it on the grass.

Nausea pulled at him again, but he choked it back. He measured the distance to the observatory. Three miles as the crow would fly, but by road much further. He wouldn't even work it out.

He eased upright, groaning at the stab of pain from his ribs, cocked the gun. The mountainside went up in front of him. It seemed too steep for the trees that clung to it. But he had to climb it.

He shifted the gun to his shoulder again and went toward the trees.

A couple of times he stopped, clinging to roots and clumps of grass, resting, sweating into the wet clothes. Evil-looking insects buzzed him, with stings that looked big enough to anger an elephant. He kept still, listening to the forest tick and scream with life. Sometimes a breath of wind blew the acrid smoke of the helicopter to him.

It was a long way up. He hadn't seen how long when they fell. It felt like half a mile, but at last he saw clear

340

sky through the trees. He took it slower then, watching for a head to appear, listening for boots in the dirt. He slid the gun off his shoulder, holding the metal buckles of the strap to stop them clinking.

He reached the edge of the road. There was nothing to hide him except the long grass and rocks. He worked himself up the last couple of inches. The car was gone. The dirt where it had stood was churned by tyre marks and footprints.

He climbed onto the road, crossed to the clearing under the rock. They had shot the helicopter down, got back in their car, and moved off, heading for the main road.

He knelt, picking at the ground-out stub of a cigarette. It was fresh, saliva still wet on the filter. He could read the brand name. French. Would rebels of the *Sendero Luminoso* have a car like that, or cigarettes like that?

The sun was above the mountains. It warmed his back. The observatory was miles away, out of sight. Back there they would have heard the firing, but could not have seen what happened. They would see the smoke, though. Picchu would know what it meant. So would Mina.

He had said he would be back. He had said he would look after her. Now he was dead, as far as she was concerned, and she was under threat. He would hear it when they started. He would be able to see when they blew the observatory to bits.

He slung the gun back on his shoulder, checking the map again. The road snaked ahead like a bad joke.

Mina.

He had been walking two hours when he heard the first shooting. It was difficult to make out at first. He was

341

down deep in the forest. He stopped, stood between the fresh tracks of the car, straining to hear.

Machine guns sputtered in the distance. It was starting, and he was on the wrong side of it.

He speeded up, telling himself he shouldn't. The air was thin, he sweated like a pig. He should take it easy to get there. But he speeded up. What if nothing was left when he arrived?

He topped the last ridge, and it was all laid out before him a mile or so away, straight across the low valley. He saw the observatory through thin white smoke. The smoke came from the trees below. He made out the accommodation block and the landing pad. No one was moving around up there. It all appeared to be happening down by the bridge. The smoke shredded in the wind, but the guns carried on. Picchu was defending as he had said he would. But there were only four men with him now. Charlie and Mina in the observatory, and four soldiers to fight off an attack. Maybe the smoke was from the bridge. Picchu had said he would blow it if there was time.

The guns stopped. He waited, almost expecting to see the white dome flash out of existence. But it didn't happen. The guns resumed, and he started down the hill, attempting to work out exactly what he would do when he got there.

Getting close, the firing loud and rapid, impossible to make out how many guns. He prowled along the road until he could see round the bend where the track to the observatory broke off the main road. He went back a way, then struck off into the trees.

He was jumpy; stuck on the wrong side of the bridge, separated from the others by whatever force was fighting over the gorge. Whoever they were, they would be experts in this line of work. The gun was his only protection, and he had fired it precisely four times. He made his way through the undergrowth with great care. The rattle of the guns off to his right was magnified by the jungle. Picchu's *guerra pequeña*.

He was using the little knowledge he had of the terrain, combined with study of the map, to get himself into a position where he could observe: a promontory on the hill above the bridge about one hundred yards downriver. If he was lucky, no one else would have found it, and he might be able to gauge where he stood from there. He worked through the wet vegetation, kicking aside the largest of the beetles that tried to crawl into his boots.

There was a lull in the firing. Suddenly he could hear every twig creak, every grain of soil underfoot grate against the next. He stopped, head raised, listening. The rush of water from below came up through the trees. He heard nothing else.

The firing resumed; stitches in the quiet, more selective now. He went on.

The promontory was where he had hoped it would be. He checked that no one else was using it, then got down on his knees and edged onto it.

Directly below, under a pall of mist, the river crashed through its narrow channel. The mountain reared in front of him, the observatory hidden by trees. To his right was the bridge, intact, undamaged, empty. Either Picchu had decided against blowing it, or had been unable to. He lay flat on the rock, feeling its coldness under his chest and hands. As he watched, the guns started another rapid exchange. He knew where Picchu and his men would be: two either side of the bridge road, in good cover about fifty feet up. They would have good views of the bridge and the approach, could pot anything that tried to cross. Picchu would be on the left, where the lines to the charges were laid.

He shifted, searching his side of the gorge for the enemy. He made out a wisp of smoke a little beyond the bridge, guessed they would be duplicating the positions of Picchu's men. They probably also had people on the ground near the approach, waiting to make a rush across if a pause in the defending fire could be arranged.

He shuffled back off the ledge, turned over and ducked into the shade. Leaves slapped him as he ran toward the road again, his cuts and bruises ached. Flies followed, buzzing him. He found the road, crossed it quickly and burrowed into the trees on the other side, climbing the gentle rise of the hill. There was a sound like a car backfire muffled with cotton, followed by an explosion. He hoped Picchu had let off a grenade launcher, not the others.

Circling, he turned downhill again, heading back toward the road, slowing, taking more care. He got within twenty feet of the trail, then skirted along the edge, looking for the turn-off to the observatory. No one there. It looked safe and empty. He started across toward the observatory road.

There was no reason why he should have been looking for a wire; he was not trained in these matters. Maybe it was what Dad had always said about being extra careful if a thing looked too easy. The fact that they had put no one to guard the way set an alarm ringing. He was almost into the side road when his eye was caught by a glimmer of something at knee level, like a trail of spider web hanging flat in a breeze. He bent down, staring, and saw the line stretched across the road. He followed it to one side, found the device it was attached to fixed on a tree trunk in the tangle of leaves and ferns there. Some kind of explosive, ready to rip through whatever broke the wire. That was their guard.

He was going to step over it, then he remembered the little gadgets Picchu had shown him in the observatory's arsenal. 'A little vibration can set them off,' Picchu had said, grinning, as he tossed one across the room. 'Only when they're primed.'

He got off the road, circling the tree, keeping his eyes on the ground for signs of it having been disturbed. All the while, the shooting continued up ahead. He worked along the edge of the jungle, gun ready, keeping the track just in sight.

Around the first bend, he saw the car. It was the one they had spotted from the helicopter. Same colour, same markings, same gear in the back. It was drawn over to the side, its roof brushed by overhanging branches. He crept in closer. The sweat on him was cold.

No one was with the car. He made sure of it before he stepped onto the track. He saw the marks of three men leading away toward the bridge. Three men to take a mountain? He moved round the car, keeping his gun on the track in case one of them should return. It looked safe enough, but they might have wired it as they had wired the road. The trouble was, he had no time to play it safe.

The car was facing down the track. He stepped round to the rear, taking cover behind it. Letting the gun swing loose for a moment, he rubbed his hands together, reached for the tailgate handle, and pressed the catch.

Nothing happened, except another *phut* followed by a ringing explosion from the gorge. It made his breath come faster for a moment, but then he released the handle. The tailgate was locked. He moved round to the passenger door, under the branches, safe from sight.

He tried it, found it secure, drew his knife and began working it up into the window recess.

It was too slow. He stooped, scratched around in the dirt to find a fist-sized rock. The one he got was rough and warm, as if alive. He gripped it, lined the knife up with the point on the glass. Then he waited for a good burst of fire from the bridge. When it came, he struck at the knife handle. The window fractured perfectly, the knife point going through. He looked up the trail again, to be sure no one had heard him, and punched a hole in the window. Pieces of it fell inside the car like diamonds. He reached in, lifted the lock. The door came open without further problems. Twisting his gun out of the way, he pulled the passenger seat forward and wormed into the back, leaning over to see what the car contained.

It was well-stocked. Guns, ammunition, some kind of rocket launcher and the snub projectiles that went with it. He moved them around, feeling the slick oil on metal. There were boxes too, sealed with red tape. He recognized them, tore one open. The *plastique* was neatly wrapped in polythene, innocuous as putty. He dabbed at it, making impressions with his fingertips.

Taking a look through the windscreen first, he hauled himself further over the seat, the ridge of it under his belly. It was more than possible that they had taken all the fuses and detonators with them. But he only needed one. He searched among the rucksacks of camping gear, coming across cans of food, gas canisters, and a couple of bottles of good whisky. Then he turned up a canvas bag lodged by the spare wheel. He yanked it open and smiled to himself. It contained everything he needed, as long as he could remember what he had watched Picchu and the guards doing that morning on the bridge.

He picked up two packs of the *plastique*, two smoke

grenades, took them and the bag of gear with him as he backed out. Passenger seat folded into position again, he eased across it into the driver's seat, unlocked the door and wound the window down, resting the gun so that he would stand a chance of plugging anyone who appeared. Then he went to work on the *plastique*.

He had watched closely when the explosives were laid on the bridge. He had always learned quickly; it was his one big achievement in the brain department. 'Show the boy somethin' once,' Dad told people, when they doubted a kid could handle some of the things he in fact did handle, 'and he's got it. Stuck in his little 'ead like them poems.' He unwrapped the explosive, moulded the two slabs together, then tore back the carpet on the floor and pressed them onto the metal, working them down firm. He sifted through the bag, found a timer. Picchu had not used any on the bridge, but had showed them to him. There were a few of the digital type. He left them alone and picked out one with a simple clockwork dial. This he understood. He leaned down and pressed the detonator into the plastic. Doing it made him nervous. One mistake and he would go up like a firework display.

He checked his watch, heard another spat of gunfire, another dull thump as someone let go with a grenade. The car was hot and close, green under the trees. He slithered over again, reaching under the dashboard, pulling down the bundle of wiring. He separated the ignition and battery leads, cut them loose with the knife. This was something he knew from the good old days in Lowestoft. Some things, he thought, wryly, you never forget. He touched the leads, blinked at the spark, held them as the engine jerked and started.

Still no one coming up the trail. Maybe they couldn't hear him. There was plenty up there to distract them.

He pumped the accelerator, revving her up to keep

her going, darted down to set the timer, licking his lips as he did it. Three minutes on the dial, three minutes on his watch. He sat up straight in the driver's seat, gripping the wheel, heard another grenade blow. The way things were proceeding, the bridge would be gone before he got there.

He propped the gun on the window ledge, wondering if he would actually be able to drive and shoot at the same time. It didn't matter. It was all new experience, all a chance to do something he had never done before. Take a positive attitude, as Charlie would say. The smoke bombs were on his lap, the timer was running down the first minute, he had to do this quickly, or he would probably never have the nerve to do it at all.

He wondered what Charlie would think of all this.

He released the handbrake and hit the accelerator.

The road fell steeply on the bend, then curved tight to the right, banking under the trees. Foot hard on the floor, he controlled the lumbering weight of the car round the bank, the big tyres kicking dirt as he swung. He drove with one hand, got the smoke grenades ready with the other. The jungle whirled past the windscreen, and he heard the guns sniping back and forth above the engine noise. He thought: They'll hear me soon. Christ! Charlie, hidden in the dome, would hear him soon. The car bucked over holes the size of serving plates, but he kept her on the trail, and took the bend fast. The watch said he had two minutes and fifteen seconds.

Sunlight burst into view at the end of a long tunnel of trees. The track sloped down, then the rails of the bridge were at a slight angle to it. No one was down there, but the firing was getting louder all the time.

He pulled the pin on one of the grenades, held the trigger open in his left hand. The car plunged toward the light.

348

Two minutes and five seconds, the watch said.

Then someone was ahead. He jumped out of the trees to the left of the bridge, surprised as hell. Not native. Looked like some kind of military, though: combat uniform, heavy machine gun of an unfamiliar type in his hands. The real point, however, was that the big red face above the uniform was getting over the shock. His gun was coming up.

Paul ducked sideways, trying to hold her on course. A stream of bullets smacked the car, like reminders of the fire that had felled the helicopter. He heard the windscreen go, punched up with the grenade still in his left hand and brought some of the glass down on his head. He risked a look over the dashboard, saw the figure sidestepping ahead, adjusting his aim.

One minute, fifty-five.

He yanked the wheel over.

He felt the slam, heard the scream, and saw the body spin past the driver's window. He reared up in his seat and smashed a bigger hole out of the 'screen. It was just in time to stop the car from shooting uncontrolled out of the trees and over the edge of the gorge. He brought her hard to the right and started pounding on the horn. It was all happening in fragments of seconds, slow enough for him to operate, but too fast to think about anything but doing it. He dropped the first grenade out of his side as the wheels hit wooden planks, got the pin out of the other and tossed it at the shattered passenger window. He was in luck. It went through.

A thundering like stones pelting the roof. They were firing on him from above. He only hoped Picchu's men wouldn't try the same, would realize he was helping them.

Halfway over the bridge now, the planks rumbling. He smelt the river, the gunsmoke. The hammering came again, splintering the dashboard instruments,

349

pocking the seat next to him. He screwed the wheel over to the right as hard as he could and slammed the brakes on.

One minute, forty-five.

The car pulled up short, smashing through the rails of the bridge. His hand went immediately for the door handle, mouth opened and he started yelling: 'Picchu, it's Paul. Don't shoot, Picchu, tell them not to shoot.' Another volley of fire drowned him out. He fell as the door opened, sprawled on the bridge, hunkering down as the machine guns on the hill peppered the car again.

One minute, thirty-five.

As he lay there, splinters of a plank digging into his cheek, he heard Picchu's voice:

'Paul?'

He turned his head and searched among the trees on the mountainside.

'Me,' he yelled.

Picchu's hoarse shout came back: 'The others?'

He started to say they were gone, but just then the opposition let rip with a barrage of fire. He heard it singing overhead, and the thwack of the leaves on the mountain trees as the bullets went in. Under the car, he could see the other side of the bridge. One of the smoke bombs had gone over the side. The other was there, but the breeze was not blowing the smoke across the line of fire. It spumed uselessly away downriver.

One minute, fifteen.

He got to his knees, trying to see a way to make a break for it. He had not judged it finely enough. The car was almost broadside on to the hill, the front bumper through the rails, but he was still a good fifteen yards from the safety of the trees. When he started to edge out toward the railings a stream of fire spattered the wood behind him.

'Picchu?'

'What is it?'

'The car's wired to blow in . . . fifty-five seconds.' He didn't hear a reply at first, but he could imagine what Picchu was saying. 'Picchu?'

'All right. We try to cover you.'

There was a lull. He began to think about stopping the timer, but the moment he moved, someone on the hill let off another burst. In telling Picchu, he had also told them. They would probably do anything to keep him right where he was until the detonation.

Forty-five.

He was beginning to think he would have to crawl to the front of the car and go over the side of the bridge. He wouldn't stand a chance, even if he actually hit the water. The current would take him. His heart made a rapid squeezing sound in his ears.

Thirty.

'Picchu, for Christ's sake . . . '

The grenade launcher coughed in the trees to his left. He thought he saw it arc through the air, then there was another from a different spot on the mountain. The first explosion was joined by the sudden splash of machine-gun fire, and in a moment it was deafening.

Twenty-five.

He was poised, hand against the hot metal of the car's wings, muscles of his calves twitching as he tried to judge the best moment to go. The second grenade went off, followed by another and another, but someone was still working the car over. He felt it shiver with each strike. The machine guns flickered up and down the gorge.

Twenty.

Picchu shouted:

'Come on, my friend. Come now.'

His breath was hard and shallow. It burned in his lungs. He was locked. A perfect line of bullets slashed across the planking, throwing up great chunks of wood.

Fifteen.

Picchu. Head down, blinking every time the fire studded the car or the bridge, he was sure he could see the burly brown figure. He was on the road, well back in the safety of the trees. 'Now, Paul. Now!'

Ten.

Another grenade split the air. The fire around him seemed to fall away for a second. He sprang up, teeth gritted to stop the scream when he was hit, and ran faster than he had ever run in his life.

Picchu was there, yelling at him. The fire broke out again behind him, came following him as he lunged toward the trees. No time to weave and dodge. Either he would do it or he wouldn't.

'Come, come, come!' Picchu roared, and he was trying to outrun the bullets, feeling them pound the wood behind him. He struck dirt. He reached shade. He threw himself at Picchu.

And the car went up dead on time.

Picchu caught him. They hit the ground as the gloom was lit and the machine guns and grenades blotted out by the crack of the detonation.

By the time he got his head up, the initial flash was over. He saw the frame of the car rising in the air, turning like an incandescent toy, and the bridge disintegrating. There had been enough explosive in the car. What was under the bridge must have doubled it. As Picchu tried to hold his head flat to the ground, he watched another blast take out the remaining rail and struts, lifting the planks in a wave that shot them whirling into the sky. Petrol was showering down in gouts of bright flame, and the car twisted beautifully and began to fall.

'Keep down,' Picchu snarled, and thumped his head against the dirt again. In a second, fragments were raining through the trees. A six-foot rail fell to earth a couple of feet from where they lay, and something heavy clouted him on the shoulder, numbing it completely. There was a rending crash from the gorge as the remains of the car struck the river.

Finally the sound of the explosion began to ebb. It was still ringing away into the mountains, though, silencing the birds.

Picchu rose cautiously.

'Okay?'

Paul rolled over and sat up, rubbing his shoulder. 'Alive.' He liked the way the word tasted.

'Come, off the road. They could see us.'

They hustled into cover again. Paul climbed behind Picchu, ears ringing in the stillness. They reached one of the soldiers, who was lying behind his gun, laughing.

Through the concealing leaves, they could make out where the bridge had been. There was nothing left. The road on the other side ended in a raw scar of dirt. Timbers were scattered on the bushes all the way down toward the river.

'You did good work,' Picchu said. 'Even the enemy is silent.' He patted Paul's shoulder and took out one of his foul cigars. 'We couldn't blow the bridge. Maybe they cut the wiring.'

'Everyone all right?'

'Corilla has a wound.' He was talking about the guard on the other side of the road. 'It is nothing.'

'Where're Charlie and Mina?'

353

'Safe in the observatory. Manaro is on the cliff.' He struck a match and held it to the cigar.

The opposition must have been getting over the shock. There was a short blip of firing, then a further rush of it. Corilla replied, the big gun burping across the gorge.

'Still awake,' Picchu said. He clamped down hard on his cigar and cocked his gun.

'Need me here?' Paul asked, as they strode down through the trees again.

'Go to them, if you want,' Picchu said. 'You've done enough here.' He smiled, shaking his head. 'We can play with them all day now, wait for the General to send more men. Better to keep them pinned down where they are no trouble. And be sure you get those cuts seen to. Go.'

The shoulder was stiff. He felt as if he had been dragged round the mountain a couple of times. But he ran up the road's twisting folds. The gunfire fell away like the river and the stench of smoke. He felt alive, eager. He wanted to get to Mina, show her he was all right. And Charlie.

The thudding of his heart in the thin air slowed him a little. He was impatient with the road. He veered off, climbing directly up the mountainside through the rocks and trees, crossing the road where it snaked back to him. He kept listening for helicopters, for the sound of rescue, and let himself think a little of her face when he came back from the dead. Schoolboy fantasies of a kind he'd never entertained when he was the right age. It was like being taught to grow up all over again, getting it right this time.

He skinned his knee on the last piece of the climb, came out of the trees at the crest of the road. The observatory was white and calm under the hot blue the sky. Nothing had touched it. Charlie and Mina were inside, the Weatherspy program working softly onward to save the world, or whatever damn thing it was.

Drawing breath deep, he ran across the grass, over the landing pad, making for the cliff. Manaro should be told what had happened. He pushed his way through the branches on the edge of the grounds, calling out:

'Manaro?'

Manaro wasn't there.

He stopped dead, confused. But while his mind worked on confusion, a coldness crept down his spine, and his hand went back to the Sterling, lifting it ready, snapping back the bolt. He ducked low.

'Manaro?' A whisper now. He shuffled forward, into the cup of rock made so perfect for a lookout post. There was nothing but Manaro's brass cigarette lighter. He swung round, slowly covering the trees and the path back to the observatory, sat on the rock and shuffled backwards until he could see down the cliff.

Manaro's body hung doubled over a branch three hundred feet below. He knew it was Manaro by the red neckerchief. And by the blood.

He looked back at the observatory, cold turning to ice.

37

The building *was* untouched. He made sure of it, skirting round the plateau. The big double fire escape doors set in the wall of the observatory building itself were locked tight, the dome was closed. When he reached the western side again, the sound of the guns keeping busy echoed up from the gorge. He thought about going down to get Picchu, but he didn't do it. He edged up to the accommodation block. There were no windows through which he could be seen, only the door. He kept out of sight of it, ran and put his back against the wall. In the far distance, the mountains were blue and green like sapphire and emerald. The sky was pale with sunlight. Everything he saw was beautiful. The air was clean. He filled his lungs with it, started crabbing along the wall, head back, listening for the first voice or step.

What if they had been and gone?

The grass was springy under his boots. He turned the corner, and the doorway was there, open and dark. He kept to the same speed. No slips, no stones dislodged, nothing to announce his coming. He let the barrel of the gun drop into the opening, snatched it back. No reaction. He did it again, slower this time, and still no one fired. He took a careful look.

The corridor into the accommodation block was empty. The doors either side of it leading to stores and washrooms were shut and locked. Down at the far end, he could see the canteen table with a coffee pot and a pamphlet lying on it. No sign of trouble. He moved into the corridor, closing the door silently.

His boots crunched on the concrete floor. He went

into the canteen, sweeping the gun over it, checking the bunks and the corners. Still nothing. Like the *Marie Celeste*; the room frozen as it had been when the men jumped up to go to their positions.

He rubbed his hands on his trousers. They were as sweaty as the rest of him had been in the heat. But now it wasn't hot. The accommodation block was cool, and dim with only the electric for light.

He moved on to Mina's room. It was undisturbed. The other room the same. He wiped his face, breathed through his nose. Everything was cold. There was a lump of iron in his belly. He stepped into the corridor. Only the main building was left. The big steel door hung open. A spurt of anger stirred his guts. Why hadn't they kept the fucking thing locked? He moved up, so carefully, so quietly, and now he began to hear voices. The first was Mina's and he breathed a small sigh of relief right then, because the worst hadn't already happened. Next there was Charlie's low murmur. It made him think for one second that maybe they were all right. But before he could react, he heard someone else talking.

He licked his lips, took another step. The steel was before him, the only thing between him and the room beyond. He turned sideways, ready to slip through the gap.

Round the door, from the half-lit, echoing cavern of the observatory, the voice sounded odd. Foreign, somehow. He could hear the words.

'Doctor Quillet, please stop the computer and give me the program.'

Charlie then. He seemed perfectly calm, stating facts to a dull student: 'Don't you understand, you can't do it now? It's that close to getting the answer. If we stop it, hundreds of thousands, maybe millions, of people could die.'

'I have my instructions, Doctor.'

'Why don't you listen? —' Mina began, clearly scared but furiously angry. There was some kind of scuffle, then a blow.

He used it to move through the doorway. Just the right eye and the gun barrel round the door.

They were side-on to him. In front of the work stations, Charlie was holding Mina by the shoulders, while she clutched her face and stared in disbelief and disgust at the man who had just hit her.

He was turned slightly away, partly obscured by the barrel of the telescope where it came down, but Paul knew the profile. It was the one from the airport, the one who had been with them all the way, who had stared at them like a pair of netted fish that night outside the blazing house on the lake. He knew it, and he was not even surprised. The iron in his belly grew heavier. He wanted to shoot the bastard there and then, but he knew he wasn't practised enough to be sure of hitting first time at this distance. And it needed to be first time. The man called Haggard held a snub machine pistol, an Uzi, dead centre on them. Even a reflex pull of the trigger might get both of them. So he waited.

'Courtesy of Robersman?' Mina sneered, rubbing the weal on her cheek.

Haggard had no particular expression. He glanced at his watch.

'We have little time. Please make this easier, Doctor. Do what I say.'

Charlie held Mina, making sure she was all right. He raised his eyes to Haggard.

'I can't do it.' The screens flicked and changed, blurring images and words. They flashed their light on the three figures in the gloom.

'Then I will have to destroy it all,' Haggard said.

The barrel of the Uzi shifted to the screens. Paul waited for the flash of the machines exploding. But it didn't come. The Uzi didn't fire. He saw Charlie's face working. There was something almost confident about it.

'They want the program, don't they?' he said.

Haggard showed no irritation, but the gun remained silent.

'You can't destroy it,' Charlie said. 'They told you to get it before you killed me. And you don't know how.'

Mina was resting against one of the work stations. Paul could see her hand searching around in the debris of paper and pens behind her back for something to use as a weapon. He wanted to shout to her not to do it.

'All right,' Haggard said. He turned the Uzi toward her. 'Step to your right, please.'

Her eyes widened. She eased slowly to a standing position.

'Over there,' he said, motioning toward the wall, safely away from the computers.

The iron began to roll, over and over. He saw her pass in front of Charlie. As she blocked Haggard's view, Charlie reached and grabbed something off the desk. Maybe a pair of scissors. It was so quick he couldn't be sure. His finger tightened on the trigger. Haggard stepped back a pace, hiding himself better behind the telescope.

Mina was by the wall. Haggard had tracked her all the way. Keeping the Uzi on her, he turned to Charlie. 'Now, Doctor.'

Braced against the work station, Charlie stared at Mina, then at Haggard. His eyes were feverish and bright behind his glasses.

Mina said: 'Charlie . . . '

He slumped suddenly, defeated. His head hung down

359

and his low whisper dropped on the floor at his feet.

'All right.'

Haggard straightened a little, as if taking his strength from the defeated man. He shifted round, presenting his back as a target. Paul lifted the Sterling a fraction.

Then Charlie moved.

Mina screamed.

Haggard went into a swift turn. Charlie lunged in with the blade, going for his stomach, but the Uzi was going to be there first.

'Charlie!'

Paul fired, the rattle of his gun running into the burst of the Uzi.

Haggard was taken in the right shoulder, thrown forward sprawling against a splash of red on the wall.

Charlie staggered back, blood spraying from somewhere. He smacked hard onto the desk and slid down, Mina going to him.

Paul steamed in. 'Charlie?' He saw Mina's shocked gaze, but Haggard was turning over. He fired again but the shots were off. They cracked the floor and whined up to the dome. Haggard was quick. Even with his shoulder leaking he was struggling over, levelling the Uzi.

Paul dived at Mina, bundled her and Charlie under the work station. The barrel of the telescope sparked as Haggard's stream of fire caught it.

He got over on his knees, stuck the gun round the corner and sprayed the general area.

'Is he all right?' Fear in his voice.

'I don't know.' Mina was cradling Charlie's head, pulling off her jacket to make a pad of it.

Charlie's blood was on him. Charlie was breathing. He could hear the gurgle of his lungs working fast

'Charlie?' He glanced quickly at his brother, saw the glasses skew-whiff on the long face. But the eyes were open and he was trying to speak through the pain.

'Hey, Parrot,' he whispered, weakly.

Paul put his hand down over Mina's.

'Shit, Charlie . . .'

He heard scuffling over by the fire doors, then the clank as the locks snapped open.

He nearly got his head removed when he bobbed out to see what was happening. Haggard fired as he heaved against the doors with his good shoulder. Paul ducked back, then darted out again and pulled the trigger. But Haggard was out. A gust of sunlight and warm air wafted into the building, stirring the hanging smoke from the guns.

No, you don't, he thought. No you fucking don't.

He jumped up and ran for the door, smelling Charlie's blood on his jacket and his hands. As he ran, the computer started bleeping, a loud piercing alarm.

He shot out into the open, heard the firing still going on down in the gorge. Haggard was limping toward the cliff, trying to replace the Uzi's magazine one-handed.

He fired, realized at once he was too high, pulled the barrel down. The gun spat twice more, then fell silent. He was empty too. Haggard turned, seeing what had happened. His awkward movements to get the spent magazine replaced became more frantic.

Paul ran at him. Behind the built-up rage and the fear for Charlie, he was thinking: This man's a professional, he kills people for a living, knows everything about it. Even with both arms shot off he could probably finish me. But he was too angry. Angry like the old days.

He hit Haggard full in the bad shoulder, and that made Haggard yell. He snatched at the Uzi and twisted it loose, throwing it aside. Haggard's good left came up

361

and found his belly. He was part ready for it, but not ready enough. It felt as if his guts had burst into his chest. He staggered back, and Haggard moved in, the good hand straightening for some kind of killer blow. He managed to block it, knew it was only because pain and blood loss was slowing the other man down. He used his forearm like a club, slamming down on the side of Haggard's neck.

Then they were down, and face to face, breathing on each other as they rolled. He looked into Haggard's face and the eyes terrified him. They were dead. It was like staring into the deepest part of the sea, where nothing lived. For a second, he was like an animal hypnotized by a predator. He saw all the killing Haggard had done.

He pulled himself together. Haggard was trying to get a hand down to grab his balls. He thrust him away, concentrating on getting clear. Spun and got on his feet, darted in while Haggard was trying to raise himself with the good hand, and kicked hard at the shoulder. Haggard howled and fell into the cupped rock of the lookout post. Paul leapt and pinned him. Suddenly he was angrier than he had ever been in his life. He started pummelling the sleek head, feeling the impact of each blow jerk up his arm and through his body, cancelling out fear or any other consideration. Doing it for Charlie, for Sam, for Penny Leman and all the others who had fallen in this mess. He made the smooth pink face dissolve.

A movement distracted him. He saw Charlie stagger out of the observatory, clutching his side with one hand, a sheet of bloody printer paper in the other. He was half out of his head, probably, but shouting triumphantly:

'Got it, got it,' He slumped against the wall as Mina

appeared. He shook the printout at the sky. 'You bastards, try and smother this. California, you bastards, California!'

He sensed Haggard moving, thought it was useless struggle. Then Haggard heaved suddenly and a fist jabbed up into his chest. The blow made his heart lurch. He was paralysed for a second, long enough for Haggard to get a boot under and force him back. He fell on the grass, spine jarring. Haggard lurched to his feet, reaching down to his boot. He started to get up at once, but the grass was slippery. He skidded and fell on his side.

When he looked up, Haggard was standing over him, a little Derringer pistol in his good hand.

Haggard's dead eyes regarding him through swelling lids.

It was over.

A flare rose from the gorge. A green and beautiful flare, the colour of new leaves. It climbed and climbed into the sky, drawing level with the observatory, going higher. Haggard's eyes followed it. Paul's did the same, despite the gun barrel pointing at his face. He saw it begin to arc. Then it erupted into a cluster of bright sparks. The sound of it reached them a moment after, a deep, ringing boom.

The guns down in the gorge fell silent.

He looked back at Haggard.

The eyes were different. He knew Haggard wasn't going to kill him.

He kept the Derringer on him, but took a look over his shoulder, down the cliff. He was searching for his way down.

Lying there, Paul found a shred of voice to speak with. He said: 'Why?'

The other started to move, grunting at the pain from

his shoulder. He glanced back. 'It's just business,' he said, the moment before he died.

The shot didn't come from the plateau. It came from somewhere down the cliff. It caught him under the left shoulder blade, tore into his upper body, arching his spine even as he was jerked forward by the impact. He opened his mouth to scream, but only blood spilled out. He pitched foward and fell dead on the rock. The Derringer clattered from his hand.

As Mina came running, Paul stared at the eyes. They hardly looked any different.

He got shakily to his feet. Taking her arm, he made his way back to Charlie. Charlie was sitting, legs splayed in front of him, holding Mina's jacket wadded to his side. The printout fluttered to the grass.

'All right?' Paul said.

'Christ, Parrot, I don't know.'

Mina edged him down by Charlie's side, and went to fetch the medical kit. Charlie reached for his hand.

'California, Parrot,' he said, and began painfully to laugh. 'Fucking California.'

They rested.

PART FOUR
Aftershock

38

Three limousines drew up in the forecourt of a shining tower in midtown Manhattan. A uniformed doorman came down the steps to the middle car and opened the passenger door. Paul got out first, then Mina, then both of them helped Charlie. He moved with some stiffness and pain: the metal attaché case handcuffed to his wrist didn't help; but finally he stood between them. The limousine whispered away. They paused there for a moment, blinking in the cold glass and metal shadows of the March afternoon like savages brought to civilization for the first time.

A flurry of snow whipped down the street, a yellow cab blared at an old woman to get out of the way. At the corner of the block a news stand was selling the evening 'papers. All were taken up with the coverage of the earthquake in California. Full page pictures of San Francisco in ruins; the Golden Gate damaged but still standing; the 'HOLLYWOOD' sign with letters missing; Malibu beachfront property belonging to the stars washed away by the sea; aerial shots of new cracks running for miles along the San Andreas fault.

But the headlines screamed only good news:

MILLIONS SAVED – POPULATION GIVES THANKS.
COMPUTER PREDICTION CORRECT – 8.2 'QUAKE
ROCKS SUNSHINE STATE – CASUALTIES LOW.
WEATHERSPY SAVES CALIFORNIA.

The doorman ushered them into the lobby.

They walked together, Charlie leaning on the arm Paul offered, Mina at his other side in case he felt weak. They didn't talk, to the doorman or each other. Paul was watchful.

Despite the numbers of people going in and out, the lobby was hushed like a great library, tall and gleaming, a monument in marble and glass to power and money. The brass plate by the door detailed only one company in the entire building. At a semicircular desk not much bigger than the average amphitheatre, a receptionist looked up with a bright, expensive smile. An armed guard was tucked away at a security monitor behind her: discreet menace. The receptionist did not need to see identification. They were expected. A uniformed flunky rushed out of nowhere to show them to an elevator.

Paul stared down for a moment at the polished floor. The ceiling lights reflected as if in deep water. The flunky was young, on the make. He ushered them along with all the calculated friendly deference of a man who expected to work his way to higher floors and greater positions than this one day.

Charlie coughed. Paul stopped, looked at his brother questioningly.

'I'm all right,' Charlie said.

They went into the elevator. The flunky pressed a button for the top floor.

Charlie breathed slowly, reserving himself. Paul glanced behind his back at Mina. She stared at the door of the lift, adjusted the collar of her blouse. Like all the clothes she was wearing, it had been provided for her. The very best names and designs. At first she had refused to take them, but Charlie had said: 'Take them. Take everything.' Like the suit he was wearing. Only Paul still wore his old jacket and jeans. He looked as out of place as an old church among the New York tower blocks.

The elevator seemed not to move, but the numbers

368

climbed, and then the doors opened, and a metallically attractive girl greeted them with another smile full of company training. She led them along a plush corridor studded with squares of modern art. Concealed lighting and concealed classical muzak furthered the atmosphere of money.

The corridor opened out on a huge reception room with a heavy set of doors on one side and a wall of glass looking out on the city in the sky. Another girl behind a massive desk picked up a 'phone and pressed a button. She spoke quietly into it. The first girl waited, hands pressed together in front of her. Then the one behind the desk put the 'phone down and smiled brightly.

'You can go right in. He's waiting for you.'

The first girl opened the doors. She gave them one last reassuring smile as they passed through into an office that made the reception room look like a cupboard.

A slender, handsome man got up from the desk on the far side and came toward them.

'Glad you decided to come,' he said, with another variation on the smile. 'Welcome. I'm Anthony Sheal.'

They were alone with him. But Paul guessed one bad move would bring a ton of security people crashing in. Sheal did not go so far as to try shaking hands with them, but he kept up the convivial front, moving around them, saying: 'Please, sit down. You've had a long trip.'

There were three chairs of brass and buttery leather on the other side of the desk. Charlie took the centre one, easing himself into it with care. Mina sat on his right, Paul on the left. The attaché case, now released from Charlie's wrist, went down on the floor at Charlie's feet. Paul noted Sheal's interest in it as he walked over to a bar.

369

'Can I get you something to drink?'

Mina shook her head. But Charlie and Paul nodded, asked for whisky. Sheal offered them a choice from several brands. They settled on Red Label. Sheal poured them and brought them over. Then he circled round the desk and resumed his seat. He turned it on the swivel slightly, then leaned back. He was as neat and polished as one of the wire and perspex sculptures on the pedestals by the wall. He had the air of a man who had come recently to greatness, who was still acclimatizing himself to new, much-desired surroundings. He clasped his long fingers together on the desk and said:

'You must be exhausted.'

'You understate,' Charlie said.

'I trust the 'plane we provided made the journey a little more bearable, anyway. I know you've been travelling for some time now, and, if all goes well, you'll have to attend a press conference soon, Doctor. But we thought it would be wise if we brought you up here to straighten a few things out before we go any further.' He regarded them benignly over the desk. 'I *am* glad you came.'

'We agreed to hear what you have to say,' Charlie said, glancing first at Mina, then Paul. 'Though some of us weren't so eager.'

'I think it's for the best.' Sheal nodded.

'So,' Charlie said. They waited.

'You have to understand that this has all been a terrible mistake,' Sheal said.

'A mistake?' Mina said, incredulously. Paul felt his stomach tighten.

'This entire unfortunate affair was due to certain renegade persons in the company, who've now been removed.'

'Tell us more,' Charlie said, softly.

'It's quite simple. In an organization as large as this,

there are power struggles. Over recent years, certain parties have gained leverage within the company, and they've tried to turn it toward illegalities, projects not wholly moral or, uh, for the benefit of anyone but themselves.' The word 'moral' sounded sickly coming from him. 'When the "Weatherspy" matter came to their notice, these people saw a chance to take it and use it for their own purposes. And so, while you were running around trying to keep the program from them we were also trying to stop what they were doing. But the corruption went very deep. It took time.'

'And lives,' Mina said.

Sheal didn't reply. He gazed at the stock reports on the desk monitor, lips pursed.

'I'm as aware as anyone that you've all been through hell these last weeks, but believe me, I was one of the people working to help you. We only gained control at the very last minute. The mercenaries who came after you were in constant contact with higher authority, they were receiving instructions from minute to minute. When you started trying to broadcast the news about California, we finally succeeded in breaking into the system and letting the news pass. At the same time, we regained control, and got the order through for those men to withdraw. In point of fact, I was the one who did that.'

'Very kind of you,' Paul said.

'I know it must be hard for you to trust us now, but I promise you, changes have been made. Positions have been vacated and refilled. It's all over. That is to say, it will be, if we can agree on where we go from here.' Since no one replied, he went straight on:

'This is the proposition, which we sincerely hope you'll want to accept. I hope you will, so that this sorry business can be put to rest finally.' He steepled his

371

fingers and stared through the gap between his palms. '"Weatherspy" has saved millions of lives, chiefly because we managed to overcome the blocks the renegades had placed on your transmission from Peru. We feel that proves to you that we're acting in good faith. Also, to be blunt, the fact that you're still alive.'

'Why not put your "renegades" up for trial?' Mina asked. 'If you're so eager to prove "good faith"?'

'Mrs Quillet, we're a very large and very respected company. To tell you the truth, we just don't want that kind of publicity. Certain terrible things were done under our name, and I admit to you that my superiors want to sweep it away as best they can.'

'Sweep away Penny Leman,' Paul said. 'Sweep away Sam, you bastard.'

'Sam?' Sheal looked surprised. 'Oh you mean your, uh, your first mate, Mr . . . Cuddy?'

Paul wanted to pick Sheal up and tear him in little pieces. 'Your people put him at the bottom of the harbour.'

'No, no, not our people.'

'Yours, theirs . . . '

'Anyhow, Mr Cuddy's fine.'

'What?'

'It was the man who planted the explosives who died. There was some confusion surrounding the incident at first. You must've received a garbled report.'

That left Paul speechless for a time. His fingers gripped on the arms of the chair. And Sheal, happy to have imparted good news, continued:

'Here's what we want to offer you. All the troubles back in England have been settled. There never were any warrants for your arrest – that was only a story the renegades hoped would trickle through. As far as the law is concerned, you can return home any time. There are no troubles waiting for you. Mr Quillet, we're

372

already paying to have your boat lifted from Lowestoft harbour. It'll be refitted, and a very sizeable cash sum will be paid to you. A *very* sizeable cash sum. The same goes for you, Ma'am.' He nodded toward Mina. 'As for you, Doctor, I think you already know what the score is here.'

Charlie took a drink. 'I know that you've already publicly credited me with the breakthrough. Taking your share of the glory for financing it, of course.'

'Of course,' Sheal said. 'The company – the good heart of this company – is very proud of its part in creating "Weatherspy". Tell me, is it true she gave outline plans of events into the next five years?'

'Not exact information like California, but enough to make provision for the future.'

'You think it's accurate?'

'I think it will be.'

'How did you do it?'

'I really don't know. The program did it, somehow made a leap all by itself.'

Sheal smiled. 'A case of the machines minding the men?'

'It looks that way.'

'So what are your thoughts?'

'I should say that you're offering me the chance to enjoy my success.'

'At least the Nobel Prize, wouldn't you say? After California.'

Charlie ignored the interruption. 'All I have to do is agree never to say a word about what's happened.' He glanced again at Mina and Paul. 'We all have to do that.'

'You're being very understanding,' Sheal said.

'And if we don't?' Paul muttered.

Sheal looked over their heads, out of the window to the blank sky and the tall spires of commerce.

Silence swung like a pendulum across the desk. Then he said:

'I don't need to tell you, do I?'

Paul started to rise. Sheal blanched, but Charlie's hand came out and restrained Paul.

'No,' he said. 'Let me tell him.'

Paul settled back, and Sheal relaxed again, but with a more nervous edge than before.

'Just so you don't think we'd any of us ever fall for this . . . this unutterable shit,' Charlie said, slowly and with great emphasis, staring malevolently across the desk, 'I'll tell you what the score really is.

'I know that there's a grain of truth in what you say about a power struggle inside the company. I saw enough activity on the computers to prove that. One lot of gangsters fighting another. And I don't doubt that you climbed over the corpses of several people who used to be your superiors to get to this office.

'But this is the real point: until the "Weatherspy" program revealed that it was California that was going to be hit, you were ready to let your people kill us and everyone on that mountain, just as they'd removed anyone who had anything to do with the project. You'd have slaughtered all of us without a thought. If it had said there was going to be a volcanic eruption in Chile or Mexico, you would have blocked the broadcast of the information. If it had been a tidal wave in India, you wouldn't have cared a damn. But there're too many of your people with homes and families in California – you sound like one yourself – too much investment. It's too close to home. You had to let that one through. So you did it. And you're taking credit for it, and to make it all look like the humanitarian gesture it was supposed to be, you want me alive to talk about it. So you've flown us here – in secret, of course. But if we don't agree to your terms, we'll never leave

374

this building alive, and there'll eventually be a story about a rebel attack on a mountain observatory in Peru where I was doing my heroic work, in which we'll all unfortunately have been killed.' He paused for breath, sweating, pressing at his side, holding Sheal by the force of his hatred.

'Further, I know damn well that, as things stand, the three of us might hope to have six months or a couple of years before the fuss about "Weatherspy" dies down, and then we'd all meet our deaths in untimely accidents. So here's something you and your "superiors" have to consider.' He looked Sheal straight in the eyes, dragging the words out with a weight of contempt. 'Over the years I worked for this company, I made myself pretty familiar with all the systems, all the operations. And while I was hiding in Peru – in my spare time, if you like – I planted the whole rotten story of "Weatherspy" and what led up to it in various systems all over the world. I know you probably already have people looking for such things, but don't forget I'm the best there is, and I wrote most of the programs they're using. Copies of the story are all over the place, and unless I key in the correct code signals at a precise time every few months, they'll start appearing in places where even Robersman, powerful as it is, can't stop them. So, if for any reason I – or any one of us – should die, the codes won't be sent, and the story will be out.'

Sheal's hands pressed against each other, whitening.

'That isn't all,' Charlie said. 'I didn't think it would be enough. So, as extra insurance, I've rigged some other bugs, bombs and viruses on the same time scales. They won't tell any stories, they'll just release incorrect information into the money markets and company files. Within a year, Robersman will be worth about five cents. All its funds will have disappeared. And they'll reappear in the accounts of relief agencies and charities involved in Third World aid. Rather poetic, don't you think?'

Sheal's bland expression was peeling at the edges now. A fine sheen stood out on his forehead.

'You know I can do it,' Charlie said. 'And none of it's written down. It's all in here.' He tapped his skull. 'It all depends on three things: me getting the backing to do the work I want to do; your many companies making appropriate amends for your past behaviour to the poorer nations; and me and mine staying alive. So, if you're going to interfere in our lives at all, it'd better be to make damn sure none of us dies in suspicious circumstances.'

'How do we know you won't do these things anyway?' Sheal said, when his voice was steady enough.

'The same reason we know you won't try to hurt us,' Charlie said. 'Trust.'

Sheal thought for a long time. Finally, he said: 'Would you excuse me?' He rose and went through a door into another office. As the door swung to, Paul saw him picking up a 'phone.

Mina twisted in her seat, about to speak, but Charlie touched a finger to his lips.

They heard Sheal talking. His voice rose in pitch and volume. Then there was silence. The 'phone went down. The door opened again. Sheal came in.

'Well, Doctor, you've been busy,' he said, with a reasonable imitation of his former manner. 'It's a pity you couldn't believe our intentions are honourable. But . . . we're prepared to let that go.' He thumbed his tie, stroking up and down the silk pattern. 'Now, if you'd be good enough to hand over the "Weatherspy" program . . .'

Charlie reached down and lifted the attaché case. He held it up.

'It's all in there?' Sheal said, almost disbelieving.

'Everything you want,' Charlie said. He handed the case to Paul, who stood and held it out to Sheal.

Nervously, Sheal came to him. Paul made him wait just long enough for his own satisfaction. Then the case was in Sheal's hands. He pressed a buzzer. A couple of heavies in dark suits came in, took the case without a word, and disappeared again.

Sheal sat down. 'Well, Doctor, that seems to be all for now. One of our cars will take you back to the airport. There's a press conference waiting for you there. Our people will brief you on your story on the way.'

Charlie sat forward. 'Thank you, Mr Sheal. You've been most helpful.'

On the way down, they were taut and silent. Mina kept reading the front page of the *Herald Tribune*, shaking her head bitterly.

They crossed the lobby, keeping their silence. Fresh-faced people in good suits passed in and out all the while. They seemed to be all nationalities, all races.

As they went past the big brass plate with the Robersman logo writ huge upon it, Mina said:

'He still thinks he's won. *They* think they've won.'

Charlie shushed her. There were too many people close by.

'We did pretty well.'

'You did all the talking,' Paul said, admiringly.

'I told you I could handle it. Maybe you won't think me such an idiot any more.'

Paul shook his head. The point didn't require an answer.

'I thought you controlled yourself rather well,' Charlie added, as they stepped out into the biting wind.

'Wanted to throw him through the window,' Paul muttered.

'No, no,' Charlie said, wincing slightly and pressing at his side. 'Better my way. So they don't connect us. So that you and Mina and I stay safe.'

One of the limousines drew up. Paul looked at it with distaste. 'I don't want that,' he told the doorman. 'Get a taxi.'

The doorman whistled up a taxi from the rank. They waited in a small huddle, their conversation covered by the noise of the streets.

'You sure it'll work?' Mina said, speaking quietly.

Charlie's eyes narrowed coldly. 'It'll work. Six months from now, the bombs I set in the company computers – the ones I didn't tell him about – will start going off. Every time they do, money will be transferred from Robersman into private accounts. The methods will be complicated, clever enough to convince the people who look into it that embezzlement's taking place; and investigation will prove that those accounts belong to certain high-ranking company employees. Robersman will deal with the problem the way they tried to deal with us. In a year or two, Sheal and all the people who were up to their armpits in this will be dead.'

His face was grey. 'I owe her that much.'

Paul put his arm around him. After a moment, Charlie responded, embraced him tightly. Then Mina too, holding both of them.

The taxi pulled up. Slowly they disengaged, except that Mina kept hold of Charlie's hand.

'Are you sure you're all right?' she said.

'I'm fine. I have a press conference to go to.' He handed her into the taxi, letting her kiss him once more on the cheek. Then he turned to Paul.

'Odd how things go,' he said.

Paul shook his head. 'You need a bodyguard, I'll stick around.'

'No.' He tilted his head toward Mina. 'She needs to be away from me now. I suppose I need it too. Nothing can be sorted out if we stay in close proximity ... Think you can make it work?'

'I don't know.'

Mina and Charlie had said whatever it was that needed saying between them in the hospital in Lima. He had left them alone, not knowing, not until she came to him the night before they were flown to New York. She had said:

'We shouldn't do it. Once a thing's over, it should be done with. Never go back.'

'We already went back.'

'I won't be pushed. I'm not a timid kid any more.'

'Don't want you to be.'

'What do you want?'

He thought for moment. 'Chance to give something back.'

She studied his face. Her eyes were the same as always. Tigereye and gold.

'All right,' she had said. 'All right. It probably can't work, but let's go on from there.'

Charlie frowned, looking for a second like the boy who couldn't understand all the fuss about Hendrix.

'It's a bastard, isn't it? All any of us can ever do is our best, and we're lucky if we get to do that. Luckier still if it actually makes a difference.'

'You made a difference,' Paul said.

'In some things.' Charlie looked at the ground, then the words came from old memory:

'To go on for ever and fail and go on again,
And be mauled to the earth and arise,
And contend for the shade of a word and a thing not
    seen with the eyes.'

They spoke the last lines together, each patching the other's recollection:

'With the half of a broken hope for a pillow at night
That somehow the right is the right
And the smooth shall bloom from the rough:
Lord, if that were enough?'

Charlie said it quietly, so that Mina shouldn't hear:
'Just make sure you treat her better this time.'

Paul held his brother's sleeve. 'We'll see each other
again?'

'When some time's gone by.'

'And you're sure?'

'I'm as safe as I can be now. We all are. It's down to
"Weatherspy".'

The doorman was waiting. The taxi's meter was
clicking up the fare.

Paul remembered something. He said:

'It really did that? Worked out the next five years.'

Charlie nodded. 'Ten.'

He shivered.

'What's wrong?'

'I don't like it,' Paul said. 'Give it time, it'll be telling
you when the world's going to end.'

Charlie looked at him with a strange expression,
half-smiling. 'It's done that already, Parrot.'

Paul got in. The taxi pulled away. The last they saw
of him, he was being helped into the limousine.

And be mauled to the earth and arise,
And contend for the shade of a word and a thing not
seen with the eyes . . .

He stared at Mina.

'What?' she said, taking his hand.

He frowned. 'I don't know if he's joking or not.'

Lord, if that were enough?